The Oyster Diver's Secret

The Oyster Diver's Secret

A NOVEL

CAROLINE SÄFSTRAND

TRANSLATED BY A. A. PRIME

Previously published as *Sanningen om ostrondykerskan* by Bokförlaget Forum in Sweden in 2022. Translated from Swedish by A. A. Prime. First published in English by Amazon Crossing in 2024, by agreement with Enberg Agency.

Published by Amazon Crossing, Seattle

www.apub.com

Amazon, the Amazon logo, and Amazon Crossing are trademarks of Amazon.com, Inc., or its affiliates.

ISBN-13: 9781662518690 (paperback)
ISBN-13: 9781662518683 (digital)

Cover design by Kathleen Lynch/Black Kat Design

Cover images: © Dmitry Ageev, © LoudRedCreative / Getty; © Magdalena Wasiczek / ArcAngel

Printed in the United States of America

For my sister Thomazine

THE OYSTER DIVER

The still surface, soft as velvet, dark as night, carried Mathilda's small sailing boat from the harbor to Oyster Bay. Where the moonlight shone like a shimmering ribbon in the water, she let go of the rudder and let the boat drift. As long as she could remember, her father had called her a daughter of the sea. He often told her that, when she was a baby, she would lie swaddled in a pale-yellow blanket in the stern of his fishing boat and breathe in time with the waves. Mathilda had just turned three when her mother was killed in a car accident, and she had since found great comfort in the idea of the sea as guardian of the motherless.

She blinked back tears and looked around. Islets surrounded her in a gentle embrace. She knew their granite surfaces as well as her own skin. She closed her eyes and breathed the air deep into her lungs. If there was one thing she wished to keep, it was this scent of seaweed and salt. It flowed through her veins instead of blood.

She put her hand in her pocket and took out the oyster shell. Inside, on its pearly surface, she had scratched the most important words she'd ever written. She held the shell in her hand. Tears welled. Tore and tugged at her insides. Telling her that this was a mistake, that she would regret this forever, that she should turn back.

But she couldn't turn back. Not now. Not after what had happened.

She leaned over the edge of the boat, caressed the water's surface, and let the oyster shell sink to the bottom, along with her tears. Her destiny went with it. A destiny she could not foresee, but which, with this decision, she was making one final attempt to steer.

INEZ

Two weeks ago, Inez had decided to get organized for death. Not that she felt particularly old. The gray streaks in her hair had nothing to do with her seventy years; they had come about as the result of intense stress fifteen years ago. No one believed her when she said this, but she'd seen an article in a reputable psychology magazine that confirmed it was possible. Apparently the legend of Marie Antoinette going gray the night before her beheading hadn't just come out of thin air.

No, her decluttering efforts had nothing to do with old age, but rather a wake-up call. Her neighbor Viola, ten years her junior, did water aerobics, yoga, and spinning, and sang in a choir. She walked with quick, nimble steps and wore blue eye shadow and pink lipstick. The complete opposite of Inez. And she had been the very picture of health that morning three weeks earlier when Inez had peered through her Persian blinds and seen her performing sun salutations in her garden. Viola was carried out on a stretcher that same afternoon. Sudden cardiac arrest.

Inez grabbed the armrest of her chair with one hand and her walking stick with the other and stood up with a grimace. Two days later, Viola's sons and daughters-in-law had come to clear out her house. They had worked efficiently, and after one afternoon there were three piles in the garden: one for garbage, one for storage, and one for sale. This had inspired Inez to walk around her own house eyeing up all her stacks of books, papers, and bric-a-brac. She realized it would take her daughter, Amelia, weeks to go through it all. And she would hate every minute. Amelia lived in a luxury apartment in Copenhagen with her partner, Aksel the architect. Their home was all white and chrome with a hint of beige. Black-and-white photographic art hung on the walls, the rooms were minimally furnished, and personal items were glaringly absent. The last time Inez had visited, the sun reflected on the white walls so brightly that she had to wear sunglasses indoors, which made Amelia say through gritted teeth—always so emotionally repressed—that if Inez was going to sit there wearing sunglasses in her home, she would be only too happy to bring a roll of garbage bags the next time she visited her mother. "Your house looks like a dusty secondhand bookstore that has collected a lifetime's worth of books but never sold any. And it smells musty. Who knows what's hiding behind those piles of books? It's actually disgusting, Mom. You live in a pigsty." By the time she had finished talking, she was ghostly pale, as if the mere thought of Inez's house made her feel sick.

These two events—Viola's sudden death and Amelia's expression of revulsion at her home—had led Inez to the conclusion that she had to organize and declutter. But no sooner had she begun than she had fallen off the stool she was balancing on to reach the top of her bookshelves. The doctor in the hospital said she was lucky she hadn't hit her head, but he did find a fracture in her pelvis that might take months to heal. When she asked if she could continue clearing out her house, the doctor replied that it was good to keep moving, but carefully. *Take gentle walks, but leave any heavy lifting to the professionals,* he said with a wink. So she had called Spick & Span Co., which agreed to send a cleaner every morning, Monday to Friday, for three weeks.

She glanced at her watch. The cleaner was due to arrive in ten minutes.

Inez sighed. It didn't seem like such a brilliant idea anymore. She never had strangers in her house. Just the thought of someone else going around her home and rooting through her things sent a shiver down her spine. *For Amelia's sake,* she thought. *You're doing this for your daughter's sake, so she won't have to stand here one day, retching, rolls of garbage bags in hand.* Inez stood at the window and moved the blinds slightly so she could see out but no one could see in.

And she waited.

MEJA

"Is that okay with you?"

Her colleague Angelika was drumming her long, hot-pink nails on the table. Meja didn't understand how anyone could work as a cleaner with those nails.

"Sure," she said, though she would have rather said no. For a temp paid by the hour, timetable changes were rarely a good thing. She had worked as a cleaner for Spick & Span Co. for nearly a month and had been lucky enough to get clients who requested cleaning while they were at work, or who at least made an effort to keep out of the way. This meant Meja could put in her earphones and clean every inch in peace without having to think about anyone or anything. She liked those shifts; they were meditative. Now she was being asked to swap them for a client who was actually scheduled for Angelika.

"It's that woman, she used to be a writer—Inez Edmark—and she needs a cleaner every morning for three weeks. To help her, like, sort through her books," said Angelika.

Meja nodded, even though this meant a guaranteed end to her cleaning sessions in contented solitude.

"Ever heard of her?"

Meja shook her head. She never read books.

"She's been a recluse for a few years, but I'm sure she's . . . nice," said Angelika. "But . . . bit of a lone wolf, you know . . . if you believe the tabloids."

The pregnant pause between "she's" and "nice," combined with the laughter from their colleague Shima, sitting nearby, told a different story. Boss Karin snapped her folder shut. "Great. Then off we go."

Twenty minutes later, Meja had parked in a small pine wood between Domsten and Gråläge, a few miles north of Helsingborg. She looked at her map app. She could have driven farther into the village and parked closer to her house, but the thought of driving around looking for a parking space in those narrow streets stressed her out, and this gave her a two-minute walk, according to the app. She needed it.

She exited the car and followed a well-trodden path past tall, windswept pines, soon coming into an open green space. The sea swirled before her with all its billowing late-summer energy. Inez's house should be somewhere on the left along the seafront.

Nerves buzzed like a tuning fork in her belly. Her colleagues' ingratiating smiles had told her that Inez was not going to be an easy client. *Lone wolf.* What had Angelika meant by that?

As she cut across the grass, she got a text from her mom, Susanne. Don't forget dinner tonight. Table booked.

Meja sighed and put her phone back into her bag without replying. Once a month she and Susanne went out for dinner. That was how they spent time together. And she already knew how the evening would go. Susanne would comment on her clothes and posture with a smile that didn't let on to the people at the next table that she was criticizing her daughter, then conclude with the words "Why don't you get yourself an education and a proper job? You're thirty-seven years old. It's high time you took control of your life. Nothing comes for free, you know. By throwing your life away you're also throwing away mine. After everything I sacrificed for you."

Meja had heard these words so often that they were practically etched into her cerebral cortex. But they clearly didn't make a difference. Here she was, still a temp with no real plan for the future.

She came to a path with orange signposts that snaked its way between two fulsome rosebushes, with sand dunes to the right, and three identical houses, each surrounded by a low stone wall, to the left. They looked like little dollhouses. All three were white-plastered, and the ones on either side had blue shutters and doors. The house in the middle had green. The first house seemed empty. The second looked locked, with drawn Persian blinds and a paved yard. The third was newly renovated, with a rainbow floral explosion of a garden. She stopped and checked the app. Inez did not live in the green oasis. She lived in the middle, behind the blinds.

INEZ

Through a gap in the blinds Inez watched the cleaner standing behind the gate and struggling with the latch. "Push it," Inez said to herself. But the woman didn't look like the pushy type. Inez sighed. Wispy women made her skin crawl. She grabbed her walking stick and went outside. The woman looked up and smiled that nervous sort of smile that gets stuck halfway through.

"Hello. Are you Inez Edmark?" she asked.

Inez walked over to the gate, lifted it slightly, and pressed the latch to open it.

"Yes," she said. "That's me." She turned around and led the way inside. The cleaner followed.

"My name is Meja, and I'll be doing your cleaning for a few weeks."

Inez chose not to respond. Her daughter used to get offended when she did this. "Are you listening or not?" Amelia would ask with an irritated wrinkle between her eyebrows. Inez would answer, "I am listening, but there's no point in stating the obvious."

Inez sighed. It was going to be a long three weeks.

"Oh," said Meja when Inez opened the porch door. "I've come to the back door."

"I tend to use this door," Inez said and went into the kitchen. "Coffee?"

"Thanks," said Meja.

Inez noticed from the corner of her eye that she was taking in the state of the living room, with its piles of books, folders, and loose papers stacked on the rococo couch and two armchairs, in front of the bookshelves, along the walls, and over and under the sturdy oak table. Without saying a word, Meja put her shoes neatly by the door and followed Inez into the kitchen.

Inez took two mugs from the dish rack, poured out freshly brewed coffee, and handed one to Meja, who shifted her weight from foot to foot a couple of times before asking, "Could I possibly have a drop of milk?"

Inez nodded to the fridge and left the kitchen. She'd had a hunch that Meja was the type to drink milky coffee. Not offering had been a test to see if she'd dare ask. Inez had observed her passive body language, but Meja had passed the test.

Maybe she wasn't so wispy after all.

Inez pointed with her walking stick to one of the armchairs in the living room, also covered in books. "You can put them on the floor and sit down."

Meja did as she said.

Inez collapsed into the other armchair with a thud and took a sip of coffee. "I decided to do a clear-out, but I fell off a stool and injured my pelvis, which is causing me great pain in the hip. Hence why you're here. I'm not used to—or partial to—having people in my home, and I think we'd best attempt to make this as pain-free as possible." Inez leaned forward. "You'd be forgiven for thinking that I have trouble letting go of things, but that's really not the case. I'm not all that sentimental."

Meja fiddled with her mug and nodded.

"I suggest we do one pile at a time. You show me a book, I tell you what to do with it. Toss, give away, or keep. After a while you might understand the way I think and be able to do a lot of the preliminary work yourself."

Meja nodded again but didn't look all that convinced.

"I only have one rule. You mustn't read these papers," Inez said and picked up a blue plastic folder from the tray table. "Not even a little bit. Not a word. Understood?"

This time Meja nodded most earnestly, as if to show that she would never dream of it.

"All right then," said Inez. "We may as well get started on the first pile."

Meja put down her mug and they began.

The only one that gave Inez pause was Märta Tikkanen's *Little Red Riding Hood*. Keep or give away? She flicked through it. Poetic prose put the book in the keep pile.

Time passed quickly, and at eleven, Inez got up to stretch her legs. They had sorted through the piles on and around the little tray table. The give-away pile was significantly higher than the keep pile. This was good. Plus, they had managed to sort through all the loose papers between the books. A hodgepodge of paid bills, fan letters, and flyers. Everything had ended up in the recycling.

"I think that's enough for today," Inez said and limped over to open the porch door. Her hip didn't like sitting still for hours.

Meja got up a little uncertainly, put on her sneakers, and walked out.

Inez squinted in the harsh daylight. The summer was squeezing out its hottest July rays now. In the distance, they could hear the joyous sounds of splashing water, beach activities, and general summer fun. Inez noticed Meja eyeing the neighboring garden. Sverker and Filip had moved in three years ago and spent what seemed like all their free time on their green space. It showed. Inez spent no time on hers. That also showed. But the weeds sprouting between the paving stones didn't bother her in the least. She suspected her neighbors were just dying to tear them out and plant something new on her side of the wall.

"Can you manage the gate yourself now?" she asked.

"Absolutely," said Meja and waved goodbye. "See you tomorrow."

Another obvious statement that Inez chose to ignore. She turned on her heel and went inside, then plonked herself down in an armchair and sighed heavily. That was the first morning over and done with. Fourteen left.

After resting her head for a moment, she reached for the blue folder and took out the manuscript that no one knew about. Her final book. The one she intended for posthumous publication.

This was also a sort of death-cleanse. Cleaning out her mind. Her dark confession of a time, an event, and a friend from the past that had sat like a thorn in her heart for many years.

It was time to pull the thorn out. She glanced at the title—*The Oyster Diver's Secret*—and read the last words she had written about her friend Mathilda.

1976

Anyone who witnessed Mathilda standing in the sea, scraping the growth off oyster shells at early dawn, understood how the legends about her had come about. Passersby and visitors who ate at the waterside restaurants or had a beer in one of the village bars of Kobbholmen would often hear tell of this water nymph who stole the hapless hearts of all the fishermen—but who loved only the sea.

Mathilda would laugh heartily at the stories. But she knew they contained a kernel of truth. Her relationship with the sea, and the oysters on its bed, was special. This was her home. Her upbringing and profession. Her life.

She loved the place, and she loved what she did in a way that defied description. It wasn't enough to say passion. Her attachment to Oyster Bay was deeper, warmer, and more genuine than that. That's why no one could believe it when, one day, without a word, she suddenly left it all behind.

It pains my heart to know that it was my fault.

MEJA

Johan had just left for work when Meja came home. As a game developer, he had no fixed work schedule. Sometimes he worked late at night, sometimes all night. *You can't just go home when you are in flow with a project,* he would say.

As usual, he had left behind him an unmade bed, wet towels on the bathroom floor, and a kitchen full of dirty dishes. Meja picked up a frying pan full of congealed bacon fat and sighed.

Several months ago, returning from a night shift at an assisted living facility, she had tried explaining to him that it was no fun coming home in the morning to chaos. Couldn't he pick up after himself? He had just shrugged and nodded at the same time—without taking his eyes off the game on his screen. He made an effort for two days. Then they were back to their old habits again.

Meja turned on the hot tap and rinsed off the frying pan. She stuffed the rest of the dishes in the dishwasher before giving the apartment a quick tidying up.

She stopped by the dresser and picked up a framed photo, studying it in detail. Her mother had taken it of her and Johan in the Sofiero Palace garden on Meja's thirty-fifth birthday. At first glance it was a lovely picture of an attractive couple in front of a pink rhododendron. But if you looked more closely, you could see that Johan was looking in one direction and Meja in another. Like their lines of sight were crossing each other. She put the photo down. It was a very telling picture. That's what their relationship looked like.

They loved each other but were rarely looking in the same direction.

She sighed, picked up Johan's socks from the couch, and put them in the laundry basket. Inez hadn't had any photos on display. At least none that Meja could see among all the piles of books and dust bunnies. Meja had never seen a house so full of clutter. Living among all those stacks of books and papers couldn't be healthy. She shuddered. Could that be why the blinds were down? So Inez didn't have to see the mess in daylight?

Meja went to the cage in the corner of the living room, where Ingrid was nibbling on the apple slices Johan had given her. That was one good thing she could definitely say about Johan: his heart was in the right place. When Meja said she was going to buy a skinny pig—a hairless guinea pig—he had protested fiercely. *Well, I'm not going to touch that freakish thing,* he'd said, looking in disgust at the dark-gray little lump of skin staring up at them curiously in the pet shop. But Meja heard how he spoke to her every time he passed the cage, and he always gave her treats while Meja was at work.

She scooped up the little animal, lay on the couch with Ingrid on her chest, and shut her eyes. She was more tired after a few hours at Inez's house than after a whole night shift at the assisted living facility. There was something in the older woman's eyes that had put her on edge. Like they were boring into her, mercilessly. It had taken a lot of energy to try to appear calm and collected. She pulled the blanket over herself and Ingrid.

Three weeks in that dark, dusty, messy home. How was she going to cope?

Meja knew where her mother would be sitting before she even opened the door to the restaurant. At the bar, in the middle, under the big crystal chandelier—always in the center for all to see. She raised her martini glass in greeting and gave her daughter air kisses.

Once they were seated at their table, the waiter asked if Meja would also like a drink to start with, but she opted for water. Susanne gave her a look. "You've got to start embracing life. Stop being so . . ." She waved her hand around, searching for the word. "Beige."

Meja gritted her teeth and called the waiter back. "I think I'll have a martini after all."

Susanne tilted her head to one side with a satisfied smile. "Are you still working at that old-age home?"

"No," said Meja. "I'm cleaning. Better working hours." It was just something Meja said. The working hours had nothing to do with it—she'd taken the only temp job that was available. "Anyway, they don't call it an old-age home any more. It's an assisted living facility."

She took the martini from the waiter. Susanne took a sip of her drink and leaned over the table with a neckline that wasn't leaving much to the imagination. Meja steeled herself. *Here it comes.*

"Why don't you get yourself an education and a proper job? You'll be forty before you know it. It's high time you took control of your life." She raised her glass in a toast and hid the harsh tone of her words behind a smile. "Nothing comes for free, you know. By throwing away your life, you're throwing mine away too. After everything I sacrificed for you."

Meja lifted her glass in a toast and nodded. Just like she always did. Then she downed the drink so fast it made her woozy. Meja ordered flounder, and Susanne chose a half lobster and a bottle of champagne. Susanne knew that Meja didn't like bubbly, be it champagne, cava, or prosecco, but she always ordered it anyway. At least this time she didn't quote Coco Chanel in English to the waiter like she usually did.

"Look," said Susanne and reached her hand over the table. A large sapphire glittered on her finger. "Bengt gave it to me."

"Bengt?" said Meja. Her mother changed men as often as Meja changed jobs.

"Yes, I've told you about him, he's the CEO of one of those big companies." She shut her eyes tight and looked pensive. "Oh, I don't remember what it's called but something global."

Meja nodded. She had a vague memory of her mother telling her she was going to move in with her new man at last month's dinner. Rich, smart, and kind—that's how she had described him. Susanne always chose a man with status.

But maybe Meja was no better. She had chosen Johan for security and companionship.

The food was served. Susanne talked about Bengt. About his villa in Marbella and apartment in North Harbor, where Susanne now lived. Meja listened and struggled to keep the fish and champagne down. The combination was not kind on her digestion. Susanne efficiently plucked the lobster meat out of the shell as she spoke and had finished her meal before Meja made a dent in hers.

"Oh, and Bengt's son works in e-commerce," she said, dabbing the napkin on her lips. "Maybe that could be a good fit for you? Everyone shops online these days."

Meja gave a little shrug, even though she knew full well that it wouldn't be a good fit for her. She wanted nothing to do with computers. The problem was she had no idea what *was* a "good fit" for her.

"You really should go on holiday, you and Johan," said Susanne, out of nowhere. Jumping from one topic to another was her specialty. Meja, who could ponder conversation topics for a long time, was equally disoriented every time Susanne changed the subject. She was just about to say that Johan couldn't take a holiday now that his company was in the middle of a big project, when Susanne continued.

"A weekend in Berlin, Amsterdam, Paris. It would do you good."

Meja picked at her fish. She and Johan in Paris. Something about it didn't feel right. But she couldn't figure out what.

"It's tricky going away for days at a time, plus we've got Ingrid to think about." She immediately regretted saying this. It only prepared the ground for another judgmental appraisal of Meja's life.

"My dear child, sometimes it's like you've voluntarily put your life in a tumble dryer at too high a temperature. Like it's shrinking into nothing. Surely your neighbors can feed that bizarre little pet of yours? You make simple things so complicated."

Meja felt her cheeks go hot but had no time to respond. Susanne stood up and waved at the door, where a man in a dark-blue suit was standing and waiting. She threw on her pale-yellow trench coat, air-kissed Meja, and said, "Must dash. So good to see you. Quit this job before we see each other next time, won't you, sweetie, darling? And book a trip. Trust your mother for once."

Meja watched her go and saw Bengt talk to the waiter, point at their table, and take out his wallet. Meja lifted her hand in greeting and thanks. Bengt gave her a nod and a smile, linked arms with Susanne, and left.

Meja was alone with the flounder fillet and champagne. Red blotches bloomed their way up her neck in embarrassment. She poked the fish with her fork. She would have much rather gotten up and left, but she couldn't stand wasting food. Not with all those worrying headlines about food waste and climate change. Johan would shake his head and say, "What difference does it make if we throw away a bit of leftover food?" and she would say, "But that's just the problem—no one thinks they make a difference, so no one does anything. No one cares."

She popped a piece of flounder in her mouth and washed it down with champagne. She might not be the most ethical person on the planet, but she certainly wasn't going to contribute to its downfall any more than necessary. She *cared*. That was something, at least.

INEZ

Through a gap in the blinds, Inez observed Meja as she lifted the gate slightly before pressing the latch. "Good," Inez said to herself and then opened the porch door. Meja was holding a bouquet of yellow daylilies, tied up with string.

"This was hanging on your fence," she said, handing over the bouquet. "So beautiful."

Inez muttered, "Merde, merde."

She had learned to swear in French from a writer colleague long ago, when she had come upon a bad review in the middle of a party. It still came in handy from time to time—something about the rolled *r* worked wonders for shaking off irritation. Inez leaned on her walking stick, opened the garbage can, and tossed the trumpet-shaped flowers inside, closing the lid with a bang.

"Coffee?" she asked without turning around.

Meja cleared her throat. "Yes, please."

Inez poured them each a cup and watched the young woman. She was curious to see whether she would have the guts to take milk without asking.

Meja took such a tentative step toward the fridge that it looked like she was barely touching the floor—and she poured herself a splash of milk.

As a reward for her courage, Inez decided to explain her reaction to the flowers.

"The flowers are from my neighbors, Sverker and Filip. They insist on leaving these bouquets from their own garden, as if to convert me and my weeds. They're like Jehovah's Witnesses, except their religion is called gardening, and flowers are their gods. I am not the type to be converted."

Meja nodded uncertainly and drank her coffee standing up.

Inez limped into the living room. Her hip was bothering her today. Maybe because she had taken an early morning walk along an uneven path, past the red fishing huts, onto the beach, and along the pier. Her fractured pelvis hadn't liked it one bit. But she had to walk to the pier to be able to write about her and Mathilda. She needed the rippling sea and briny air to help her tune in to the story. Her senses evoked the memories.

She sat down heavily in an armchair. Inez observed Meja's darting eyes and leaned back to sip her coffee. Meja reminded her of the heroines in her books. At first, they were unsure of themselves and their place in the world. But over the course of the story, they underwent a transformation. Usually thanks to a strong, charismatic girlfriend who showed them the way. Rarely a man. That was why her books were so beloved by a female readership and lambasted by male critics who—if they even deigned to review her—called her books trashy.

"Do you have a close girlfriend?" asked Inez.

Meja looked up. After a moment's silence she said, "I live with someone."

"Aha," said Inez. "You live with a female friend?"

"Hmm? No, no." Meja shook her head. "But he is my best friend. I have colleagues and, uh, some old childhood friends I see sometimes. But my closest friend is probably Johan."

Inez nodded. These little words of uncertainty. *Probably.* Either her partner was her best friend or he wasn't. Meja definitely reminded her of her characters. The advantage of fictional characters was that they really could change. Real people rarely did. That was probably why Inez had become a writer and not a therapist. "Shall we begin?"

Meja's tense shoulders sank with relief.

They worked through the pile in front of the bookshelves and then moved onto the next. When they were halfway through the second pile, a photo fluttered to the floor. Meja picked it up and handed it to Inez. It was a picture of her and Amelia in the Danish neighborhood of Nyhavn a few years ago. Amelia had asked a stranger to take it, and they had posed in front of the red, blue, and yellow buildings typical of the district. Inez had managed to blink in the picture. Or maybe she had done it on purpose, she couldn't remember. But she did remember the words exchanged over an expensive bottle of wine and bite to eat at one of the open-air cafés. Inez had questioned her daughter's latest relationship, and Amelia had taken issue with her "biting bitterness," as she called it. But Amelia had just turned forty, and her new man, Aksel, was fifty-six, with two grown-up children. Inez had only said that Amelia's train was nearing its terminal, and if she wanted a baby, she had better get on with it. Inez considered this neither biting nor bitter. She was simply pointing out a fact. Her daughter had taken a gulp of wine so big it caught in her throat, and once she had finished coughing into her napkin, she said, "Aksel is done with children. He's had a vasectomy."

Inez turned the photo over and nodded to Meja to continue showing her the books, but her thoughts kept returning to the photo.

When Amelia had said that children were not in the cards, Inez had been surprised. She couldn't remember what she had said now, but she remembered Amelia's answer only too well. "I don't have a father, and my mother spent more time with her fictional characters than her own daughter. Why on earth do you think family life would appeal to me?"

It was one of the few occasions Amelia had talked back to her, and she had turned very pale afterward.

Pain blazed in Inez's hip as she stood up. She went over to the window and tilted the blinds. Sverker was pruning withered roses from the bush on the other side of the wall, and he raised his hand in an eager wave. Inez bit her cheeks and pulled the cord until the room was plunged back into darkness, then she sighed and turned around.

"I think that's enough for today," she said.

Meja looked at the clock on the wall uncomfortably.

"You don't have to tell your boss I've let you go a little early. You'll stay a bit longer another day. It'll balance out." Inez gestured to the porch door.

Meja put on her shoes and jacket and went outside. Sverker greeted her with pruners in hand. Inez couldn't hear what he was saying through the door, but when Meja turned around to wave goodbye to Inez, she stuck her head out and mouthed as clearly as she could, "Jehovah's Witnesses." Then she gestured with her hand for Meja to keep going.

Like a marionette guided by invisible strings, Meja hurried toward the gate and disappeared around the corner. Inez smiled to herself and shut the door. She glanced around the room. Her home didn't look much different after two days with Meja. Was she really going to sit here clearing out the living room for weeks? It remained to be seen.

Her thoughts were interrupted by a murmur of voices outside. She walked back to the porch door. The sound wasn't coming from Sverker and Filip's garden but from Viola's house. Her son was walking around with a man in a suit that wouldn't have looked out of place at a wedding. They were talking and pointing, and the man was filling in some forms. Definitely a real estate agent. Inez hadn't thought this far—that someone else would move into Viola's house. *What if they were even worse than Sverker and Filip? A young family.* Inez shuddered and hobbled over to the display cabinet with her walking stick. Only one door opened. The other was blocked by boxes and god knows what else. She took out a bottle of white port, poured some into a crystal glass, drained it, and poured another. Maybe the drink, with flavors of plum, spices, nuts, and pomegranate, could inspire a few more words in this book—the hardest she had ever written.

With the glass in one hand and her walking stick in the other, she went into the bedroom, where her laptop stood on her antique writing desk. Not very ergonomic, but beautiful.

She took a deep breath and started to write about her first meeting with Mathilda.

1969

When I was nineteen, I was offered a job at a bookstore, where I had been helping out now and then. It allowed me to move out of my parents' house. I found a little studio apartment in the village where I had lived as a child, Kobbholmen. My mother looked unconvinced and asked what on earth I was going to do there. I had no answer to give her. It might have had something to do with my roots. I had lived there until the age of four and always liked that little community, even though I didn't have many memories of it. Perhaps I needed to embark on my adult life in the same place as my life had begun, in order to go on to spread my wings and fly.

I was off work that day and had just unpacked the last of my moving boxes. To celebrate that the move was over and done with, I had gone to the café on the pier. It was an unusually hot day for early September. I leaned my head back and felt the sun's rays prickle my skin.

I knew, then and there, that I had made the right decision. This was my home now. At least for a while.

The sunshine in my eyes blurred my vision and made the woman walking toward me along the pier in rubber boots and orange waterproof pants seem like a mirage. The red tinge of her hair shone brilliantly in the sun. She was carrying a plastic basket of oysters. She stopped by the café and asked if anyone wanted to try one. Some people wrinkled their noses and others shook their heads. I raised my hand gingerly.

She stopped and smiled, not only with her lips, but with her eyes and freckled cheeks, then put down the basket, picked out an oyster, and showed me to how to open it with a little nick from a Mora knife. Then she held the shell up to her bottom lip, tipped her head back, and let the oyster slide down her throat. I had never seen anything so beautiful, almost sensual. She handed me the knife and an oyster. When I couldn't get the shell open, she took my hand and guided my movements until it opened. Then she looked deep into my eyes and nodded.

Carefully I raised the shell to my mouth, let the salty scent of the sea tickle my nose, and swallowed. The oyster was smooth and slimy, like nothing I'd eaten before. It didn't taste good, but there was a certain carnal pleasure to its flavor and consistency.

She let out a contented laugh, picked up her plastic basket, and carried on into the restaurant with the rest of her oysters.

I sat there, unmoving. Intoxicated by my first oyster and my first meeting with Mathilda.

MEJA

Meja watched Johan as he shoveled spaghetti and meatballs into his mouth while scrolling on his phone. Always on his phone. Sometimes she wished that smart phones had never been invented.

She turned to face the window. The apartment blocks were so closely clustered that she could see straight into her neighbors' place across the way. They had just put their baby down to sleep. Meja had seen the dad walking around, rocking the little one. Now he was opening a bottle of wine as the woman lit a candle on the table. Meja swallowed hard and looked at Johan. At the blond fringe hanging over his eyes.

"Did you have a good day at work today?" she asked.

He hummed in response.

"Are you leaving early in the morning?"

Johan looked up from his phone. "Why?"

Meja fidgeted. "Just wondering if we should open a bottle of wine."

Johan frowned. "It's Tuesday."

"Well, yeah . . ."

He smirked and went back to his phone.

After ten minutes of silence, Meja said, "I'm cleaning at an author's house now."

Suddenly interested, Johan looked up and put his phone down. Of the two of them, he was the one who sometimes read books. He only read English-language fantasy and sci-fi, but still. "Oh really? What's his name?"

"It's a she. Inez Edmark."

Johan reached for his phone again, scrolled a bit, and turned it to show Meja. "Is that her?"

Meja looked carefully at the picture. "Well, she looks a lot younger in that picture, but it's her all right. What does it say?"

Johan began to read.

"Inez Edmark is one of Sweden's most prolific writers, who, over the course of her career, published thirty-four novels and was translated into fifteen languages. Her principal theme is female friendships. *Twist of Fate*, published in spring 2005, was her last novel, and she has kept out of the limelight ever since and given only a handful of interviews."

He looked up. "What's she like?"

"Strange. Kind of harsh. She has this stare that, like, drills into you." Meja shuddered. "Her home is a mess, and I'm helping her clear it out."

Johan leaned back in his chair. "You could probably earn a bit on the side if you took pictures and sent them to a tabloid."

"You know I would never do such a thing."

"I know," he said. He kissed her on the cheek and put his plate on the counter.

She almost asked him to put it in the dishwasher but decided against it.

In the other building, the woman was laughing at something the man had said. Meja sighed, took out her phone, and looked up Inez Edmark. She saw lots of pictures of Inez wearing flamboyant hats and beautiful dresses at various literary events, mixed in with those of her trying to hide her face from reporters' cameras. Words like *bestseller* came up, along with *accused* and *misleading*. The most recent photos looked like they had been taken around 2006. Something had clearly happened that not only made her stop writing, but also made her stop appearing in public.

Meja put her phone facedown on the table. This felt like snooping into Inez's private life, and Meja wasn't the type to snoop.

◆ ◆ ◆

The next day another bouquet of flowers hung on Inez's gate. Meja carefully removed it, lifted the gate slightly, and pushed the latch. The gate glided open without protest. She smiled to herself.

Inez came out of the porch door in a sun hat, sunglasses, and pink lipstick. She waved her free hand to encourage Meja to hurry up. "Can I lean on your arm? These level changes are impossible for my hip."

"Where do you want to go?" asked Meja.

"Not me, us," said Inez.

"You've got flowers again," Meja said, trying to hand her the bouquet.

"Bring them," said Inez.

Meja took her by the arm and supported her over to the gate. She opened it, with the same ease as before, and led Inez out. They veered off to the left, slowly following the uneven path, and just before they emerged onto the asphalt road, Inez gestured to a house.

"You can hang the flowers there."

Meja hesitated but did as she was told. When they continued walking, Inez chuckled.

"A nice couple live there who do nothing but work all the time. Maybe a little drama will make them spend time together again."

"Drama?"

"Yes. Maybe they'll both think the other has an admirer, or better yet, a lover."

Meja glanced back at the bouquet and bit her lower lip. This didn't feel right. But Inez seemed pleased with herself. They continued walking.

"Why do you have a walking stick instead of a crutch or cane?" Meja asked.

Inez scoffed. "Crutches are for the injured and canes are for the elderly, whereas walking sticks are for those of us who are perfectly healthy but just need a little temporary support."

Meja was fairly sure a fractured pelvis counted as an injury but said nothing.

When they came to a few red fishing huts and a strange, white-painted stone pyramid, they veered off toward the water. Inez grabbed hold of Meja's arm and they walked slowly across the soft sand and then up to the pier, where a bench was strategically located by a stone wall to give shelter from the wind. Inez sat down and tried to catch her breath.

Meja walked farther up the pier, where the wall was replaced with a blue-and-white-painted handrail. At the end was a ladder leading into water so crystal clear that she could see shoals of fish below the surface. When she returned to the bench, Inez was sitting with her eyes closed. Meja wasn't sure what to do. Sit down next to her or keep some distance? She chose to sit next to her, and after a while, she did the same as Inez—shut her eyes. But her eyelids were twitching and trembling. She didn't feel peaceful enough to sit still and do nothing. She opened her eyes, observed a man in a yellow kayak, and counted how many dogs and their owners passed by. She got to nine before Inez opened her eyes.

"The sea slowly rolling into shore, only to sweep straight back out again, might be the most beautiful sound in the world, and the most melancholy. Imagine struggling so persistently, never to arrive at your destination," Inez said. Then she got up, leaned on Meja, and started walking back.

Back home they went into the kitchen and put on some coffee. This time Meja didn't hesitate to open the fridge to help herself to milk.

Inez sat down in her armchair. Meja sat in the other, as before.

"We can do this pile here," said Inez, pointing at a stack of books leaning against the wall.

Meja lifted the top book, but Inez didn't look at it. She was looking at Meja.

"You don't read books."

Meja slowly put the book down again. How could Inez know she didn't read books? Or was it a question, even though she had made it sound like a statement?

"I can see it in your eyes," said Inez. "They don't have the depth that one acquires after visiting a thousand worlds with a thousand people."

Meja shrugged and raised the book again.

"Books aren't just stories, you know. They are lessons. About life. About ourselves," said Inez. She looked at the book in Meja's hand. "Keep."

They went through the books for an hour. Then Inez stood up and stretched. She grumbled about her painful hip and walked over to the window, peered through the blinds, and sighed. "Now they have a 'For Sale' sign up."

Meja didn't know whether she was talking to her or just thinking out loud, but she answered anyway with a soft "Oh, really?"

Meja could see the blue folder tucked by the armrest of Inez's armchair. She felt guilty just looking at it and blushed when Inez turned around.

They went through a few more books, and when Meja held up the final one of its pile, Inez said, "You can have that one. Read it. It will teach you a lot about the mother-daughter relationship."

Meja could feel redness creeping up her cheeks again as she looked at the book. *Divine Secrets of the Ya-Ya Sisterhood.* Surely Inez couldn't know how complicated her relationship with her mother was. Or could she see that in her eyes too?

Inez got up and opened the porch door. "That's enough for today."

"Thank you," said Meja, nodding at the book in her hand before leaving the house.

"No need to say thank you for something you didn't ask for in the first place," Inez said, shutting the door.

Meja walked down the path. She wanted more than anything to pick up that flower bouquet stuck on the gate a few houses away, but she suspected Inez was watching her and went straight to her car instead.

INEZ

The phone was just out of Inez's reach. She swore, grabbed her walking stick, and got to the phone at almost the precise instant it stopped ringing. The only people who ever called her were salespeople; Amelia; her doctor, Aron; and her publisher, Cristy. She hoped it was Cristy, who was still a human whirlwind at age eighty-four. Cristy had worked on all of Inez's books and stayed in contact even though Inez had stopped writing fifteen years ago. Sometimes she nagged Inez about doing another book, but less often these days. Cristy hadn't just been her publisher—she had been the one holding all the threads. Of her professional life and her private life. When Inez used to go into a writing bubble or out on book tours, she became like a sister and a friend, as well as a second mother to Amelia.

Inez sighed. Amelia and Inez didn't speak to each other about that time. It was better that way. They had such different interpretations of how things had been. Inez defended her decisions by saying that times were different then. Children weren't coddled, they had to adapt. It usually did them good. And indeed it had for Amelia, who had developed a keen eye for design and achieved a successful career curating art exhibitions.

Amelia had her own interpretation and underwent years of therapy on account of her "traveling childhood with a mother who wasn't always mentally present even when she was physically present." Inez picked up the phone. It had been Amelia. She dialed her daughter's number.

"Hello, you called?"

"Yes, what's happened to your hip? Cristy told me you had a fall and went to the doctor."

Inez asked her to hold on a moment while she limped to the porch door and went outside. Beyond the path, the tall grass, and the pebbly beach lay the sea. She shut her eyes and inhaled its salty scent, distinct even from a distance. A sense of calm spread through her.

"It's no big deal. Just a fractured pelvis."

"That's not what I heard from Cristy," said Amelia in a reproachful tone.

"You know what Cristy's like—a total drama queen."

"She's not more of a drama queen than you are stubborn and proud. You'd say it was no big deal if you broke both your legs. So who am I supposed to believe?"

Before Inez could answer, Amelia continued.

"And what were you doing up on that stool anyway?"

"Cleaning."

"Cleaning?"

"Yes, sorting and clearing stuff out. Decluttering."

"Why on earth are you doing that?" said Amelia.

"Why not? It's time."

"Wow. Wonders never cease!"

Obviously pleased at this turn of events, Amelia became more light-hearted as she spoke about her work and art exhibitions. Inez wasn't listening particularly carefully. She shut her eyes and took a deep breath. So many memories, so many feelings wrapped up in this sea scent. They were all coming back to her now that she was writing this book. She was going to pour her whole self into this book; it would be unlike anything she had written before. This one would be true. But truth always came at a price.

She opened her eyes. "You have to promise me that you'll scatter my ashes in the sea."

"What?" Now Amelia's voice had gone into falsetto. "What are you talking about? You're not sick, are you? You said it was just a fracture."

"It is. But I'm going to die someday. You might as well know my wishes."

She imagined the deep creases in Amelia's forehead. She had probably just gone into the kitchen, grabbed a cloth, and started polishing an already sparkling surface. Just like she always did when Inez was visiting and the conversation turned to something deeper than what new restaurants had opened in town. *Why make life more complicated than it already is?* Amelia would say while fluffing a pillow. Apparently, this is where years of therapy had gotten her.

"I promise I'll let you know when I go back to the doctor," Inez said, returning to the original topic.

"So you don't need me to come over and help with anything?"

"That's very kind, but there's no need. I've hired a cleaner."

"What? Finally!" said Amelia. "How many times have I nagged you about that?"

"Well, you can come over, once it's all done. We can celebrate."

Inez could imagine her daughter's face breaking into a smile of relief. Decluttering and celebrating were more Amelia's style than sickness and plans for after her death.

Just as Inez put the phone in her pocket, Sverker appeared on the other side of the wall. He was holding out a bright-pink peony.

"A beauty for a beauty. Sarah Bernhardt—the world's most beloved peony. The plants can live over fifty years and still bloom in abundance, and the flowers emit a gorgeous fragrance."

Inez suppressed an eye roll as she took it.

"What's happened?" he said, pointing to her walking stick.

"Cleaning incident."

"Do say if you need help with something. Anything. We're right here, you know. Just a wall away."

His eager expression made Inez bite her lip. Such a kind soul didn't deserve her acerbic comments. And yet only acerbic comments came to mind. She turned around to go back inside.

"Hey," he said. "You've still never taken us up on dinner. Maybe you'd like to come over this evening? Bring that young woman who has been coming in the mornings. Is she a relative?"

"That's my cleaner," Inez said shortly and opened the porch door.

Sverker and Filip had been inviting her over ever since they had moved in—to no avail. The first thing Sverker had said when they introduced themselves was that he loved her books. And she could tell from his eyes that he meant it. He was a fan. It had made Inez put up a high wall between them. A wall she had no interest in bringing down.

"We have to work together to make sure we get a decent new neighbor in Viola's house," he said.

Inez stopped in her tracks.

"We know the real estate agent," he continued.

She turned around and squinted at him. Was he telling the truth or grasping at straws? She nodded slightly and shut the door.

She put the peony in the garbage can.

She didn't throw it away because she hated flowers. It was more about not feeding her bitterness. Trying to avoid being "bitingly bitter," as Amelia would say. Flowers were associated with success and happiness. And even though it had been her choice to retire, it wasn't an easy decision. She had felt compelled. And in order to live with this decision, she had to remove herself from certain things that reminded her of what had been. Flowers were one such thing. That's why all she had on her windowsill was a cactus.

She sat in the living room. She had made two crucial decisions in her life. Both had changed everything. Changed her and all the people around her. One had been to stop writing. A betrayal to many. But that decision was nowhere near as difficult as the one she had made when she was twenty-six. Her carefully guarded secret. The one she was writing about now in her new book. She had tried to shut the memories up in the deepest, darkest place inside her. But burying something always meant someone else could dig it up. And journalists were like a combination of detectives and badgers. That's why she had given up writing fifteen years ago. So that the people who were starting to scratch beneath the surface of her writing career wouldn't get deep enough to stumble upon something else entirely. A story from her past. A much uglier one. Through quiet withdrawal she had managed to calm the storm that could so easily have grown into a tornado. But no one knew this. No one knew the secrets she carried.

She reached for her computer and opened it on her lap. She hadn't gone down to the pier today, but that didn't matter. She still had words left from yesterday. She took a deep breath and continued to write her story, the one she had been so afraid of someone else finding and telling in words that weren't hers. About her life with Mathilda. She was glad she was still at the beginning of the story, when everything was filled with wonder.

But she was already dreading the end.

1969

Every day that I was free, I went to the café on the pier in the hope of seeing that young woman with the oysters again. A week later, she appeared. Dressed in the same orange waterproof pants and carrying a plastic basket of oysters. She recognized me and gestured to say she would come over after she had delivered the oysters to the restaurant.

She came back fifteen minutes later, her basket empty and her pants in a bag. She sat down at my table, introduced herself as Mathilda, and ordered a coffee. I said my name was Inez and I had just moved here, and she nodded slowly. I don't remember what else we spoke about that day, but I remember feeling like we had been talking all our lives.

An hour later, when she had to go, she told me what day and time she planned to come back. I was already sure that I would be there then too. We met three times at the pier café before Mathilda asked if I wanted to go with her out to sea.

We took the boat out countless times after that. In all seasons, all weathers.

If I had to describe Mathilda, I would say that she was as wild and sensitive as the oysters under the sea. I would definitely say that she carried a primordial strength within her. Without it, her slender body wouldn't have been able to handle the freezing water, thrashing winds, and physical exertions of her work. When she dived at Oyster Bay in winter, she wore more than her own body weight in diving gear. Going out on the boat with her on those days was more of a religious experience than Sunday mass at church.

At first she spoke in high spirits, turned her face into the wind, and let it play with her hair. As we approached Oyster Bay she became more and more closed. When we arrived and she put on her diving gear, she often said nothing at all. A curious calm resided in her silence. As though it didn't matter if harsh winds blew and dragged the boat or if thunder rumbled in the distance. Right there, right then, everything was perfectly still, surrounded by reverence and respect. One time I told her it was like she was taming nature when she stood there in the boat, ready to dive again. She looked at me and said, "It's the exact opposite. It's not about taming, but following."

MEJA

Meja was just about to lock her front door and go to Inez's house when her phone beeped.

Shift postponed to 5pm. Wear something nice.

Inez hadn't formulated it as a question—she'd just taken it for granted that Meja would change her plans. Was a client even allowed to do that? Change the schedule on such short notice? And what did she mean by "wear something nice"? Her mother had said the same thing to her umpteen times, but she didn't really have anything "nice" in her wardrobe.

Meja sighed, locked the door, and left the building. Her apartment was by Mariatorget Square in central Helsingborg, with its gothic church in the middle, encircled by restaurants. Once Meja had been on her way to one of her temp jobs, she couldn't remember which, and seen long tables covered with bones and skulls outside the church. Renovation in the square had uncovered the remains of buried bodies that were now in the hands of archaeologists. Meja had found it utterly bizarre that these skeletons were just lying there on the table, not even ten feet from the outdoor seating of local establishments where people were eating pasta and burgers; everyone else seemed to think the skulls were a fun, kooky feature of their surroundings. Johan did too. He went down to take pictures on his phone. She, on the other hand, couldn't eat for days and had terrible nightmares.

She dodged prams and tourists with the same vague anxiety she always felt in crowds. She really wasn't a city girl at heart, but the apartment was Johan's, and he had no intention of moving. She turned onto Kullagatan and into the nearest clothes store. Before her was a mannequin in a navy-blue wrap dress. She found one in small, paid for it, and left.

She regretted it as soon as she got home. A dress. Why hadn't she gotten a pair of light pants and a simple blouse? She took off her clothes and slipped the dress over her head. It was beautiful, but it made her feel uncomfortable. Maybe she could wear jeans and a slightly nicer sweater? Should she text Inez and ask what her plans were? She hated not knowing. But something told her that Inez wouldn't answer. She sighed and collapsed onto the couch.

On the table in front of her was the book Inez had lent her. Meja googled the title and saw that there was a film version starring Sandra Bullock. She drummed her fingers and considered her options for a moment before downloading the film and starting to watch. It was cheating, of course. And she would never be able to tell Inez that she had watched the film instead of reading the book, but at least she could probably answer vague questions about the characters and plot.

Two hours later she was staring up at the ceiling. Thoughts were swirling in her mind. The film's message was clear. Nothing was ever black-and-white. There were often explanations lending nuance to the blackness. In order to understand, it was necessary to go beyond the surface. Look at the whole picture. Not just at the sticking points.

Inez had told Meja that the book would teach her a lot about the mother-daughter relationship. Memories of her upbringing flashed through her mind. Susanne had always had this way of looking out the window and sighing that made her desire to leave obvious. From an early age, Meja had learned to take care of herself. She never asked for help with homework, made her own breakfast, and packed lunch for school trips. She had worked hard to avoid being difficult or getting in the way. Words like *strength* and *purpose* had been among Susanne's favorites, and Meja had striven to embody them. Except she had also longed fervently for the occasional gentle embrace.

She went into the kitchen and made some instant noodles, which she ate standing up, leaning against the counter. Now that she thought of it, she realized that Susanne was still trying to do the same thing: push her to have strength and purpose. All the nagging about education and getting a good job. Johan always said that Susanne didn't mean anything by it, that Meja viewed her mother through the eyes of a child and took everything the wrong way. Surely Susanne was only commenting because she wanted her to be happy? But Johan was blinded by Susanne's dazzling charm; he hadn't had to grow up with that razor-sharp tongue. The one that waited behind that smile and jabbed whenever she least expected it.

The harshest jab of all had come in an argument when Meja was a teenager. Susanne told her that Meja had destroyed her dreams with her very first breath.

What these dreams had actually been, Meja didn't know. But they had clearly been incompatible with the life of a young single mother working two jobs.

And ever since, Meja had lived with the feeling that everything was her fault.

She shook off these thoughts and took the rest of the day at a relaxed pace.

Later, as the clock approached four thirty, she put on the dress, despite herself. A quick glance in the mirror told her it would have looked better with suntanned legs. Oh well. At least it was "nice."

She parked under the pine trees again, followed the little path to Inez's house, and took a deep breath when she arrived at the gate. *Please let this evening pass quickly.*

INEZ

Inez took out an unopened bottle of white port labeled "Graham's." A decent present for her hosts. She had caught Sverker in the garden yesterday afternoon and accepted his dinner invitation. He had struggled to sound politely restrained when he said "how lovely," but she could hear his voice tremble in excitement.

She sighed. It had been a long time since she last attended a dinner party, and it was *not* like riding a bike. She was already tired. She used to be able to party all night. But now it wasn't for the sake of festivities that she had accepted the invitation, but rather to potentially get a say in who their new neighbor might be.

If Sverker weren't so wide-eyed, he would have understood that their acquaintance with the real estate agent was the only reason she had agreed to come over after three years of invitations.

She didn't plan on hiding it. On the contrary. No need to tiptoe politely around one another; why not get straight to it? How could they make sure the right person moved in?

She glanced at the clock. Meja would be here soon. She was always punctual. The decision to bring her cleaner along mainly came down to needing someone to help her walk home if her neighbors served wine. Which presumably they would. She often saw them from her living room window, sitting under the pergola with a glass in the evening. She peeked through the blinds and waited for Meja to appear on the other side of the gate.

She came five minutes before the appointed time. Inez picked up the bottle and opened the porch door.

"Oh," said Meja. Inez assumed this was at the sight of her tidied hair and rouged cheeks. "So, where are we going?"

Inez didn't answer, but she noted Meja's relieved smile when they walked out of her gate and straight in through the neighbors'. Meja had probably expected something a lot worse than a visit to Sverker and Filip.

It was clear from the outside that their garden was a green oasis. But it was impossible to really appreciate just how lush it was until they went in. Each section of the garden merged into the next, offering peace and beauty in many different forms. A bountiful rose arbor led to a minimalist Asian-inspired section with a Japanese maple in the middle, which in turn led to an herb garden.

"Oh," said Meja again.

Sverker and Filip came onto the veranda carrying a tray with four glasses of sparkling wine.

"Welcome," Sverker said ceremoniously, dressed for the occasion in a pale jacket and gray bow tie. Filip had gone for a simpler short-sleeve shirt, and he shivered slightly in the cool wind that had intensified since the afternoon. Inez handed over the port, which was received with wide smiles. She took a glass, raised it slightly to the other three, and took a sip. So she still remembered some of her old social skills, at least.

"What a wonderful garden," said Meja, looking around at the brightly colored dahlias framing the veranda.

Inez nodded, happy that Meja was socially competent enough to praise their hosts. That way she didn't have to do it herself.

"I hit the proverbial wall a few years ago," said Sverker. "Then Filip introduced me to the world of gardening. I knew nothing about plants and flowers, but when my burnout was at its worst, gardening became my medicine and then my rehabilitation. Today it is the air I breathe." He looked at Filip and broke the mood with a broad grin and a playful shove of his partner's side. "Sorry, *you* are the air I breathe, of course."

41

Filip laughed and shook his head slightly. "We'd planned on sitting outside, but it's gotten a bit breezy. Is it okay if we sit indoors?" he said.

Inez nodded, knocked back her drink, and walked in last, leaning on her walking stick. Just like the garden, the inside of the house was the exact opposite of hers. Every single thing was thoughtfully placed. This house was cozy, soft, and welcoming. Rich colors, thick rugs, and large candelabras. She heard Meja's third "oh" of the evening. Inez tried to imagine what her home must look like. She would bet good money that most of it belonged to her partner. To picture how her apartment was decorated, she would have to know more about him.

Sverker took Inez's arm and led her to the table, while Filip pulled out her chair. A gesture which normally would have produced a smile and a thank-you from Inez, but which now, on account of her walking stick and aching hip, mainly just made her feel like a decrepit old biddy. So she did not smile or say thank you. Filip disappeared into the kitchen and came out with small plates of scallops served beautifully in seashells. Now Inez couldn't help but smile.

"Scallops with pea-and-wasabi mayonnaise," said Filip as he put the plates down on the table.

Inez mused on whether people were simply born with one of two DNA types—chaotic or refined. She had come across many people in her life and noticed that a beautiful garden most often came with a beautiful house and almost always good food too. Whereas she worked at home in what her daughter called a pigsty, had a yard that consisted of algae-green paving stones and weeds, and cared so little about food that she often cooked in bulk and ate the same meal for a whole week.

Meja was across from Inez and looked at her from under her fringe. Inez understood her expression. How on earth were they supposed to go about eating this work of art? She pushed her fork straight into the scallop, stuffed it in her mouth whole, and chewed. Meja hid her smile behind her napkin, then did the same. Filip and Sverker split their scallops into three neat pieces and enjoyed small bites.

"So you work as a cleaner?" said Filip, looking at Meja.

She washed the scallop down with wine and nodded. "As a temp."

She wiped her mouth and quickly deflected further questions from Filip. "And you two, what do you do?"

"I'm the head gardener at Sofiero Palace. But cooking is my passion."

"And I'm a biomedical analyst at a laboratory in Lund," said Sverker. "And, as you have already gathered, my husband's line of work is my passion."

Meja and Inez both nodded. Sverker continued to talk about his work studying microorganisms and cells until they had finished their starters. Filip took away the plates and returned presently with the main course. He carried two plates in each hand like a proper waiter and presented them with an elegant bow.

"Beef filet medallions with chopped herbs and roasted pine nuts," he said.

Inez inhaled the delicious aroma. Three years of nagging her to come for dinner were forgiven. Filip sat down and gestured for them to begin. All that could be heard was a unanimous murmur of enjoyment.

"This is without a doubt the most delicious thing I've ever eaten," said Meja, closing her eyes before taking another bite.

Filip smiled. "So good. Cooking is a bit like gardening. You have to respect the ingredients, tend them carefully, and take time to enjoy the result."

Sverker went back to the original topic of discussion: work. "I truly love my job, and Filip his, but you must have the best job of all of us," he said, looking at Inez. "Oh, to guide people into fictional worlds. To make them laugh and cry, give them insights and an escape from reality."

Inez took a bite and shrugged her shoulders slightly. She wanted to keep this conversation floating on the surface.

Filip nodded to Sverker. "He's read all of your books. At least once."

Sverker blushed a little. "Books, including yours, have always afforded my brain a much-needed break—they cut straight to my heart."

Inez finished chewing and wiped her mouth with a napkin. He obviously admired her as a writer, but she was done with being admired. There was no way of saying so without seeming rude.

"There is healing power in even the most lighthearted entertainment," she said eventually and made up her mind to steer the conversation elsewhere. To the reason she was there.

"If I may change the subject, what a tragedy it was that Viola left us so suddenly," she said.

Filip shuddered. "Yes, it came as a complete shock. One day she was doing yoga in her garden, and the next day she was gone."

"You said you were in contact with the real estate agent dealing with the sale?" said Inez, looking at Sverker, who nodded and looked at Filip.

"My sister's brother-in-law works for the real estate agency. He doesn't really work in this area, but if we bribed him with good food, we could certainly get some information out of him," said Filip.

Inez smiled properly for the first time that evening. "Perhaps an evening like this, getting information, could also include some requests from the neighbors. We live so close together, after all."

Filip smiled. "It's the seller who decides in the end, and they usually go for the buyer with the highest offer."

"But more or less anyone can be influenced if you find the right buttons to push." Inez took a sip of wine, raised her glass to Filip, and said, "Surely Viola's children will want someone who will take good care of their mother's beloved house? To preserve her memory."

"Not a boisterous young family, in other words," Filip said with a wink.

Inez flashed a dazzling smile. "I can just imagine a football flying over my insignificant little yard and straight into your beautiful African lilies."

Filip raised his eyebrows, and Sverker, who had just come in carrying a silver tray with four portions of lemon curd topped with edible violets, made a squeaking sort of sound.

Inez smiled and stretched her back. "Those look delicious."

Her task for the evening was accomplished. She had gotten them where she wanted them. Now she could just enjoy herself. She poured them all some of the dessert wine that stood on the table. Filip and Sverker leaned in to one another and exchanged a few words.

"We'll arrange a dinner with the brother-in-law," Filip said after a little while. "We want to avoid footballs in our African lilies at all costs."

"I understand," said Inez and raised her glass. "Well, now. The night is still young, isn't it?"

MEJA

Meja didn't say much over the course of the evening, but she thoroughly enjoyed herself. The flavors, aromas, and decor, the jazz tinkling in the background, and the beautiful table setting with a lavender centerpiece. Every detail was a ten out of ten. She had felt nervous at first, afraid of doing the wrong thing or saying something stupid. Afraid that she would embarrass Inez. But from the first scallop, she had understood that Inez didn't care much about manners and decorum, and she had been able to relax.

Sverker shifted his chair nearer to hers, clinked glasses, and looked over at Inez and Filip, who were deep in conversation about local excursion destinations.

"I almost want to pinch myself," he whispered. "For three years we've been trying to convince her to come over. And then suddenly she agrees."

Meja saw his eyes glitter.

"Well, I know she's only come so that she can influence who moves in next door, but still." He smiled at Meja, who smiled back. Then he tilted his head slightly. "You don't read books, do you?"

Meja squirmed. He said it just like Inez had—a statement disguised as a question. Did it really show in her eyes? Before she could respond, he continued, "She writes fantastic books about friendship and life-changing decisions." Then he looked at Meja again. "Does she ever talk about her writing?"

Meja shook her head. "Never. She hasn't said a single word about it."

"And I don't suppose she's writing anything new," Sverker said with a conspiratorial wink.

Meja thought about the blue folder in the house that she was absolutely not allowed to touch and shook her head. "Not that I know of."

She poured some water. The wine, and perhaps all the excitement, had given her a slight gnawing ache in the temples. She decided to speak plainly without getting involved in subjects that weren't her business. Like whether or not Inez was writing a book.

"You're right, I don't read books. And I didn't actually know who she was when I started this job."

Sverker nodded. "I suppose she likes that. She must have become a recluse for a reason. The newspapers weren't very kind to her fifteen years ago, but no one thought it would make her stop writing altogether. On the contrary, people expected her to fight back fiercely in book form."

Sverker rested his gaze on Inez again. "Filip told me to butt out, but I'm just trying to brighten up her life behind those blinds with some flowers. I hope she appreciates them."

Meja felt her cheeks flush pink when she thought about the beautiful flowers that had ended up in the trash, but she gave a little nod. "They look beautiful on the living room table."

Sverker smiled widely. "Really? That's what I told Filip. He thought she probably threw them away." He scoffed at the mere thought.

Meja giggled and hoped she didn't sound nervous.

"One day," Sverker said, leaning closer, "I hope those flowers might encourage her to open her blinds. Heal her like her books have healed me time and time again."

Meja nodded and saw Inez push back her chair.

"Well, you know what? Tomorrow is another day. I would like to thank you both for a wonderful evening."

Meja stood up too, thanked her hosts, and gave Inez her arm in support. Sverker stood next to Filip and smiled. "We're the ones who should be thanking you. If you only knew how much we've been looking forward to this."

Inez muttered something inaudible and then said, "Now don't forget to invite that real estate agent over for dinner. The viewings are bound to begin soon."

They nodded and Sverker opened the porch door. He looked with concern at Inez's wobbly steps, but she waved her hand dismissively. "We can manage just fine."

The solar-powered lights in the garden were on, and it was like walking through a mini paradise.

Meja adjusted to Inez's slow pace through the garden and onto the path. Once there, Inez stopped and gazed up at a sky that looked like an acrylic painting in pink and navy tones.

"Not even the most beautiful garden can compare to that."

Meja agreed and led Inez through the gate. Every step seemed to be a struggle for Inez after so many hours of sitting in the same position. Inez clung tightly to Meja's arm. They stopped at the porch.

"To think that such a small step can feel like climbing a mountain." Inez sighed.

"Maybe it would be better to use the front door?" Meja suggested.

"There's a step at least as high. And it's stone. If I fell there, I'd hurt myself more than here."

Inez mumbled something angry. It sounded like Spanish or French.

"We'll count to three. Then go for it."

"We could ask Sverker if he . . . ," said Meja.

"Dear girl, there is a limit to the humiliation I'm willing to undergo. Hold on now. One . . . two . . . three."

Inez pressed down as hard as she could on her walking stick at the same time as Meja pulled her up. They both wobbled but succeeded. Inez sighed with relief and let Meja open the porch door. The room was in darkness. Meja led her over to the armchair and turned on two table lamps.

"I can help you into bed."

Inez shook her head. "Just leave a glass of water here. I'll be fine."

"It's no trouble for me, I've worked doing that sort of thing before as well," said Meja.

"That sort of thing? Helping old people into bed?"

Meja nodded.

Inez laughed dryly. "May I have a glass of water?"

Meja disappeared into the kitchen and came back with a glass of ice water. On the little tray table she saw the blue folder. She was just about to push it to one side to put down the glass when Inez quickly put her hand over it. Their eyes met. Meja swallowed hard. Inez took the glass in her hand.

"You can go now. Thank you for today," she said.

Meja reluctantly picked up her bag. "Text me if you need anything. Anything, at any time. Promise me."

Inez shooed her to the door.

Meja pressed her lips together and left. It didn't feel right leaving Inez there in that armchair, but she was a stubborn old woman. Too tipsy to drive home, she opened an app on her phone and found the bus schedule. There was one coming in ten minutes. She hurried to the pine trees that looked like eerie arms reaching up into the darkness. When she saw the bus coming, she let out a deep sigh.

The evening was over.

INEZ

Inez was woken up by a loud banging on the front door. The sudden sound made her heart race. She groaned. Her head throbbed, and her dry lips had a metallic taste when she licked them. Memories from the night before slowly came back to her, one by one. The food and laughter at Sverker and Filip's house, Meja's reluctance to leave, her decision to sleep in the armchair when she felt pinned down by exhaustion, pain, and drunkenness. That had been a mistake.

The person on the other side of the door banged again, and she whimpered as she reached for her walking stick.

"I'm coming! Calm down!" she called.

She took hold of her walking stick and pushed herself up. One dragging step at a time, she made her way through the hall and opened the door. On the other side stood her daughter.

"Amelia?"

"Oh, dear god," Amelia said and slapped her hand over her mouth.

"Do we not call before visits anymore?" asked Inez and turned around as abruptly as she could. It turned out to be a slow and rather clumsy pirouette.

"I tried ringing last night and this morning but you never picked up, and I thought . . ."

"That the old witch had croaked? I told you, no one dies from a fractured hip."

"I thought you'd had another fall," Amelia said shortly and hung up her jacket. She kept her shoes on.

"I see. Well, now that you're here, maybe you can make some coffee?"

Amelia went into the living room and opened the blinds, as she always did when she visited, then disappeared into the kitchen. Inez hid the blue folder on the bookshelf and went to the bathroom. Her reflection in the mirror made her laugh. She looked absolutely terrible. No wonder Amelia had been concerned. Her hair stuck out in all directions. Her eyes were red and her lips were flaky. She rinsed her face with cold water, applied some lip balm, and combed her hair.

"I was at a party last night," she told Amelia when she came out. "In case you were wondering why I look so disheveled."

"Party?"

"Yes, at the neighbors' house."

Amelia's frown softened. "With those two men?"

"Yes, Sverker and Filip."

"But you've always said you would never give in to their nagging about a dinner."

"Yes, but now it turns out they know the real estate agent dealing with the sale of Viola's house. I thought I'd lobby for someone without young children."

"I see. In other words, you had an agenda. Why couldn't you just have a little fun for once?"

The frown was back in her forehead as she walked past Inez with a tray of coffee, bread, and butter. Inez followed slowly. She glanced at the windows. She wanted to pull down the blinds again, but she'd have to wait until Amelia left.

"I had fun *and* an agenda. Life isn't all black-and-white, you know. There's a broad color palette in between."

Amelia scoffed in that way she always did when she wanted to swear but couldn't because she disapproved of profanity. They sat down at the edge of the table that wasn't cluttered with objects.

"We drank sparkling wine in their beautiful garden, and they served up incredible food and wine that accompanied the flavors perfectly in their delightfully decorated home. Why do homosexuals always have such good taste and eye for detail?"

Now an even deeper frown appeared in Amelia's forehead. "For someone talking about the palette between black and white, you have a surprising number of preconceptions. Not *all* gay people have beautiful homes and are amazing cooks. I know plenty who are just normal people, kind of sloppy, prefer eating out to cooking, and have zero taste when it comes to interior design."

Inez took a piece of bread and spread a substantial amount of butter on it. She murmured in pleasure as she took the first bite.

"Are you eating properly?" Amelia said. "You look thinner."

"Pain burns calories."

"No, it doesn't." Amelia squinted. "How bad is the pain? Are you taking painkillers?"

Before Inez could answer there came another knock on the door. The porch door this time. A much gentler knock than Amelia's. Even though the blinds were up, they hadn't noticed Meja arrive. Now there she was, waving awkwardly outside the window.

"Come in," called Inez.

Meja opened the door and stepped inside.

"My cleaner, Meja," said Inez.

Amelia stood up to say hello. "It can't be easy working on this house," she said and laughed a little nervously as she shook Meja's hand.

Inez gestured for her to sit down.

"Amelia is my daughter. She thought I'd died and came rushing over from Copenhagen."

"You weren't answering your phone," said Amelia.

Inez took some more bread and butter and nodded to Meja. "She was with me next door last night."

Amelia looked up. "Oh really? How nice."

"My extra crutch," said Inez, taking a big bite.

"I've never eaten such good food," said Meja, glossing over the fact that Inez was referring to her more as a personal assistant than as a cleaner. She turned to Inez. "Did you sleep well? I felt so bad just leaving you in that armchair."

Inez finished eating and got up. "Absolutely, like a princess in a feather bed."

From the corner of her eye she saw Amelia shake her head and mouth "armchair" to Meja.

"Oh," said Meja in her typical way.

Interesting, Inez thought, to use such a small and insignificant word in so many different contexts: surprise, amazement, horror, joy, concern. Everything was "oh" for Meja.

Inez sat down in her armchair.

Meja came and sat next to her. She leaned in toward her. "I can come back later, seeing as your daughter is here."

"Absolutely not. She showed up uninvited. Besides, this is like her birthday and Christmas rolled into one—seeing her mother tidying."

Meja squirmed and glanced uncertainly over at Amelia, who smiled in response.

"I have some errands to run, so I'll go and come back again after lunch. Does that work?"

Inez nodded and pointed at a pile by the bookshelf. Meja carried it over, and they began to go through the same procedure as usual.

As soon as Amelia left, Inez got up and pulled down the blinds. Fatigue made her legs feel like lead.

"I'm going to lie down and rest for a bit. Yesterday's festivities have taken a toll. You can go home if you want, or do a provisional sorting of that pile. I can check it later."

Inez yawned widely and went into the bedroom with Meja's hesitant gaze boring into her neck. She lay down on top of the bedspread, fully clothed, and sank immediately into a deep sleep.

When she woke up three hours later, her forehead was sweaty. She couldn't remember what she had dreamed, but she knew where the dreams had taken her. Her book about the oyster diver was opening a window to the past. So far the story had been seeping through a crack, but with time she knew it would probably burst through in full force and gush out like a waterfall. The risk was that it would take Inez with it.

Whether she would sink or swim remained to be seen.

She got up slowly and went into the living room. Meja had gone home but she'd left a note.

Sorted through some things. Found some photos that I left in a pile. Didn't want to wake you, but didn't know if I should stay until the end of my shift. Call if you need anything. I can come over any time. —M

If the girl can come over any time, then she can't have much of a life, thought Inez. Her eyes fell on one of the photos and she sat down to flick through the rest. They were pictures from book launches, signings, writers' seminars, and parties. It was like looking at a different person. She was always smiling and laughing. Always well dressed in silk blouses and high heels. Often holding a champagne flute. Amelia was in some of the pictures, too, holding on to Inez's skirt or Cristy's hand.

Inez bit her bottom lip and turned the pile upside down. She had loved every second. Even though she had missed her daughter's graduations, been left by men who thought she worked too much, and lain on the floor in the fetal position crying with exhaustion until Cristy came and put her to bed with a glass of whiskey and a few soothing words. She had loved being able to feel. Loved being passionate about words. About stories. About her characters.

She looked around the room. The life she lived today contained little trace of that other life. But there was no halfway. It was one or the other. So she had replaced her career and celebrity with the exact opposite: quiet, solitude, isolation. It was the right thing to do.

She heard the front door opening and quickly hid the photos under a newspaper.

"I've brought some lunch." Amelia stepped in with three plastic trays of Caesar salad. She looked around. "Oh, has the cleaner finished for the day?"

"Yes, she's only here in the mornings." Inez nodded at the third salad. "You can leave that in the fridge."

Amelia went into the kitchen, came out again, and started talking about everything she had done since she'd been gone. About the exhibition she had seen in Dunker Culture House, the perfume she had bought, and the vanilla latte she had drunk at Espresso House in the harbor. She had done this when she was little as well—reported every detail of what she had done while Inez had been away. After Amelia had gone to therapy as an adult, she called Inez one day to find out why she had never asked her how her day had been or what she had done. Inez had answered that there was never any need because Amelia always told her anyway. Amelia had countered by saying that she told her because she knew she wouldn't ask. Never cared. Inez had said that a person could care without knowing every detail of someone's day.

"That sounds nice," she said this time, to maintain a civil atmosphere.

"And you've been working hard?" Amelia said, looking around the room.

"Yes, we're taking one pile at a time. It's not going quickly, but progress is being made."

Amelia nodded but looked like she thought it was going very slowly indeed. "You have the money to hire a second cleaner, of course. They could work in different rooms in parallel. Efficiency, you know."

"Then I might as well rent a locker and just shove it all in there."

Amelia shrugged her shoulders as if to say that wasn't such a bad idea. They ate, and when they finished Amelia glanced at the clock. "I'd better go home. Are you sure you'll be all right? If you need help, you're always welcome at my place, you know that."

"Absolutely," said Inez and gave a dismissive wave with her walking stick.

Inez stayed where she was until she heard Amelia start the car. Then she took out the blue folder and sat down in the armchair to read the last pages she had written. To her surprise, she felt a tear well up in the corner of her eye. It slowly rolled down through the furrows in her skin. She wiped it away. It would have been easier to put the lid back on, decide that this book was a silly idea, and destroy what she'd written. But now she realized that she wasn't telling this story for her own sake, but for Amelia's. It would be a form of explanation and apology. An answer to why she had become the person she had, and why she had taken her writing so damn seriously. It would show the color palette between black and white. The answers to all questions.

She owed it to her daughter.

1971

Mathilda loved teaching me about her world just as much as I loved being in it. So she taught me all about the bizarre wonders of life beneath the surface, as she called it, when we went out in her boat. With stubborn conviction, she filled me with information about bycatch and lime worms. I forgot most of it by the time we returned to land. But some of it I would remember for the rest of my life. Like that you could tell whether oysters had lived deep underwater or near the surface just from their color: the paler the green, the shallower their waters. Mathilda liked the darkest greens best, the ones from the deepest water; but I liked the ones closer to the surface best. I guess that said a lot about us as people as well.

Mathilda was complicated. Transparent and impenetrable at the same time. I curiously scratched at her layers to find the magic formula that put her in such perfect harmony with the natural world. Every time she broke the sea's surface and disappeared into the deep, it was like everything held its breath, then slowly breathed out: now she was where she belonged. Anyone who experienced that moment with her would forever search for their own sense of belonging.

We grew very close, but I'm not sure I ever really knew her. Still, through my search to understand her, I learned more and more about myself. Through watching her break boundaries, I learned how to transcend my own. I was happy with my job at the bookstore, liked my little apartment in Kobbholmen, and enjoyed spending my free time with Mathilda. But I also felt that there was more waiting out there. At twenty-one years old, I knew my calling lay just around the corner. I just didn't know what it was.

Looking back now, I see that my calling was there in the ripples on the water caused by Mathilda's dives. When she was under the surface, I sat on a rock and wrote in my little black notebook. I sat there as the summer sun warmed up the stone slabs, and I sat there as the snow creaked beneath my shoes and the letters came out almost illegible due to the thick gloves holding the pen. I wrote about nature, about Mathilda, about my innermost thoughts and dreams. I didn't know it then, but all those times Mathilda was following her calling, it sowed the seeds of my own.

Writing. It was to become my greatest joy, but it also led to my greatest tragedy.

MEJA

Meja wandered aimlessly. As always, she had asked Johan if he wanted to join her for a walk. And as always, he had answered, "Some other time." She walked past the bustling side streets lined with stores and restaurants, past Dunker Culture House, like a white meringue on the North Harbor, and along the waterside. Outdoor tables were full of people talking and laughing. Which was precisely why she rarely came here. Places like this reminded Meja that the world was filled with cheerful people. And that she was not one of them. She didn't belong.

She stopped outside one of the restaurants and looked up to the top floor of the building. This was where Susanne lived with Bengt. She took out her phone and fiddled with it a little before making her mind up to call her mother.

"Susanne speaking," she heard after a couple of rings.

"I was just out for a walk, and I think I've ended up outside Bengt's apartment. Wondered if I could pop in for a coffee and a chat?"

There was silence on the other end, but when Meja looked up again, she saw her mother leaning over the railing of the top-floor balcony.

"There you are," said Susanne. "Yes, come up. I'll buzz you in."

As soon as the gate opened, Meja had second thoughts. What kind of whim was this? She and Susanne didn't drop in on each other out of the blue.

She started walking up the stairs. Meja never took the elevator, even in an eight-story building. She wasn't scared of getting stuck or falling down the shaft—as had actually happened to a former colleague of hers. It was the mirror. *That* was her phobia. She couldn't stand being trapped in a confined space, watched by her own reflection.

She had to stop to catch her breath three times before she reached the top floor, where Susanne was waiting.

"Bengt is in Stockholm for a meeting and won't be home until tomorrow," she said.

Meja nodded, hung her denim jacket up in the hall, put her shoes neatly on the shoe rack, and followed her mother through the spacious apartment to the living room. Susanne's hair and makeup were flawless and she was dressed in a salmon-pink silk blouse; a tight, dark-gray skirt; and a pair of indoor shoes with a heel. *Wear something nice,* Inez had written when they were going to dinner at her neighbors' the other night. The dress that Meja had bought was nowhere near as nice as the outfit her mother was wearing just home alone. *No wonder we don't get each other,* she thought.

"Isn't it a gorgeous apartment?" said Susanne, making a sweeping gesture to indicate the large windows looking out on the strait separating the Swedish coastline from Denmark.

"It sure is," replied Meja, stepping forward to admire the view.

"So," said Susanne, going into the kitchen and turning on the espresso machine. "Are we celebrating a new job?"

"No, I have to finish this temp job before I can apply for something else."

They sat down on the white leather couch in the living room, and Susanne placed a tiny cup and saucer on the glass coffee table for Meja.

"So how's Johan?" Susanne asked.

Meja shrugged. "Fine. Probably playing video games."

Susanne raised her eyebrows at the disappointed tone in Meja's voice.

"His hobby is his job. You should get yourself a hobby—and a job you like," she added with a wink.

Meja sipped her espresso. Strange that her mother, who freely criticized her choices in life, never said a word about Johan's choice to spend most of his free time playing games despite pushing forty. Anyway, she did have a hobby—Ingrid. She had always wanted a dog but was never allowed a pet as a child. Then her work schedule wouldn't allow it. And Johan claimed that he was allergic to all animals with fur, but Meja suspected that was just an excuse to avoid responsibility. If it were up to her, she'd have birds, turtles, hamsters, rabbits, and even more guinea pigs.

"You used to like taking photos when you were younger, didn't you?" said Susanne.

Meja looked up. Yes, that was true. But then cell phones took over, and her old digital camera had ended up in a cardboard box somewhere.

She'd always thought there was something special about photographs. The last time she had been at Inez's house and found those photos between two novels, she couldn't help but look at them. If she gazed at a photo for long enough, she felt as though she could step right into it. The sounds, the background hum, the smells and tastes. Inez had looked happy living in the moment. Meja had become so engrossed in them that she had lost track of time and had to hustle to get the job done.

"Yes, I like photography," she said.

"Well, that's a hobby if ever I heard one," Susanne said and reached for her cell phone, which was ringing with some Spanish melody.

"Lizette!" she exclaimed, glancing at the clock. "Damn, I forgot the time. My daughter came over in need of life advice. You know how it is." Susanne smiled at Meja. "I'll be right down. Order a bottle of champagne—in an ice bucket. Bye." Susanne stood up. "I totally forgot I'm supposed to be meeting Lizette. Remember her? Kent's sister."

"I remember," Meja said, standing up.

Kent and Susanne had been married for a few tumultuous years. He had no children of his own, so when he died of lung cancer after years of heavy smoking, Susanne and his sister inherited all his money. Susanne hadn't worked a day since, and she still hung out with Lizette.

"Ah, so that's why you're so dressed up," said Meja as she got ready to leave.

Susanne laughed. "I always dress up. Like Dolly Parton, no one, absolutely no one, will ever see me without makeup and coiffed hair. Not even myself."

She applied another layer of red lipstick in front of the mirror, smacked her lips, and said, "That's my only stipulation for my funeral— for a proper beautician to do my hair and makeup so I can go into the furnace as my most beautiful self."

"Oh, Mom." Meja laughed.

Susanne fluffed her hair and turned to Meja with a dazzling smile.

"You know why some people are afraid of death?" She didn't wait for an answer. "Because they never really lived."

Meja nodded and sighed to herself. "Shall we go down together?"

"No, you go. I have something to do before I leave."

Meja said goodbye and left. Her pulse was racing, and not just because of the stairs. Because she had visited her mother, just like that.

She walked home slowly. She was about to go in to see Johan when she paused and glanced at the stairs leading up to the attic. Why not dig out that camera she used to love so much? Live a little, as her mother would say.

INEZ

For the first time since her fall, Inez had actually taken her pills as prescribed by her doctor. The right dose at the right time, just before bed. And funnily enough, it did help the pain. She fixed herself a cheese on rye sandwich and a cup of Earl Grey tea, one sugar, and went into the living room. Glancing at Meja's suggestions of which books to give away, it occurred to Inez that Meja had a coldhearted approach to books. Just like Amelia. Clear out the clutter.

She had no idea what time it was. Time didn't interest her these days. Peering through the blinds, she saw it was a beautiful morning. Gloriously drowsy, soft and disheveled, as only late-summer mornings could be.

She finished her breakfast and put on her cardigan to go out, but paused. Slowly, she turned toward the living room table. The photographs Meja had found the day before were lying there, half-hidden under a newspaper. She walked over, picked up the pile of photos, and put them in her pocket. Then she left the house and walked slowly toward the pier.

Thanks to the painkillers, she managed to walk all the way to the end. She breathed deeply. Memories washed over her like a wave. She closed her eyes, letting them ebb and flow. Then she walked slowly back to the bench and took out the pictures.

She had lived an incredible life. Which wasn't to say it had been easy. She had worked hard, and she'd known that her sacrifices would only be worth it if she took full advantage of every moment. She looked at the top photograph of her smiling widely at the photographer at yet another book signing. She couldn't recall whether this was in Sweden, Germany, Holland, or somewhere else. Not that it mattered much. What mattered was meeting the long, winding lines of women. She always took the time to say a few positive words to each and every one. She enjoyed it, giving people encouragement. It didn't take much. But those days were gone, never to return. She didn't have any encouragement to give these days, even to herself.

She tossed the photo into the water and watched it float on the surface for a moment before a wave washed over it and pulled it under. Inez felt a flurry in her stomach.

The next photograph was from some party or other. She was standing next to Cristy, clinking glasses with a man. He was an author of detective stories, if she remembered correctly. She threw that one in the water, too, watched it disappear, and picked up the next one.

When she only had five left in her hand, she saw a figure approach out of the corner of her eye. Meja? The cleaner looked just as surprised as she was.

"Is it nine o'clock already?" said Inez, frowning.

"No, no." Meja waved her hand. "I just . . ." She held up a camera. "This place is so beautiful, and I couldn't sleep."

Inez was still frowning. "So you thought you'd come early and take some pictures?"

"Yes, the sea . . ." Meja's cheeks paled. "Just the sea, nothing else."

Inez nodded shortly, turned her gaze to the water, and dumped all five remaining pictures. For a moment she thought Meja was about to jump in after them.

"What are you doing?" she said, staring at the photos sinking one by one.

"Decluttering," said Inez.

"But . . ."

"Take your sea pictures now. There's an unusual image for you."

Meja fumbled with the camera, knelt down on the pier, zoomed in on the water's surface, and snapped a picture just as the last photograph started to sink.

Inez had already started walking back.

"See you at nine," she called without turning around.

A couple of minutes past nine, Meja was standing outside the porch door. Inez opened it.

"The camera will have to stay outside," she said and walked over to the piles of books.

Meja carefully set the camera down on the porch and followed Inez.

"So you think all of these should be given away?" Inez nodded at the pile that Meja had sorted on her own.

"Well, I thought you'd probably go through them yourself first. It's so hard to choose. Maybe I was a little hasty . . ."

Inez hummed and pointed to some other piles.

"You can start with those. I have something else to do now."

Mathilda's story was itching to come out and left no head space for tidying today. She went into her bedroom, sat down at the desk, and set her fingers loose on the keyboard.

A few hours later, she skimmed what she had written about the oyster diver and pressed print. When she heard the printer fire up in the living room, she went out to pick up the papers and tuck them into the blue plastic folder. Meja watched Inez as she put the folder as high up on the bookshelf as she could reach. Then she sat down in the armchair next to Meja.

"Save?" Meja asked.

Inez nodded, barely glancing at the book. She leaned back. "So, you're into photography?"

Meja squirmed. "Not really. I used to be. Then I found my old camera and thought I'd just give it a try. For fun."

Inez sat quietly for a while, looking at Meja. Her eyes revealed everything. That was probably how psychics performed their role. They read the look in people's eyes and pretended they saw signs in the cards.

Meja always sounded a little uncertain when she talked about herself, and when Inez looked into her eyes, she got the sense that this was a woman who had never had the courage to find herself. Who had never followed her dream—or even worse—never had a dream in the first place.

"Tell me about your partner," she said.

"My partner?" Meja looked up at the ceiling. "We've lived together for eight years."

She went quiet. Inez raised her eyebrows. Meja cleared her throat and continued.

"We live in the center of town, on Mariatorget, in his apartment. He works as a game developer in Malmö."

Inez yawned demonstratively and stood up. Meja blushed.

"On Monday, I want you to tell me something that you actually *feel* about your life with your partner. In here," Inez said, bringing her hand to her chest. "Clear a few more piles and then you'll be free to go. And don't forget your camera."

Inez went back into the bedroom and closed the door.

Normally, a few hours of writing was enough to empty her head of memories, but today they just kept coming. Mathilda's laughter echoed in her ears, light and thunderous at the same time. Like a storm on a summer's day. One image in particular lingered. It had been a cold and windy day and Mathilda had told her she simply must dive with her. That she must hear the fizzling plankton, swim with the fish, crustaceans, clams, shells, starfish, and oysters. They were like gold coins on the seabed, she said. *Like treasure?* Inez had asked, and Mathilda had laughed and said *Yes, exactly like treasure.* Didn't she want to join her on a treasure hunt?

Mathilda was always drawn underwater, to what she called her forest of kelp and red algae. Inez never understood the appeal, and on that particular day she refused to go in. It was too cold. Mathilda rolled her eyes and said that if treasure were easy to find then there wouldn't be any treasure left. Only those who were the most persistent, the most stubborn, and maybe a little crazy found it. Inez responded that she did not belong to the stubborn, crazy crowd.

So Mathilda jumped in without her, shouting, "Forget it then, I'll take the treasure for myself."

Inez closed her eyes.

She hadn't known it at the time, but spending all those days in the boat and experiencing Mathilda's passion firsthand changed her life. It made it impossible for Inez to settle for mediocrity. She would be forever searching for her own treasure.

She took a deep breath, got up, and pressed her ear to the door to hear if Meja had gone home. When the porch door finally closed, she went to the kitchen and heated up some sausage casserole, her batch meal of the week.

She sat down in the living room. Mathilda's voice had fallen silent, leaving enough room for thoughts about Meja. Had she pushed her too far? Meja was there to help tidy her house, not reveal juicy details about her relationship. But she couldn't help it. That lost look in Meja's eyes awakened something in Inez. A desire to give her a push. *You can do it. You are brave.*

She found herself actually looking forward to Monday, and hoping that Meja would surprise her.

She reached for a book, *The Three Miss Margarets* by Louise Shaffer. No more memories today. No more writing. She would spend the rest of the day reading about other people's secrets instead.

MEJA

Johan had texted to say he was on his way home. Meja was sitting in the kitchen, gazing at the apartments across the street. Ingrid lay in her lap, cooing. Meja liked to sit in the kitchen. She preferred to avoid the bedroom, which was Johan's gaming zone, and the living room felt a bit dry and impersonal. This was where she was most comfortable. Maybe because it was the only room she had decorated. She had hung up a picture with a powder-pink magnolia motif and chosen drapes to match. When they moved in together, Johan had explained in great detail how annoying he found it when his friends moved in with their girlfriends and suddenly had homes filled with floral cushions and pastel colors. But the kitchen was not Johan's favorite room, and Meja had managed to sneak in a few things without his commenting.

She ran her hand over the little tuft of hair on Ingrid's head, the only fur she had, and thought back to the time she had spent at Inez's house. She didn't know which had been more awkward—sorting through the books on her own or with Inez. Since she had no idea which books Inez wanted to save, she had devised a system. For every five books she threw away, she saved the sixth. No wonder Inez had looked at her strangely when she'd seen the pile of books that Meja had suggested she save. It was a completely random mix.

The blue folder on the bookshelf had caught Meja's eye that day. She reached up, just to touch it, and before she knew it, she had taken it down. The folder was made of semitranslucent plastic that she couldn't quite see through, but Meja did glimpse a title and lots of text. A book manuscript? She carefully put it back again and thought Inez was lucky it was her working there and not her colleague Angelika, as was originally planned. There was no way she would have respected Inez's wishes not to look in the folder.

Meja sighed and looked out the window. Inez had asked her to tell her something she felt in her heart about her life with Johan, and she could only mumble something about his apartment and job. It bothered her that she couldn't come up with anything better to say. Then again, she rejected the idea that everyone had to *feel* things about their life all the time. Wasn't just living enough sometimes?

Clearly not according to Inez. Or her mother.

She heard the door open and Johan's bag land on the floor with a thud. He peeked into the kitchen.

"I didn't think you were home. You're so quiet."

Meja didn't know what to say. She didn't put music on as soon as she walked through the door like Johan did. Before she could answer, he had disappeared into the living room, started a Spotify playlist, put his feet up on the couch, and started fiddling with his phone. Meja came in and put Ingrid in her cage.

"I was thinking . . . ," she said.

"Mm?"

"Why don't we go out for dinner tonight?"

He looked up. "Out?"

"Yeah. I can't remember the last time we went out to eat together."

He shrugged. "I eat lunch out every day. It kind of loses its appeal after a while."

But I don't, Meja thought. Usually the conversation would have ended there and she would have started preparing dinner. But on Monday she was going to have to look Inez straight in the eye and tell her something that she *felt* about Johan. It would make it easier if she could say they had gone out for dinner together.

"Please," she said. "My treat."

Johan shrugged. "Fine. But let's go now, I'm hungry as a bear."

Meja suggested they go to one of the restaurants along North Harbor. They could sit and watch the boats and passersby. Be some of the cheerful people. But it was not to be. Johan headed straight for the pizza place around the corner. The fast-food joint with three plastic tables, plastic chairs, and fluorescent lighting. This is where they went for takeout pizza. She had never seen anyone sitting at those rickety tables.

Meja bit her lower lip and told herself that at least they were out. Together.

Johan ordered a kebab pizza, and Meja got a Greek salad.

"Why not have a beer?" she said to Johan. She knew he was planning on ordering a Coke. He looked at her in surprise.

"Yeah, okay," he said and nodded to the guy behind the counter. "I'll have a Carlsberg."

"And I'll have a glass of house white," said Meja, feeling a tiny tinge of excitement. Even though they were just at the local pizza place. She and Johan only drank when they were hanging out with their friends, which they did less and less these days because everyone had children and busy lives of their own. Now Johan only went out on boys' nights when his friends needed a break from home. Meja had thought many times that she should get her old friends together for a night out too. But it never happened.

She got her salad, which turned out to be iceberg lettuce, pale tomatoes, and mealy black olives. She popped an olive in her mouth and washed it down with wine. She and Johan never spoke about family plans. They had said long ago that they would get around to that later. But what did "later" mean?

"Do you want children?" she asked.

Johan bit into his pizza and chuckled. "Not after listening to my colleagues complain about sleepless nights, the terrible twos, and problems at school."

Meja forced down another olive.

Johan tilted his head slightly. "Is this why you wanted to go out? To ask if we should procreate?"

Meja took another sip of wine. It was far too sweet for her taste but better than nothing.

"'Procreate'? I don't like the sound of that. So impersonal. 'Start a family' sounds better," she said.

"Okay. Do you want to start a family?"

Meja squirmed. She hadn't really meant to start a conversation about it. "No. I don't think it's the right time. Do you?"

Johan shrugged. "I'm easy. I can afford to wait, but maybe you can't, so it's really up to you."

Meja pushed her salad plate away, finished her wine, and ordered another. How could Johan be so flippant about something as huge as whether or not to have children? Then again, a lot of people seemed to be. Meja saw it as a monumental, life-changing undertaking. To be someone's mother. Could she do it?

Johan had already moved on to talking about work and a new retro-inspired game they were developing. It was going to revolutionize the market. Meja was only half listening but didn't think it sounded particularly groundbreaking. Didn't all companies create games with retro influences these days? She didn't say anything. It occurred to her that she probably shouldn't have had that last glass of wine on a near-empty stomach. When Johan had finished his pizza and drunk his beer, she paid, and they walked the mere five hundred steps home.

"That was a great idea," Johan said with a smile. "We should do it more often."

He kissed her on the cheek and headed for the bedroom.

"Mind if I play for a while?"

Meja shook her head and went to get ready for a night on the couch. She met her gaze in the bathroom mirror as she brushed her teeth. It was the only mirror in the apartment. She had wanted to get rid of it, but Johan wouldn't let her. "I need it to shave in the morning," he had said.

Ordinary—that was the first word that came to mind. She was very ordinary looking. It had always been her salvation, allowing her to blend into the background at school and various workplaces. Her facial features didn't attract attention. Nothing stood out, like dimples or a lazy eye. She splashed water on her face and smeared on some night cream. *Tell me something you feel.* She supposed she would just have to tell Inez something about their apartment on Monday.

With a sigh, she went to make herself comfortable on the couch. She picked up her camera and looked at the pictures she had taken; they were hard to see on the small screen, so she transferred them to her laptop. Among the seventy or so pictures she had taken that morning on the pier, one stood out. The one that Inez had encouraged her to take, capturing the very moment when half of her old photograph was submerged and the other half was still visible on the surface. The latter half showed Inez laughing happily. Meja had zoomed in and chosen a short shutter speed to freeze the movement of the water. It didn't look real.

She printed it out and inspected it carefully before putting it in an envelope. Now *this* she would bring to Inez on Monday.

INEZ

Over the weekend, Inez was sucked into a writing bubble like a black hole. She wrote, slept for short periods, and ate a small snack every now and then. She didn't know if it was day or night behind the drawn blinds. There was no such thing as time or space inside the black hole, there were only memories, which became words, which became pages. Sometimes she laughed to herself, reliving the emotions, the places, the lust for life. But every time she momentarily emerged from her bubble, she found her cheeks stiff with dried tears. She knew how the story ended.

On Monday, when she woke up to the persistent sound of birds chirping outside her window, she looked around the room in a daze. Meja was due at nine.

She got up slowly, took some painkillers, and started collecting the half-drunk coffee mugs dotted about the place. After a hot shower, she sat down in her armchair and waited. It was time for round two with the cleaner.

Meja arrived punctually, as ever. She was carrying her camera over her shoulder and opened the gate with more determination than before. Inez left the porch door open while she made coffee. Soon she heard a "Yoo-hoo!" from the living room. What young woman said "yoo-hoo"? Inez shook her head and went to meet her.

Meja flinched when Inez entered the room. "Oh, I wasn't sure if you were in."

Inez fought the urge to roll her eyes. This constant uncertainty. She handed Meja a cup of coffee and sat down. Her body ached from the weekend. She could only assume from Meja's frown that it was obvious.

"Shall we begin?" Inez said, hoping to avoid questions about how she was feeling.

Meja nodded and picked up some of the books. She lifted the top one. Inez took a deep breath and tried to remember whether the book was worth saving, but she couldn't concentrate.

After the first hour, the books in the save pile and the discard pile may as well have been chosen at random. Inez leaned her head against the backrest.

"Have you read the book?" she asked.

Meja turned to look at the cover of the book she was holding and shook her head.

"I mean the one you borrowed. *Divine Secrets of the Ya-Ya Sisterhood.*"

"Well . . ." Meja swallowed. "I've made a start . . ."

Inez caught her eye. "You watched the movie."

At least Meja had enough sense not to respond. Sometimes it was best to neither confirm nor deny. Few people Inez encountered seemed to understand that.

"Read the book," she said.

Meja nodded. "I will."

"Preferably before you finish here. It should be in the save pile by then."

"Absolutely," said Meja.

Inez could hear the nervousness in her voice. She pointed to the book in her hand. "Give away."

Though Inez was tired, they managed to clear everything in front of the bookshelf. The empty space made the room look bigger. Meja stretched and Inez looked at the clock. Ten minutes left of Meja's shift.

"So, tell me something about this man you live with. Something from the heart," she said. She noted that Meja clenched her jaw.

"We went out for dinner last Friday," she said.

"How lovely," said Inez. "Some cozy little spot?"

"Well, I wanted to go to a restaurant on North Harbor, but we ended up at the pizza place around the corner."

Inez raised her eyebrows. "How romantic."

Meja shrugged. "Not really. Fluorescent lights, plastic chairs, a stream of people who made the smart decision to get their pizza to go, disgusting olives and sickly wine."

Inez laughed. Now Meja raised her eyebrows. It occurred to Inez that she might not have heard her laugh before. When was the last time she had really belly laughed? Certainly not since Viola had died. She felt out of practice. Inez leaned on her walking stick to open the porch door, her shoulders still shaking with laughter.

"Thank you for sharing your feelings," she said.

Meja smiled weakly and pulled an envelope out of her purse. She hesitated, then handed it to Inez.

Only when Meja was out of sight did Inez open it carefully. It was a picture of Inez's half-submerged old photograph. She saw her youthful smile about to sink to the bottom of the sea, where it would dissolve into tiny particles. The image felt almost painful in its significance. That smile belonged to another time.

She put the picture facedown on the living room table and stepped out onto the porch. A scream emanated from the other side of the fence. A little boy appeared to have pushed a slightly littler boy off Viola's porch, and the littler one was now shrieking at the top of his lungs. A woman scooped him up in her arms and comforted him while also trying to listen to her husband, who was eagerly pointing toward the upper floor of the house.

Damn that sea view from the balcony, Inez thought with a sigh. *Too bad there isn't a big tree outside Viola's house to block it.*

Before long, more couples appeared and walked around the yard. It must have been an open house. Inez clenched her jaw as she looked at the narrow footpath, the rose hips, and the sea.

When the fracture in her pelvis healed, she would go down to the beach again, like she used to—in all weather. Take her shoes off, roll up her pant legs, and walk on the stones. The pressure against the soles of her feet was like shiatsu. She missed that wholesome part of her daily routine. Now that she was forcing herself to write again, she needed it more than ever.

The boy in the garden let out another deafening howl. Inez scowled.

She missed Viola. Now that she was gone, Inez realized how much the small interactions with her neighbor had meant to her. Viola never read novels, only nonfiction about health, and had no interest in Inez's past. "The present, my friend," she used to say, "the present is all that matters." What would Viola have said if she knew Inez was digging up the past she had buried long ago?

A woman peered over the wall and smiled, but instead of smiling back, Inez turned on her heel and went inside.

She wasn't ready to write again after her intense weekend. She puttered around the house, an unusual feeling of restlessness crawling around her body like tiny, itchy ants. Exhausted and energized at the same time, she wanted to do something, meet someone. But who? Amelia was in Copenhagen and Cristy was probably in London, or some other glamorous far-flung location. You never knew when it came to her publisher.

Without thinking, Inez called for a cab. She felt a little flutter in the pit of her stomach. This wasn't like her.

She put on her poncho, sunglasses, and pale-pink lipstick, slung a rarely used, fancy-branded purse (a gift from her daughter) over her shoulder, and went out to wait for the cab. She didn't know where she was going until the driver slammed the door behind her.

"North Harbor, please," she said, then looked out the window so the driver wouldn't feel compelled to talk to her. He followed the coast in the direction of the city center and stopped at Gröningen, the popular small park on the water's edge.

It was buzzing with people. Families with children, dog walkers, romantic couples, lonely old folks, gangs of exuberant teenagers. Stepping out of her solitary existence and onto this summery movie set of life and sound was rather dizzying. In the distance she could see summer restaurants with palm trees outside, people swimming from the wide pier, a large playground, and an outdoor gym.

Inez walked leisurely in the other direction, toward the harbor, and stopped at the first restaurant. The waitress showed her to a table in the outdoor dining area with a view of the boats. She ordered a glass of white wine. This was where Meja had wanted to eat with her partner when they had ended up at an unromantic pizzeria. She chuckled at the memory of her story, picked up her cell phone, and typed: Are you busy? The answer came almost immediately. No, do you need help? Inez thought for a few seconds before she wrote: Restaurant in North Harbor, at the bottom, by Gröningen. Outdoor seating.

She waited awhile. Then the answer came: OK.

Inez sipped her wine and glanced at the neighboring tables, safely hidden behind her sunglasses. No one was paying any attention to her. Fifteen years behind blinds had had its benefits.

Twenty minutes later, she saw Meja walking along the quay. Her eyes were fixed on the ground until she reached the restaurant and lifted her gaze to wave gingerly to Inez, who nodded back. Inez had already ordered her a glass of white. The young woman looked embarrassed.

"You wanted to eat in North Harbor," Inez said and picked up the menu as Meja sat down. She made it sound like she was doing this for Meja's sake, when really she was doing it for herself. She needed company. Needed to enjoy the present. She heard her daughter's voice in her head: *Don't you ever do anything for someone else without benefiting from it yourself?*

Inez took another sip of wine. "What do you want?"

"The tomato soup looks good," said Meja after carefully perusing the menu more than once.

Inez looked at the menu. The tomato soup was one of the cheapest starters. "As an appetizer?"

"No, I was going to have it as a main," said Meja.

"But you do eat meat, right?" Inez said.

"Yes . . ."

Inez put the menu on the table, turned to the waiter, and said, "We'll both have the grilled beef filet with baked silver onions and mashed potatoes." She looked at Meja. "My treat, of course."

Meja bit her lower lip and nodded.

They sat in silence. While Meja watched the people buzzing around the harbor, Inez watched her. During her writing career, people had been like commodities for Inez. She had listened, observed, analyzed, and distilled the information about them into personality descriptions that later gave life to the characters in her novels. When she stopped writing books, she also stopped being interested in people. But observing Meja gave her a tickling sensation in the pit of her stomach, something she hadn't felt in a long time. Curiosity.

Based on Meja's cautious uncertainty, Inez assumed that she was, consciously or unconsciously, a people pleaser. Not only with her partner, but with her family and friends, colleagues, strangers she passed in the stairwell, and the cashier at the local store. Inez would bet she turned her groceries the right way to show the barcode and didn't pile them up high on the conveyor belt. Right now, she was no doubt looking forward to the beef that Inez had ordered while also feeling guilty about its environmental consequences. Wondering if she should have gone for soup after all. She would have made a good character in one of Inez's novels.

"Have you googled me?" Inez asked.

Meja answered with wide eyes and silence. Inez smiled. This woman was really incapable of lying.

"My partner has," she said in a whisper.

"Does your partner read?"

"Fantasy mostly."

Inez nodded. Now she liked her partner a little better.

"I didn't read any of the articles. Just a few sentences on Wikipedia. And saw some pictures."

Inez smiled again. She liked being with someone who couldn't lie. Meja's obvious honesty made their conversations easier.

"If you know about me from Wikipedia, isn't it only fair that I learn something about you, other than the fact that you live with a game developer?" she asked.

Meja squirmed.

"I'm an only child. My mother, Susanne, and I . . . are very different."

"How so?"

Meja shrugged. "She likes being in the spotlight, she knows what she wants. I prefer staying on the sidelines and don't know what I want."

Inez smiled. "Once I knew what my dream was, what I wanted to do with my life, I made sure I got it. But it came at a cost."

"My mother always knew what she wanted, but she didn't get it."

"Interesting," said Inez. "Like three characters in a novel. The woman with no dream, the woman whose dream came true, and the woman whose dream amounted to nothing."

The waiter came to their table and served their dishes.

"Oh," said Meja.

This time Inez smiled at the little nonword. The woman who didn't know what she wanted certainly knew what she liked, at least.

"What was your mother's unrealized dream?" she asked, popping a piece of tender meat into her mouth.

Meja started coughing and covered her mouth with a napkin, which she then folded carefully and put back on the table.

"I don't know," she said.

Inez nodded. All these unspoken truths with the power to cloud our realities.

They went back to eating in silence.

"That was absolutely delicious," Meja said when they had finished.

Inez beckoned to the waiter, who removed their clean-scraped plates.

"Do you want dessert?" she asked.

"Oh no, I'm fine, thanks," said Meja.

After Inez had paid the bill and Meja had thanked her several times, they left the restaurant and strolled along the harbor. Meja automatically fell into rhythm with Inez. They walked quietly side by side. When they came to Dunker Culture House, Inez called for a cab.

"You don't have to wait. I'll be all right," she said, leaning against one of the rabbit statues outside the entrance.

Meja stayed by her side. "It's no trouble. I'm happy to wait with you."

Inez nodded, again grateful for her honesty. If Meja said she was happy to wait, she meant it. Inez squinted at her.

"You may have seen on Wikipedia that I stopped writing fifteen years ago?"

Meja nodded.

"I was the subject of a scandal, you might say," said Inez. "And I lost my drive."

"I figured something must have happened when I saw the pictures."

"It was deeply unfair. None of it was my doing, but I was forced to take responsibility anyway."

"Sounds tough," said Meja.

The cab pulled up.

"Thank you for today," said Inez.

"I'm the one who should be thanking you," said Meja.

Inez patted Meja's hand. "No, my friend. The pleasure was all mine."

The driver helped Inez into the cab and Meja waved her off.

Inez leaned her head back and closed her eyes. The conversation with Meja had brought back memories of her writing days. Her books had all been about female friendships. They hadn't won any literary prizes, but they had told stories that women all around the world really wanted to read. Inez had written entirely out of desire and curiosity about humans. Yes, it had been light entertainment, but entertainment that could move mountains. Well, a boulder here and there, at least. She had received many letters over the years. Women sharing their stories, telling her that they had been inspired to shake up their lives, overcome barriers, find themselves. These stories were more beautiful than anything Inez wrote. The poetry of life.

She narrowed her eyes as she thought about how it had all ended. There was a woman who, after reading Inez's novel *Twist of Fate*, decided to leave her husband after years of abuse. This decision led to the enraged man strangling her with his bare hands. A terrible tragedy, but nothing to do with Inez. Until a young columnist honed in on something the perpetrator had said in police questioning: that his wife had decided to leave him after reading Inez's book, and that was what had made him see red. This statement had resulted in a bizarre think piece about the possible harmful effects of romanticized literature. And a summer news drought meant more journalists jumped on the bandwagon. Inez would never forget the last words she read before deciding not to open another paper until this had all blown over: *Can a writer manipulate vulnerable readers into believing happiness is easy to find? Yes. Can such naivete be a death trap? Evidently. If so, who should be held accountable?*

"We're here."

The driver's voice sounded far away. Inez opened her eyes, fumbled for her card to pay, and waited for the driver to help her out.

She thanked him and limped slowly into the house.

She looked at herself in the hall mirror. Saw the gray strands, the furrows around her eyes, the slightly slumped posture. When that horde of journalists had hounded her with idiotic questions she had wanted to shout, *Why don't we talk about the men instead? The ones who kill. Isn't that the conversation we should really be having?*

Cristy had thought that she should say exactly that to the press. Show them who was boss.

But Inez had said nothing. She had cowered under her hood, moved to Domsten, and pulled down the blinds. Why? Because she was terrified that the journalists would shift focus from her romanticized fiction to her own past. She couldn't risk it. Couldn't risk anyone revealing her well-kept secret.

MEJA

Meja didn't go straight home as she had intended. Instead she walked back along North Harbor and stopped at her mother's new building. The light was on in the top-floor window. A man came out of the lobby, and Meja managed to slip her foot in the door before it slammed shut. After walking eight stories up, she had to pause to catch her breath before ringing the bell.

Susanne didn't even try to hide her surprise at seeing Meja on her doorstep—again.

"I was passing and thought I'd drop in," said Meja, hearing how wrong that sentence sounded. They didn't have a "drop in" kind of relationship.

"Okay . . ." Susanne let her in and disappeared into the kitchen.

"Bengt not home?" Meja asked as she hung up her jacket. She could hear cupboards opening and closing.

"He's working late today."

Meja looked around the living room. There wasn't much of her mother here. The home Meja had grown up in had consisted of heavy silk drapes, a plush burgundy couch, ornate gold mirrors, crystal chandeliers, and colorful art on the walls. Susanne used to have a vase of multicolored ostrich feathers, which Meja had loved, and two grotesque theater masks, one comic and one tragic, on the hall wall. Meja had had to shut her eyes every time she passed them. Her mother was nowhere to be seen in this sterile, white, airy, elegant apartment. Maybe they weren't so different after all—because where was she visible in Johan's apartment? A painting of a magnolia that she had bought in a supermarket?

Susanne served some tea and sat down in the sheepskin armchair.

"Out for a walk without Johan again?"

"I was at a restaurant in the harbor," Meja said. It felt good.

"Oh really? With a friend?" Susanne's expression softened.

"Not really. More of a client, you might say."

"Client? Have you finally changed jobs?"

"No. It's the woman I clean for."

"I thought you cleaned several households."

"Not at the moment. Just one woman's house. She is seventy years old, a writer, and she had a fall and broke her hip so she needs help cleaning her house."

Susanne blew on her hot tea. "So when you finally go out and have fun for once, it's with some old lady that you clean for?"

Meja clenched her jaw. Put that way, it admittedly sounded a little strange.

"Is that even allowed?" said Susanne.

That hadn't occurred to Meja. What had been in the fine print of that work contract she had signed without reading?

Susanne dropped the subject. "How are you and Johan doing?"

"How are we doing? I'm pretty sure we're doing fine," said Meja.

Susanne squinted. As she always did when she disapproved. "You're pretty sure?"

"Yeah, as usual. So, good," she said, drinking her tea too quickly and burning her mouth. Why had she come here when she was actually in a good mood for once? Her dinner with Inez had almost made her feel like one of the cheerful people.

But deep down she knew why. It wasn't really a random, spontaneous visit at all. Inez asking about Susanne's dream had piqued Meja's curiosity. What was the dream that Meja's birth had prevented her mother from pursuing? She wanted to know the answer to the mystery that had tainted her entire childhood with guilt.

She cleared her throat. Her cheeks were hot. Why was it so hard to talk about important things?

"Inez, the woman I clean for, and I were talking about big life dreams." Meja swallowed hard. "And it got me thinking about your dreams when you were young. I don't really know what they were."

Susanne laughed. It was an artificial laugh.

"Oh, you know," she said, looking out the window. "Life, movement, excitement, color, drama."

Meja knew this wasn't the whole truth. From what she remembered of her childhood, her mother had a life filled with friends, color, parties, hustle and bustle. It was something else. Something that had wedged itself between them and forced a distance. But what?

Susanne quickly changed the subject. "I forgot the cookies," she said and disappeared into the kitchen.

Meja sipped her tea and wondered whether Susanne ever even thought about her daughter's childhood. Did she remember what she had said in that argument all those years ago, that her dream had died with Meja's first breath? Such cruel words.

"Help yourself to thumbprint cookies," said Susanne, laying a plate on the glass table.

Meja took one. "Delicious."

"I got them from Fahlman's," said Susanne. "Never been one of those cookie-baking moms, as you know."

Meja did know. Every time her school had held a bake sale, Meja had to bring in store-bought cakes. It was mortifying.

Susanne glanced at the clock. "Oh, look at the time. I don't mean to rush you out, but . . ."

"No problem," Meja said, finishing her cookie. "I just wanted to say hi."

They got up and went out into the hall.

"Thanks for the *fika*," said Meja.

Susanne gave her a quick hug. "Maybe give me a call next time you're passing? To check if it's a good time."

Meja felt her cheeks redden. There was that thorniness again. She said goodbye and left.

Her lighthearted mood following dinner with Inez was ruined.

Johan had once said she should talk to a therapist about her relationship with Susanne. She never had and probably never would, though he was probably right.

Meja emerged onto the street, took a deep breath, and headed for Johan's apartment via a back route. When she came in, he was watching a cop show in the living room.

"Where have you been?" he said.

Did he look a little worried? Meja had just slipped out so as not to disturb his gaming. She sat down next to him on the couch.

"I had dinner with Inez and then a cup of tea with Mom."

"Inez?"

"Yes, the writer."

Johan looked as surprised as Susanne had. "Why?"

Meja shrugged. "Because she wanted to."

Johan frowned at her irritated tone. "Okay, sorry I asked."

"Sorry," said Meja. "I shouldn't have gone to see Mom afterward. You know how that turns out."

Johan put his arm around her shoulders and pulled her close.

Meja swallowed hard.

"Do you love me?" she heard herself ask.

"Sure I do."

"*Sure* you do?" she said, just like Susanne had when Meja had said she was *sure* they were doing fine.

Johan released his grip on her shoulders. "The word 'love' feels so big and contrived. But if I love anyone, I'm sure it would be you."

Sure again, thought Meja. Then again, hand on heart, did she love Johan? She liked him, was comfortable with him, felt safe with him. But love?

That's probably why they were such a good match, she thought with a sigh. Because they both felt the same.

"I'm going to bed. It's been a tiring evening."

Johan nodded. "I'm going to watch one more episode."

Lying in bed and staring at the ceiling, Meja thought about Inez. About the scandal that had made her stop writing. It must have been pretty bad. Inez didn't seem like the sort of person to give up without a fight.

She turned on her side and closed her eyes. Behind her eyelids, she saw the blue folder. Sometimes it was at the top of the bookshelf, sometimes Inez had it in her room. What kind of story was in it? Might it be a new novel?

INEZ

Inez had spent far too long out on the pier early this morning, and now her hip ached. But it had been worth it. The sea, the cries of seagulls, and the smell of seaweed had taken her back to Kobbholmen.

She had seen Mathilda's red hut, with ropes, tools, diving equipment, and skipper clocks hanging on the walls. She had seen all the rakes and plastic baskets stacked on top of each other. The memories were so clear, their outlines so sharp. She remembered that a little farther away was a stand for hanging up nets and a strip of beach made entirely of oyster shells. She remembered trying to describe the shells in her little black notebook and what a challenge it had been to convey in words the contrast between the delicate beauty of their insides and the coarse ruggedness of their outsides.

Inez had thought that those memories were long since buried and forgotten. But suppressing memories didn't destroy them. In truth, memories of Mathilda had continued to haunt her over the years. Like the time Amelia took her out for dinner in Copenhagen to a restaurant with seaweed kimchi on the menu. Naturally, it brought back the day when she and Mathilda were lying on a sun-warmed rock and Mathilda started chewing on a piece of seaweed and said she bet that it would become a delicacy in the future. She had been right. She had been right about a lot of things.

Whenever the past had whispered through Inez's mind, she had drowned it out with other sounds, other thoughts. Not anymore. Now she listened. The question was what would happen next, when she had finished writing the book. Would Mathilda's voice then be silenced forever?

A knock on the porch door interrupted her thoughts. Inez opened the door for Meja and greeted her briefly, then grimaced, swallowed a painkiller with some tepid coffee, and sat back down. The pain left no room for conversation, so she pointed her walking stick at the piles along the wall next to the bookshelf.

Meja sat down, put a stack of books on her lap, and lifted up the top one.

"Save," said Inez.

They continued sorting at a good pace. Once they were through the first pile and a box of papers, the painkiller had kicked in. Inez leaned back and looked at Meja.

"Thanks for yesterday."

"Thank *you*. You invited me," Meja said.

"I enjoyed the company," said Inez.

She really had enjoyed sitting in a restaurant and having a conversation with another human being. Enjoyed feeling curious again.

"How did you and your partner meet?" she asked.

Meja fiddled with the book in her lap. "I was working at the deli counter of a supermarket, and he worked in the produce section. He was quitting to study programming, and on his last day of work our shifts ended at the same time so he asked if I wanted to hang out. We had worked at the same place for two years without speaking. So we exchanged numbers that day. And never looked back."

Inez smiled. "Sounds very romantic to me."

Meja shrugged. "On our first date we went to the movies, then for a coffee on our second, then for a burger on our third. On our fourth date I moved in with him."

"Gosh!" Inez raised her eyebrows. She had assumed Meja was the type of person who took a long time to make big decisions.

"We quickly slipped into a situation that suited us well, but . . ."

"But what?" Inez said.

"Sometimes I wonder if liking each other is enough."

Inez nodded and considered this.

Meja glanced at her from under her bangs.

"Have you ever been married?" she asked in barely more than a whisper.

Inez laughed. "Three times. In the end they all left me because they couldn't stand coming in second place. Writing always came first. Well, and Amelia."

Inez got up laboriously, went into the kitchen, and prepared a tray with four small glasses, two of port and two of vodka on the rocks. She supposed Meja wasn't used to such strong drinks, so she threw a lemon slice into the vodka as well.

"Can you help me with this?" she called.

Meja came into the kitchen and looked wide-eyed at the tray. "Is it really a good idea to mix that with your meds?"

Inez snorted in response and led the way into the living room.

"Okay," she said as they sat back down. "One glass is for pleasure, the other is necessary. Which do you want first?"

"The necessary one," said Meja with a grimace.

"Wise decision," said Inez, picking up the vodka.

Meja squinted, sipped, and shuddered.

Inez smacked her lips. "This, my friend, cleans the blood and the heart. It makes everything so much cleaner and clearer afterward."

"Maybe that's why they say drinking it 'neat,'" said Meja, grimacing again as she took another sip.

Inez chuckled. "Maybe."

When her glass was empty, Meja looked up. "Finished," she said with a relieved smile.

Inez nodded toward the other glass, the port with flavors of plum and black cherry. "Now this is for pleasure. Think about it: What gives you pleasure in life?"

Meja sipped the sweet drink.

"It's good," she said, surprised.

"Well?" Inez said.

Meja fixed her gaze on an arbitrary point.

Inez frowned. This young woman clearly needed help answering her question.

"Come on," she said. She got up, got dressed, and left the house. Meja followed and they walked down the path to the sea. At the point where swaying beach grass gave way to sand, there was a wooden bench overlooking the sea.

"What a perfect location," said Meja.

Inez laughed. "The local council was setting up some benches along the coast. When the men were on their lunch break, Viola, my recently deceased neighbor, and I seized our chance to move one to exactly where we wanted it."

"You stole it?" Meja said.

"No, we put it here." Inez drew a deep breath and smiled. "What do the authorities know about where to put benches?"

Inez shuffled to the side and pointed to the backrest where the words *Viola's bench* were scratched into the wood. Meja smiled and shook her head. They sat in silence and watched the waves wash slowly back and forth.

"I had a friend once upon a time," said Inez. "She always said that dreams were rooted in pleasure. So if you want to find your dream, you follow your pleasures."

Meja nodded slowly, still looking at the sea. They sat in silence again, until eventually Inez struggled to her feet.

"Damn hip," she muttered. Then Meja helped her slowly walk home.

As they approached the house, they saw Sverker in his garden. He waved.

"I have news," he called. "The house has been sold."

Inez felt a nervous flutter in her stomach, but his smile suggested good news.

"It was bought by a man in his forties, divorced. He has a child, a thirteen-year-old girl, but she doesn't live with him full-time." Sverker looked pleased. "Worth celebrating, right?"

"Indeed," said Inez, raising an invisible glass.

She pretended not to understand the insinuation that they should celebrate for real. Dinner at their house had been lovely, but it had served its purpose. The house was sold. No more dinners. No celebration. She waved goodbye and went inside.

Before Meja had time to take off her jacket, Inez said, "Why don't you knock off early? This next pile is more complicated; it'll take longer."

"Right," said Meja. "See you tomorrow then."

Inez nodded and shut the door. Through the blinds, she saw Meja turn around at the gate to wave to her. Inez didn't wave back.

Instead, she went to her desk and brought her fingers to the keyboard.

1972

When I had days off from the bookstore I usually spent them with Mathilda. We went out on the boat, swam with seals, pulled up the day's catch, cleaned oysters, shipped them ashore, and delivered them to customers.

One day when we were cleaning the oysters, she said, "Look carefully at each one. Even an empty shell can hide a secret."

I worked as carefully as I could but didn't find any surprises in those baskets. Until one day when an empty shell appeared. I was just about to throw it back into the sea when I remembered Mathilda's words and turned it over. On the inside there was a word engraved: *Friendship*.

Mathilda ran her hand over the birthmark on my temple. She was fascinated by its heart shape, perhaps because she saw signs in everything.

She said, with great seriousness in her voice, "Now you'll never throw away a shell until you've really looked at it first. Life is full of surprises. It's up to you to find them!"

I put the shell in my pocket and placed it on my bookshelf when I got home. It was my first shell with a message from Mathilda, but not the last. And cleaning those oysters, though not an especially enjoyable task, suddenly became something to look forward to. What if another special shell was waiting to be found? I learned to look at all the seemingly inconsequential moments in life with a new kind of curiosity. Was there anything more on the other side?

MEJA

Meja was sitting on the couch when Johan opened the front door. She hadn't moved since she'd gotten home. Three and a half hours ago.

"Hey," he called, dropping his work bag on the hall floor and picking up his gym bag. "I'm going straight back out. Lucas has booked a slot for paddle tennis."

"Okay," Meja called back and heard the door close.

A few minutes later, the door opened again and Johan strode into the living room. "Where's the car?"

"Oh," said Meja. "It's at Inez's . . ."

"Why?" Johan's cheeks were flushed with stress.

"Because we were drinking vodka and port." It sounded wrong when she said it out loud.

Johan frowned. "What? You'll be out of a job before you get your first paycheck."

Meja swallowed. "It was kind of hard to say no."

"Oh, Meja." Johan shook his head as he picked up the phone. "Hey, Lucas. Sorry, I don't have a car. Can you pick me up? Thanks." He hung up and turned to Meja. "I'm getting bad vibes from that writer."

"There's nothing wrong with her."

"Maybe not, but I think *you* have been acting weird since you started there."

He left before Meja could respond.

She leaned her head back on the cushion. Had she been behaving differently? Maybe. She had started taking photos again, and she had been out for dinner three times: with Inez's neighbors, Johan, and Inez. Well, and once with her mom, too, but she did that every month so it didn't count. She had found the courage to ask difficult questions that had rubbed both her mother and Johan the wrong way. She hadn't gotten the concrete answers she had hoped for, but at least she had asked them about love and dreams. Was that weird?

Inez's question about pleasure came to mind. She sighed. Her attention turned to the book Inez had lent her. She picked it up and flicked through a little before finally opening it to the first page and starting to read.

Meja didn't look up from the book until the door opened and Johan shouted, "Hello!" with a cheerful tone this time. She had read forty pages.

Johan stopped short when he saw her with a book in her hand.

"Is she making you read that too?" he said.

"You say that like it's a bad thing."

Johan was always trying to get her to read. Shouldn't he be happy?

"I'm concerned about how much influence she's having on you."

Meja closed the book. "You're being melodramatic. She gave me a book to read—we're clearing out her book collection, as you know, so it's hardly strange, is it?"

Johan tossed his gym clothes into the washing machine. "It *is* strange. It just is. You're reading books, you're drinking at work, you're starting up weird, deep conversations." He paused in the doorway. "Your mom called yesterday. She wanted to know if you were okay. She thought you've been acting strange lately too."

"What?" Meja grit her teeth. "A daughter drops in on her mother a couple of times, and her reaction is to be suspicious? Which of us does that make strange?"

"Well, you don't usually see each other that much. And hardly ever spontaneously. So it is strange."

He was about to disappear into the bedroom when she called, "Hey. Tell me something that gives you pleasure in life."

Johan sighed. "Drinking a beer, reaching a new level in a game, flashes of genius at work, getting a good hit on the paddle court . . . Lots of things. But see? You asking me that is weird. It isn't you."

Meja bit her lower lip, picked up her book, and continued reading.

INEZ

Inez was standing on the porch with a cup of tea. The sea was tinged gray and dark clouds moved across the sky. Like Inez's mood. She closed her eyes. Last night some doubt had crept in. Was writing this book really a good idea? What value was there in even remembering it, let alone writing it down? She wouldn't let anybody read it until after her death. So what was the point? If she was too cowardly to share her story, wouldn't it be better if it died with her?

The creaking gate startled her. Meja. Inez sighed. She really didn't feel like cleaning today.

"So strange, the weather almost seems like fall!" said Meja.

Inez nodded and continued gazing out to sea. A gust of wind blew so strong that it almost knocked her off her feet.

Meja grabbed her arm to steady her. "Talk about fall weather!"

Inez knew that the wind was trying to take her to the sea. Back to the force of nature that knew all her darkest secrets. Maybe the waves could tell her whether or not she should write this book?

She put her cup down and started walking toward the gate.

"Where are you going?" Meja said, following behind.

They walked along the path and across the undulating coastal meadow. Meja was about to stop at Viola's bench, but Inez urged her on. The wind whipped at their hair. Inez staggered against its force.

"Maybe we should go back?" Meja shouted.

Inez didn't answer. Instead she carefully bent down, removed her shoes and socks, and rolled up her pant legs.

"What are you doing?" Meja asked.

Inez ignored the concern in her voice. "Take your shoes off and come with me."

Meja pursed her lips but did as she was told.

Inez took a few steps toward the water's edge. A surge of anger arose inside her and brought tears to her eyes.

"Come on then," she whispered to the dark forces of the water. "I'm ready."

She went out a little farther, supported by Meja's arm. A big wave retreated, gathered strength, and hurled itself furiously at them, splashing up to their knees. Inez's feet sank into the soft sand as the water receded to recharge. Watching the next wave rumbling toward her, she felt Meja trying to pull her back, but she refused to move.

"Go on, say it," she whispered.

As the wave unleashed itself, Inez heard her own despairing voice in her mind: "You left me." And Mathilda's calm answer: "I didn't leave you. You never followed me."

The wind calmed slightly. Inez lowered her head and screwed up her eyes to force back the tears. That thought was like a blow to the head. *I didn't follow her. After everything Mathilda did for me, I didn't follow her.*

Her spilled tears tasted as salty as the sea. Inez extracted her feet from the gritty sand. They picked up their shoes and walked home barefoot, in silence. Back on the porch, they cleaned their feet as best they could.

A shiver rippled through Meja's whole body.

"Ugh," she said. "That almost got nasty. It looked like a storm was brewing but then it died down, just like that. Weird."

Inez nodded. "The sea said its piece for today."

Meja frowned questioningly.

"Could you make us some coffee?" Inez asked as they came in.

"Sure." Meja slipped into the kitchen.

Inez put on her slippers and sat down in the armchair with a thud. She closed her eyes. Just that brief time by the sea had drained her strength. Meja clattered about in the kitchen for a few minutes before producing a tray of coffee and raisin cookies.

"I found these in . . ."

Inez nodded. "That's fine. Thanks. We need some sweetness after our salty sea excursion."

Meja sat down in the armchair opposite and they each took a cookie.

Inez observed the younger woman. "Do you know what 'Meja' means?"

She shook her head.

"It comes from the Old Swedish word *mäghin*, which means power and strength."

Meja choked on a cookie crumb and coughed. "Well, that doesn't suit me then," she said, shaking her head.

"Join the club. Inez is a Spanish form of Agnes, meaning pure or chaste. So nothing like me."

Meja giggled. Inez tilted her head. She had such an honest laugh. She was honest through and through. Inez had been fooled at first by her uncertainty, but there was more to Meja than that.

"You should have been called Emina."

"Really? How come?" asked Meja.

Inez sipped her coffee. "You'll have to find out for yourself."

She got up from the armchair. Her night of writing had taken its toll on her hip. As had their seaside walk.

"I have to lie down and rest for a while. If you start with the last piles by the bookshelf, we'll soon have freed up an entire wall."

Meja nodded. "Shout if you need anything."

"Will do."

As soon as Inez got into the bedroom, she lay on her bed and shut her eyes. She pictured Mathilda's green eyes, which could smile just as well as her lips.

"I'm sorry," Inez whispered. "I'm sorry I didn't follow you."

MEJA

After Meja had sorted a few piles, she looked around. It didn't look much different yet, but once they actually got the books out of the house, most of the floor space would be free. Meja looked at the singular plant on the windowsill. A cactus. Meja didn't know much about plants and assumed cacti were pretty hardy. But this one looked sad. Pale and sort of droopy. She carefully watered the dry soil and wondered if she should pick up some cactus feed from the plant store.

She angled the blinds to let light in and saw how dusty the living room was. Dust particles swirled through the air in a gentle dance. She ran a damp cloth over the surfaces, resisting the urge to vacuum and mop as well. She didn't imagine Inez would appreciate her taking initiative. Inez had told her to finish the piles by the wall, but maybe it would be better to do the bookshelf? Then they could use it to store the books she was going to keep. She started taking down the books from the top shelf and dislodged the blue plastic folder, which fell to the floor. When she bent down to pick up the spilled papers, the writing on one of the pages caught her eye:

1972

Mathilda used to swim with seals. At dawn or dusk, when the animals were at their most playful, she would row her boat out to the rocks where she knew they liked to congregate. They got used to her company and started coming to meet her. She would shore up her boat on an islet, undress, and swim out. I'll never forget the first time I witnessed it. I wasn't a fan of swimming, or of shedding my clothes, so I sat on the rocks and watched her circle like a sea creature until the herd closed in. It was one of many magical moments with Mathilda. The joy of the seals, rolling around in the water, inviting Mathilda to join them—it was surreal. They all swam around the rocks together, and the seals adjusted their speed to hers. Sometimes they would follow her up onto the rock where I was sitting and sunbathe for a while before disappearing into the water to go in search of food. The friendly animals looked at Mathilda with wide eyes, bobbed their heads, and barked. They didn't give me so much as a glance.

Meja looked up from the paper. Inez was standing in the doorway staring at her. Her face was pale. At first Meja was concerned, then she remembered what Inez had said on her first day. There was only one rule: do not look in the blue folder. Meja had promised.

She gulped. "I was just . . . it fell."

With a trembling hand, Inez snatched the folder and papers away. Then she pointed at the door with her walking stick and hissed, "Out."

"But . . ."

"And don't come back."

Tears burned behind Meja's eyelids as she grabbed her things and hurried to leave, and Inez slammed the door behind her. Meja jogged all the way to her car under the pine grove and didn't let the tears flow until she was safely inside.

"Shit," she whispered, slamming her hand on the steering wheel. "Shit, shit, shit!"

Twenty minutes later, she was home. It seemed unnaturally quiet. She slumped against the hall wall and buried her face in her hands. How could she have been so stupid? It wasn't like her at all. She had never snooped on a client before.

Meja didn't know how long she had been sitting in the hall when Johan came home, but she was so stiff that she had difficulty getting to her feet. He helped her up and brought her to the kitchen. With tears streaming down her face, she told him what had happened.

Johan made tea and listened.

"I bet that was her new book," he said once she had gotten it all out. "And she was adamant that she'd never write another one, so it must have been top secret."

He smiled. Meja looked at the little laugh lines spreading out from his eyes. He didn't get how serious the situation was.

"I've lost my job. After a week and a half!"

"Honestly," he said, "it's probably for the best. It was turning you a bit weird."

He whistled a cheery tune as he did a little tidying, then gave her a peck on the forehead and went to start gaming. Soon she could hear him chatting to someone online.

Meja blinked quickly to hold back the tears. Why couldn't she have just minded her own business?

She went into the living room, where Ingrid was whining for food. She gave her some fresh hay.

"You've got a good life, you know," she whispered, sitting on the floor next to the cage and watching the guinea pig eat greedily.

Inez had said her name should be Emina. She googled the meaning on her phone: reliable, honest. Meja put her phone screen-down on the floor and leaned her head against the wall. No, she wasn't reliable at all. She had done something that Inez had expressly told her not to. Johan laughed loudly from behind the closed bedroom door. Meja clenched her jaw. She couldn't bear the sound of his laughter. Couldn't bear another night on the couch. Couldn't bear him calling her strange.

She grabbed a bag out of the hall closet, packed her charger, toiletry bag, and a change of clothes that were drying in the bathroom. Then she went back into the living room and stroked Ingrid's head.

"I'll be back tomorrow," she whispered. As she left the apartment, she texted her mother: Minor crisis. Can I sleep in your guest room? Just one night.

INEZ

Inez was trembling with anger, disappointment, and fatigue. The thought of someone reading what she had written about Mathilda made her feel sick. It was so private, from her innermost hiding places, from the most beautiful and ugliest parts of her heart. No one was allowed to read her words without her permission. No one.

She swallowed a double dose of painkillers and went out, walking stick in hand. The wind had died down, but the sky was still dark gray. A bouquet of lavender hung on the gate. She took it down, grumbling to herself, tore up the flowers, and threw the remnants into Sverker and Filip's garden. *Maybe now they'll get it into their thick heads that I don't want their flowers,* she thought as she limped toward Viola's bench for the second time that day.

The waves that had charged at Inez and Meja so furiously that morning were now rippling gently. She clasped her hands in her lap and recalled Meja's despairing face on being caught red-handed. Inez's initial outrage had subsided, leaving only loneliness behind. Of course it had been awkward letting a stranger into her home, but she had also enjoyed having someone there to share things with—coffee, conversation, time. Sighing heavily, she got up to go home.

If the folder was really so private, why had she left it on the bookshelf?

When she got back, she did her best to sweep the torn lavender under Sverker and Filip's bushes with her walking stick. It wasn't fair to take her anger out on them. Maybe she should go over for a coffee one day, to make up for the flowers.

As she opened her gate, she caught sight of a man in Viola's yard. He raised his hand in a tentative greeting. She appreciated that. Appreciated the implied respect for her privacy demonstrated in that small gesture. Inez took a couple of steps closer to the fence. The man did the same.

"Hello. My name is Andreas Lundh, and I've just bought the place. Since it's vacant, I'll be moving in right away. I've come to take some measurements." He smiled.

Inez nodded. "It's bigger than it looks from the outside. Will you be living here alone?"

"My daughter will be here sometimes. But she and her mother live in Gothenburg, so only when she has the time and inclination. She's thirteen . . ."

Inez observed the streak of sadness in his velvety brown eyes and nodded.

"Come and knock on my door in a few days, once you've settled in, and we'll go and visit the neighbors on the other side of the wall. They're very . . . sociable."

Andreas smiled a crooked little half smile. He seemed to understand. "Well, I'd best get back."

"Yes, of course, see you later." Inez turned back to the house. This could be good. Very good. Finally something positive to balance out all the negatives of the day.

She went inside, swapped her shoes for slippers, and stood in the middle of the room. Her eyes were drawn to the armchair that Meja usually sat in. Had she overreacted by telling her to never come back? No. Meja had broken her only rule. She had read the words engraved in Inez's heart. The ones that bled. Inez had lost trust in her, and she couldn't have someone in her house that she didn't trust.

She sighed deeply. Her encounter with her new neighbor had softened her anger somewhat, and she resolved to pull herself together and make an action plan. She got out a paper and pen, sat down in her armchair, and wrote a list. 1. Email Spick & Span: thank them for their help and cancel any further work. 2. Take painkillers on schedule. 3. Continue decluttering efforts at a reasonable pace. 4. Coffee with Sverker and Filip. 5. Finish writing book.

She decided to start with point three: declutter. For Amelia's sake. She planned to complete this project and have a tidy house to show for it. For once in her life, she was doing something purely out of love for her daughter. All the more important that she reach the finish line.

She started taking books off the shelf and piling them up on the tray table by the armchair. Suddenly something caught her eye. Hidden at the back of the shelf was an oyster shell. She trembled as she picked it up, brought it slowly to her ear, and listened. Tears welled up. *Don't cry*, she thought, *write*. She went into the bedroom, placed the shell on her desk, and started typing.

1973

At the entrance to the bakery, I almost passed by Mathilda without recognizing her. I was on my way out; she was on her way in. We both ended up going in and sitting at a table.

She found it very amusing that I almost hadn't noticed her. In my mind, she was so connected to the sea. Here in the village, wearing ordinary clothes and with her hair up, she looked like any normal person.

She leaned back, squinted at me, and said, "How's the story going?"

"What story?" I asked.

"The one you're writing in that little black book of yours."

I smiled shyly and replied that I wasn't writing a story, just random words, feelings, descriptions of places. Nothing special.

"You should write a book," she said.

I laughed out loud. "There's no way I could write a whole story, with a beginning, middle, and end. I don't have any of that."

Mathilda pulled something out of her jacket pocket. An oyster shell. She slid it across the table.

"My lucky oyster. Take it, hold it up to your ear, close your eyes, and listen. It will give you your beginning, middle, and end. I promise."

I shook my head, smiling at this good-natured lie, but put the oyster shell in my pocket.

When I got back to my apartment I took out a pen and brand-new notebook, held the oyster shell to my ear, and listened. Then I started to write the beginning of what would, many years later, become my first novel.

MEJA

Susanne flinched when Meja dropped her bag on the hall floor with a thud.

"What happened?" she asked.

Meja shrugged. It was too difficult to explain. Susanne pursed her lips unhappily and nodded toward the guest room, where Meja took her bag before following Susanne to the kitchen.

"I've just made some pasta with tomato, mozzarella, and olives. Do you want some?"

Meja nodded. It smelled of garlic and basil. She sat down and took a small portion.

"You're not going to find a better man than Johan," said her mother, continuing to eat.

"I haven't left him. It's just for one night. So that I can think."

"That's the problem," Susanne said between bites. "You think too much. Johan thinks it's that writer putting ideas in your head."

"It's not," Meja said shortly. "Besides, I'm not working there anymore. We've finished sorting out her house."

She thought about the message she had received from Karin a few hours earlier. She wanted Meja to come into the office at eight o'clock tomorrow. Presumably to fire her. Meja's heart skipped a beat just thinking about it.

Her phone beeped: Where are you?

Meja keyed in a reply to Johan: Didn't want to disturb your gaming. Got tired of the noise and my back hurts from sleeping on the couch. Staying with Mom for the night. Back tomorrow.

Weird to just take off like that without saying anything, he wrote.

This time he was right. That was weird. But it was what it was.

The front door opened. Susanne leaped to her feet and went to greet Bengt. They exchanged a few whispered words. Typical that the man who always seemed to be out working happened to be home today of all days, thought Meja. But this was his apartment, and she had basically invited herself to stay.

She stood up when he entered the kitchen.

"Sit, sit," he said, waving his hand. "So nice to have you here. Please make yourself at home."

"Thank you," said Meja and sank back into the chair. "It's just for one night."

Bengt smiled warmly. Susanne pursed her lips. He sat down and helped himself to pasta.

"Smells great," he said. "Susanne tells me you work as a cleaner."

"Temporarily," said Meja.

"Temp work is better than none at all," he said.

She nodded in response.

"I've tried to tell Meja that she should study," said Susanne. "It's not like she has a mortgage or children to worry about, so she's free to invest everything in her career."

"Studying is good," Bengt said, smiling at Meja. "If you have the passion and drive to do so."

Meja smiled weakly. He was actually a nice person.

"You never studied, Mom, and you've done well," she blurted and then instantly regretted it. She didn't usually say such thoughts aloud. Susanne's cheeks paled while Meja's blushed.

"Well, you know why that is," Susanne said through gritted teeth.

Meja bit her lower lip. She knew perfectly well. Because she had been a single mother without the time or finances to study. Why was she coming out with things like this now, when she was spending the night? Maybe Johan was right: spending time with Inez was making her act differently.

They finished eating and Meja helped her mother clear the table.

"Sorry," she whispered.

Susanne avoided eye contact. "Leave that, I'll do it," she said, nodding in the direction of the guest room.

Meja swallowed hard and thanked Bengt once more for his hospitality before going into the guest room and shutting the door.

She stood in the middle of the room. There was a bed, a dresser, and an orchid on the windowsill. She longed to go back home to Johan. Why hadn't she just put in earplugs while he was gaming? She messaged him a heart. He responded with a surprised emoji.

She sank down on the bed with a sigh. When she opened her bag she found Inez's book about those Ya-Ya girls, which she barely remembered packing, lying on top. Soon she could hear Caro's southern accent and feel the sticky heat of Spring Creek. When Vivi had a mental breakdown and Sidda was desperate to help, Meja cried. She finished the whole thing.

She brushed her teeth and crawled back into bed. *Tomorrow is another day,* she thought. But she couldn't imagine it being any better.

Meja slept on and off for a few restless hours and felt like a wreck when she woke up the next day. She got up and made herself some toast in the silent apartment.

She sat down at the kitchen table, ate her toast, and thought about the book. It had moved her greatly, even though she already knew the ending from the movie. Two words that resonated in her mind were *understanding* and *reconciliation.*

The living room clock struck seven. The gilded antique was an odd feature in Bengt's otherwise modern apartment. She cursed and gobbled up the last of her toast. She didn't have a car. It, like everything in her life, belonged to Johan. She would have to hurry to make her eight o'clock meeting with Karin. She got washed and dressed, ran a comb through her hair, and scurried out to the bus that would take her to Spick & Span.

She ran into her manager's office fifteen minutes late and gasping for breath. Karin raised her eyebrows slightly, nodded for her to sit down, and glanced at the computer screen.

"Sorry I'm late. I didn't have a car . . ."

"The bus is better for the environment," answered Karin, still with her eyes on the screen. Then she looked up, clasped her hands, and smiled. "Everything went well with Inez Edmark, then?"

Meja held her breath. *Well* wasn't exactly the word. Or was she being ironic?

Karin looked at the screen again. "She sent a very nice email praising your efficiency in getting everything done earlier than expected."

Meja let out the breath she'd been holding. "Really?"

Did this mean she wasn't fired?

"So I'm placing you in an office. You start tomorrow." Karin returned to her screen. "Come here first thing in the morning for a briefing and cleaning supplies."

Meja thanked her and left the office. As soon as she rounded the corner, she jumped up and down, clapped her hands, and let out a small squeal of joy. She was keeping her job! Despite everything.

She walked with a spring in her step to the bus stop, but instead of going back to Bengt's apartment, she went in the direction of Höganäs and got off at the pine grove in Domsten. She followed the path to Inez's house. Then she took out the borrowed book, in a pink plastic bag she had found in Bengt's kitchen. Pink like the peonies that were hanging on Inez's gate. She hung the bag up next to them and turned to leave.

She had left a little note in the book. There was so much she had wanted to say, but she hoped her few words would be enough.

INEZ

Inez saw someone moving by the gate and angled the blinds slightly to get a better look. Meja? Her pulse quickened. It looked like she'd hung something on the gatepost before quickly walking away. Inez draped her crocheted shawl over her shoulders and went out. On the gate was a pink plastic bag. Inside was the book about the Ya-Ya sisterhood that Meja had borrowed. She wondered if she had actually read it. Probably not.

Her thoughts were interrupted by cheerful voices. Sverker and Filip appeared in their garden and waved at Inez.

"We're having coffee in the rose arbor. Fancy joining us?" asked Sverker.

Inez was just about to decline when she remembered her list of action points. It would feel like a positive step to tick off the fourth: coffee with the neighbors.

"Thanks, I'd love to," she said.

Sverker stopped in his tracks. "You would?"

Inez enjoyed the calming, spicy scent of wild honeysuckle as she walked along their gravel path. She stopped at the ornate wrought-iron lawn furniture where Sverker had already laid out a third place setting under the parasol.

"Gosh, it's so nice to have company," he said, his cheeks flushed.

They sat down and Inez was served coffee.

"It finally feels like summer again," said Filip. "What terrible weather we had yesterday. I thought all our rose petals would be blown away."

Inez nodded. "I ran into our new neighbor," she said. "Have you met him?"

"Not yet, but my brother-in-law was confident that we would be pleased," said Filip.

"His name is Andreas. Seems very pleasant," said Inez, sipping the hot coffee.

Sverker broke into a smile.

"Yes, I'm quite pleased." He pushed forward a tray of cookies. "Help yourself. They're homemade."

Inez took a raspberry jelly–filled cookie and hummed contentedly. It was perfectly fluffy and crunchy.

"Meja not with you today?" asked Filip.

Inez lifted the cup to her lips to buy a few extra seconds before answering.

"No, she's gone."

Sverker raised his eyebrows.

"Our decluttering went faster than expected. We finished in half the time."

"Oh, that's good. I got the impression that she was a very neat and organized person, so it's no surprise she was a fast worker," said Sverker.

Inez nodded, avoiding eye contact.

They continued to chat about the weather and the roses.

Inez finished her coffee and thanked them both. When she got up to leave, Sverker followed her to the gate while Filip cleared up.

"Don't forget the peonies and your bag," he said, handing them to her. "It looks like a book."

"It's an old favorite. You can borrow it if you like."

"Can I?" Sverker took the book out and smiled. "I read this a long time ago, but I would love to read it again." As he flipped through the pages, a small note fell out and fluttered to the ground. Inez pinned it down with her walking stick, and Sverker bent to pick it up. He glanced at it quickly before handing it over to Inez.

Thank you! And sorry. —Meja

Inez swallowed hard, folded the note, and put it in her pocket. "Well, thanks again for the coffee."

"Thank you," said Sverker and raised the book in the air, a little embarrassed.

When Inez was back home, she took the note from her pocket and smoothed it out. Why had she lent Sverker the book? Completely unnecessary. And why had Meja put a note in the book? Also unnecessary.

Thank you and sorry.

Inez sat down and cast her eyes over the remaining piles of books. Could she really sort through them all herself? Did she even dare to climb that stool again? Mathilda's oyster shell was on the table next to her. She raised it to her ear, closed her eyes, and listened. Then she emailed the cleaning company, saying that on second thought she probably needed help clearing the attic as well. Would Meja be able to complete the work period as planned?

An hour later she received the reply: No problem. She's coming by the office tomorrow morning. I'll tell her to go straight to your place after.

Then she took out the blue folder and placed it on the small tray table between the armchairs. She felt a flutter in the pit of her stomach. She had an idea. Whether it was a good idea, or a disaster waiting to happen, remained to be seen.

MEJA

The day Meja had been dreading turned out completely differently than expected. On finding out she still had a job, she had, in a great surge of joy, returned Inez's book and bought some tulips for Susanne and Bengt and a breathable sports shirt for Johan to wear when he played paddle tennis. Now she was sitting opposite her mother in Bengt's living room, messaging Johan to say she would be home that afternoon and asking if she should pick up anything on the way.

"So you're free today?" said Susanne.

"Yes, there's a gap between clients. Tomorrow will be work as usual."

Susanne nodded and started to leaf through the latest issue of *Femina* magazine. Meja's phone beeped. Johan had replied: Maybe we should give it a bit more time? I'll feed Ingrid.

Meja's mouth went dry. What did he mean? Susanne looked up and sighed, as if she could tell just from Meja's face what the text had said.

Meja typed back: More time? How long?

The answer came immediately. Just a day or two.

Meja pursed her lips. Easy for him to say—he had his own apartment. But he had added a heart to the last text. That was something.

She looked up at Susanne. "Slight change of plans. Could I stay another night?"

Susanne closed the magazine. "I'm guessing you have no choice?"

Meja shrugged. No, she didn't. Otherwise there was no way she would impose herself on her mother. The whole situation made her feel ten years old again. The little girl who always seemed to be in the way.

Susanne went to get her a spare key. Meja leaned her head back and closed her eyes. At least she still had her job. And tomorrow she would be back with Johan, even if she had to get down on her knees and beg.

The next morning, she was back in Karin's office, awaiting instructions.

"New plan for today," Karin said while fiddling on the computer.

"Oh?" said Meja, feeling goose bumps of tension form on her skin.

"I had you down for an office, but Inez would like to hire you back. To tidy her attic."

Meja swallowed hard. She didn't understand.

"So you can carry on as before. Weekly meeting here, but otherwise just go directly to her place." Karin looked up from the screen. "Okay? I told her you would go today, straight after this meeting."

Meja picked up her bag and left the office. Her breathing was so shallow that she became lightheaded. Back to Inez?

She reluctantly made her way to the bus stop and traveled to Domsten, where she was greeted by the straight-backed trees in the pine grove. She, on the other hand, plodded with a stooped posture toward Inez's house. Nerves were giving her a slight grinding headache around the temples. Thank goodness it was Friday at least.

She knocked on the door, and Inez called for her to come in. Meja blinked a few times to adjust her eyes to the darkness. She felt sick. Inez said nothing. She just sat in her armchair with an inscrutable look on her face. Meja could feel her pulse throbbing in her eardrums as she took off her jacket and sat down.

"Hello," she said softly, unsure of how to continue. Should she apologize or act like nothing had happened? On the tray table between them was the blue folder. Inez pushed it forward.

"So. This is the manuscript for my next book," she said. "And I want you to read it. Aloud."

Meja swallowed. Now she was really confused. But she didn't dare say no. With trembling hands, she opened the folder and began to read.

1972

Mathilda taught me how to shuck oysters like a pro. Lay the oyster flat side up on a tea towel, insert the knife in the hinge, and wiggle carefully until the opening gives way. Rotate the knife to pry open the shell and cut out the oyster sitting in the flat top half. She also taught me the trick of gently poking its edge to see if it contracted. Apparently that meant it was alive and could be eaten. I thought that sounded horrible, but she just laughed. She made sure I chewed each oyster properly. "That's how you get all the flavor of the ocean. You mustn't swallow it whole. Otherwise it has sacrificed its life for nothing," she said. That was how seriously she took it. Of course, I did as she said. Prodded the oyster, checked that the oyster was alive, and chewed a couple of times before swallowing.

She told me that you never cut or break oysters free, you pick them with care and respect. Sometimes a smaller oyster sat atop a larger one, and then the smaller one would be gently broken off and put back, while the larger was harvested. Her dedication was admirable—sometimes to the point of irritating.

I remember one cold February day sitting in the boat, waiting for her to surface. I was exhaling warm air into my gloves to keep my fingers from freezing, thinking I wasn't going to be able to stand the cold much longer, when her head finally popped up above the side of the boat.

"You're crazy for doing this," I shouted. "Crazy!"

Mathilda just laughed as she pulled her fourth basket up. She paused to catch her breath, then began loading them onto the boat with my help. On the way back I was shaking with cold.

As she steered the boat, she turned to me and said, "I read that if you represent the age of the Earth as twenty-four hours, a human life would be only a fraction of a second. So, what then is the meaning of life, you may wonder?" She didn't wait for an answer. "To follow your calling. Even on cold days." Then she laughed and began humming some old sea shanty.

I sat hugging myself tightly and thought my answer would more likely be to *find* my calling. We were starting from different positions. But thanks to Mathilda, I found mine eventually. Maybe I would have anyway. Maybe not. But I know this much: Finding one's calling requires a touch of madness. Or madly following someone. Like me, following Mathilda.

Inez leaned back in her chair.
"Any questions?" she asked.
Meja tensed. Questions? About the text? The job? She didn't know what to say, and a question slipped out completely unplanned. "Why do you always have your blinds down?"

The unexpected question made Inez laugh. "Well," she said in a slightly softer tone, "maybe because I'm just a little mad."

She hummed in amusement as she took the paper from Meja's hand, put it back in the blue folder, and nodded toward the bookshelf. "We can start by sorting those, then fill the bookshelf with books that I'm going to keep."

By the end of Meja's shift they had sorted three large piles of books and papers. Meja glanced at the clock. Weren't they going to talk about what had happened before she left?

But Meja got the hint when Inez stood up and opened the porch door.

"See you on Monday?" Meja asked on her way out.

Inez replied with a curt nod and shut the door behind her.

Meja breathed in the sea air and squinted into the sun. Sverker was on the other side of the fence, smelling a flower. He lit up when he saw her.

"Sweet pea," he said, snapping one off and holding it out to her. "Glad to see you're back."

"Yes, there was a change of plans."

"Small words can bring about big changes."

Meja nodded, embarrassed. Did he know about her note? Surely Inez wouldn't have told him about it.

"I've got a bus to catch," she said and left, sweet pea in hand. Small words could bring about big changes. It was true. Should she apologize to Johan too? What for? *Sorry I don't want to sleep on the couch, sorry I want to go out to eat once in a while, sorry I want to have conversations . . .*

Neither Bengt nor Susanne was home when Meja returned to the apartment. She sat down on the couch, utterly wiped out after the day's unexpected turn. So she was going to continue working with Inez. She shook her head. She had desperately wanted to ask if that text she had read was fictional or autobiographical, but hadn't dared. Maybe next time.

She ate some broccoli quiche she found in the freezer, then perused Bengt's book collection. All crime fiction. She flipped through a few at random but none grabbed her. She looked through one of Susanne's monthly magazines wearily instead. Time passed slowly. Finally she sat in the sunshine on the balcony, counting down the minutes until she could go back home to Johan. He had said a day or two, and it had been a day, so that was enough. She was going to set everything right again.

When Bengt's antique clock struck four, she wrote a note to thank Susanne for her hospitality, gathered her things, and left.

The city was buzzing with the atmosphere of a Friday evening. Summer vacation was finally here. People laughed louder on days like these. Meja felt a kind of elation too. She still had her job, things with Inez were going well after all, and now she and Johan were going to put an end to their spat and everything would go back to normal.

She passed the ferry about to set sail for Denmark and walked inland toward the city center, past Saint Mary Parish and to Johan's building. She ran up to the third floor, two steps at a time. She could hear voices and loud music coming from inside the apartment. She texted: Home soon!

A few seconds later the answer came. I have a few friends over. How about tomorrow?

Meja looked down at the screen, bit her bottom lip, left the package with Johan's shirt outside the door, and went back down the stairs.

All her excitement drained away as she trudged back to Bengt's apartment. Susanne cast a displeased glance at the bag hanging over Meja's shoulder as she entered the hall.

"Sorry," said Meja. "I wanted to go home, but Johan was having a boys' night."

"Of course he was," she said, leading her into the living room. Susanne poured a glass of red wine in the same shade as her lipstick. "Want some?"

Meja nodded. It was Friday, after all.

"Is Bengt at work?"

"He's at a conference in Brussels all weekend," said Susanne, holding the glass out to Meja.

"Oh," said Meja, accepting the glass and going onto the balcony. She gazed out at the boats bobbing in the harbor and thought of the story she had read at Inez's. About having to be a little crazy in order to find your calling. And maybe even crazier still to follow it.

She glanced back into the living room, where her mother was watching some old movie. She had been denied her calling. Perhaps that was even more tragic than never finding one to begin with.

INEZ

At five thirty in the morning Inez woke up with a jolt and looked up at the calendar hanging on the wall above the bed. Saturday. She stepped out onto the balcony and took a few deep breaths. Had it been the right decision to let Meja read the story? It was a risk. But it was done now. Hearing her words from someone else's lips helped her get a feel for a text. Cristy used to do the same thing back when Inez wrote most intensively. She usually wrote at night, then Cristy would bring her breakfast, get Amelia to school, and read the previous night's words aloud.

Inez closed her eyes. The sound of the waves brought her back in time. To Kobbholmen. Salt-sprinkled rocks and carefree days. To a time dedicated to living, not responsibilities. She felt surprisingly light today. She took a deep breath and stretched her arms high in the air like Viola used to. Suddenly her new neighbor, Andreas, appeared on the adjacent balcony with a cup of tea. He flinched when he saw her, then smiled and raised his cup in greeting.

"Good morning."

"Good morning," said Inez. "You're up early too, I see."

He nodded. "I'm going up to Gothenburg to pick up some things."

"Yes, I saw you rented a little van," said Inez, who had noticed it in the driveway the night before.

"Then I'll be officially moved in," he said, shrugging his shoulders nonchalantly. But his eyes betrayed his true feelings. Moving his things wasn't going to be easy.

Kobbholmen fluttered through her mind again. Inez hadn't been there for forty-five years, and had never intended to return. But this book she was writing . . . did it require her to go back? A rush of nerves bubbled through her chest.

"Gothenburg, you say? I don't suppose you want company?"

He raised his eyebrows. "You have business in Gothenburg?"

"A little outside the city."

He thought about it. "That would work. I'm leaving at seven."

"Perfect." Inez nodded curtly and went back inside.

Her heart was racing. Was she really going to Kobbholmen? Should she tell Andreas she had changed her mind? She sighed deeply. If she did have to go back for the sake of the book, she might as well do it today, when she was feeling light on her feet.

A little over an hour later, she was waiting in Andreas's driveway. He came out punctually and helped her into the van.

"Off we go." He smiled, and Inez's concerns that she was intruding disappeared. He seemed grateful for the company.

"How did you come to move here?" she asked when they had left Helsingborg behind.

"I grew up around here. I love the sea."

She nodded. "But your daughter still lives in Gothenburg?"

"Yes. She seemed okay about her mother and me divorcing, but made it very clear that it wasn't her decision and she wasn't going to suffer because of it. In other words, she didn't want to swap homes every week." He smiled his crooked half smile. "She came apartment hunting with me, and after the fourth place she looked at me and said she would prefer it if I moved exactly where *I* wanted to, and not where I thought I ought to be for her sake."

"Smart girl," said Inez.

He nodded. "Kattis, my daughter, and her mother, Sandra, love city life. I could never get used to it. So I thought I'd give this a year and see how it goes. When you're fumbling around for something to hold on to, I figured it's probably best to start by going back to your roots." He shrugged his shoulders in embarrassment at the poetic digression.

Inez smiled. That was exactly how she had felt about that apartment in Kobbholmen in her youth.

She took a couple of thermos mugs out of her bag. "How about some *fika*?"

Andreas smiled and nodded.

Inez shared coffee, and cheese and cucumber sandwiches, and looked out the window at the passing scenery.

"How about you?" he said. "Have you lived in Domsten for a long time?"

"Fifteen years. I was in Stockholm for many years but needed to get away from the big city. A good friend of mine suggested Helsingborg so I could be closer to Denmark and the continent." She shrugged. "Not that the proximity has made me travel more. And it was a coincidence that I ended up in Domsten specifically."

"So what are you doing in Gothenburg today?" Andreas asked.

"I'm not actually going to Gothenburg, but to Kobbholmen."

"Oh, that's quite far."

"I'll take a bus," she said.

He didn't ask any more questions. Instead, he turned on the radio and let her snooze the rest of the way. That made her like him even more.

When they arrived in Gothenburg, Andreas dropped her off at the bus terminal.

"Are you sure you'll be all right?" He didn't look comfortable leaving her there.

"Of course," Inez said and promised to let him know when she was on her way back into the city.

As she boarded the bus to Kobbholmen, she saw that Andreas was waiting in the car until she got on safely. She shook her head. Did she really come across as that frail?

She sat down in an empty window seat. They were due to arrive around midday. She was sweaty and her blood was fizzing with nerves. She took off her poncho and fanned her face with her hand.

The bus started with a jerk. Inez leaned her head against the headrest. She had never intended to go back. Not after what had happened. She closed her eyes and tried to rest but couldn't fall asleep. She should have brought something to eat. Or a book to read. Someone had left today's *Gothenburg Post* in the pocket of the seat in front. She reached for the newspaper, flipped through the pages haphazardly at first, and then skimmed every article, just to distract herself from the purpose of her journey. Of course, she could try to trick her brain, but her body knew. It sensed where she was going and was bracing for it.

Her mouth was dry and her legs were trembling when she got off the bus in Kobbholmen a couple of hours later. She was struck by the heat. The sun seemed warmer here, and the sky bluer. There was a lively market full of people buying fruit, flowers, and souvenirs, beyond which she caught a glimpse of the water. She began walking in the direction of the sea, pausing now and then to consciously draw breath. There was so much to see that made her want to hold her breath: the rocks and skerries, the high mountains in the background. It was so different from Domsten's swaying beach grass. So familiar—and yet so foreign.

There was a long line for the fishing boat about to set out on an archipelago tour, and a steady stream of visitors strolled along the pier, lined with red boathouses, restaurants, and little shops.

Inez gripped her walking stick tightly and walked slowly so as not to topple over in the crowd.

Her stomach growled and she stopped at a restaurant with a few empty seats. Her hip ached—sitting for hours in the car and bus was worse than long walks. The couple next to her had ordered a proper West Coast platter of freshly caught lobster, crayfish, shrimp, and clams. It was a treat for the eye as much as for the taste buds. The waitress came to her table.

"Can I take your order?" she asked.

Inez nodded, glanced at the couple's overflowing dish of delicacies, then realized how awkward it would be to fiddle around with all the shells. She opted for a shrimp sandwich and a glass of the house white wine instead.

While she waited for the food, she gazed at the pier. It was more commercial than she remembered it. More stores and large signs boasting sales and special offers. It didn't matter to her; she wasn't one of those sentimental types that wished everything would stay the same all the time. Change was usually a good thing.

The waitress came back with her sandwich and wine. Inez popped a shrimp in her mouth, closed her eyes, and savored it. It had a good bite to it and tasted of the sea. Nothing like frozen shrimp from the store.

She ate slowly, wishing she could just stay where she was. Spend the day people-watching and drinking wine before returning to Gothenburg. But that wasn't an option.

Oyster Bay was calling to her, whispering that it was time to come back. That it was waiting for her.

Having managed only half the shrimp sandwich but the whole glass of wine, she paid and walked slowly back to the square and hailed a cab.

"Oyster Bay, please."

She felt a flutter in her stomach as she settled into the passenger seat. Now she wished she had drunk another glass of wine to soothe her nerves.

It took less than ten minutes to get there. Inez looked out the window at the bay with high cliffs on both sides and a small island in the middle. Her eyes were moist and her heart was beating alarmingly fast. The bay looked smaller than she remembered it.

The driver stopped in a parking lot.

"This is the closest I can get you to the water," he said regretfully.

"That's fine," Inez said, hearing her voice tremble.

In Inez's time, this had been a hidden place where few people went. Now it looked like a recreation area. A family was sitting at one of several picnic tables, and next to the parking lot was a large information sign with marked hiking trails. On the other side of the bay was a jetty, also new, surrounded by small fishing and leisure boats. Tears welled up in her eyes.

"Could you wait here for fifteen minutes?" she whispered.

The cabdriver nodded and came to help Inez out. Her legs were shaking so much she wondered if they would carry her all the way.

Mathilda's hut was still there but had been rebuilt or renovated, and the sign saying MATHILDA'S OYSTERS was gone. Now it was TORSTEN'S OYSTERS. Inez slowly made her way toward it, passing some children lying on the pier and fishing for crabs. Every yard felt like an eternity, but also like a time machine, hurling her back to a life she had left behind and thought she would never return to. When she had made it all the way to the oyster shack, the sounds of the children on the pier had disappeared. She was alone with this place. With her memories.

She walked past the hut, lightly touched the large plastic baskets where the oysters were collected when in season, and cast her eyes across the rakes hanging on the wall. Then she gazed out at the island, the one she had swum to so many times. She walked a few more yards and saw the strip of beach littered with empty oyster shells. The same as it had always been! She had loved looking for the prettiest shells here while Mathilda was busy tinkering with her fishing gear.

She sank to her knees. The pain in her pelvis burned like fire. Laying her walking stick beside her, she ran her hands over the oyster shells and let the tears flow. They dripped down slowly and pooled in the shells' crevices.

The sound of a small boat engine some distance away made her turn around. Laboriously, she rose to her feet and limped to the stony shore. The boat glided over the mirror-like water. Inez could picture Mathilda at the wheel, her long reddish hair fluttering in the breeze. She clutched her heart with both hands to make sure it was still beating. Then she slowly raised her right hand in the air.

"Here," she whispered. "I'm here now."

Someone cleared their throat behind her, and she was snapped out of her trance. She turned and stared at the man for a moment before realizing he was the cabdriver.

"It's been fifteen minutes," he said.

Inez looked out over the water. "Did you see a woman in a boat?"

The man squinted. "You mean that boat? Looks like a man to me."

Inez used her hand to shield her eyes from the sun. He was right; it was a man. Of course it wasn't Mathilda. She looked down at the seabed, where she saw some white spots glistening.

"Treasures of the sea," she said, smiling through her tears and pointing. But the cabdriver didn't look at the oysters. He looked at her shoes, which were now completely submerged. Inez felt water seeping in between her toes and took a few steps back.

"Are you okay?" he asked, looking concerned.

She wiped her tears and nodded. "Perhaps you could drive me back to the bus station in Kobbholmen now?"

They didn't speak on the way back. Inez tipped extra for dragging water and sand into his car. She headed for the bus, and her whole body ached as she sank into the seat.

She texted Andreas to say she was on her way back to Gothenburg but that he absolutely did not have to wait for her, that she could take the train. He promptly replied that he would be waiting.

Inez leaned her head against the headrest, closed her eyes, and remembered a conversation from long ago.

"Do you want to live in Kobbholmen all your life?"

"The sea is my blood, the waves my heartbeat, the winds my oxygen," Mathilda replied while rowing her boat with expert movements.

"But don't you want to see other places? Stockholm, Berlin, Rome, Amsterdam . . ."

Mathilda looked up. "I would suffocate in a big city. But I can breathe anywhere in the world as long as I'm by the sea."

"Then we'll go somewhere where there's sea," I said.

Mathilda smiled and dipped her hand into the water. "Did you know that all the world's seas are joined together in one vast global ocean? Perhaps that's why this is where the feeling of freedom is greatest."

Three hours later, Inez got off the bus and made her way, painfully, to Andreas's moving van. He helped her in and looked curiously at her pants, which were damp up to the knees, but said nothing.

"How's your day been?" he asked.

The pain in Inez's hip made her grimace.

"Did you know that all the world's seas are connected in one big global ocean?" she said. She looked out the window and muttered to herself, "That means she could be just about anywhere."

MEJA

It was nearly lunchtime when Meja emerged from the guest room. It was dead silent. Had Susanne gone out? No, she was sitting on the couch with a glass of red wine, staring out the window. She appeared lost in thought. When Meja cleared her throat, she flinched.

"Hi," she said.

"Hi," Meja said and plonked herself down beside her. What was she supposed to do with this long Saturday? She checked her phone. Johan hadn't replied to her latest text.

"Have a glass," said Susanne and nodded toward the serving trolley.

Meja really wasn't in the mood for red wine so early in the day, but poured a glass anyway. She had nothing better to do. She looked around the room.

"Where are all your things?" she said.

"My things?" Susanne shrugged. "In storage. They don't fit. All I have here is a dresser in the bedroom."

Meja's belongings didn't require storage; they fit in a suitcase. A medium-sized suitcase. She sighed and fixed her gaze on a photograph on the sideboard. It was of Susanne and Bengt under a palm tree.

"Do you have our old photos in your dresser or are they in storage too?" Meja asked.

Susanne shrugged again.

"I'd love to see pictures from when I was little."

Susanne pressed her lips together in irritation but went into the bedroom and soon returned with a small pile of photographs. Meja started looking through them. The flash had turned people's eyes red in several of the pictures taken indoors. Many were blurred, and the composition of others clearly hadn't been thought through. She saw herself. She was rarely smiling. But she didn't look sad either, more surprised. As if life surprised her even then. Susanne was smoking a cigarette in most of the pictures.

"I can't believe you used to smoke," said Meja, holding up a photograph.

"Everybody did back then."

"I've never smoked," said Meja.

Susanne raised her eyebrows. "But I'm sure you tried it?"

"No, not really." She picked up a picture of them on vacation somewhere. Meja was just a little baby. "Where is this?"

Susanne went into the kitchen and returned with a pack of cigarettes. "I'll tell you where it was taken if you smoke a cigarette."

"What!?"

Susanne went onto the balcony and nodded for Meja to sit in the other chair. Reluctantly, she joined her mother and watched as she lit a cigarette with a well-practiced movement. She inhaled smoke deep into her lungs before holding the cigarette out to Meja.

"I'm not a smoker anymore. Just a puff every now and then when I feel like it. Sometimes a year passes between smokes, sometimes a few weeks," she explained.

Meja didn't know what to say. She took the cigarette in her hand and wrinkled her nose at the smell. It was disgusting. But she wanted to know about the photograph, so she screwed up her eyes, inhaled, and coughed out the smoke. Susanne laughed as she relieved her daughter of the cigarette, then took another drag.

"So you've really never smoked?" she said. "I suppose I shouldn't be surprised."

"There is nothing cool about smoking," said Meja. Her mother's derogatory tone stung, like it had so many times before.

Susanne shrugged. "It's a question of pushing boundaries, living a little."

"Not worth dying of lung cancer for," said Meja.

"Better than being a health nut and dying of bone cancer," said Susanne.

Meja shook her head. It was impossible to argue with her mother. "So," she said. "Tell me about the photograph."

Susanne leaned back and looked up at the sky. "It was taken in Barcelona."

"I didn't know we'd been there on vacation," said Meja.

Susanne ashed her cigarette into a flowerpot. "No, why would you?"

"Why did we go there when I was so small? We never went abroad when I was growing up, did we?"

Susanne held out the cigarette. Meja took as small a puff as possible.

"No, there was no money for it. There was a reason I went that year."

Meja took the cigarette from Susanne, took another quick puff, and looked at her with wide eyes, urging her to say more.

"I went to see if I could find your father."

Meja coughed and spluttered until her eyes watered.

Susanne looked at her, amused. "Would you like a glass of water?"

Meja waved her hands to say it was okay. She wasn't about to let her go now. Her father? Susanne had barely mentioned him before.

"Did you find him?" she asked hoarsely, though she knew the answer.

Susanne shook her head. "He was from Germany, worked in a bar in Barcelona. We spent one night together, and you were the result of that night. The following year I went back to see if he was still working in the same place. He wasn't."

"Did you keep looking?"

"No," said Susanne. "How could I? I didn't know where in Germany he came from, didn't know his last name, how old he was. I had nothing to go on. And of course the bar had no records of employees and paid wages in cash."

Her mother took the cigarette back and blew out a perfect smoke ring. Meja smiled and poked her finger through it like she remembered doing as a child.

Susanne stubbed the butt out in the flowerpot and went inside.

Meja stayed where she was and gazed out to sea. Her heart was racing. Susanne had actually looked for her father. She had never spoken about him. Meja had told her friends that he was dead. But he wasn't dead. He was out there somewhere. So strange. When she got her life back together, she would definitely try to find him. Maybe post an announcement on social media?

Her phone beeped. It was Johan. He said he'd had too much fun last night and was paying for it now. He wouldn't be good company today and hoped they could speak on Monday.

Meja closed the message without replying. He was slipping through her fingers. She could feel it. And it was all her fault. Because she had started making demands and asking strange questions. Their relationship wasn't stable enough to withstand rocking the boat. She should have known that.

INEZ

Sunday turned out to be a day of pain. Ten hours of sitting in the car and bus on Saturday had taken its toll. Inez stayed in bed most of the day and only got up to do some reluctant shopping and cooking for the coming week. Oven-baked chicken with rice.

She had bought seven different packets of sauce to make the dish feel new every day: curry, béarnaise, spicy béarnaise, café de Paris, green pepper, cream sauce, and red wine sauce. Then she went to bed and slept all evening and night and woke up so early on Monday morning that the birds hadn't even started chirping yet.

She pulled her crocheted shawl over her shoulders and stood on the porch. The day was overcast and gloomy. A band of mist swirled along the shore like dancing fairies. She shivered and pulled the shawl tighter around her when she sensed movement in the garden next door. Andreas turned his head in her direction, gave her a crooked half smile, and nodded toward the sea.

"It's at its most beautiful now."

"You think?" Inez said. She had assumed he would be the type of person who liked beautiful sunrises in red and blue. Misty gray days were for those of a dark disposition.

He looked at her again. "Have you recovered from the Gothenburg trip?"

She nodded.

"You look a little pale. Let me know if you need help with anything."

"Thanks. I will."

He put his hands in his pockets and went back inside.

Inez sighed. Her pale cheeks weren't just about the pain in her pelvis, but also about the pain in her heart. She regretted going to Kobbholmen. Before, the place had felt like a dream, a little fuzzy around the edges. And it was from that dream that she had written her story. Now it had become real, developed solid outlines. She couldn't fool herself anymore. This time she was writing a true story, not fiction. She had a duty to tell Mathilda's story as it had really happened—not as she wished it had.

She went back inside, sat down at her desk, and continued writing.

At nine o'clock there was a knock on the back door. It slowly dawned on Inez that it must be Meja. She had completely forgotten that she was coming. When she opened the door she saw a weary-looking woman on the other side.

"I thought I had a tiring weekend, but it doesn't look like yours was any better," said Inez. She went to put on some strong coffee. "Well?"

Meja shifted her weight from foot to foot. "Yeah, it was a rough weekend."

"How so?"

"I've been staying with my mother. And, well, we're only used to seeing each other once a month for dinner. So it takes a lot of effort."

"That sounds tiring all right."

"She also made me smoke my first cigarette, so I felt pretty sick for half the weekend."

Inez laughed. "I think I like your mother."

"Most people do," said Meja.

Inez nodded. The mother-and-daughter relationship. The most complicated relationship of all.

"So what did you do this weekend?" Meja said.

"Wrote, walked, cooked."

Meja squinted at her. "I thought you said you had a tiring weekend?"

Inez waved her hands. "Bah, it's just my hip acting up, as usual."

They sat down in the armchairs and drank their coffee. Inez had taken down the blue folder. She didn't know if she wanted Meja to continue reading aloud, but she wasn't sure there was any turning back now. She pushed the folder toward her, and Meja picked it up and began to read in a soft voice.

Inez leaned her head back and listened.

The description of the friendship between the narrator and the oyster diver got under Meja's skin. Words about women who became such important parts of each other's lives, despite, or perhaps because of, their differences. Words about belonging and dreams. But more than that. She had gotten to the point in the story when the bond between them was obviously becoming strained. Would it survive?

Meja took a deep breath and started reading the most recent part:

"I rarely accompanied Mathilda out on the boat anymore. Instead I would sneak away from the men in my bed on the weekends and follow the path up the rocky outcrop above the pier. Then I would sit there with my little black notebook, gaze at the sea stretching out in the morning light, and wait for her. She always came on time. Seven in the morning. Prepared the boat, drank a cup of coffee standing up, and set sail. Just before she rounded the island, she would always look back. As if she knew I was sitting there in the bushes on the rocks. And every time she disappeared, I gasped. As if a piece of me had been removed."

Meja looked up. "Is this fiction?"

Inez put the paper back in the folder with a short chuckle. "I only write fiction. The trick is to make it so realistic that readers believe it's true."

"But where does it take place? It doesn't feel local."

Inez cleared her throat a little. "No, it takes place in Kobbholmen, in Bohuslän. Where people dive for oysters. I read about the place in an article once and thought it would make a good setting for a book, but I've never been there."

"How can you write about a place you've never been?"

"Google. It's got everything." Inez looked at one of the piles of books on the floor. "You can start on your own today. My hip is acting up; I need to rest awhile longer."

Inez went into the bedroom, sat on the edge of the bed, and took long, deep breaths to bring her pulse down. Inez's words, which Meja had just read out loud so tenderly, reopened wounds that Inez thought had healed. But they had never healed; they hadn't even scarred over. They were just scabs, easily picked and ready to bleed again. She squeezed her eyes shut to avoid reliving all those mornings on the cliff, but they had been set free now and wouldn't go away.

After an hour's rest, Inez shook off the memories and went back out into the living room. Meja was sitting in the armchair with her hands in her lap, tired and waiting for her. They really were a sad duo right now. They could both do with cheering up. And Inez could think of someone else who could probably do with the same.

She went into the kitchen to make some sandwiches and a pot of coffee and packed them in a picnic basket. Then she beckoned to Meja to follow her.

"It's not really picnic weather," said Meja, shivering as she buttoned her jacket up to the neck.

Inez didn't answer. She stopped at Andreas's gate.

"Wait here," she said to Meja and walked over to knock on the porch door.

He opened presently.

"How about a picnic on what I like to call Viola's bench?" she said.

He looked hesitant, but half smiled, pulled on a knitted sweater, and followed.

"This is Andreas, my new neighbor," Inez said to Meja. "And this is Meja, my . . . assistant."

Andreas and Meja said hello and followed Inez to the seaside bench. Meja gave her a quizzical look, but she didn't know whether it concerned the neighbor, or her new title of "assistant." It didn't matter. They were here to forget their troubles for a little while—Inez's memories, Meja's domestic issues, and Andreas's move away from his family.

They sat down on the bench with Inez in the middle, and she shared the picnic. Andreas gazed at the sea, momentarily far away in thought. Then he looked at Inez and smiled.

"Funny that we drove all the way to Gothenburg and back together but hardly know anything about each other." He turned to Meja. "So you're Inez's assistant?"

His mention of Gothenburg had made Meja frown, but she answered his question politely.

"Yes, I help with this and that. A little bit of everything, you might say. Papers and stuff."

Meja looked at Inez as if to confirm that she was saying the right thing.

Inez nodded briefly and looked at Andreas. "What about you?"

"I'm an art teacher and was lucky enough to find a position at a junior high school in Helsingborg around the same time as I had the idea of moving here. It kind of felt like it was meant to be. But every day I wonder what the hell came over me. It's not easy starting over."

Inez nodded. She knew all about that.

They finished their coffee in silence. On their way back, Inez felt much more balanced than before.

They said goodbye to Andreas and, once back inside, Inez checked her wristwatch. "Well, your shift is over, so see you tomorrow."

But Meja didn't move. "I thought you said you hadn't done anything special this weekend?"

Inez shrugged without answering. "He's nice, don't you think?"

Meja pursed her lips, then relented. "I suppose so, but it's hard to tell after half an hour."

Inez couldn't help but smile. Meja was annoyed with her. Presumably because she had lied about what she'd done that weekend. It was almost amusing.

"It takes seven seconds for a person to establish their first eleven judgments about another person. So no, it's not hard to tell whether he seems nice," she said.

"Okay. He seemed nice," Meja said resignedly and waved goodbye.

Inez stood and watched her go with a smile on her face.

She hoped their little picnic had helped to brighten Meja's day. And Andreas's.

MEJA

Should she knock or just let herself in? Meja was dithering outside Johan's apartment door. She decided to knock first and then let herself in.

"Hello?" she called and set her bag on the floor.

Johan emerged from the kitchen.

"Nice to see you," he said. "Coffee?"

"Please," said Meja. Something about his vaguely cheery tone made her pulse quicken. She had felt anxious ever since he'd sent a text saying they needed to talk.

He served her a mug of coffee as she sat down on her usual kitchen chair. She glanced around the room as she sipped her drink. It was as if the apartment had already shut her out; the kitchen had never felt so alien to her. She looked up at Johan and knew what he was about to say.

"I've been doing some thinking while you've been away, and I've come to the conclusion that we should take a break."

"A break?" Meja said.

She had never understood the concept. Surely you were either together or you weren't. Besides, hadn't they just had a break?

"I just needed one night away because I was exhausted from work and needed some peace and quiet. I didn't mean for this . . ."

"I know you didn't, but when I was here alone, I realized that we might need a proper break to figure out what we really want. It's easy to get stuck in a relationship rut without noticing."

He was tapping on his leg. She wanted to tell him to stop but didn't. He could drum on his own leg in his own apartment as much as he wanted. She blinked back the sudden tears.

"Just for a little while," he said, embarrassed.

Meja tried to wipe her tears away discreetly. The tears weren't just for their disintegrating relationship, but for her life in general. Her heart skipped a beat at the realization that, without Johan, she was nothing but a homeless temp.

She refused to start begging and pleading, so she removed the apartment key from her key ring, despite Johan's protests, and placed it on the table. Then she went straight into the bedroom to pack the rest of her things into her medium-sized suitcase and one of Johan's large sports bags.

Johan remained in the kitchen. Meja went to pick up Ingrid and buried her nose in her neck. How would she transport her cage to Bengt's apartment? Would they even let her? She had better ask.

"I'll come back for you," she whispered.

Johan walked her to the door. "Let's talk soon," he said.

She gave a curt nod and hurried out, painfully aware that she would burst into tears if she said anything.

She hauled her heavy luggage downstairs and outside. The bag refused to stay on her shoulder, and she struggled with the suitcase over the cobblestones. Then a wheel got stuck in a pothole and she couldn't pull it out. That's when the tears came. She bent down to pry the wheel out, but her vision was blurred with tears. When that didn't work, she stood up and yanked the handle with such force that the case shot backward and into a passerby. He leaped out of the way.

"Sorry," Meja whispered, wiping away the tears. "It was stuck."

The man tilted his head. "Meja?"

"Yes?"

"It's Inez's neighbor," he explained when he saw her baffled expression.

"Of course," said Meja, clearing her throat to try to hide the weepiness in her voice. "Sorry, I've forgotten your name."

"Andreas," he said and took the handle of the suitcase from her. "Let me take that. Where are you going?"

She was about to say she had no idea, but then realized she had to go to North Harbor, to Bengt's apartment. She had no choice.

Before she could answer, he said, "Wherever you're going, you look like you could do with a coffee first."

She nodded weakly and followed him to Fahlman's café. He held the door open for her and told her to sit down while he got her a drink.

She surrendered to the comforting embrace of the old-fashioned café and watched Andreas as he stood in line. He was very average. Average height, semi-broad shoulders, medium brown hair. Average people were actually quite attractive. Johan wasn't average. His blond hair was slightly too long, which gave him a mischievous look, and his bright-blue eyes were mesmerizing when you first met him. She looked elsewhere when Andreas turned around with a tray of coffee and two slices of almond cake.

"You looked like you needed something sweet."

Meja smiled weakly. They ate and drank in silence. Andreas was right. The cake did make her feel a bit better.

"What are the odds of us bumping into each other here?" he said. "It's not like Helsingborg is a small village."

Meja had thought the same thing, but changed the subject. "How come Inez went with you to Gothenburg this weekend?"

"She went on to somewhere else from Gothenburg. Had some business in Kobbholmen. I think she said she lived there once upon a time."

"Kobbholmen?" Meja frowned. Wasn't that where Inez's novel was set? "Is Kobbholmen famous for something?" she asked.

"Yes, oysters!" he said, smiling.

Meja nodded. The oyster diver. Inez had said that the story was made up and that she had never been there. Why did she lie?

"She shouldn't have traveled so far with her bad hip," she said.

"As assistant, I suppose you feel responsible for more than just her papers." He smiled.

Meja looked up. "I'm not really her assistant. That was just something she said. I'm a cleaner, and I'm currently helping her clear out her books. And sometimes I read aloud to her."

"I see," said Andreas, surprised.

Meja looked out the window and sighed so deeply that Andreas raised his eyebrows.

"Sorry. That seems to sum up my life at the moment," she said. "One big sigh. I'm thirty-seven years old, no home, no proper job, a relationship on the rocks . . ." She trailed off. "Sorry, I'm babbling."

"Thirty-seven? You look younger," he said with a smile.

She shrugged. Most people would probably take that as a compliment, but not her.

"I'm forty-three. Divorced. Have a teenage daughter who mostly just thinks I'm embarrassing, and I've moved to a new place where I don't know anyone."

"Forty-three? I thought you were older," she said and returned his crooked smile.

He laughed and shrugged. They both fidgeted bashfully.

"I should probably . . ." She nodded toward the door. "How much do I owe you?" she asked, picking up her wallet.

"Nothing," he said. "And if you don't like feeling indebted, you can buy me a coffee another time."

She nodded. They left the café and paused on the street.

"Thanks for the coffee and for intercepting an imminent emotional breakdown," she said.

He shoved his hands into his pockets. "It was nothing. Sure you don't want help with your bags?"

"No. It's fine. Thanks."

He smiled. "See you."

She gave a short wave with her free hand, slung the bag on her shoulder, and started dragging the suitcase more carefully this time.

By the time she got to Bengt's apartment, sweat was running down her back and temples. She was just about to unlock the door when she heard noises coming from inside. It was her mother's voice. It sounded like she was arguing. The discussion got more and more heated, but Meja couldn't hear a second voice. Strange.

Meja knocked on the door and waited for what felt like an eternity before it opened. Susanne's cheeks were flushed red and her eyes were moist. Her hair was even somewhat disheveled.

"What are you doing here again?" she said, her eyes falling on the suitcase.

Meja cleared her throat. "Just a couple more days?"

Susanne still didn't open the door.

"Uh . . . now isn't a good time."

"Oh, okay." Meja felt stress rise inside her. She had nowhere else to go. "What if I just left my bags and came back a little later?"

Susanne reluctantly opened the door. Meja dumped her things in the guest room and went to get a glass of water. Glancing curiously around the apartment, she saw nobody else there. When she came back into the hall, Susanne was still holding the door open. Did she look a little embarrassed? Very unlike her.

"Come back in a few hours," Susanne said shortly and closed the door.

A few hours. Meja left the building and sighed at the appealing sight of a waterfront restaurant. The little money she had was too precious to fritter on fancy restaurants, even though her stomach was rumbling.

She walked slowly along the boardwalk in the direction of Viking Beach, where the kite surfers were struggling to raise their sails in the light wind, then turned around and went back again. Eventually she sat on one of the docks in the harbor and listened to a podcast on her headphones. After exactly three hours, she went back to Bengt's apartment. Susanne wasn't home.

Meja helped herself to a bowl of yogurt and went into the guest room. She couldn't bear thinking about Johan, so she let her thoughts turn instead to Andreas. What a strange coincidence to bump into him on the same day they had been introduced. And even stranger that Inez had gone with him to Gothenburg, considering what an antisocial person she was. There had to be something significant about that trip. Otherwise why keep it secret?

The next morning, Meja woke up early. She had gone to bed with her clothes on and without dinner. She slipped into the kitchen to get something to eat and saw a silhouette in the dark. She jumped.

"You scared me! Why are you sitting here in the dark?"

"There's coffee if you want some," her mother said and left the room.

In the dim light, it looked like Susanne wasn't wearing makeup. She had great skin.

Meja switched on the light, squinted in the brightness, and prepared a simple breakfast of bread and cheese, which she ate with relish. Soon Susanne came out of the bathroom, fully made up as usual. Meja wanted to tell her she was beautiful without all that makeup, but didn't dare.

Susanne cleared her throat. "I need some alone time today."

"Okay, I'll just stay in the guest room. I won't disturb you."

"Meja . . ." Susanne sighed. "You really can't be here right now, and I can't explain why."

"You mean now, like *right* now? You can't wait until I start work in . . ." Meja looked at the clock. "Three hours?"

"I'm afraid not," said Susanne.

Meja looked out the window. It was pouring rain.

"Where am I supposed to go at six in the morning?"

"Darling, we're both grown-ups here."

Meja grudgingly grabbed her purse and left. She lingered outside the apartment door and soon heard her mother's voice again. Speaking as though to herself in that same upset tone. Was she talking on the phone at this time in the morning? To whom?

She sighed deeply and left the building, pulling her hoodie over her head. The city was slowly coming to life.

Her phone beeped. She snatched it out of her pocket, hoping it would be Johan. It was from Inez: Take the day off today. I have some things to do. Come back tomorrow as usual.

Meja clenched her jaw. Inez was going to be her salvation today. She shivered. The rain was cold and, in her haste to leave, Meja hadn't brought an umbrella.

She headed toward Helsingborg Central Station and wandered around inside for a while before settling on a bench. She watched people sitting in cafés, rushing to work and school, dragging suitcases behind them, double-checking tickets. Some were taking the train, others the bus or the boat to Denmark. She imagined all the places she could go if she had her suitcase with her. Would anyone even miss her? She bit her lower lip. Inez probably would, at least.

A couple of hours later, a guard came to ask if she was all right, and another couple of hours later she got up and trudged through the rain back to Susanne's. She could still hear her agitated voice coming from inside. She fell silent when Meja knocked. Not wanting to disturb her mother, she took off her wet things, went straight into the guest room, and collapsed on the bed.

She drifted off and woke up in the afternoon with her stomach growling. She crept out for some more bread and cheese and took it back to her room. This kept her going until nine o'clock, when she skulked out again for a bowl of granola and yogurt. When she took it into the living room, she found Susanne in an armchair with her eyes shut and her lips moving but making no sound. She flinched when Meja cleared her throat, then looked at her with the same expression Johan had worn when he said he wanted to take a break.

"I'm sorry, Meja. I know you need the guest room, but your spat with Johan has come at a very inconvenient time. I want to help, but I just can't right now. I need the apartment to myself until Friday when Bengt comes home."

Meja could hear her pulse throbbing in her eardrums.

"But I'm not making a peep. I won't bother you. I can eat in the guest room as well."

"The answer is no, you can't be here right now. Come back on the weekend."

"But . . ." Meja had no words. The weekend? As if she were choosing to be here for the fun of it.

She had nowhere else to go.

"You must have somewhere else you can stay, right? It's just for a few days," Susanne said hopefully.

Meja looked down at the floor. She hadn't seen her friends much lately, and they all had their own lives with partners and children. No, she couldn't impose on them.

"Please don't make me feel bad," said Susanne when Meja didn't answer.

Meja felt her face get hot. She knew she had no right to intrude on her mother's life, but this was the only time she had ever asked her for help. Why couldn't Susanne just extend a helping hand, from mother to daughter?

Susanne remained still with her hands clasped in her lap.

Once again, Meja had no choice but to hastily pack her things and leave, with nowhere to go.

"You don't have to take everything with you. Come back on Friday, if you haven't worked things out with Johan by then, which I'm sure you will," said Susanne, who had come out of the living room and was watching her.

Meja turned around. The emotions she had spent her whole life carrying spewed forth like hot lava.

"All my life I've felt like I've been in your way," she barked in a trembling voice. "And I've never understood why. I've always done my best to be quiet, polite, considerate. Never bother anyone, take care of myself. But I can never do anything right. Maybe we should just stop seeing each other altogether—it's not like either of us actually wants to."

These last words struggled to come out through sobs. She wasn't used to making such dramatic statements. Susanne opened her mouth to speak, but said nothing.

Meja left the door open behind her and lugged her things downstairs. Tears flowed. She stopped at each floor to wipe them away. Susanne wasn't worth her tears.

All she could think to do was return to the station to get out of the rain. On the way, her phone beeped and she dropped her bag immediately to check it. Could her mother have changed her mind? No, it was from Johan.

What are we going to do with Ingrid? I think she gets lonely when I'm at work, it said.

Her horrible day with Susanne fueled a blazing anger. Was he kidding? He couldn't just keep Ingrid for a couple of days while she figured out where she was going to stay?

She dragged her bags to his apartment as fast as she could and knocked on the door.

"Oh," he said. "I didn't mean you needed to come right away. I meant more, like, going forward . . . She squeaks a lot when you're not here." He fell silent when he saw Meja's swollen red eyes and all her luggage.

Meja marched straight into the living room and transferred Ingrid into her small travel carrier. Then she emptied out the large cage and loaded it up with bags of hay, wood shavings, and food.

"There's really no need to . . . ," he began, looking at her anxiously. "Where are you going?"

Meja heaved all her stuff out into the stairwell and slammed the door right in his face.

Ingrid squeaked in her little cage. Meja bent down. "Sorry," she whispered. "I know it's cramped in there. But everything will be okay soon."

Wiping her wet cheeks with the back of her hand, she lugged all her belongings into the elevator—no more stairs today—and didn't avoid the mirror this time. She looked herself straight in the eye. "You have to get a hold of yourself. Don't be such a darn wimp. Get a grip, for flip's sake."

The elevator stopped at the ground floor with a jerk. Meja dragged everything out onto the street and called a cab. It would eat up her last krona but she had no choice. There was only one place she could go, and that was to Inez's house.

The cab showed up in less than five minutes. The driver loaded her bags and the cage, and Meja sat in the passenger seat with Ingrid's carrier in her lap.

"Wow," said the driver. "Unusual pet."

Meja nodded and said she wanted to be dropped off at the pine grove in Domsten.

A message came from Johan: You're staying with your mom, right? Because if not, of course you can come back until we've figured this all out.

Meja quickly typed back: I'm staying with Susanne.

The driver chatted the whole way about how much his children wanted pets but they couldn't have any because of his allergies. Maybe a hairless guinea pig was the solution? Meja half listened and nodded wearily now and then. When they arrived, she paid without tipping. She wasn't proud of it, but she couldn't afford to pay more than absolutely necessary.

She looked at the clock. It was past ten. She couldn't bother Inez this late. She took Ingrid and her luggage and headed to the small wooden shelter she had seen among the pine trees where tourists sometimes spent the night.

She placed the guinea pig in the farthest, most sheltered corner and brought in the rest of her things. She stuffed plenty of hay into Ingrid's carrier and pulled a fleece jacket and knitted sweater out of her suitcase. This would have been a perfectly pleasant place to stay if it weren't for the drizzle and chilly winds. There was even a toilet and fireplace. But it was cold. Not only was the weather making her shiver, but also the shock of it all. She had actually stormed out on her mother. There had always been friction in their relationship, but could she have pushed her away for good? It was a painful thought. But maybe some intense, temporary pain was better than a lifetime of razor-sharp jabs? And what about her and Johan? She couldn't bring herself to think about it.

She took a few more pieces of clothing out of the suitcase and rolled them up to use as a pillow. A few dog walkers passed by. They looked at her but said nothing.

Meja slept on and off until five in the morning, when she woke up so cold and damp that her teeth were chattering. She got up, packed her things, and took two trips to drag her belongings to Viola's bench. She could sit there for the next four hours, until it was time to start work. Then what?

This was a new low.

Ingrid squeaked in her cage. Meja held out a shivering hand to her. "What would I do without you?"

INEZ

Yesterday's writing session had stretched far into the night. Inez had tasted the salty sea spray on Mathilda's boat. Heard the sound of oysters rattling in plastic baskets. Felt the pain of their friendship veering off course, and the burning hope that it would recover.

She looked at the clock and yawned. Already half past seven and she hadn't even had her morning coffee on the balcony. When she stepped out into the gray morning, she took a few deep breaths. She thought she could see someone down on Viola's bench. Yes, someone was sitting there with a hood up and a suitcase. How strange. She swapped her slippers for rubber boots and set out to investigate.

"Good morning," she said. The person flinched and turned around. "Meja?"

Meja nodded and bit her lip. Inez frowned. This didn't look good. Meja's teeth were chattering. Inez picked up Meja's bag and beckoned for her to follow, dragging the suitcase in one hand and holding the carrier in the other. It was slow going through the dunes. They left everything on the porch and Meja went back to get the large cage. Inez bent down and peered into the smaller cage. Two brown eyes peered out of black skin with a tousled tuft of fur on its head. Inez shuddered—she was not a pet person, least of all rodents—and took the suitcase instead.

"You take a hot shower. I'll make some tea," said Inez.

Meja's hands were shaking as she put down the carrier and rummaged in her suitcase for dry clothes. She trudged into the bathroom.

Inez shook her head. She had never seen anyone look so miserable. She made some tea with plenty of honey and a sandwich with roast beef, mayonnaise, and fried onions. Her survival sandwich. She always used to keep roast beef in the fridge in case she got into a writing flow and forgot to eat. That sandwich had saved her from fainting many times.

Half an hour later, Meja emerged from a steamy bathroom. Inez was sitting down at the oak table, as far away from the carrier as possible. She could hear the creature nibbling inside.

"Thanks for the shower," Meja said as she sat down. She waited for some encouragement from Inez before biting into the sandwich with her eyes closed.

"So . . . ?" Inez began.

"There's been a lot going on lately. I'm really sorry. Coming here with my whole life in a duffel bag and using your shower . . . I've really crossed the line for a cleaner. I promise I'll have myself sorted out by tomorrow."

Meja looked so contrite that Inez almost wanted to give her a hug. Almost.

"Aren't you going to introduce us?" she said instead, nodding at the carrier.

"Oh." She got the leathery little creature out of its cage. "This is Ingrid. She's a hairless guinea pig."

"Ingrid?" Inez had to bite her tongue to keep from blurting out something nasty.

"Yes, after Ingrid Bergman. My fondest childhood memories are of the times when my mother would make some popcorn and pour some wine, and I would drink raspberry cordial out of a wineglass, and we'd snuggle on the couch and watch old movies. Ingrid Bergman was our favorite. Well, Mom's favorite, but I loved those moments, so she became my favorite too."

Inez saw Meja's lower lip quiver and understood not to press her on the mother topic. But she needed to know what was going on.

"And . . . you've packed up your things to get *away from* something, not go *toward* something?" Inez said.

"I guess you could say that."

"So you have nowhere to live?"

Meja hesitated, then shook her head.

"Right then," said Inez. "Upstairs there is a small guest room with a fantastic sea view. It's hardly ever used. Rooms get lonely, so you would be doing both me and the house a favor if you lived there for a while, until you find your feet."

Meja looked longingly at the stairs but shook her head. "I can't do that."

"Yes, Meja. You can."

"But my job . . ."

"You know what? You can call up and resign; it's just a temp job. And then I will hire you as my assistant—for real." Inez continued before Meja could protest. "Don't think I'm doing you any favors. You'll have to work. I have a book to write and could do with help cooking, sorting through my things, and reading the manuscript aloud. And if you found some time to weed the yard, that would certainly make Sverker and Filip happy. Not that I give a damn—a plant is a plant."

Meja considered the offer, though Inez could tell she had already made up her mind.

"Of course you wouldn't need to pay me. Room and board would be enough," said Meja meekly.

"Dear girl, you do yourself a disservice. I'll go by the book and give you the correct legal wages and pension."

Meja swallowed hard and glanced at the stairs again. "Okay, just for a little while."

"You have a month's notice," said Inez with a wink. "Go—get yourself settled in. Then we have work to do."

Meja carried up her things. Inez heard her bustling around in the room. It sounded like she was talking to that freakish hairless guinea pig.

She went out onto the porch and resumed her deep breathing exercises. Suddenly her phone rang.

"Yes?"

"Mom, that's a rude way to answer the phone," said her daughter. "What are you up to?"

Inez glanced up at the guest room balcony. "I'm cleaning."

"Still? That cleaner of yours can't be all that efficient."

"Oh, she's still beavering away. She's going to live here for a while, too, so we'll get the last of it done soon."

"*Live* there? Why?"

"Because she is temporarily homeless."

Amelia scoffed. "That doesn't sound like you, to take someone under your wing. What's your ulterior motive?"

Inez took a deep breath and exhaled straight into the receiver.

"What are you doing?" Amelia said in a slightly irritated tone.

"Deep breathing. Good for your health."

She heard her daughter sigh. "Okay. I just wanted to check in, but everything seems to be under control."

"Absolutely."

Amelia was quiet for a moment before adding, "Call if you need anything."

"Will do."

Inez put the phone down again and tried to resume her deep breathing, but she couldn't get back into it. Had Amelia sounded unusually tired and grumpy? Inez should have asked her how she was, of course. Maybe she should call Cristy to make sure everything was okay. If something was wrong, Cristy would know. It had always been comforting to know that Cristy was such great support for Amelia. Still, Inez was her mother.

She thought about Meja and her relationship with her mother. Inez didn't need to know the details to understand that they had old wounds that had never healed. It wasn't that bad between her and Amelia, was it? They had done pretty well, hadn't they? Yes, Inez had put her work first, but would Amelia have been better off growing up with a bitter mother like Meja's? Hardly.

The problem was that they focused on different memories. Inez remembered all the times when Amelia had been the center of attention because she was surrounded by adults who adored her cute, precocious ways. She remembered all the trips they had taken together, when her daughter would fall asleep on the train with her head in her mother's lap, then look out the window in a daze and ask what country they were in. She remembered the times when her daughter sat on Cristy's lap and flipped through a picture book while Inez played around with narrative arcs and characters.

Amelia, on the other hand, remembered only the loneliness.

She promised herself that when she finished writing this book, she would get better at talking to her daughter. Better at asking how she was.

Inez went into the living room, sat down, and waited.

The stairs creaked loudly as Meja came down. She sat opposite Inez and they sipped coffee in silence. Inez liked that Meja didn't feel the need to fill every silence. Once they had finished, Inez handed Meja the blue folder.

"Can you manage some reading?"

Meja nodded but instead of starting to read, she looked up at Inez.

"Why did you say that you had never been to the place where this book is set? You used to live there, didn't you?"

Inez squinted at Meja. How had the girl figured that out?

"Andreas told me you were in Kobbholmen on the weekend, and that you said you used to live there. We bumped into each other in town."

"How funny," Inez said with a smile.

"You haven't answered my question."

"No," said Inez. "And I don't intend to. Not now." She nodded to indicate the folder.

Meja sighed and started reading.

1974

We thought our friendship would last forever. The fact that it didn't was my fault. I guess I was impatient to grow up. I got a new job in an office, met a man, and fell in love. Mathilda didn't say much about it, but she seemed happy when the relationship ended and I spent all my spare time out at sea with her, like before.

That lasted for a while, then a new man appeared in my life. And then came Nikolas. He was fourteen years older than me. Worldly and mature. We met at a party thrown by one of my colleagues. We made eye contact as soon as I stepped in the room, and he didn't look away all evening. I broke up with my boyfriend for him, enraptured by the fact that such a charismatic man was so taken with plain little me. I was intoxicated and spoke about little else. It was Nikolas this and Nikolas that. Mathilda instinctively disliked him. I could see it in her frown when I introduced them. Then again, Nikolas didn't think much of her either. It was hardly surprising. They were polar opposites; Mathilda cherished her independence, while Nikolas was all about partnership. And I mean that in the narrowest sense of the word.

At first I felt flattered that Nikolas held on to me so tightly, that he got jealous if another man so much as looked at me and didn't want me hanging out with friends when I could be with him instead. Mathilda was concerned and warned me early on not to become an anchor for the wrong boat. She said I ran the risk of never breaking free, never choosing my own direction in life. Deep down I probably knew she was right, but I told myself she was just jealous because she didn't have a man of her own. Our bond stretched to the breaking point, and Mathilda disappeared from my life.

I didn't give myself time to mourn the friendship I had lost, because it fed Nikolas's devotion to me. He took me out for dinners, bought me presents, and showered me with compliments. I was blind to what was happening. Nikolas worshipped me as long as I turned down every invitation to see friends or join colleagues at the pub. But what would happen if I did accept an invitation one day?

MEJA

Inez's guest room contained no stacks of books or piles of papers. The walls were painted a grayish blue, like the sea, and the furniture was dark brown, like the beach grass. The bedspread was beige like the sand, and on the Gustavian desk was a writing pad, a pen, and some seashells. Meja gently pulled the brass handle of the narrow drawer. Locked.

She stepped out onto the small balcony. She could see down to Viola's bench. Funny to think that she'd been sitting there trembling like a wounded animal only this morning. She was just about to go back in when Andreas appeared on his balcony next door.

"Good evening," he said, smiling.

"Good evening," replied Meja with a wry smile. It sounded a bit old-fashioned.

"Going to be a nice day tomorrow," he said.

"How do you know?"

"You can tell by the sky. The calm blue beyond the heavy gray. A premonition of what's to come."

Meja scanned the horizon for this calmness he spoke of.

"You feeling better today?" he asked.

Meja nodded. "It's amazing the difference an almond cake can make."

Andreas laughed, shoved his hands into his pockets, and turned to go back inside. "See you later."

Meja lingered on the balcony. She thought about the chapter she had just read. The story had taken a completely new direction with the arrival of Nikolas. She dreaded what was coming next, but was also curious.

Her phone buzzed in her pocket. Eight missed calls. One from her mother. Seven from Johan. She listened to his message: *Can you call me, or at least send a message? I called Susanne when I couldn't get hold of you, and she said you weren't there but might come on Friday? But you'd left things on an unpleasant note so she wasn't sure. And then I called your job and they said you quit. Call me. I'm worried.*

Meja went back into the guest room. What would Inez do? Let them sweat. That's what she planned to do as well.

She opened Ingrid's cage and fed her a piece of carrot she had smuggled out of Inez's fridge.

"It's going to be okay, Ingrid. We don't need Johan, do we? Or Mom."

The next day she woke up groggy after a night of troubled dreams. She shivered when her feet touched the cold floor. A light veil of fog lay over the strait. She didn't feel as thick-skinned today. Slowly she texted a reply to Johan. It's OK. Don't worry. Her stomach clenched, yearning for what she had lost.

She sighed. Time to face the day. She had no idea what kind of Thursday lay before her.

Meja reached the bottom of the stairs just as Inez came inside from the porch.

"Good morning," they both said at the same time.

Meja thought her steps looked lighter today. Inez fixed them a breakfast of coffee, toast, and marmalade, and they ate in silence. When they had finished, Inez fixed her gaze on Meja and said, "Put your bathing suit on and meet me outside the gate in ten minutes."

"Bathing suit?" Meja looked out the window. It was still only dawn. "I don't swim in the sea."

But Inez was already getting ready. "Ten minutes," she said, pointing to the clock.

Meja clenched her jaw. Was this what it was going to be like, working for Inez? She was expected to be subject to her every whim?

She dragged her feet upstairs, put on her bathing suit—she wasn't sure why she even owned one when she never went swimming—and wrapped a bathrobe around her.

Meja had a healthy respect for lurking deep-sea currents. They had dragged her underwater once when she was six years old. She remembered flailing around in the water, the current grabbing her legs, and struggling against forces that refused to let her go. Luckily, a man had noticed her distress and rescued her. Her mother had been reading, and she let out a little chuckle when the man told her that Meja's rubber dinghy had capsized. Then she wrapped her in a bath towel and hissed that she was all right now and should stop crying. Meja had hated swimming in the sea ever since.

Inez was waiting impatiently by the gate. Instead of turning left toward the pier, she turned right. They followed the path, past the pine grove, to where the tall beach grass swayed in the wind.

Inez stopped when they reached a spot with benches, an information board, and public binoculars.

"Grollegrund," she said. "A marine nature reserve." Without a hint of self-consciousness, she took off her bathrobe, revealing a dark-blue bathing suit with large white polka dots, and went to look through the binoculars. "Take a look."

Meja was too shy to take her bathrobe off as she leaned forward to look through the binoculars. Some seals were lying on the distant rocks.

"Wow," she said, turning to Inez. "I had no idea there were seals here."

Inez nodded for Meja to remove her bathrobe and come with her. With a tight grip on Meja's arm, Inez balanced carefully on the stony shore. Seabirds made disgruntled noises and flew a little farther away.

"Is this really good for your hip? The water is very cold," said Meja. But of course she had no choice but to go with her. What if she slipped?

A little farther out, the pebbles changed to sand. The water quickly got deeper. Meja felt seaweed caress her thigh.

"I don't like to go too deep," she said.

"Neither do I," said Inez. "I never put my head underwater. Snorkeling makes me hyperventilate. Which is a pity, because there is a fantastic world beneath the surface."

"So can we just take a dip here?" Meja said hopefully.

But Inez continued walking, then started to swim. Meja grit her teeth and followed. Just as Meja was about to tell Inez not to go too far, she heard her make a strange noise. A bit like a seal. Meja swam quickly to catch up with her.

When Inez made the same noise again, Meja started laughing so hard that she swallowed a mouthful of seawater and completely lost her ability to swim. She couldn't feel the bottom and splashed wildly with her arms.

"I have to . . . go back," she said weakly and sank below the surface.

She was struck by the same panic as when the currents had dragged her down as a six-year-old. The more force she exerted to rise to the surface, the deeper she sank. Oh god.

Suddenly a dark body approached. Meja found herself looking straight into a pair of brown eyes and stared into them as though paralyzed. The seal swam beneath her and lifted her to the surface, dived down again, and emerged about ten yards away. It glided through the water on its back for a while before swimming up onto the rocks.

Meja trod water and gasped for breath. "Thank you," she whispered.

Inez smiled in amusement. As they returned to shore, Meja's legs were shaking so much that Inez had to hold her arm to support *her*.

"What just happened?" Meja whispered and sat down on the bench, exhausted.

"I had a friend who used to hang out with wild seals," said Inez.

"Mathilda?" Meja asked. Wasn't there something about seals in Inez's story?

Inez laughed. "I told you, I only write fiction."

"Then you're very good at making things up."

"Of course I am. I'm a writer—it's my job. Anyway, she taught me how to make that sound. Good job I did it right, because there are small-spotted cat sharks in the water too."

"Sharks!?"

Inez nodded, looking very pleased to have given that information *afterward*.

On their way back, they passed Sverker out on a brisk walk. He gave them a cheery wave.

"First day of vacation!" he said. "I'm celebrating with a morning walk, and Filip is celebrating by sleeping in. Opposites attract." He laughed. "And you've started the day with a lovely swim, I see. We're going to raise a glass to our time off with a little bubbly tonight. Won't you come over?"

"Maybe," Inez said and continued walking.

Meja wondered why she spoke to him so bluntly when he was always so friendly.

Back at the house, Meja showered and settled into the armchair. Inez sat beside her, seemingly deep in thought.

"There's something I'd like you to do for me," she said at last.

"What?" Meja said.

"I'd like you to take some pictures."

"Of what?"

"Of this. Our work. Document it."

"Okay . . ." Meja wasn't sure she understood.

"Well?" Inez said, waving her hand.

"What, now? Shall I get the camera now?"

"Yes, of course now."

Meja went upstairs to get her camera. She pointed the lens out at the strait where the fog had now dissipated and made room for blue sky. Had she really swum out into deep water and been lifted to the surface by a seal? It felt like a dream. Time and space felt strange with Inez sometimes. Almost unreal.

She went out on the balcony to snap a picture, looked down, and saw Inez on the porch. She was standing with her eyes closed and her head angled slightly skyward. Meja clicked. All was calm. And blue. Just as Andreas had said it would be.

When she came back downstairs, Inez had settled into her armchair. The blue folder was on the round table. Meja snapped a picture before she opened it, took a deep breath, and started reading aloud.

1974

Mathilda was right. She often was. I became an anchor for the wrong boat—Nikolas's boat. Attached to a heavy colossus that was impossible to control. He shrank my world and my self-esteem. In retrospect, it amazes me how rapid the decline was. How quickly his aggression began to dictate my existence.

I missed Mathilda so much it hurt, until finally I felt like I needed to just catch a glimpse of her in order to breathe. So I began a ritual of hiking up to the rocky outcrop above the jetty, hiding behind a bush, and watching her in her boat. Most often on Saturday and Sunday morning when Nikolas was still recovering from a party the night before. The partying that had been so much fun at the beginning of our relationship had become both my prison and my freedom. Alcohol brought out violence in him, but his hangovers gave me some time alone. So I sat there and watched Mathilda's boat calmly putter away for a day at sea.

Mathilda had always been special. It was as if she had a sixth sense. She intuited things. And one day as she was sailing away from the jetty as usual, she suddenly turned the boat around and came back to the dock.

She jumped out of the boat and started up the path that led to my hiding place. My heart was pounding so hard I thought she might hear it echoing around the rocks. It only took her a couple of minutes to make her way to the top. There I was, sitting motionless behind a bush, staring at her. She said nothing. Not a word. She just walked straight up to me, tenderly caressed the black eye Nikolas had given me the night before, took me in her arms, and rocked me for a long time, until my tears dried. Then she went back to her boat and set sail again.

Before she rounded the island, she turned and raised her hand.

I lifted mine back, and in this small gesture, life returned. Once again, Mathilda's breath became my oxygen, her embrace my healing.

MEJA

Inez looked tired when Meja finished reading the painful chapter about the recovery from Nikolas's violence. Still, she went into her room to continue writing. Meja was shocked and didn't know what to do. At lunchtime, she knocked on the door of Inez's combined bedroom and study to ask if she was hungry, but got no answer. She heated up some chicken and rice anyway and added green pepper sauce. She left a tray outside the closed door and, after eating her own lunch, began tidying piles of books and papers at random. In the afternoon she removed the tray, untouched but for the coffee cup. She knocked again. Still no answer.

In the evening there was a knock on the porch door. It was such an unusual occurrence at Inez's house that it startled Meja. She opened the door only a crack. Something told her that Inez wouldn't want people peeking inside. It was Sverker, holding a bouquet of violets.

"So how about that drink to celebrate vacation season?" he said, craning his neck with curiosity.

"Uh . . . now isn't a good time," said Meja. "Inez is working."

Sverker's eyes widened.

Meja swallowed. "Or well, not *working* exactly . . . answering her fan mail. Maybe another night."

Meja was a terrible liar and she knew it. Sverker held out the violets.

"Please give her these when she's done. We'll meet another day when it's more convenient."

"Absolutely. Thank you," said Meja, taking the flowers without opening the door more than necessary. Then she went to put them straight in the trash. It hurt her heart but she knew that's what Inez would want.

She made a cup of tea for Inez, left it outside her room, and knocked gently. A few minutes later she heard the door being opened and closed.

Meja photographed a few piles of books and the neglected cactus and then sat down to wait for Inez. But she didn't emerge from her room. At just past eleven, Meja went up to the guest room, got into bed, and fell asleep almost instantly.

Friday followed the same pattern. Meja realized that Inez must have an en suite bathroom, because she didn't see her all day. All she heard was the clatter of the keyboard.

Meja carried on sorting the books, took her camera out for long walks along the coast, angled the blinds to let light in. Inez continued to ignore the chicken and rice placed outside her door, so Meja tried a toasted sandwich and fruit instead, which was better received.

Friday bled into Saturday. Meja sneaked downstairs a few times during the night to hear if Inez was sleeping. She wasn't. Didn't she ever take a break?

It wasn't until Sunday night that the sound of typing in Inez's room stopped. Meja knocked gently. No answer. She pressed her ear against the door. She was seized by worry. She must have been sleeping, surely, but still . . . Inez had barely eaten over the past few days—what if she had fainted? Meja carefully opened the door.

The darkened room smelled stuffy. Inez was sleeping in her chair with her cheek against the desk. Meja walked over and put her hand on her shoulder.

"Inez," she whispered. When Inez raised her head in confusion, Meja saw that her eyes were swollen as though from crying. Meja took her hand and helped her up, slowly leading her to the bed and putting a blanket over her.

"Can I get you anything? Water?"

Inez nodded. Meja fetched a glass of water, waited for her to drink half, then put the glass on the bedside table.

"Shout if you need anything. I'll sleep on the couch tonight," said Meja.

Inez closed her eyes. Meja went up to the guest room, put on her nightgown and one of Inez's cardigans that she'd found hanging on a hook, and went out on the balcony. There she took a deep breath and let the air out in a long exhalation.

"Your life is still like one big sigh, I suppose," she heard a nearby voice say.

"Oh." She smiled thinly at Andreas on the balcony next door. That was what she'd said when they'd had coffee at Fahlman's. "It's been a rough weekend."

"Has it?" Andreas leaned against the railing and looked at her.

Suddenly the draining weekend took its toll. She bit her bottom lip. She hadn't slept much more than Inez. She felt exhausted and alone. It would be so nice to talk to someone.

"Can you keep a secret?" she said.

"Of course."

"I'm serious. It has to stay between us. Forever."

"All right," he said with emphasis.

"Did you know that Inez is a writer?"

"No, I didn't actually."

"A pretty famous one, but she stopped writing fifteen years ago." She paused and looked out over the dark strait where the Danish ferries shone like fireflies. "Now she's writing again, but being very secretive about it. The problem is she works for days on end and barely eats or drinks. I just went in to see her, and she looked like a wreck. I know she doesn't want to be disturbed, and she's extremely stubborn, but what if something were to happen to her? I would be the one held accountable, because I'm the one letting her stay in her room for days without food. But it's not like I can force-feed her."

Andreas nodded slowly. "Artistic souls. They burn with passion. Sometimes it consumes them. I think that's why I never really dreamed of becoming a great artist and dedicated myself to teaching art instead. I like structure too much—planning, order. I think eating and sleeping well are important. My passion doesn't burn brightly enough."

He smiled. Something about that crooked little smile of his made Meja's shoulders relax slightly.

She leaned against the railing. Of course, she shouldn't have told Andreas that Inez was a writer. And *really* shouldn't have told him that she was writing a new book. If Inez found out, she would throw her out again, headfirst. But she needed someone to talk to.

"Promise you won't say anything?"

"I promise," he said and smiled.

"I should probably try to get a few hours' sleep while she's sleeping," said Meja.

Andreas nodded and turned his gaze back to the sea.

Meja went back inside, cuddled Ingrid for a while, and made up a bed on the living room couch. What had Inez been typing so intensely in the next room? She hoped that Inez was telling the truth and that the story really was fiction. That Inez hadn't been the one sitting on those rocks hoping for Mathilda to save her.

The next day she woke up to the sound of the porch door being closed. She sat up and looked around groggily. It took a few moments for her to remember where she was. She stretched and noticed an oyster shell on the coffee table. Inez must have put it there before she went out. It hadn't been there last night.

Inside was a small handwritten note. *Thank you.*

Meja ran her hand over the corrugated shell. Memories of the weekend came back to her. She hoped Andreas was better at keeping promises than she was.

Meja still hadn't moved by the time Inez returned. She looked calm and rested, nothing like the previous night when Meja had had to help her to bed, shattered and pale.

They said nothing. Inez went into the kitchen, and Meja heard her pottering around before she emerged with coffee and toast for them both. She sat down at the large oak table, which, thanks to Meja, was now decorated with a tablecloth and candlestick instead of piles of papers and books.

"We've made progress," she said, running her hand over the cloth.

Meja nodded. She wanted to say something about how worried she had been. But she assumed that the note in the oyster shell was all Inez wanted to say on the matter. She joined her at the table.

"Could I ask you a favor?" Inez said.

"I'm your assistant," Meja said and tried to smile, but it came out awkwardly.

"I need to pick up my painkillers at the pharmacy, but I can't bring myself to go into town. Maybe you'd like to get out of the house for a bit?"

Meja nodded. "I can go after breakfast."

When Inez finished her coffee, she got up to shut all the blinds that Meja had angled open the day before. The room was dark again.

Meja got off the bus at Helsingborg City Theater and walked up to Kullagatan. The shops had just opened, and people were rushing around, on their way to and from work, school, and errands.

Unusually, Meja felt at ease among the noise and bustle on the streets. She walked slowly, taking her time to look in the storefronts before eventually arriving at the pharmacy. She picked up Inez's tablets and checked the time. There was no rush to head back.

She went into a café and was struck by the aroma of coffee and sweet treats as she walked up to the counter. She ordered a chai latte and settled down at a window table, but no sooner had she taken her first sip than a shadow descended over her table.

"Meja?"

She looked up and straight into Johan's pale-blue eyes.

"Wait there," he said and hurried away to order a coffee. When he came back, he sat down at her table without asking permission.

"How are you? What are you up to? Where are you staying?" His voice carried a note of worry and anger.

Meja tilted her head. "Are we still together?"

"We're taking a break . . . but that doesn't mean—"

She interrupted him. "I don't ask you what you're doing with your time."

"That's different. You already know where I am and what I'm doing. You just disappeared."

"Nobody just disappears."

"You know what I mean." He looked at her. "This has all gone so wrong. I thought you were just staying with your mother for a few days. If you don't have anywhere to go, then of course you can stay with me. For now."

"I have a place to live," Meja said shortly.

Johan raised his eyebrows. The penny dropped. "You're living with that author!"

Meja shrugged.

"But Meja . . ." He placed his hand on hers.

His tone of pity made Meja withdraw her hand at once.

"You know what?" she said firmly. "I really care about you, and I miss you. But . . . this break is over. You were right: our relationship did get stuck in a rut, and we've grown apart."

She carried her half-finished mug away on the tray and returned to the table to pick up her jacket.

"Take care. I'm sure we'll talk again at some point," she said and left.

Her heart was pounding so hard she thought it might burst out of her chest when she sat down on the bus. Had she really just ended their relationship? Were she and Johan truly over? Was it just her now?

When she came back, Inez was standing on the porch with her arms crossed, gazing out to sea. She looked peaceful. Meja came to join her.

"I've made an important decision," she said without looking at her.

"Oh?" Inez asked.

"Yup. It's just me now."

"There's no 'just' about it," said Inez. "Make sure you take your 'me' seriously."

Meja nodded and remained on the porch when Inez went inside.

Me, she thought. *Who am I?*

INEZ

Inez and Meja stacked all the books to be given away in the hall. It took a long time. When they were finished, they stood on the threshold and looked into the living room.

"Goodness," said Inez. "The room looks so much bigger."

"A quick dust and mop and it will be like new," said Meja.

Inez nodded in amazement. Amelia would cry with happiness.

"Shall we heat up some chicken?" Meja said. Then she paused. "You know, I'm not a great cook, but if you want I can try some simple dishes next week. For some variety."

Inez shrugged. "As you please. Personally, I hate cooking and would never ask anyone to do it either. But if you want to, I won't object."

They prepared lunch and ate in silence, but Inez could tell that Meja had something on her mind. Something other than cooking.

Finally, she put the cutlery down and said, "I had an idea. I mentioned to Andreas that we're sorting through your books and have several piles destined for the secondhand store. I asked him if he liked reading and wanted a book or two, as a joke." Inez raised her eyebrows, and Meja looked down at the table. "He said he mainly reads nonfiction, but he offered to rent a trailer and drive all the books to the store."

She uttered this last sentence so quietly that Inez could barely hear it.

"Is that so?"

"Well, only if you want." Meja's cheeks turned red.

Inez leaned back and observed her. Meja knew it had been a mistake telling the neighbor that they were clearing out her books. Inez never told her neighbors anything. Meja may not have known much about Inez, but she knew *that*.

Well, at least it had just been Andreas and not Sverker. And they did have to get rid of all the books, so a little help wouldn't hurt, even if Inez hadn't asked for it. Right?

"Why not?" Inez said. "Maybe later today?"

The thought of Andreas hauling her books off to some thrift store made Inez feel fidgety. She truly loathed any kind of invasion of her privacy. But she may as well get it over with.

"I'm going to rest for a while," she said to Meja. She took a painkiller and went to lie down.

After recharging her batteries for a couple of hours, she opened the bedroom door and almost collided with Meja, who was carrying a pile of books. Her cheeks were flushed with exertion. Through the open front door, Inez could see Andreas backing into her driveway with a trailer. She came out onto the front step. At the same time, the door to the house on the other side opened. Sverker emerged, with Filip close behind. Inez bit her bottom lip. Did the whole neighborhood have to watch?

"What's going on here?" said Sverker, eagerly.

"I'm giving away some books," said Inez. "I've amassed rather a few over the years, as you can see."

Sverker's gaze swept over all the piles of books. "Giving away? May I?"

Inez nodded. Soon he was enthusiastically perusing the piles, picking up book after book.

"Well, if you're going to take so many books, there was no point in us renting a trailer," said Inez, glancing at the growing pile on Sverker's front step. He blushed and laughed sheepishly.

"You're right. Just one more." He went through the piles, his movements almost reverential, until eventually he settled on one last book.

Then he looked at the remaining piles and let out a sigh. "So many good books. I hope other people have the sense to appreciate them."

Inez couldn't help but shake her head in amusement. This was clearly more sentimental for him than for her.

When they had helped to get all the books onto the trailer, Andreas asked Inez if he could borrow Meja to help deliver them. Inez nodded.

Sverker lit up. "What do you say we start up the barbecue in the meantime? To celebrate vacation season!"

Those two can always find an excuse to celebrate, Inez thought. She was about to say that they had already eaten when she noticed Meja's and Andreas's eager faces. She didn't want to be a stick-in-the-mud for the young people.

"That sounds lovely," she said. "In a few hours?"

Sverker gave a thumbs-up and disappeared into the house with Filip, who was already discussing what to cook.

Dinner was magnificently arranged, as Inez was beginning to understand was always the case when Sverker and Filip were hosting. A fire crackled at one corner of the porch, and the grill was covered with corn on the cob, onions, lemons, and marinated chicken skewers. On the table were small bowls of sauces, large bowls of sweet potato fries and coleslaw, sliced baguettes, and a carafe of white wine. Before they settled down, Sverker proposed a toast. Then he pulled out a chair for Inez and sat down next to her.

"Doesn't it feel strange to have gotten rid of books you've collected over a lifetime?" asked Sverker, who still couldn't seem to grasp the idea of all those stories being given up so freely.

"The only strange part is that I have suddenly gained a living room," said Inez.

Sverker laughed. "Oh, I recognize that dry humor from your books. I love it." He leaned in a little closer. "I don't suppose you're writing anything new?"

"No," she said. "Absolutely not."

Sverker smiled, embarrassed. "I just thought . . . it was . . ." He looked at Meja, who looked away.

Andreas raised his glass and thanked their hosts, and everyone else raised their glasses in response. Inez squinted at Meja. She wouldn't have told Sverker and Filip that she was writing again, would she? It seemed unlikely. Then again . . . she had broken her only rule once before. Who was to say she wouldn't ignore this rule too? She would ask her tomorrow. Now she just wanted to relax and enjoy the moment, the conversations, the food. It would help her cope with what was coming next. The story.

Everyone helped themselves to the treats. Andreas started talking to Sverker about beautiful excursion destinations in the area, and Filip and Meja talked about food. Inez found it difficult to participate in their conversations. Her eyes kept being drawn out to sea, which made her think of Mathilda. When dusk fell, Filip grilled pineapples and served them up with Italian ice cream. Inez tried to eat a few bites but had to leave most of it. She met Meja's worried gaze across the table, pulled her shawl tighter around her shoulders, and cleared her throat.

"All this tidying has wiped me out. I have to accept the fact that I'm not young anymore. I think I'll turn in and get my beauty sleep."

Meja got up to leave, but Inez raised her hand. "You stay here. Enjoy your evening. Many thanks, Sverker and Filip, for another unforgettable dinner, and Andreas for helping with the books."

Sverker stood up. "Can I escort you?"

Inez shook her head. "Thanks, but I'll be just fine."

She nodded goodbye to them all and walked through the flamboyant garden. It was as beautiful as a fairy tale in the evening light but only made her long to be back home. Opening her own gate, into her paved, weedy yard, she breathed a sigh of relief.

Once inside, she headed straight for her bedroom and shut the door. She read through the last chapters she had written and continued from where she had left off.

A couple of hours later, she heard Meja return.

The stairs creaked as she walked up. Then creaked again as she came back down. Inez listened. The porch door opened and shut. She went into the living room and peered through the blinds. Meja was going over to Andreas's house. *Well, well, well.*

She took out a bottle of port, poured herself a drink, and sat down. She hadn't printed the last chapters she had written. She was beginning to doubt whether she should really tell the whole story. But what was the alternative? Make it up?

She closed her eyes and heard Mathilda's voice in her head. *I would do anything for you. You know that. Anything.*

1974

Every weekend morning I sat on the high rocks, no longer hidden behind the bushes, but with my legs dangling over the edge. Some mornings Mathilda would go out on her boat and turn and wave just before disappearing from view. Other mornings she would come up and sit with me for a while. She would put her arm around me and let my head rest against her shoulder.

I don't remember if we talked. I don't think we did. But her mere presence healed me. It was enough. No, more than enough. It was my salvation.

So why did I let this happen? Why did I let Nikolas hit me? I can't explain. Perhaps I was lost and sought security in strong people. In Mathilda, but also in Nikolas. He was strong in a different way. Good at his bank job, sociable, confident, knew what he wanted and how to get it. When he entered a room, all eyes were on him. He courted me with grandiose gestures, and I fell like a pine tree. Just as he wanted. Once I had fallen, he wrapped me around his little finger, stopped wooing, and started demanding. When I didn't do the right thing, didn't understand, didn't show up, he hit me. Because he got tired of me, he said.

Why didn't I leave him after the first time? Because he begged for forgiveness. He sounded so genuine.

I don't want to be the type of person who has regrets. But I regret not leaving him after the first time he hit me. If I had known what that first smack would set into motion, I would have left him even if doing so risked my life.

MEJA

Andreas and Meja helped Filip and Sverker clean up after the evening's festivities and accompanied one another on the short journey home. Andreas asked if Meja wanted to come over for a nightcap, to which she replied that she had drunk a little too much wine already. When he suggested that a cup of tea could also count as a nightcap, she bashfully declined anyway, saying she had things to do tomorrow and needed to get some sleep. Andreas nodded and said good night.

Meja could hear Inez still typing away in the bedroom as she went up to the guest room and out on the balcony. She leaned on the railing and looked out at the sea where the moonlight had rolled out a glittering carpet. It had been a wonderful evening, but she felt a knot in her stomach. She was all too aware of having broken Inez's rule to not tell anyone about her newest writing project. Even if Andreas kept the secret forever, she had still broken her promise. And she couldn't lie. Why did she always sabotage herself like this?

She looked down into Andreas's garden. He had already put up some solar-powered lamps along the edge of the lawn, which emanated an inviting glow.

If there was a risk she might lose her job tomorrow, she might as well take him up on that nightcap. She tried to slip downstairs silently, but the stairs creaked worse than ever. Meja heard a pause in typing as she tiptoed out of the house as quietly as she could.

She knocked on Andreas's door. Maybe he had already gone to bed? Silly to say no first and then show up fifteen minutes later. Meja was just about to turn back when the door opened.

"Changed your mind about that cup of tea?" he said.

She nodded with a little smile.

"Welcome," he said, ushering her in. "Well, it doesn't look all that welcoming in here. I've just sort of shoved all my things inside. It doesn't feel very homey yet. Maybe you could give me some advice?"

Meja went into the living room and looked around. "It's very . . . white."

He laughed. "Yes, that might be problem number one."

He went into the kitchen and came back with a tray so quickly that Meja realized he must have already set it out: two mugs, a teapot, a sugar bowl, and some oatmeal cookies. She raised her eyebrows.

He half smiled. "I was hoping you'd change your mind."

When they sat down it was clear that the buoyant atmosphere at Sverker and Filip's was gone. This just felt awkward. Andreas spun around on his chair.

"So . . . how do you think I could get this place into shape?"

Meja looked around until her focus landed on an easel, canvases, and paints in one corner of the room.

"Do you paint?"

He nodded. "It's my main hobby. A way to distract myself from my thinking mind."

Meja thought of the guest room where she was staying.

"Inez's guest room is like the coast. You can almost feel the waves of the sea lulling you to rest, the warm sand between your toes, the seaweed softly swaying." She smiled, suddenly embarrassed by her digression. "I don't know her very well, but I know that the sea is very special to her. That used to be her bedroom. I don't know . . . it's nice to decorate a room according to a feeling. By choosing a theme that means a lot to you."

"A feeling as theme?" said Andreas thoughtfully. "I don't know how I'd do that."

Meja knew. A theme that distracted him from his thinking mind. She got up and walked over to the window, where Andreas had yet to hang drapes but had placed a potted kalanchoe that looked a little neglected.

"Instead of flowers you should just have big glass jars full of paintbrushes." She pointed. "That's where I would put the easel and canvases." She looked at the living room table. "I would push this to the other side of the room and put a workbench here instead, a glorious mess of sketches, clippings, inspiration." She went back to the couch and looked at the large wall beside it. "I'd paint this as a feature wall and hang one of your own paintings right in the middle."

Andreas looked at her with an amused smile. Meja was on a roll now.

"Do you have any with you?" she asked. He shook his head. "Hmm, then maybe hang up the canvas you're working on. So you can see its progress step-by-step. Or something."

"Now I'm very curious as to what your apartment looks like," said Andreas.

"I don't have one right now. It's complicated."

"But if you did?"

Meja shrugged. "Unfortunately, it would probably have just been . . . white."

Andreas laughed. "My daughter is coming this weekend. Do you have time to help me rearrange the living room before then? As per your suggestions?"

Meja didn't know what to say. She was both flattered and embarrassed.

"I can't promise anything. Like I said . . . it's complicated," she said at last.

Andreas looked puzzled.

Meja shrugged. "I'm just staying with Inez temporarily. She offered me her guest room because I had a few problems on the home front and needed somewhere to stay. In return, I'm helping her with a project."

"The book?"

Meja looked down. "That's the other thing. I was absolutely *not* supposed to tell anyone about the book. And I told you. So now there's a chance she won't want me working for her anymore. If she finds out."

"I won't breathe a word to anyone," said Andreas.

"I know. But Inez has a way of seeing through me. And I'm a terrible liar."

"There are ways to avoid lying by not telling the whole truth."

Meja smiled weakly, sipped her tea, and glanced at the clock. "I'd better get to bed."

Andreas nodded. "Well, if you do have some time to spare, I would really appreciate your help. My daughter would be overjoyed to see her father actually living—as opposed to surviving."

"I'll try," said Meja and went onto the porch.

Andreas stopped in the doorway and leaned against the frame.

Meja smiled. "Thanks for the nightcap."

"Thanks for the good advice."

She raised her hand slightly in an awkward goodbye, embarrassed by how quickly her heart was fluttering. He just smiled back.

Meja tried her best to sneak inside silently but winced as she approached the armchairs. Despite the darkness, she could make out the shape of Inez sitting there, very still. Meja swallowed hard and slowly sat down in the armchair next to her.

As her eyes adjusted to the darkness, she could make out Inez's face. Her expression was completely different from usual. Vulnerable somehow. And she had seemed distracted during dinner at Sverker and Filip's. How could she let her writing consume her this way? Was it really worth it?

Their eyes met. And suddenly Meja *knew*. This wasn't a fictional story, as Inez had claimed. The narrator of the story was Inez herself. That was why she was writing so intensely and finding it so draining. Because she was reliving it all.

Meja took Inez's hand and gave it a light squeeze. Inez responded by gently pushing her hand away.

INEZ

Waves lapped gently at the pier. Inez's mind moved with the rhythm. Since she had started writing about Mathilda, it was as if she had forged an invisible bond with the sea. When it was troubled, troubled memories arose. When it was calm, happier memories came, or no memories at all. The weekend had been challenging, and Inez was grateful for some peace today. Maybe she would even let this be a writing-free day. To gather her strength for what was to come. She knew that a violent storm lurked beyond the calm waves—her story's end.

She got up and headed homeward. When she opened the gate, she glanced into Andreas's garden. She missed Viola today. If she were alive, she would have no doubt been sitting there on her yoga mat, uttering some clichéd words of wisdom as Inez tried to pass by unnoticed. Probably something about finding balance in life. Balance salt with sweet. What could Inez sweeten her life with?

Meja was working in the kitchen and shooed Inez away when she came in and tried to help.

"Just sit down and I'll bring you some breakfast."

Inez did as she was told. She thought back to the day before. The events of the previous night looked very different in the light of day. She had never admitted that the book was autobiographical, but the way Meja had taken her hand showed she must know. Was it fair to drag Meja into this? Could she handle it?

Meja came out with a tray of juice, boiled eggs, toast, butter, marmalade, and cream cheese. It looked good.

"So, where did you go last night?" Inez said, spreading butter on a piece of toast.

Meja fiddled with her napkin. "I went over to Andreas's briefly. He needed some interior design tips."

"Aha. Did you give him some?"

Meja squirmed in her seat. "A few."

"The best ideas tend to come at night," said Inez.

Inez recalled the way Sverker had asked her if she was writing anything new, as if he had an inkling that she was.

"Did you tell Sverker that I'm writing a new book?"

"No," said Meja, shaking her head. "But the other day he wanted to invite us over for a drink while you were totally absorbed in writing, so I said we couldn't come because you were busy working. Then I realized he might assume you were writing, so I said you were probably answering fan mail."

Inez laughed. "Fan mail? You think he bought that?"

"I hope so, but I couldn't say. Would you like me to talk to him? I would never tell him—"

Inez interrupted. "No need."

She peeled an egg, put plenty of herb salt on it, and bit off half. Chewing carefully, she thought of Viola again and her constant praise for balance. She regarded Meja. Inez's life wasn't the only one that was too salty. They both needed a good dose of sugar. Maybe what they really needed was to feel exhilarated and wild, if only for one day.

"I think we should go on an adventure today," she said.

"Like what?"

"Why not let fate decide?"

Inez tore two pieces of paper from a notebook on the table. On one she wrote *walk* and on the other *cab*. She folded them, shook them around in her hands, and presented them to Meja to choose.

Meja took one and unfolded it. "Cab," she read aloud.

"Right then," said Inez. "In half an hour there will be a cab waiting for us."

"But where are we going?"

Instead of answering, Inez just nodded at the clock. Meja quickly finished eating and went to get ready.

Inez called the cab and wrote a few more notes, which she put in the pocket of the bright-yellow summer jacket she found at the back of her closet. The right attire for an adventure. Then she plugged in the curling iron to add a flick to the ends of her hair. This was probably what inspired Meja to exclaim "Oh!" twenty-five minutes later, or maybe it was the smell of her sweet perfume.

The cab dropped them off at Helsingborg Central Station. Inez took out two more scraps of paper and told Meja to choose one.

Keep traveling, it said.

"Okay," Inez said, offering Meja more options. The next said *Boat.*

"Well, then," said a smiling Inez. "We're going to Denmark."

She took the lead toward the ferries, bought tickets, and looked up at the big board of departure times. They were just in time to catch the *Aurora.*

They had to hurry to board and made it in the nick of time. The conductor wished them a pleasant journey, to which Inez gleefully replied, "Thank you very much. I'm sure it will be." She was feeling invigorated.

They settled into the cafeteria located opposite the shop with tempting offers on alcoholic beverages, perfumes, and candy. Inez presented Meja with three new scraps of paper. Meja unfolded one. *Beer.*

Inez unfolded another. "'Wine.' Phew. The third said 'water,' which would have been a great tragedy on the ferry to Denmark!" She nodded at the shop. "Shall we?"

Meja nodded. "Except I don't drink beer."

"That's the point. We are letting fate make our decisions, pushing our boundaries a little. It's good to try new things sometimes."

Meja didn't seem to agree with this philosophy, but she came back with a green can of Tuborg for herself and a small bottle of white wine that perfectly filled a glass for Inez.

A couple settled down next to them. The woman looked about Inez's age. Was she looking at her with that same curious look as Sverker did? Or was Inez just being paranoid? They whispered between themselves. For fifteen years, Inez had loathed being out in public for this very reason.

Balance. That was why they were here.

The woman leaned forward slightly. "Sorry to bother you, but aren't you Inez Edmark, the author?"

Inez felt a cold shiver run down her spine and nodded.

"Your books are wonderful," the woman said with a smile. "I'm such a fan. I really wish you'd written more. No one writes like you."

Inez let these words sink in. Allowed herself to bask briefly in the praise, like she used to. Before the storm of criticism swept away all the joy.

"Thank you," she said. "That's very kind of you to say. Unfortunately, I don't write anymore."

"What a shame," said the woman. "Well, don't let me disturb you. But it was great to meet you briefly."

Inez nodded and even managed a smile before turning back to Meja.

Meja waited until the couple had left before saying, "You said before that you were the victim of a scandal. Was it the journalists that made you stop writing?"

Inez shrugged. "I might have decided to stop anyway. At least that's how I choose to see it."

"But what about the book you're writing now?"

Inez raised her hand. "We're not talking about books today."

Meja nodded and asked no more questions.

Twenty minutes later they arrived on the Danish coast and followed the stream of travelers along the walkway and outside the ferry terminal. Inez gave three new pieces of paper to Meja, who opened one that said *Stay.*

"Wonderful," said Inez, gesturing to the street beyond the small square filled with flowers of every possible color for sale. "Fate has delivered us to our destination, where we can sweeten our lives and feel wildly alive."

MEJA

"Town or Kronborg Castle?" Inez asked.

Meja was just about to say that she didn't mind and Inez could choose, when she realized that she actually did have a preference.

"I feel like town today."

"Me too," said Inez.

They followed a narrow alley up to the main street, Stengade. It was teeming with people. They passed baskets full of wine bottles with handwritten signs saying **Special Offer** on the sidewalks, the cheese shop that spread its aromas far out into the street, and cozy little outdoor restaurants. They stopped at a café to have a cup of coffee and watch all the scurrying tourists before moving on.

Inez headed for Munkgade, with its cobblestones and red-and-yellow half-timbered buildings. She began to lecture Meja about its history, like a tour guide.

"The Black Friars built a monastery here in the Middle Ages. They were so called because of the black cloaks they wore outdoors. Can't you just feel the history?" she said, running her hand over a bumpy building wall.

Meja couldn't help but giggle a little but tried to sound serious when she answered.

"Yes, it's like entering a fairy-tale world."

They continued toward Axeltorv, then stopped again. They were lucky enough to find a place to sit in the shade, where they ordered a glass of wine each and listened to a live jazz band.

Then they walked down a few store-lined streets, window-shopping, until Inez pointed to a sign advertising a small tavern with outdoor seating in the backyard. It was a picturesque courtyard with an abundance of flowers, peaceful in the warm afternoon sun. There were cobblestones on the ground and a high wall all around. A few people were already eating, but there was a table free for Meja and Inez.

Inez sat down unusually gracefully, instead of with her usual thump. Meja wondered how many painkillers she'd taken and, on seeing Inez pick up the drinks menu, wondered if mixing them with alcohol was a good idea. But before she could say anything, Inez told her to choose a number between one and twenty. Meja said eighteen.

Inez smiled at the waiter and pointed to number eighteen on the drink menu. "Sex on the Beach, please. Two."

Meja blushed.

When their cocktails arrived, Inez clinked her glass with Meja's. "Thank you for coming along on this little adventure."

Meja nodded. "And the idea is for us to feel 'wildly alive'?" she asked, sipping the drink with notes of peach and orange.

"Something like that. It's been a while," Inez said, taking off her jacket.

Meja couldn't help but think that Inez was looking for life in the wrong places.

"You should open your blinds," she said.

Inez laughed.

"Why do you have them down all the time?" Meja pressed. She knew she'd asked this before, but she hadn't been satisfied with the answer.

"I don't do things by halves. It's one extreme or the other. During my career, I put everything I had into writing books, appeasing the industry and the press, being there for my readers. When I couldn't carry on that way, I chose a different path. Solitude, seclusion. The opposite. It's different, but it's also good."

"Is it? Surely no one really wants to live in a darkened home with a withered cactus?"

Inez smiled and sipped her drink. "Seeing as we're speaking so candidly, what exactly happened a week ago when I found you sitting on the bench early in the morning with a suitcase?"

Meja popped an olive in her mouth and shrugged. "Johan wanted a break. And I guess I'm like you: I'd rather not do things by halves."

"Quite right!" Inez said. "None of this ridiculous middle ground."

"So I was hoping to stay with my mother for a while. But, as I've said, my mom and I usually only see each other for dinner once a month. We talk about the same things every time and focus more on getting it over and done with than actually enjoying it. Anyway . . . I couldn't stay there because she had something going on, don't ask me what. And I said some hard truths that I probably should have kept to myself."

"Don't say that," said Inez. "Sometimes it's better for these things to come out."

Meja shrugged.

Inez glanced at Meja's purse hanging on the back of the chair. "Did you bring your camera?"

Meja nodded. She had completely forgotten about it. She would have to remember to take some pictures of Inez in a quaint alley on the way back.

"May I see some pictures?"

Meja handed the camera to Inez. "You can scroll back from there. But I haven't deleted the bad ones yet."

Inez raised the camera to see the small screen better. She stopped at one photo in particular and turned the screen toward Meja. "This is a fantastic picture. You've captured the fleeting truth beneath the surface that often goes unnoticed."

In the picture, Andreas had his hands in his pockets, which Meja had noticed was typical for him, and was inspecting the lavish display of food at Sverker and Filip's barbecue. Meja had captured a streak of sorrow in his eyes.

"He obviously wishes he could share it with his daughter. The one he will never live with again. Every now and then he realizes that she is no longer part of his everyday life," said Inez.

Meja looked at the picture. She had never thought about a photo of hers that way before. She just snapped instinctively without thinking. But Inez was right—if a little bombastic. Meja had captured something deeply sad in his expression at that moment.

Inez scrolled further and stopped at the picture of herself that Meja had taken from the guest room balcony. Inez was standing with her head tilted upward and her eyes closed. She looked at it for a long time, before putting the camera down and turning her gaze up to the sky.

"I should have taken more pictures. To remember. I wish I had a photograph of a friend I had once."

Meja glanced at Inez. She wondered if Inez was referring to Mathilda but didn't dare ask. Inez had implied, but still never admitted, that the book she was writing was true and Mathilda had been a real friend of hers.

Inez finished her drink and held up the second menu, the one with food. "We may as well eat here, right? It's a cozy spot."

Meja nodded, happy to stay in this little pocket of peace and quiet. They ordered traditional Danish open sandwiches with battered cod and rémoulade, and a bottle of Riesling.

"So, are you feeling wildly alive yet?" Meja asked, sipping the cold, dry wine.

Inez laughed. "No, but I feel balanced. Which is very pleasant and allows room for feeling wildly alive. I feel a sort of tingle of expectation. Don't you?"

The waiter came with their food before she could answer.

"When else have you felt wildly alive? You said it's been a while."

Inez mused on the question as she chewed a piece of fish. Then she put down her cutlery, dabbed the napkin against her red-painted lips, and said, "I remember one time when I had just finished writing a book. I had typed the all-important final period and was filled with adrenaline, separation anxiety, and relief. It was late at night and I decided to just take off. I took the train to Copenhagen and sat down in one of my favorite places, a book café. I was on my second cup of coffee by the time Cristy, my publisher and all-around assistant, called."

"Wow," said Meja.

"I know. Suffice it to say . . . *then* I felt alive."

"How long did you stay?"

"Just the night. Amelia was at home and Cristy couldn't change her whole schedule just to look after her, even though she was usually there for her."

Meja frowned. "You left Amelia home alone?"

"Yes," said Inez.

"How old was she?"

"Now you're talking in the same tone of voice as Amelia. She was five years old and always slept like a log. Besides, I knew Cristy would show up at seven in the morning."

Meja pursed her lips.

"Wipe that look off your face," said Inez. "There was no harm done. Amelia didn't notice. Cristy was there when she woke up."

"But what if . . . ?" said Meja.

Inez sighed. "I've never done things by halves, and I've never thought *what if.* What on earth is the point?"

Meja shook her head slightly. How could she have left Amelia all alone like that—and gone to a whole other country?

Inez's eyes narrowed. "Don't judge me on one incident that you don't even fully understand. It doesn't suit you."

Meja felt herself blush. They finished their meal in silence, and when the empty plates were taken away, Inez ordered a coffee and chocolate each. Meja tried to think of something to say that might bring back Inez's good mood.

"Sorry," she said. "I'm probably just angry at my own mother and taking it out on you."

Inez nodded briefly. "It was a chaotic time in many ways. I was high on life, making spur-of-the-moment decisions that might seem a bit reckless nowadays." She looked at Meja with a wry smile. "But we all survived, and I regret nothing. I'm glad I was a bit wild back then."

Meja nodded. The wildest thing she had ever done was buy a naked guinea pig.

Inez patted Meja's hand gently, as if she knew that Meja had a poor record of wild experiences. "The best days of your life are yet to come. You have time."

A couple of hours and another cocktail later, they left the restaurant arm in arm. Dusk was falling over Elsinore and making the town look even more like a fairy-tale land. They strolled around for a while before heading for the ferry.

Once they were on board, Inez got another glass of wine. Meja opted for water. They didn't speak much. The day had taken its toll and, considering how tired Meja felt now, she couldn't imagine how drained Inez must be.

It had been a fun day, but they were both grateful to arrive back home.

"It sure feels good to have exhausted your whole body," said Inez and yawned widely.

Meja nodded and smiled faintly. "Good night, and thank you for today."

"Thank *you*," said Inez.

Meja took a quick shower and collapsed into bed, her head slightly dizzy from the wine. She closed her eyes and felt sleep creeping in.

A couple of hours later she woke up with a jolt. She could hear something out in the yard. She stepped out on the balcony and saw the door to the shed wide open. Inez emerged holding something. Meja squinted in the dark. Were those fireworks?

"What are you doing?" she half whispered.

Inez looked up at the balcony and laughed.

"You're not going to light those, are you? Don't you need a permit?"

"Not those, plural. Just one firework. Amelia bought it on New Year's Eve, but we never set it off. I feel like now's the time," Inez whispered back.

"Inez, stay there and don't move. You can't light that!"

Meja ran downstairs and outside just as Inez lit the string, which crackled before it released a firework that shot up into the air and exploded in a cascade of colors. The sound ricocheted between the houses.

Inez had huddled up to Meja and was clapping her hands with delight at the light show that never seemed to end. When the explosions stopped, she turned to Meja, laughing and rosy-cheeked.

"Isn't it wonderful to feel wildly alive, if only for a short while?"

Meja heard Andreas's balcony door open and pulled Inez back so he wouldn't see them. The fireworks display hadn't brought her the same effervescent joy as it had to Inez—quite the opposite. Still, she couldn't help but feel warmly toward the slightly crazy woman by her side.

INEZ

Inez woke up early. The burned-out firework was lying in her little flower bed. She went outside to pick it up and throw it in the trash, then returned to her room, sat on the edge of her bed, and sighed deeply. Her body felt a hundred years old. Gone was yesterday's wildness and exuberance. Now she was just hungover and tired.

She popped a painkiller and curled up in bed like a baby bird. She had dreamed about a storm, with wild waves striking the little boat she and Mathilda were sitting in. Suddenly her friend fell overboard, into the dark depths. She heard herself cry out for the sea to spare her. *Take me instead!*

She was woken up by Meja knocking on her door. "Is everything okay?"

Inez ran her hand through the hair stuck to her clammy temples.

"I'm fine," she replied in a gravelly voice.

"Do you want some lunch? I've made fried pork chops and mashed potatoes."

"No," Inez replied, then added a faint "Thank you."

Inez heard her feet shuffling outside the door for a few moments, as if Meja was deciding what to say, before she left.

Inez went back to sleep. It was evening when she finally got up, put on her slippers and shawl, and crept onto the porch. She shivered when a brisk gust of wind caressed her cheek. Like a cold hand.

Stuck somewhere between waking and dreaming, she walked through her yard and down to the beach by the pier. The wind stirred up the waves. Pulling her shawl tighter around her, she recalled Mathilda's intense gaze in the boat that day when she spoke about the sea as mother of the motherless. "I would do anything for you. You know that," she had said. When Inez asked why, she replied, "Because true friendship is stronger and more beautiful than any other bond."

Inez picked up a blue shell and ran her fingers over its ridged surface. Mathilda's words about friendship had become the final sentence of Inez's first novel. It had also become the consistent theme of all her later novels. Friendship as the strongest bond of all. That which heals and shows the way. A good theme for fiction. Better than in reality. *I would do anything for you.*

Inez looked up. Mathilda's voice was so clear in her head.

"You shouldn't have," she whispered, squinting at the sea.

Some distance away she thought she could see a lock of Mathilda's hair. Close, but out of reach. She moved forward, taking one step, then another. The water came up to her ankles, thighs, waist—she didn't care. Her shawl flew away. *Just one more step. Then I can reach her.* Inez was pulled below the surface. She reached out, grabbed the strand of hair, and held on. The air was squeezed out of her lungs, making her dizzy. Her clothes weighed her down. She was sinking, still gripping the strand of hair, until two strong hands pulled her above the surface.

She coughed and gasped for air. Her body dangled limply in someone's arms. She didn't have the strength to do anything but float and be taken. Her rescuer pulled her onto land with one final jerk before collapsing in the sand and letting out a deep breath.

Now she could see that it was Andreas. Meja was there too. Her lips were moving, but Inez couldn't hear what she was saying.

Inez wasn't sure what had happened or where she was. She opened her hand and saw that she was clutching a thin, reddish-brown piece of seaweed. Laboriously, she sat up and looked at Andreas, who was lying next to her, soaking wet and panting.

She began to cough violently and shake all over from cold and shock. Andreas stood and held out a hand to help her up.

"You need to get out of those wet clothes and have a hot cup of tea," he said, helping her to her feet while Meja ran down to the water's edge, where Inez's shawl was drifting in the surf.

"So do you," Inez replied.

He smiled warmly at her, and it made her well up with tears. The three of them walked slowly back to Inez's house.

Andreas put the kettle on while Meja helped Inez out of her wet clothes and into a fresh T-shirt, pair of sweatpants, and soft fleece dressing gown. Inez didn't protest. Meja sat her down in her armchair, and Andreas handed her the tea.

"Hot with lots of sugar," he said.

"How did you know that's exactly how I wanted it?" Inez said, accepting the drink with trembling hands.

"Intuition," he said with a smile.

"I thought I was dreaming," Inez said to comfort Meja, who looked completely distraught. "I wasn't trying to drown myself. And it won't happen again. I was probably still giddy from our excursion. I think that's enough wild adventures for a while."

She tried to say it with a twinkle in her eye, but Meja did not look amused.

Andreas looked back and forth between the two women. "Well, I'm going to head home. Take care now, Inez," said Andreas, putting his hands in his pockets.

"I will," said Inez. "And once again, thank you."

He just smiled in response, and Meja walked him to the door before coming back to join Inez.

"Sorry about all this," Inez said. "Get to bed now. You look more tired than I am."

Meja hesitated but went upstairs anyway. Halfway up, she turned around. "When Andreas pulled you ashore, you said you'd reached her. What did you mean?"

"Did I?" Inez said with a shrug. "I don't remember that."

Meja squinted at her as if trying to read whether she was answering honestly, but then continued upstairs with heavy feet.

Inez looked down at the hand that had been holding the seaweed.

"Where did you go, Mathilda, daughter of the sea?" she whispered.

1975

"Aren't you going to come with me?" said Mathilda early one Saturday morning when she came to sit next to me on the cliff. I had sneaked out while Nikolas was sleeping again. It had been over six months since I was last out at sea, and I desperately wanted to join her. Watch her steer the boat toward the oyster bed, soak up her calmness. Just exist in the moment. That's what I loved about it most of all. Maybe Nikolas would sleep for a long time today? He had been at a party last night and probably wouldn't know I was gone. I nodded weakly.

Mathilda smiled and took my hand, and we walked down to the jetty together, unmoored the boat, and let the still morning guide us out onto the water. Everything was magical. The red and orange tones of the sun were dazzlingly beautiful. I could immediately feel the place envelop me in security and comfort. Here I was free.

I watched Mathilda dive into the water and resurface with plastic baskets filled with oysters. We cleaned them together in reverent silence. The ones that were too small were put back.

I found an empty shell. I looked up at Mathilda, who was smiling mischievously. Slowly I turned the shell around and read the word she had engraved: *Write.*

I blinked back the tears. Mathilda was clearly trying to remind me what was important in life. She wanted me to continue writing the story I had started long ago. The one she had told me to write. There was nothing I found more pleasurable than disappearing into my fiction bubble. I caressed the shell with my fingers and suddenly I could hear them again. The characters in my head. I looked up at her.

"I hear them," I said with a wistful chuckle. "The people in the story who got their beginning, middle, and end thanks to your oyster shell. I thought they were gone forever. They've been so quiet lately."

They had stopped the day Nikolas hit me for the first time.

Mathilda understood that, of course. She understood everything. Including all the unspoken words, everything that simmered between the lines.

"What's it called? The story in your head?" she asked.

I hadn't thought of a name for the story yet, but the moment Mathilda asked, I knew. "*The Daughters of the Sea.*"

Mathilda smiled softly. "That will be your first book. If you choose to follow your calling."

She carried the last baskets into the boat and got ready for the journey back.

"Shall I tell you what my father told me about the daughter of the sea when I was little?" she said, starting the engine.

I nodded, leaned back, closed my eyes, and let Mathilda's words wash over me.

"The daughter of the sea is motherless, and so the sea offers her protection. She is carried through life in water's strong arms; she knows that she is always part of something greater and hence learns the most important lesson of them all."

I looked up expectantly.

"To extend a hand to those who need it."

MEJA

Meja woke up with a jolt. As she padded down the stairs, she heard the clatter of the keyboard in Inez's room. She didn't know how Inez could bear it; she certainly didn't envy her artistic soul, as Andreas had put it. She thought back to last night and shuddered. She had been standing on the balcony when she saw Inez walk down to the beach. She was instinctively concerned, perhaps because it looked like Inez had gone out in her morning slippers.

When she rushed down to follow her, she came across Andreas and asked if he would come with her. And he said yes, thank goodness. What if he hadn't? Meja would never have had the strength to pull Inez out of the water herself.

Meja decided to knock on Andreas's door. He opened it wearing a dark-blue dressing gown with a coffee mug in his hand.

"Good morning," he said, raising his mug in greeting.

"Good morning," Meja said, suddenly embarrassed to have come over so early. He wasn't even dressed yet.

He eagerly invited her in for coffee, and she accepted, though she would have preferred to just go home again. She felt she owed him a proper thank-you for yesterday's heroic deed.

"I just wanted to say thank you again," she said.

"Don't mention it," Andreas called from the kitchen, where he had gone to get Meja a cup of coffee. "Anyone would have done the same thing."

Meja glanced at the windowsill, where Andreas had displayed a glass jar full of brushes. He came back, handed her the coffee, and half smiled when he saw what she was looking at.

"Yes, I took your advice, as you can see. I liked your ideas for the living room and thought I'd do some shopping today. I don't suppose you'd have time to help me arrange everything?" he said.

"I think I can slip away for a while," Meja said, settling on the couch. "I don't have specified working hours, I just do things as and when she needs."

"How unusual."

Meja couldn't help but smile. She would have said the same thing if the roles had been reversed.

"It is unusual, but necessary. For both of us."

Andreas nodded thoughtfully. "Hey, um, did she set off a firework the other night?"

"Yes. She wanted to feel 'wildly alive,' as she put it."

"It scared the life out of me. And all the seabirds, too, I bet."

Meja nodded. "She's stubborn when she wants something."

Andreas fiddled with his mug. "You might want to think about setting your boundaries."

"Oh sure," said Meja, touched by his concern. Then again, she wondered what boundaries she really had right now. Her whole life felt fluid. As if she were sitting on a raft and being moved by the current. She finished her drink. "I'd better get back, but I can come over around two o'clock, if that works?"

Andreas got up and opened the door. "Sounds great. Looking forward to it."

Meja walked back through his yard and reflected on the way it represented Andreas perfectly. Like him, everything was just right. Pretty flower beds, but nothing lavish. All very pleasant.

Inez's yard was anything but pleasant. The tiles had turned mossy green in places, and dandelions and thistles were poking up all over the place. It looked pretty depressing. She was pulling up a few dandelions at random when she heard someone clear their throat behind her. She turned around.

"Mom?" she said, startled.

Susanne was standing on the other side of the gate.

"What on earth are you doing here?" continued Meja.

"I—"

Meja cut her off before she could continue. "How did you even know I was here?"

Then she realized that of course it had to be through Johan.

"Johan said you used to park by the pine grove and walk along the sea front," said Susanne. "He thought you worked in the second house but wasn't quite sure." She held out an envelope. "I have an invitation for you. It's this weekend, and I really hope you can come."

Meja took the envelope and opened it. It was a ticket to a production of *The Queen's Tiara* at Helsingborg City Theater.

"A play?"

Susanne adjusted the purse on her shoulder. "If you want."

"I'll think about it," Meja said and headed back to the house. She turned around before going in, but Susanne was already gone.

Meja's heart was pounding from the shock. If it hadn't been for the ticket in her hand, she might have thought she'd imagined it all. A theater ticket. A peace offering? This must be Bengt's doing.

When she went inside she found Inez sitting in her armchair and staring into space. She slowly turned to look up at Meja.

"Maybe we could open the blinds after all," she said.

Meja raised her eyebrows in surprise and slowly pulled open one of the blinds. Light flooded the room. Inez squinted and Meja could see just how tired she looked. Her complexion seemed to have paled over the last twenty-four hours. She looked nothing like she had on their Danish adventure.

"Shall I whip us up an omelet? I think you need to eat something."

Inez just stared out the window without answering. Meja took that as a yes. She found eggs, chives, and tomatoes and set to work. Fifteen minutes later she came out with a tray.

"Do you want to stay in the armchair?" she asked.

Inez nodded, and Meja served her food on the small side table and sat down opposite.

"I thought I heard voices outside," said Inez.

"What, just now? My mother came by."

"Oh really?" A little spark appeared in Inez's eyes.

"Yes. Even though I never told her I was here. She and Johan must have been gossiping."

Inez smiled weakly. "Tell me more. I like gossip."

"There's not much more to tell. She gave me a theater ticket for Saturday. My mother is not the kind of person to hold out an olive branch, so I can guarantee it was her partner's idea."

"Well, that's nice anyway," said Inez, taking a bite of omelet.

"Not really," said Meja. "I'm doing just fine without her. I'm sure she is fine without me, too. This is like poking a hornet's nest. Totally unnecessary and guaranteed to get you stung."

Inez chuckled quietly. "Don't make the same mistakes I have. I mean that. Take every chance for reconciliation."

"So you think I should go?"

"Of course."

Meja sighed. Go to the theater with Susanne and Bengt? Better than a meal out, she supposed—they wouldn't have to talk!

"But will you be—?" She didn't get to finish the sentence.

"Of course I will," Inez said quickly. "Besides, I'm surrounded by three men who are more than happy to come to the rescue of this confused old authoress if need be."

Meja smiled. "Hey, how's the writing going? It's been a long time since I read anything."

Inez looked out the window again. "I don't think I want you to read aloud to me anymore. But I would like you to read it yourself and write any comments in the margin. Would that be all right?"

"Absolutely," said Meja. "But this Mathilda . . ." She trailed off and looked at Inez to see if she had crossed the line.

Inez nodded slowly. "Yes. Mathilda was my friend. A very special friend. She's the one I wish I had a photograph of."

"What happened to her?" The question slipped out of Meja's lips even though she knew Inez wouldn't answer. The answer was in the book she was writing.

Inez met her gaze. "People come and go in life. You have to think carefully about who to hold on to. Otherwise you run the risk of letting the good ones go."

Meja nodded and thought about her own life. Johan and Susanne. Was she letting them slip away from her now? Was that what she really wanted?

That afternoon, Inez gave Meja the blue folder to read, then returned to her writing. Meja sat in bed with Ingrid on her lap and devoured page after page. The words took hold of her and swept her away to Oyster Bay and Mathilda's world. To a friendship unlike any she had ever experienced. So profound, so significant.

By the time Meja had finished reading, she was utterly captivated. Evening had settled over the strait, and she stared at the sea for a little while before heading downstairs with Ingrid in her arms. Inez flinched when she saw her.

"Sorry—maybe I should leave her in the cage?" said Meja.

Inez squinted dubiously at the little creature. "No, it's okay. As long as I don't have to touch her."

Meja smiled. "She's very soft."

Inez scoffed and beckoned to Meja to join her in the living room for tea.

"What a friendship," said Meja. "I don't know if I'm envious or grateful that I've never experienced anything like it. It seems equally wonderful and devastating, almost like . . ."

"Love?" Inez said.

"Yes, actually. Were you . . . ?"

Inez shook her head, smiling. "No, we were just friends. She said once that even friendship can blaze like a crackling fire."

Meja looked at Inez's wall clock and winced. "Oh no!" she said. "Speaking of friendship, I promised to help Andreas with something at two o'clock. I completely lost track of time."

Inez smirked. "Could there be a little flame crackling there too?"

"Huh?" Meja widened her eyes. "Oh no!"

Inez shrugged playfully, a sly expression on her face.

Meja shook her head. At herself, at Inez's comment, at losing track of time.

"Go over and say it was my fault because I made you work. Which is true," said Inez.

Meja nodded. "Hold her," she said, handing Ingrid over to Inez.

The guinea pig waved her little legs in the air as Inez received her, holding her away from her body like a bag of smelly garbage.

"Put her in your lap and stroke her. It'll do you good. Feel-good hormones, you know."

Inez muttered, put Ingrid on her lap, and hesitantly ran her hand over her back. The guinea pig grunted contentedly.

"You can put her in this when you've had enough," Meja said, pointing to the travel carrier, and left for Andreas's house.

When he opened the door, music spilled out of the house. He had paint in his hair and rosy cheeks.

"Oh. Hello," he said.

"Sorry I'm a little late."

He looked at his watch. "Just six and a half hours."

"I got stuck with . . ."

He waved her in. "Ta-daaa!" he said cheerfully and gestured at the wall that Meja had suggested be a feature wall. He had gone for a blue-green tone that brought to mind the depths of the sea.

"It looks great," she said.

"I have you to thank."

"Hardly," she said.

"No really, I would have left it white if it weren't for you."

"Is there anything I can help you with now?" she said.

He pursed his lips and thought. "I'm wiped out after doing all this work on my own." He winked at Meja. "And now the paint has to dry before I can do anything else. But if you'd like to have a glass of wine with me, that would be very helpful. I'm craving a glass of red but can never bring myself to drink alone."

Meja raised her eyebrows. "Neither can I. When Johan was out with his friends on the weekends and I was home alone, I'd fancy a glass of wine, pour one, and then pour it back. It's just not the same without company."

"Well?" He nodded toward a row of wine bottles in a cabinet.

"Sure," she said, smiling.

He chose a bottle, poured them a glass each, and set out small bowls of olives and nuts.

"When is your daughter coming?" Meja asked.

"Tomorrow night. I'm kind of nervous. Which is ridiculous."

"No, it's not. You want her to see that you're doing okay."

"Could you pretend to come over spontaneously to ask for a cup of sugar, so she can see that I've already settled into the neighborhood?" He chuckled.

Meja nodded. "That's actually a good idea." She looked around. "But first, what about the rest of the room?"

Meja had already gotten up and started inspecting all the painting utensils that he had pushed into a corner. She placed another couple of glass jars with brushes on the windowsill and pushed the work table up next to the dining table. Together they sorted out the lighting, rolled out some rugs, and plumped up the newly purchased throw pillows that matched the feature wall. Andreas had bought several large green plants—weeping fig, golden cane palm, and monstera—which they arranged. Candles spread a cozy glow and scent of vanilla.

A couple of hours later the wine was drunk and the room was ready. Andreas walked around and admired it all. "It looks great." He stopped at the feature wall. "And you really think I should set up a blank canvas here?"

"Yes. It won't stay empty forever. Work in progress."

"That's such a fun, creative idea."

Meja smiled. "It's not often that I get called fun and creative."

Andreas looked deep into her eyes. His were hazel. Now that Meja thought about it, they were anything but average.

She tore her eyes away and cleared her throat. "Time to go. Thank you for a lovely evening." She walked over to the porch door and fumbled with the handle.

He put his hand on hers and pressed down. The heat of his skin shot through Meja's body like an arrow.

"See you later," he said, leaning gently against the doorframe after letting her out.

She nodded in response, afraid her voice wouldn't hold if she tried to speak, and hurried back to Inez's house, where the blinds were down again. This time she was grateful. It made the house into a protected zone. Everything that happened outside stayed there.

Life was different inside. Protected. Where no one could reach.

INEZ

It was eleven o'clock when Inez took the tray of mushrooms on toast out of the oven. Meja hadn't emerged from her room yet. Just as she served up two portions and sprinkled parsley on top, Meja appeared in the doorway.

"Good morning! Late night?" Inez said with a cheeky smile.

"Yes, I reread your final pages when I got home from Andreas's house. Then I couldn't sleep. Mm, that looks delicious."

They sat down to eat at the oak table.

"So, tell me," said Inez.

"On page 151 you write that . . ."

Inez waved her fork in the air. "No, tell me about your evening with Andreas."

Meja took a big bite and chewed slowly before answering. "We were decorating his living room for when his daughter comes to visit tonight."

Inez leaned forward slightly. "And you ate and drank . . . ?"

"Wine and olives," said Meja, frowning at Inez's smug grin. "There's nothing going on between us, if that's what you think."

"If you say so," said Inez. She was enjoying gently teasing Meja. It was a rare and welcome distraction from thinking about her book. A few rays of sunlight penetrated the blinds.

"It looks like a beautiful day. Shall we go for a walk?"

"Now?" Meja said with surprise.

Inez couldn't help but smile. Meja knew her well by now. A glorious summer day with lots of people outside wasn't usually her idea of fun. But Inez needed it today. She needed to feel like a normal person.

Five minutes later they were on their way to the pier. Inez was wearing her large sun hat. The surrounding gardens already smelled of barbecues, and they could hear the gleeful laughter of children on the beach. Young people were carrying surfboards and speakers. Thumping bass could be heard from a long way off.

Meja was about to veer toward the place where they usually sat, but Inez frowned and said, "Not today. Much too crowded."

Instead, they continued straight until they reached the small harbor. People were chatting and laughing. Children were running up the pier or catching crabs while boater types were loading picnic baskets from their cars onto boats for a day out. Inez pointed to a red hut.

"They sell coffee, fresh fish, ice cream, all sorts. What would you like?"

"Coffee and a cookie would be good for me," said Meja. "Do you want the same? Why don't I get it while you find us a seat?"

Inez nodded and walked over to a table that had just become vacant. She angled her sun hat slightly to hide her face from four chatty ladies at the next table.

"Good size," Meja said, nodding at the sun hat when she came back to the table. "No chance of anyone recognizing you under that."

Inez smiled wryly. "Some days I'm allergic to people's stares."

"I thought that was every day."

Inez chuckled. "True."

Meja looked around. "What a perfect little summer oasis."

Inez nodded. Everybody was out enjoying the sunshine. Waves of chatter and laughter surged over the harbor. She was just about to say something about it when she noticed that Meja looked distant.

"Penny for your thoughts," said Inez, dipping an oatmeal cookie in her coffee.

Meja looked up, pinched her lips together, leaned forward, and whispered, "If what you're writing is autobiographical, does that mean you were beaten by that man, Nikolas?"

Inez took a deep breath. She watched a passing dog walker.

"This is why I want you to read it. To see what you react to. The violence isn't the most important thing. It's more about the consequences. The book is about what one person is capable of doing for another. Not about abuse."

Meja leaned back in her chair again, sipped her coffee, and appeared to be contemplating what Inez had just said. Inez squinted at her. She liked observing Meja. She liked her unaffected authenticity.

"What do you think is the meaning of life?" she asked.

Meja's coffee went down the wrong way and she started spluttering.

"I'm the last person you should be asking," she said after she had stopped coughing. "I really have zero idea."

"Don't think about it too much. Just say the first thing that pops into your head."

Meja looked at her. "Wake up, eat, sleep, die."

Inez smacked Meja's arm with her napkin. "That's the worst thing I've ever heard. Have I, the great author of life-affirming trashy literature, taught you nothing?"

Meja laughed and held up her hands to deflect the napkin. "What do you want me to say?"

"Well, you could at least give the same boring answer as everyone else: *love*."

"Pah. Overrated."

Inez laughed. A wave of tenderness moved through her chest for this young woman with no home and tangled relationships. With it came a realization. Meja might need her for a salary and accommodation, but she needed Meja too. Not to read the manuscript and clean the house. But to be there as a human shield and pillar of support. As a friend.

She had taken Meja with her on her most private journey, one that no one else knew about. Wherever their futures might lead them, there was a bond between them now that could never be severed. She wished she could tell her this. But she wasn't ready. Instead, she patted her hand lightly and stood up. "You're right, love is overrated."

They started walking home and Inez linked arms with Meja.

"I read a survey about what makes people happy. It turns out that what makes us happiest is helping others. Maybe that's the meaning of life?" Inez said as they reached her gate, where another bouquet of flowers hung. A gorgeous arrangement of red bell-shaped tiger lilies.

"Maybe that's why Sverker always seems so happy," said Meja and removed the bouquet.

"Maybe."

When they entered Inez's dark house, Meja brought the flowers straight into the kitchen to throw them away, but Inez laid a hand on her arm.

"Wait," she said, looking at the bouquet. "What if *this* is the meaning of life? Letting beauty heal the pain."

Meja looked from the bouquet to Inez. "You mean I should . . . ?"

"Yes," said Inez. "We'll open the blinds and put them on the windowsill."

Meja found a vase in Inez's kitchen cupboard and placed the tiger lilies in the window. As Inez adjusted the vase slightly, she caught sight of Sverker, who had just come out to prune the wilted flowers from the rosebush between their two yards. When he saw the flowers a huge smile spread over his face. From the corner of her eye, Inez saw Meja give him a thumbs-up. She shook her head, but smiled. Now she had the energy to go back and face Oyster Bay. Thanks to Meja, and maybe just a little bit thanks to Sverker's flower bouquet.

1976

I stopped going up to the cliff to watch Mathilda on weekend mornings. Nikolas had started keeping a closer eye on me, making it impossible for me to sneak out, but that wasn't the only reason. It was also the look in Mathilda's eyes. There was a resentment there that I hadn't seen before. She never said anything, but I could see the intensity of her contempt for Nikolas—and for me. Not only was I still with him, but I was now also pregnant with his child. She thought I was throwing my life away. My talent. My dream of writing. And risking the safety of my unborn child. Or maybe that was what I was thinking, somewhere deep down. I don't know. There's a lot I don't know about that time. It's all so hazy. Blurred around the edges. What I do know is that I was spending all my energy trying to anticipate Nikolas's wishes in order to reduce my chances of getting beaten.

When he was at work I daydreamed about my child. I could sense she was going to be a girl. This made me happy, but also anxious; I assumed Nikolas would prefer a son. In my dreams I whispered words of love that would create a link between us that was stronger and more important than the umbilical cord. *You and me against the world. You will always be the most important thing in my life, and I promise I'll do anything for you.*

The Daughters of the Sea had been hidden away. And forgotten.

MEJA

After five changes of clothes, Meja settled on jeans and a T-shirt. Then she went downstairs to join Inez, who was flipping through a book in the living room. Meja sank into the armchair next to her.

Inez looked up. "Aren't you going to the theater?"

"No. I've got nothing to wear, and besides, what's the point? It feels weird and forced. And the show starts in twenty minutes, so it's too late now anyway."

Inez frowned. "Put on that navy-blue dress you wore to Sverker and Filip's that time. I'll call you a cab. Go on . . . hurry up."

Meja sighed and dragged herself back up to the guest room. Just the thought of watching a play, sitting between Susanne and Bengt like a rambunctious child who needed to be calmed down, was utterly humiliating. She changed, ran a comb through her hair, and went downstairs.

Inez came out of her bedroom with perfume, two glittery clip-on earrings, and a clutch purse to match the blue dress. She clipped the earrings onto Meja's lobes, spritzed some perfume, and handed her the clutch. "There! Not bad."

Meja couldn't help but smile. "Thanks, but I feel like I'm going to a costume party."

"Much of life *is* a costume party," said Inez.

They saw the cab pull up through the kitchen window.

"Good luck," Inez said as Meja ran out of the house.

Meja's mouth was bone-dry by the time she ran into the empty foyer of Helsingborg City Theater, five minutes late. The woman who walked her to her seat wasn't impressed by her late arrival.

"This isn't like the movies, where you can come and go as you please. Latecomers disturb the actors," she whispered.

"Sorry," said Meja, feeling her palms become clammy. She followed the woman through the darkened room and had to squeeze past half the row to get to her seat. She double-checked the number on her ticket. Yes, this was right. She glanced at the people next to and behind her.

Susanne and Bengt were nowhere to be seen. Anxiousness was replaced by irritation. So much for their reconciliation. If they had been held up or had to cancel, couldn't Susanne have called?

The reverent silence in the theater made Meja feel restless, and she glanced at her wristwatch, wondering how long she was obliged to stay. A woman came on stage, shortly followed by a man. Meja tried to pay attention to the dialogue but just kept thinking about how much she wanted to leave. Theater, she quickly realized, really wasn't her thing.

Another actress entered. Meja sat bolt upright and leaned forward. She recognized that voice. Surely it couldn't be . . . ? She tried to get a good look at the woman's face. The actress turned to the audience, said one line, and turned away again. Meja let out a squeal. What was her mother doing on stage!? She put her hands on the seat in front and leaned even closer. The woman next to her shifted awkwardly in her seat.

"The rest of us want to see, too," she whispered.

"Sorry," Meja said quietly. "That's . . . my mom."

The woman's stern expression softened slightly. "Oh really? Still, please sit back so the rest of us can see your mom as well."

Meja leaned back in her seat. She felt faint, even though she was sitting down, and couldn't compute a single word of what was said on stage. Her ears were buzzing too loudly. No matter how hard she tried, she just couldn't concentrate.

Then she remembered how Susanne had been speaking angrily to no one in Bengt's apartment. How she said she had something she needed to do which required privacy. Had she been rehearsing a play? If so, why not just tell her? Meja didn't understand.

Meja was taken by surprise when the curtain came down and the lights turned on at the end of act one. While most of the audience streamed into the foyer for wine and coffee, Meja stayed where she was. She read the program. "*The Queen's Tiara*. Nineteenth-century author Carl Jonas Love Almqvist's classic work is an interplay of ever-burning themes such as desire, sex, identity, and guilt."

Meja flicked through to the cast. There, among the supporting actors, was Susanne Skoglund. Meja swallowed hard, tilted her head back, and stared up at the ceiling until the bell rang for act two and the audience poured back in with animated chatter.

The lights went down, the curtain went up, and the actors continued with the performance.

Every time Susanne came on stage, Meja's heart pounded so hard she felt on the verge of tears. Her body felt like Jell-O by the end. The audience gave a standing ovation, whistles, and cries of "Bravo!"

The ensemble ran back onto the stage three times to bow and receive the audience's praise before waving and disappearing behind the curtain.

The audience filtered out. Meja stayed behind. Dead still.

A woman came out from a door at the side of the stage and approached her.

"Are you Meja?" she asked.

Meja nodded.

The woman extended her hand in greeting. "My name is Elin. I'm Bengt's niece, and I work as a makeup artist here at the theater." She took Meja by the arm and led her down the stairs. "Come on. I'll take you to see your mother."

Susanne was still wearing her wig and stage makeup when Meja entered the dressing room. She looked embarrassed.

"If I'd known, I would have bought flowers," said Meja.

Someone uncorked a bottle of champagne, and Meja had a glass in her hand before she could protest.

"My daughter," Meja heard Susanne say to some of the actors.

Susanne finished her drink before eventually looking Meja straight in the eye. "I just have to change, and then hopefully we can have a little chat?"

Meja nodded. *Have a little chat.* She fiddled with her glass and stood back from the others in the room. She couldn't really handle the exuberant atmosphere. She longed to go home to Inez.

Susanne came back without her stage makeup and wig and gestured for Meja to follow her to the foyer bar. She ordered two glasses of white wine and chose a table where they could have a little privacy.

"So," said Meja. All the questions that had been buzzing around her head were suddenly gone.

"So," Susanne said, then also went quiet.

"How are you?" Susanne asked at last.

"Fine," said Meja.

"Good." Susanne sipped her drink. "Thank you for coming."

Meja shrugged. "Inez made me."

Susanne looked at her. "Oh?"

Meja cleared her throat. "So *this* is why I couldn't stay in the guest room?"

Susanne nodded.

"Why didn't you just say so? Why so much secrecy? I don't get it."

Susanne took another sip and put her glass down.

"I can't remember how old I was when I first went to the theater with school. Seven, maybe. We got to go backstage before and after the play. All the other children thought it was boring, but I felt like I was in paradise. Not just the play—everything. The smell of the makeup and old wood, of sweat and wigs. The sound of the actors' voices overlapping, singing and rehearsing lines backstage, the sight of them applying makeup and trying on costumes that were scattered all over the place.

All the stories to be told, to consume the audience and spit them out two hours later, ruffled, shaken, and hopefully moved. I caressed the velvet fabric of the chairs in the audience and gasped as the curtain rose. I cried during sad scenes and laughed during funny ones."

She glanced briefly at Meja and then looked out the window as she continued speaking.

"I ran errands for neighbors to earn money to buy theater tickets. I saw *Oliver Twist* and *Fanny and Alexander* and made up my mind that someday I would come to the theater not as a spectator, but as a performer. All of a sudden my life had purpose, meaning. There was a reason for my existence."

Meja stared at her. "And then you got pregnant, became a single mother, and your dream was shattered."

"I had gotten into the Swedish Institute of Dramatic Art in Stockholm. It was extremely competitive—a lot of people apply two or three times. I got in on the first try. I went on holiday with some girlfriends to Barcelona to celebrate."

"And that's when you got pregnant after a one-night stand with a German bartender."

Susanne nodded.

The revelation took Meja's breath away. All the anxiety that had swam around her head growing up. The feeling of having ruined something, but not knowing what. Susanne could have made it all so much easier if she had just told her. Meja felt the sharp thorns of her mother's disappointment digging into her skin.

"You could have put me up for adoption. Or had an abortion."

Susanne's cheeks turned red.

"Never," she said. "I loved you. I just had such a hard time loving myself when I realized I was never going to be the person I thought I was meant to be. I felt cheated by life. Disappointed and hurt. I wanted to do both—be a mother and an actress—but it didn't work out."

Meja bit her lower lip to force back the tears that were welling up.

"Bengt brought me to this theater because his niece works here. I mentioned my childhood dream, and Elin arranged for me to have an audition." Susanne shook her head. "It was completely surreal. And I got the part, which was incredible considering I have no real theater experience!"

Meja was about to say that she had been acting her whole life, but decided against it and let her mother continue.

"When I got the role, I was so incredibly happy, but also sad." She sighed. "If only I had known when I was younger that my time on stage would come. I might have approached life a little differently."

Meja didn't answer. She was still trying to digest the fact that this had been Susanne's dashed dream all along.

"Don't you understand how much easier everything would have been if you had just told me?"

"I know, but it was easier to pretend the dream never existed. It hurt too much."

Meja sighed, pushed her glass away, and put on her jacket. "Lucky that I don't have a dream, in that case. At least I won't have to go through the same pain." She could hear how childish she sounded.

Susanne looked at her. Her eyes were moist, perhaps from the makeup.

"Of course you have a dream," she said softly.

"No. I really don't," said Meja. "I'm content with a perfectly ordinary life without big dreams. Right now that means living with a slightly crazy writer and a guinea pig with no fur. No more, no less. And you know what? You might not understand this, but I *am* happy. And I hope you are too."

She stood up and got ready to go.

"Well, thank you for coming," said Susanne. Her voice sounded very small.

They looked at each other. Meja swallowed hard. Tears were making Susanne's eyes moist, not makeup.

"Thank you for inviting me," she said and left.

She didn't have to wait long for a bus. When it started to pull away, she let the tears flow.

Back in Domsten, the pines greeted her with their lofty straight backs. She paused and ran her hand over the bark. Warm from the day's sun. It slowed her pulse. Then she continued home to Inez.

Meja found her sitting in her armchair. Inez frowned, got up, and walked over to the drinks cabinet.

"Salty tears can only be wiped away by sweet port," she said, holding out a small glass.

Meja smiled weakly, sank into the other armchair, and sipped the sweet drink.

"Was it a tragedy?" Inez wondered.

"It's always a tragedy when me and my mother get together." Meja leaned back in the armchair and sighed deeply. "But now I know the answer to the biggest mystery of my life. I know what her dream was."

Inez leaned forward. Meja suppressed a smile at her curiosity and enjoyed the suspense.

"Well?" Inez said.

"She wanted to be an actor. She had been accepted into drama school. But then she got pregnant and became, well . . . a single mom. That's where her dream died."

Inez leaned back again and nodded. "You poor thing," she said at last.

"*Me*? Poor *her*!"

Inez shrugged. "Poor both of you. I can't judge single mothers, but her troubled relationship with her own dream must have suffocated yours."

"Does everyone have some big dream? Because I don't think I've ever had one. I just want to live a simple life."

"I disagree," said Inez.

"Oh really?" Meja smiled at Inez's stubborn expression.

"Because I know what your dream is."

"You know what my dream is, even though I don't know myself?"

Inez nodded.

"Right. So what is it then?"

"I'm not going to tell you. You have to figure it out for yourself."

Meja shook her head in amusement and drank the port. "Thanks for the nightcap. You were right. Sweet balances out the salty."

Upstairs, Ingrid was scratching about in her cage. Meja put her on the pillow next to her and thought about the evening. Her mother on stage in the theater. It suited her. It was where she belonged, like Inez and the sea.

"You were the best on stage today, Mom. You really were," she whispered.

INEZ

Rain pattered against the window. Inez peeked through the living room blinds and watched the wind rustling in the rosebush on the other side of the gate, where a bouquet of flowers was whipping around on its string. She sighed, stepped into her rubber boots, and opened the porch door, which flew wide with such force that she almost lost her balance. She swore with her favorite French profanity, *merde*, and went to the gate to untie the string. Rain splashed on the pavers, and she glanced up at the lead-gray clouds before hurrying back inside with the windswept bouquet fluttering in her hand.

She put the flowers in a vase of water and placed them in the middle of the oak table. *You'll be all right*, she thought, even though she wasn't sure if she would be all right after her upcoming writing session.

She brewed a pot of strong coffee and took a shower so hot it turned her skin bright pink. Then she gently smeared on some aloe vera and put on a soft velour dress with no bra. No rough fabrics or seams. She needed everything to be soft today, to protect her from the thorns about to scratch her.

She tidied her desktop so all that remained was her computer, a vanilla-scented candle, a notebook, and a pen. Then she went to put her latest chapter in the blue folder, which she placed beside the flower vase with a note for Meja.

Hi, M. I have to work alone for a while now. Read these chapters. If you feel like making some simple food like soup or hot sandwiches, please leave them on the tray outside the door. Go over and visit Andreas! —I

She took a deep breath. It was time. This was what she had been dreading ever since she started writing this story. The ending.

Before entering the bedroom, she opened all the blinds. She didn't know whether this was for Meja's sake or her own. The clouds were rushing across the sky. She raised her hand and waved. A hello or good-bye. Then she went into the bedroom and shut the door, knowing that when she opened it again, everything would be different.

MEJA

The moment Meja knocked on Andreas's door, she regretted it. When it swung open, a girl with the same warm brown eyes and hair as Andreas was standing on the other side. Meja cleared her throat.

"Sorry to bother you," she said, shifting her weight from one foot to the other. "I'm Meja, and I live next door, or, well, not 'live' exactly, more of a guest, you might say." She was babbling. "I was just wondering if I could borrow some sugar."

Andreas appeared behind his daughter and gave a discreet thumbs-up at the word *sugar*. Meja smiled, a little embarrassed.

"Kattis," said the girl, holding out her hand. "Come in. Dad's just made some coffee. Would you like some?"

Meja was just about to come up with an excuse when Andreas nodded enthusiastically.

"Yes, we'd love for you to join us."

Meja and Andreas sat on the couch while Kattis eagerly fetched the coffee and some oatmeal cookies, then jumped into the armchair and crossed her legs. She leaned forward and looked intently at Meja.

"So you're a guest?"

"Well, it's complicated," said Meja. "I'm staying temporarily with the older woman next door, Inez, who needs some help with, like, organizing her papers and books and stuff."

Kattis leaned back and smiled. "If you'd been accused of a crime, you'd probably have to stay in custody."

Meja looked up in surprise.

"I mean, your story doesn't sound entirely believable. It sounds like you're hiding something."

Meja felt a blush rise, which made Kattis nod in satisfaction.

"Yup. I was right."

"Kattis wants to become a forensic scientist and is watching a lot of cop shows at the moment," Andreas explained.

"I see," said Meja. She watched Kattis sipping her coffee. Didn't thirteen-year-olds drink juice? Or soda at least? Meja hadn't drunk coffee until she was in her thirties. She had trained herself to like it because everyone else did.

"You're right," said Meja. "I'm on a secret mission for Inez."

Kattis lit up and gave Andreas a high five. "I knew it! Am I the best or what?"

Meja smiled. The girl certainly had confidence.

"Dad was very vague when I asked him how he managed to get all this decorating done. But now that I see you here, I get it."

Meja took a deep breath to try to keep from blushing again. Otherwise the girl might get the wrong idea.

Andreas smiled. "Okay, I must admit that I got a little help from my neighbor, the guest with a secret mission."

Kattis smiled widely. "Good job. I kind of prepared myself for a really uncomfortable, messy house, and then I got here and felt like I never want to leave. Plus I found my dad happy, and not all depressed, like I was expecting. Could that also have something to do with the mysterious neighbor?"

Meja shook her head and cleared her throat, and Andreas waved his hand dismissively and mumbled something inaudible.

"We're all friends here. There's Sverker and Filip, too, who live on the other side of Inez," she said. She sounded like a teenager pretending to be an adult.

Kattis smirked and Meja saw a twinkle in her eye from the conclusions she was drawing.

"So you're into photography?" Kattis said, pointing at Meja's camera on the table. She had brought it out to photograph the storm.

"Sometimes," said Meja.

"Can you take a picture of us?"

Andreas opened his mouth as if to protest, but Meja nodded and removed the lens cap. Kattis sat down next to Andreas and smiled widely.

"I prefer to take candid pictures, when people are absorbed in what they're doing and aren't really aware that they're being photographed," said Meja.

Kattis jumped up from the couch. "Okay. Dad, why don't you show me your paints and how you use them?"

Meja let them start a conversation and kept her distance. Soon Andreas was so engrossed in his paints that both he and Kattis actually did seem to forget that Meja was there. She took lots of pictures.

"Can I see?" Kattis said when Meja put the camera down after a while.

"Absolutely."

Kattis silently scrolled through the pictures. When she looked up, her face was different. Captivated.

"Can you email these to me? If you don't mind, that is."

Meja nodded. Kattis showed Andreas one of the pictures.

"Wow," he said.

Meja smiled. "Well, I'd better go."

Andreas walked her out, and Kattis disappeared into the kitchen. Meja was just about to leave when Kattis reappeared holding a small plastic container.

"The sugar," she said.

Meja didn't understand at first, then smiled. "Right. The sugar."

Kattis rolled her eyes. "I see. The secretive neighbor used sugar as a sly maneuver to meet the daughter."

"Oh no!" said Meja. "We did need sugar. For a cake. Inez likes to bake and didn't want to go out in the rain. She can't risk a fall because she cracked her pelvis about a month ago and—"

"Too many details make a story less believable. See ya," Kattis whispered and winked at Meja before closing the door.

Was that girl really only thirteen years old? Meja pulled up her hood and ran over to Inez's house.

She could hear Inez typing from her room. She made lunch—pea soup and grilled cheese—and left some outside Inez's door, per her instructions. Then she took her own lunch and the blue folder up to the guest room.

She ate at the desk and read chapter after chapter. Rain whipped against the window. By the time she had read the last page, she felt broken. She started bustling around and tidying in an attempt to rid her body of this uncomfortable feeling.

As she hung up yesterday's dress, she recalled the play. It still didn't feel real. She put the borrowed clip-on earrings into a jewelry box that Inez kept on a shelf above the bed, and something in the box caught her eye. A small key on a necklace. The key to the desk drawer? She tried it in the keyhole and heard a faint click. With a gulp, she carefully pulled on the small brass handle. The drawer was empty but for one thing: a small, black, well-thumbed notebook. Meja held her breath and stared at the book. Could it be *that* notebook? Inez's journal from Kobbholmen?

She shut and locked the drawer, as quietly as possible, and put the key back in the jewelry box on the shelf. Her heart was racing.

She went onto the balcony and looked up at the dark clouds and pouring rain. There were two conflicting feelings in the pit of her stomach. Warmth at the sight of Andreas's garden illuminated by the lamps in the rain. And dread thinking of the chapters she had just read. How was this story going to end?

1976

I don't know what provoked Nikolas's rage. Maybe I had asked him to take the baby for a little while because she had screamed constantly for the first two weeks of her life and wouldn't let me sleep. Maybe I had asked him to change her diaper for once. Or maybe I just happened to look at him in the wrong way, with too much fatigue in my eyes. But the first blow on that day was unlike any other. More enraged. It usually started with a slap. This time it was a clenched fist.

I lost my balance and fell onto a table edge, piercing my temple. Metallic-tasting blood ran into my mouth. I couldn't get up. He kept doling out the punches. The baby was screaming desperately, as usual. It was so awful when her little lungs ran out of air; her skin turned blue before the convulsions eased and let her draw breath again. Then she'd resume howling and start the process all over again.

I grabbed the table leg and tried to rise to my knees, but couldn't. Blood vessels burst beneath my skin, but I was numb to the pain. I couldn't think of myself. I could only think of my daughter in need of comforting.

I don't know how long it lasted. Shock makes time elastic. It might have only been a few minutes; it felt like a day. By the end, my body couldn't take any more. My eyelids had swollen shut and I couldn't see. My lungs wheezed when I breathed. All I could think was: *I'm sorry.* Sorry for my daughter.

What happened next was a blur. The smell of the sea wafted past my bruised face. I felt Mathilda's hair fall over my cheek and her warm fingers search my neck for a pulse. I mustered all my strength to try to move my hand but couldn't so much as lift a pinkie.

Soon I could smell baby skin and feel a trembling little mouth searching for the breast while Mathilda called for an ambulance. Before I was lifted onto the stretcher, I heard her whisper, *I would do anything for you.*

It was the last thing I ever heard Mathilda say. Only several weeks later did I understand the true meaning of those words.

INEZ

It was three in the morning, and Inez had been staring at the computer screen for several hours. Her hands were clasped in her lap, as though in a straitjacket. She got up and went into the living room. The rain had stopped but the sky was still dark—angry—and the wind was tearing and tugging at the bushes outside. She put on her rubber boots and windbreaker and walked to Viola's bench, struggling to keep her balance in the violent gusts.

She thought about what she had written and what came next.

Mathilda called an ambulance. Inez underwent four operations for internal injuries, came close to losing her life twice, and miraculously survived. She focused on her own slow recovery and Amelia's well-being.

Two weeks after her ordeal, she found out that Nikolas was dead. He had died that same night. Two weeks and one day after her ordeal, she found out Mathilda had been accused of his murder.

Inez sat down on the bench and closed her eyes. Mathilda had disappeared after Inez was admitted to the hospital, and no one knew where she was. She had left an oyster shell on the bedside table in Inez's hospital room. It was the first thing Inez saw when she opened her eyes after ten days under sedation. Her heart raced so wildly she thought it might burst out of her chest as she slowly picked up the shell. She turned it over and saw the message carved on the underside. *You know where the answer lies.*

She stayed in the hospital for a total of three months before she was allowed to go home. During this time, she wrote *The Daughters of the Sea* while Amelia slept. The nurses told her to rest, but she just wrote and wrote. Not only for her own sake. For Mathilda's too. She would write the book Mathilda had encouraged her to write. It was the least, and the most, she could do. By the time she left the hospital three months later, she had finished a first draft. Beginning, middle, end. A book about friendship. A fictional story, whose power and pulse had come from real life.

Inez stared at the sea until her teeth began to rattle in the icy wind. Then she went home.

She took off her outdoor clothes and sat down at the computer. She didn't clasp her hands this time. She set them free to tell the story of what happened next.

1976

There are no words to describe the surreal feeling of opening the front door to our little house in Kobbholmen after three months in the hospital. My brain refused to accept that Nikolas wasn't there anymore, and I spent the first few days tiptoeing around and constantly looking over my shoulder.

My daughter was three months and two weeks old and would lie on her blanket on the floor, gurgling contentedly. No more colic. I mainly just sat next to her, unable to do anything. A woman from the Red Cross, Katarina Ek, whom I had gotten to know during my hospital stay and now considered an invaluable friend, had been kind enough to clean out the fridge, collect the bills, and water the plants. Now she had put a fruit platter on the table with a card: *Welcome home.*

But it didn't feel like my home.

On the third day, I put my daughter in her stroller, put the oyster shell in my pocket, and went to Mathilda's hut.

Amelia slept soundly in the fresh evening air, and I sat on a rock gazing at the calmly lapping sea. I picked up the oyster shell and read the words once more. *You know where the answer lies.*

Yes, I knew. Mathilda used to write little messages in oyster shells and drop them on the sea floor for me to find. Usually it was just a beautiful word or two. *Friendship, Love,* or similar. I had kept them all in a shoebox hidden in my closet so Nikolas wouldn't find them and throw them away.

I put the shell back in my pocket. The next day I would ask Katarina to watch Amelia and go search for the message at the bottom of the sea. Then I would take my daughter to live where we belonged. With Mathilda.

MEJA

Rain was hanging in the air when Meja woke up. Downstairs, she found no new chapters on the table and heard no sounds coming from Inez's bedroom. She made tea, toast, and boiled eggs, knocked gently on Inez's door, and sat down at the oak table in the living room.

She had slept badly, tossing and turning, her head full of thoughts. It had finally dawned on her: She was never going back to Johan's apartment. She didn't live there anymore. This wasn't a break; it was *the end*. She needed a home of her own. And to get one, she needed a proper job. There was no more cleaning to do at Inez's house, and there couldn't be much left of the story she was writing. Once the final page was written, there would be nothing left for her to do here.

She pushed her breakfast away and drank the tea while looking out the window. Fat raindrops had started to fall. There was one task that she hadn't even started. She may as well get on with it.

She fetched a kitchen knife and went out to Inez's paved yard. There were no lights on in Andreas's house. He and Kattis were probably still asleep. She dropped to her knees and began scraping weeds from between the tiles. Raindrops fell into her eyes, and her dressing gown became heavy with moisture and dirty with mud. Meja continued scraping, picking, pulling. Images of Inez, the blue folder, Johan, Susanne flickered past. She let them come and go. Her body was trembling with cold and adrenaline. Occasionally she wiped the rain—and maybe tears, too, she wasn't sure—from her eyes. It left earthy trails on her cheeks.

She carried on pulling weeds until her arm was almost numb and didn't raise her chin until she felt a hand on her shoulder. It was Sverker. Meja stared at him. He gave her a kind smile, then helped her up and led her into his house. He fetched a towel and dry dressing gown and started the shower for her.

Without a word, she closed the bathroom door, let the wet, earthy bathrobe and pajamas fall to the floor, and stepped into the hot shower. What had come over her? Had she really been on all fours pulling up weeds in a rainstorm? Sverker must have thought she'd lost her mind. She turned off the shower, put on the three-sizes-too-large dressing gown, ran her hands through her hair, and went into the living room. Sverker was sitting there with a pot of tea and two mugs. He nodded for her to sit down.

"Thank you," she said, gesturing to the soft terry-cloth dressing gown he had lent her. "I don't know what happened . . ."

"It's good to weed in the rain. They come out easier." He smiled.

Meja nodded slowly. "But maybe better in a raincoat."

"Yes, maybe," said Sverker.

They sat in silence for a while, sipping their tea. Meja looked around. The whole room was like a warm embrace. It made her well up. She tried to wipe the corners of her eyes without Sverker seeing. But he saw.

"Sometimes the uphill parts of life are really steep. But there is always a downhill when you get to the top. Believe me. And when you rush down, you'll feel that glorious flutter in your belly again."

"Have you ever had a dream come true?" Meja asked.

Sverker didn't have to think. "Yes, I wanted to find love. The great love of my life."

"And then you met Filip."

"Exactly. Once I had fulfilled that dream, it was as if all the other pieces of the puzzle fell into place as well. I guess the word would be *harmony*."

Meja sighed. "At the moment I have no harmony, no dream, no corner pieces in my life puzzle."

"They are there somewhere. Keep searching."

Meja tried to smile, but it came out as a grimace.

"Promise," said Sverker.

Meja drank up. "Thanks for the tea and clothing. I'll bring it back later."

Sverker nodded and followed her onto the porch. He craned his neck to see into Inez's yard.

"Every cloud has a silver lining. You've managed to remove a lot of weeds."

Meja smiled and scurried through the rain back to Inez's house. She went up to the guest room and had just lain down on the bed when her phone beeped. It was a message from her mother.

Are we going to continue with our dinners? If so, see you tonight, same time, same place.

Meja bit her lower lip. Were they really going to continue like everything was normal? Nothing was normal anymore.

She sent back an OK, pulled a pillow over her face, and made a whimpering noise before turning onto her side and falling asleep.

In the afternoon, she removed the untouched tray from outside Inez's room and replaced it with a bowl of minestrone soup and a note saying that she was going out but would be back in an hour or two. *Call if you need anything,* she concluded and went to the bus stop.

Nerves gnawed at her stomach. It felt strange going to see Susanne again. Now that she knew. She figured Susanne had already returned to her old self. Perhaps with slightly more animated gestures and a laugh an octave higher now that she had finally fulfilled her life's dream.

Meja leaned her head against the window and kept her eyes closed all the way to Central Station. The restaurant was a couple of minutes' walk from there. She dragged her feet in an attempt to put off the inevitable.

Susanne was sitting where she always sat: at the bar under the crystal chandelier. She raised her hand slightly when Meja entered. Meja did the same. They were seated at their table, and the waitress asked if they would like to start with something to drink.

"A glass of champagne, please," Susanne said and turned to Meja. "What do you want?"

Meja raised her eyebrows. It was the first time Susanne hadn't just ordered for her, too, without asking. Maybe this dinner would be different after all.

"A glass of white, please. Chardonnay."

Susanne smiled. "Knowing what you want suits you," she said, laying her cloth napkin in her lap.

"I've always known what I want," said Meja. "*Not* wanting anything in particular is also a preference."

Susanne smiled. They both ordered fish and shellfish soup and Meja fiddled with her wineglass.

"So, how's the play going?"

"Very well," said Susanne. "Sold out and standing ovations. We couldn't ask for more."

"But how does it *feel*? Is it everything you dreamed it would be?"

Susanne sipped her drink. "It's better."

Meja had expected bragging, but Susanne focused on Meja instead. "You look tired," she said with concern.

"I didn't sleep very well last night."

"Won't you move into our guest room for a while? It can't be good to live at your place of work."

Meja was saved by the food being served.

"It smells wonderful," she said, inhaling the aroma.

Susanne dropped the topic of Meja's temporary accommodations and started talking instead about Bengt's fantastic cooking skills and all the conferences he had planned for the fall. Harmless topics. Meja murmured in agreement and slipped in a few words about how he seemed very nice, but mostly sat in silence. Susanne put down her spoon and dabbed her lips with the napkin.

"What are you going to do when you've finished cleaning that lady's house?" she asked.

Here it comes, thought Meja.

"I've already finished the cleaning. We're working on a new project now."

"Project?" said Susanne.

"Yes, a writing project. We'll see what happens next."

"Well, I know what you *should* be doing."

"I bet you do," said Meja, glancing at the time.

They had both finished their mains and didn't usually order dessert. Soon she could excuse herself and leave.

"I have to confess something," said Susanne. "When you were staying in the guest room, you left your camera in the living room one day. I looked at your pictures. Sorry, I know I should have asked first, but I couldn't help it."

Meja glared at Susanne. She didn't mind showing people her pictures. But looking at them without permission was like reading her journal.

Susanne leaned forward. "They're good, Meja. Better than good."

"Mm-hmm." Meja didn't know what she was implying, and Susanne didn't elaborate. She just beckoned to the waitress and paid.

They both got up at the same time. It was still gray and windy outside. Susanne folded up the collar of her coat and adjusted the thin shawl around her neck.

"Well, then. Take care now," she said and nodded goodbye.

"You too," Meja said and watched her mother walk away.

She didn't know which was more difficult to digest, the fact that Susanne had sneaked a peek at her pictures, or that she had praised her for them.

When Meja walked through Inez's now almost weed-free garden half an hour later, she hoped she would find Inez sitting in her armchair. She needed her company and harsh comments. It was in the silence of solitude that Meja doubted everything. But she found the house dark and the soup untouched.

Meja hung up her coat and went to take the tray away. She pressed her ear against the door. Not a sound.

Out of the corner of her eye she saw the blue folder on the living room table. New chapters. Her stomach clenched.

She made a pot of coffee, left one cup outside Inez's door, and took the folder into the guest room. Was this the beginning of the end? Of the story, and of Meja's time with Inez?

1976

I woke up and looked over at the crib where Amelia was fast asleep. As usual, she had kicked off her blanket. I sat up and stretched my back, stiff from my abysmal sleeping position on the couch. I hadn't opened the bedroom door since I'd gotten home from the hospital. In fact, I had stayed exclusively in the living room and kitchen. Close to Amelia at all times. When darkness fell, I would hold her tightly in my arms and stare out the window, half expecting to see Nikolas return, even though I knew he was dead. His presence was so pervasive in the house and in my memory that I even apologized to him when I dropped the cheese on the floor.

I gazed at Amelia and carefully put her in the stroller in a snowsuit and under a blanket. She grumbled a little but settled down. I dressed warmly in a coat, scarf, and gloves and greeted the early morning. The air was heavy, as if anticipating snowfall. When I came to the cemetery, I began searching for his grave. Katarina from the Red Cross had said to turn right from the gate and go straight for twenty yards. I pulled the stroller slowly behind me along the gravel path and read the headstones. *Beloved, missed* . . . There. I stopped. My pulse raced. I leaned forward. On the tombstone was written: *Nikolas Fridén Born 4/5 1936 Died 8/8 1976*. The stone was decorated with an engraved dove of peace.

I took a deep breath, rocked the stroller to soothe Amelia's whines, and hurried back home to feed her.

Today was an important day. One of the most important of my life. I was going to look for the oyster shell with Mathilda's message about her destination. There was already speculation in the local paper that she had killed herself, because she had left a note confessing to Nikolas's murder and was unlikely to escape punishment.

I changed Amelia's diaper, fed her, and prepared myself for what was to come. I had to think like Mathilda for a while. I knew that she would have made it easy enough for me to find the shell but too difficult for anyone else. Which meant it wouldn't be in the shallow oyster bank where you could stand in wading boots and see the bottom with an aquascope. That would be too risky. I would have to dive into the cold water. Even though I hated it. Where? *With the seals. It must be with the seals.*

The thought made my stomach flutter. There were still four hours left before Katarina would come to babysit Amelia. I would travel as light as possible, with only a backpack. I couldn't risk arousing suspicion and leading the police to Mathilda's trail. I sterilized a couple of baby bottles, packed some diapers, my passport, money, two changes of clothes for me, and five for Amelia. Then I sat down and waited for Katarina.

A knock on the door made me jump. I crept up to the window and peered out from behind the curtain. The mailman? I opened the door a crack.

"Hello, I have an envelope that's too big for your mailbox," he said, holding out a large, thick padded envelope. I saw that it was from Alma Britzelius Publishing.

"Thank you," I said and closed the door.

I had submitted my manuscript to the publisher but didn't think I would hear back so soon. I put Amelia on the blanket and opened the envelope.

Thank you for your manuscript. Your story about friendship was gripping and entertaining. We would like to publish it. Please find enclosed your submission with some comments in the margins—I couldn't help but start on it after reading in your lovely letter that you sent it to us exclusively. Call when you receive this and we can discuss the contract and how to proceed. Very much looking forward to our collaboration. —Cristy McDonald

Amelia lay perfectly still, brought her hand to her mouth, and looked at me seriously. As if she understood the significance of the situation.

Tears started to flow at the same time as laughter bubbled up.

"Look," I whispered, holding up the contract. "Your mother is going to be a writer. An author!"

I took her in my arms and was dancing around the living room when there was another knock on the door.

Katarina. I must have looked confused because she asked gingerly if today was the right day. Should she take Amelia now? I stared at the girl in my arms and then at my new friend from the Red Cross.

"Yes, of course," I said. "I just got such good news that I totally lost track of time and space."

Katarina took Amelia in her arms and smiled. "That's great to hear. You deserve some good news."

I brought my hands to my flushed cheeks and smiled. My whole body was fizzing like a carbonated drink. My book was going to be published. I couldn't wait to tell Mathilda. She would be so happy. After all, it was thanks to her. She had shown me the way to my words.

I went to my closet and got out the shoebox with all the engraved shells I had collected over the years. I would leave them at the hut. I couldn't take them with me and didn't need them anymore. I just needed one shell. The one I was about to look for.

I put on my coat and scarf and ran all the way to Mathilda's hut, lonely where it stood on the pier. But instead of going in and getting the snorkel equipment and other things that I would need to find the oyster shell, I continued up to the cliff where I used to sit every Saturday morning, battered and bruised, watching Mathilda take her boat out. I sat down and looked out over the bay. The water was so still. Perfect weather for oyster diving.

"I've got a book deal, Mathilda," I whispered. "A contract. Just like you always said I would. It's thanks to you. Because you said I had a beginning, middle, and end. Soon we'll celebrate my first published book. You and I."

INEZ

In the old days, Inez always used to smoke a cigar when she finished her first draft. She never smoked otherwise. Maybe she should . . . She got up from the armchair and slowly walked up the creaking stairs with a firm grip on the banister. One careful step at a time so as not to strain her pelvis too much. It was getting a lot better.

Upstairs was a small space: a bathroom and two small rooms. One was the guest room, where Meja was staying, and the other was . . . well, what was it exactly? Inez opened the door, fumbled for the switch, and squinted as the room was illuminated. This was where she kept all her clothes, hats, jewelry, high-heeled shoes, and sparkly shawls. Framed articles and gold certificates for numbers of books sold were hung on the walls. Along one side was a built-in bookcase displaying all her books in all the languages they had been translated into, and in the bureau under the window were letters from readers. On top of the bureau, next to the only upholstered piece of furniture in the room, a green velvet armchair, was the humidor Cristy had given her when her first book was published. It had been fifteen years since she had smoked her last cigar, but she came in here periodically to check the humidity. It had been a while.

She sat down in the armchair, opened the lid of the humidor, and let the sweet smell of tobacco tickle her nose. She was just about to reach for a cigar when Meja appeared in the doorway, sleepy-eyed and wearing a nightgown, her hair tousled.

"You have a walk-in closet!" she said in a hoarse voice. Inez smiled and nodded for her to sit on the Indian stool covered with patchwork silk fabric. Cristy always used to sit there and jot down to-do lists while Inez got dressed up for some gala.

Meja looked around the room.

"Wow," she whispered.

"I should have gotten rid of all this stuff long ago," Inez said, taking a cigar out of the humidor and sniffing it. "Maybe this should be your next cleaning project?"

Meja shook her head. "Never. You should keep it. It's your life, after all. May I?" She looked at the wall of clothes. Inez nodded. Meja browsed through the clothes, pausing now and then to caress a fabric.

"A gold mine of vintage," she said.

"Try something on."

Meja shook her head at first, but then her eyes locked onto a dark-blue corduroy pantsuit with a wide belt at the waist and breast pockets. She looked from the suit to Inez, who nodded eagerly. Meja carefully took it off the hanger, stood with her back to Inez, and put it on.

Inez grabbed the armrests and stood up to take a closer look. "I don't believe it. It looks tailor-made for you."

Inez walked over to the hat rack, poked around for a while, and found what she was looking for. A matching fluffy beret. She put it on Meja's head and turned her to face the full-length mirror in its ornate gold frame. Meja stared at herself. Inez smiled.

"This is you," she said. "You don't think you like fashion or have style. But that's only because you haven't found your style yet. *This* is it."

Meja swallowed hard, caressed the fabric with her hands, and admired herself from different angles. "This *is* me. I'm vintage."

"You sure are. Let's celebrate with a cigar." Inez cut the cigar, but Meja snatched it away.

"Not here among all these beautiful clothes."

Inez laughed. "Okay, downstairs then. Keep that outfit. It fits you like a glove."

"Can I?"

"Of course. I'll never fit into it again."

Meja smiled, took Inez by the arm, and led her down the stairs and out to the porch.

In one corner stood two stacked rattan chairs. Meja set them in the middle of the porch and brushed them off as best she could.

"Is madame happy now?" said Inez, sitting down, lighting the cigar, and puffing to get it going.

"I didn't know you smoked," said Meja, wrinkling her nose.

"I don't. Only one cigar to celebrate finishing a first draft."

Meja widened her eyes. "You've finished?"

Inez held out the cigar. "Don't inhale. Hold the smoke in your mouth and then let it out."

Meja did as she was told, carefully drawing in the smoke, holding it in her mouth, then exhaling. They took turns a few times before Meja shook her head and let Inez have the rest.

"So, when do I get to read the ending?"

"Soon," said Inez. She looked Meja up and down. "But first you need to go somewhere to test whether your new style feels right."

Meja laughed. "Like where?"

Inez shrugged. "Go and see Andreas. Make up a reason. See how it feels. I have lots of clothes in need of a new owner."

"It's only nine o'clock, isn't it?"

"I've run into him early in the morning a few times. I'm sure he'll be up and about."

Meja shook her head with a smile, adjusted her beret slightly, and left to go next door.

Inez sighed contentedly. It was satisfying watching Meja blossom. She probably wasn't aware of the transformation she was going through, but Inez could see how much she was changing with each passing week.

She looked up at the sky and thought about how grateful she was to Spick & Span for sending her here. It hadn't always been easy, but Meja's light balanced out Inez's darkness. Without Meja, this book probably would have killed her. Her gentle care and unassuming personality were like cotton wool; they cushioned Inez's fall. Inez pushed the cigar stub down into the flower bed, which contained nothing but a few scrubby bushes, and went inside to make breakfast.

MEJA

The world felt fuzzy around the edges when Meja left Inez's garden. Was it the cigar on an empty stomach? Or was this pantsuit and beret combo making her feel like a new person—invincible? Either way, laughter bubbled up inside her and her footsteps felt more floaty than heavy. She saw Sverker in workout gear approaching at a vigorous pace.

"My new habit: a brisk walk every morning!" he said with a wave. He looked her up and down. "And there was me lamenting the lack of sunshine. Who needs sun when you look so luminous!"

"Today is a better day." Meja smiled.

"So I see. Maybe the downhill is near?"

"Maybe," said Meja, thinking that she did feel an undeniable flutter in her gut. He said a cheery goodbye and went home.

The light was on in Andreas's living room. Excitement turned into nerves. Suddenly she felt ridiculous in this beret and pantsuit from the 1980s. She was just about to turn back when the door opened.

"Oh," said Andreas. "I thought I saw someone standing outside."

"I just wanted to . . . borrow some sugar."

Andreas laughed and let her in. "Coffee?"

"Please."

Meja rubbed her hands together. She had to come up with a good excuse that didn't make her sound crazy, but her head was blank.

"Nice outfit," he said.

"It's Inez's. I got to peek into her closet. It's like a treasure chest." Meja smiled sheepishly as he sniffed the air around her. "That's cigar smoke. Also from Inez's closet."

"Sounds like a very curious closet."

Meja sat on the couch and looked up at the canvas on the wall, which was no longer white. She recognized the place represented in the brushstrokes.

"Viola's bench!" she said.

Andreas smiled. "Yes, I figured there was no need to look elsewhere with such a great subject right on my doorstep." He tilted his head slightly. "Thank you, by the way, for coming to visit when Kattis was here. She was so happy when she went home."

"I hope she didn't . . . you know . . . jump to any conclusions," Meja said.

Andreas laughed. "If she does, that's on me."

Meja sipped her coffee.

"Stay right there," he said, hurrying over to his painting corner.

He dragged out an easel, a blank canvas, and a palette of leftover paints. Then he stood opposite her and started painting. Meja was embarrassed at first but soon forgot to be self-conscious. He was so easy to talk to. Afterward she could hardly remember what they had spoken about, she just felt pleasantly calm.

"Can I see?" said Meja as he put down the brush.

"Not yet. I need to refine it first. I'll let you know when it's ready."

They had long since finished their coffee. Meja put the empty mug on the table and got ready to leave.

"Thanks for the coffee and chat. And good luck with the painting," she said.

"You didn't need any sugar this time either, did you?" he said when he opened the porch door.

She shook her head with a smile and concentrated on looking casual, even though she could feel his eyes boring into her as she walked away.

Inez was waiting for her at the oak table with breakfast laid out. Meja sat down with a thump just like Inez usually did.

"The outfit went down well," Meja said.

"Excellent." Inez smiled and passed her some bread. "Then you can go upstairs and carry on browsing through the clothes."

Meja's eyes fell on the blue folder on the other side of the table. The final pages. She swallowed hard and looked at Inez, who patted her lightly on the hand. It was a comforting gesture. The only question was whether Inez was comforting Meja or herself.

They said nothing. Meja's jubilant mood seeped away and was replaced with a niggling ache in the pit of her stomach. She forced down her breakfast and tidied up.

Inez remained seated. Suddenly she looked so old and lonely. Meja bit her lower lip. She wanted to hug her and tell her that everything was going to be okay, but instead she picked up the folder, carefully, as if it were made of delicate glass, went up the creaking steps, and shut herself in the guest room.

Three hours later, she put the folder down and stared up at the ceiling.

It was a good ending. Inez had found the shell saying that Mathilda had gone to Palermo, Italy. She had visited her there but ultimately continued to live in Stockholm with Amelia to focus on her career and not draw attention to Mathilda.

A feel-good ending. The readers would want Mathilda to be safe. She deserved it. And yet . . . Meja narrowed her eyes. Something wasn't right. Something about Inez's style of writing. Every single sentence on the previous pages had felt as if it were written in her own blood. The words cut straight to the heart. The last chapters were different. No blood. No pulse. No authenticity.

Something occurred to Meja. She took the desk key from the jewelry box and let it rest in her palm for a moment. Then she opened the drawer and took out the little black notebook. She ran her fingers across the leather cover and flipped through the pages at random. The journal entries became denser and sloppier toward the end. She was just about to start reading when her mobile phone beeped. It made her jump.

It was from Inez. Shall we fix lunch?

Overwhelmed with guilt for snooping, she quickly put the notebook and key back with trembling hands. Then she took a deep breath, scolded herself, and went downstairs.

Inez was standing in the kitchen. "Omelet?"

Meja nodded. "But I can make it. You just relax in the living room."

Inez didn't protest.

Meja prepared an omelet with tomato and leek and served it on two cobalt-blue plates. Inez didn't seem to have much appetite, despite lunch having been her suggestion.

"We should buy some plants and put them there," Inez said, staring at the windowsill.

Meja put her cutlery down. They needed to talk.

"It was a good ending," she said. "Does she still live in Palermo?" No answer. "What are you going to do with the book now?"

"I'll put it into my bank deposit box for storage."

"But you're going to publish it, right?"

Inez turned to look at her. "Yes. Posthumously."

Meja, who had just drunk a sip of water, choked and coughed into her napkin.

"I don't understand," she said.

Inez looked out the window. "I wrote this book because I had to. Not for pleasure, not for work. It's an explanation for the books I have spent my life writing, for why I am who I am. It's an explanation for Amelia. For her to understand, and maybe forgive me. But you're the only one who knows the story, and I want it to stay that way for the time being. You might call it my final statement, balancing the accounts."

"But—" Meja began.

"I don't want to answer any questions about my past. I don't want to explain any more than I have already. I just want to tell my story. As I have."

"You're not sick, are you?" Meja said. "Is that why you've written this now?"

Inez smiled weakly. "Now you sound like my daughter again. No, I'm fit as a fiddle. My neighbor Viola passed away shortly before you started cleaning my place. She was in excellent health before she died suddenly. That's when I decided to get my story down on paper. You never know when your time will come—even if you're healthy."

"You promise you're telling the truth?"

"Promise," said Inez. "You'll have to put up with me for a little longer yet."

Meja smiled, but the smile quickly died on her lips. She had to bring up the subject she had been avoiding for long enough.

"So if you've finished the book, does that mean my job here is done?" she said softly.

Inez nodded. "But I enjoy your company, believe it or not, and I hate cooking, as you know, and would never buy flowers and dress the windows myself. And I have money to pay someone else to do it. Besides, I think rooms languish without people to inhabit them, and I'm glad that the guest room, which is actually my favorite room in the house, has an inhabitant to take care of."

From this mess of words Meja came to the conclusion that she wanted her to stay. But she couldn't stay here forever.

"Of course you have your own life to live," Inez added. "But just for now, until you find your way. You have taken one step on the road, and that is to find your style. It may seem superficial and frivolous, but it isn't. Presenting your style to others means putting your self-esteem on display. And self-esteem can lead to opportunities beyond your imagination. Now get up there and rummage through my closet!"

She tried to sound jovial, which once again made Meja want to hug her. But Inez wasn't the kind of person you could just hug.

"How was it at Andreas's house?" Inez said.

Meja felt her face get hot. "I posed for him."

"What?"

"Well, fully clothed, of course," said Meja.

Inez chuckled. "I should hope so. How did it come out?"

"I don't know—he wouldn't show me."

"Exciting."

This seemed to cheer Inez up. She ate her cold omelet and hummed to herself as she carried the plates into the kitchen.

"I could go shopping for food and flowers now," said Meja.

"Yes, please do. But first, look in the closet for a red leather purse. It would go perfectly with your outfit."

Meja shook her head but did as she was told. She paused to admire herself in the large mirror.

Was Inez right? Was this her? The real Meja?

INEZ

Inez wrapped a shawl around her shoulders and went outside. Warm winds caressed her cheeks as she followed the path down to the pier, nodding briefly at dog owners and passersby. The sea's waves were calm. Inez stood at the end of the pier and listened to its gentle breathing.

"Is it okay that I wrote your story like this, Mathilda?" she whispered.

She tried to tell herself that a gentle lapping wave at the pier arm was a sign of approval. She bit her lower lip to keep from crying. The truth stuck like a thorn in her heart. It would sit there until the day she died.

She shivered, despite the warm weather, and pulled her shawl tighter around her. What if some journalist started digging into her past, searching for the true ending? But why would they? Her life wasn't all that interesting. And anyway, they'd never find Mathilda. If she could be found, Inez would have found her a long time ago.

When Inez got back, Sverker was in his yard.

"How would my favorite neighbors like to come over for afternoon tea in the garden today? It's such wonderful weather," he said.

Inez considered the offer. Meja would certainly enjoy it, and she deserved a little fun.

"That would be lovely," she said. "Shall I ask Andreas too?"

Sverker smiled. "Please do. In an hour?"

"Can we bring something?" Inez said.

"Absolutely not," said Sverker, who was already on his way inside to prepare.

Inez went to knock on Andreas's door.

"Back-door guests are best!" he said, wiping paint from his hands on a rag.

"It's been a long time since I was included in the 'best guests' category," she said with a smile. "Sverker and Filip want to invite the neighbors for a spontaneous afternoon tea in the garden. Would you like to join us?"

"I'd be delighted."

Inez craned her neck to catch a glimpse of Andreas's painting.

"Go in and look if you want, but it hasn't dried yet."

Inez entered without taking off her shoes. Andreas seemed to have captured the newfound self-esteem that Meja had radiated in her blue pantsuit. The sense of a long-missing puzzle piece finally finding its place.

She nodded slowly. "Spot on," she said.

Andreas half smiled and put his hands in his pockets in that characteristic way of his. Inez gave him a gentle pat on the arm and turned to the painting on the wall.

"Viola's bench!" she exclaimed.

Andreas laughed. "It's for you. It was supposed to be a surprise."

"Oh, I hate surprises. I much prefer looking forward to something I know is coming."

They said they would see each other in an hour and Inez left. But she didn't feel like going home. She went to Viola's bench instead, where she sat and took a deep breath.

"I've written the book, I've survived rehashing the memories, I've made friends with the neighbors I've been avoiding for so long, I've got both an assistant and a project in Meja. I'll make a woman of her yet.

I've even opened the blinds, for pity's sake! It's time to move on. To live," she said softly to herself.

"Did I hear my name?" a voice said behind her.

Inez turned around to see Meja holding shopping bags, red in the face and sweaty around the temples. Inez patted the bench for her to sit down and took her by the hand.

"Now she has found peace," Inez said, more to herself than to Meja.

"The sea?" Meja asked.

Inez nodded. "Yes. The sea."

They sat gazing at the sea and sky for a long time.

"Come on," Inez said eventually. "Let's go back and freshen up a bit. We're invited to Sverker and Filip's for afternoon tea."

Back home, Meja unpacked the groceries while Inez put on a fresh white blouse and linen pants.

"Go and see what you can find in my wardrobe," she said when Meja was finished in the kitchen.

"I couldn't. They're your clothes."

"Don't be silly. They don't fit me anymore, and I'd rather they were used."

Meja was hesitant but went upstairs anyway. Half an hour later she came downstairs, showered and wearing a formfitting orange dress with wide sleeves and a white psychedelic pattern. She did a twirl.

Inez applauded. "You look like a younger version of me."

"Oh, I wish. But not even close."

Inez snorted. "Much closer than you think. You have to get into the mindset." She tapped her fingers to her temples for emphasis.

They were about to leave when Meja stopped. "Shouldn't we bring something?" she said.

"How about some of the flowers you bought?"

"I think you should give them one of your books—signed," she said. "Sverker is, like, your biggest fan."

Inez sighed. Maybe Meja was right. Maybe this was a necessary part of her fresh start—accepting her past self. Actually enjoying her identity as a successful author. Enjoy being remembered, if only by some.

"You're right," she said.

She went over to the bookcase, took out a copy of her last novel, and wrote: *For Sverker and Filip, with thanks for all the lovely occasions in your home. Your friendship is as beautiful as the ones in my books.* And she signed her name. Her autograph was the same as ever.

Meja smiled contentedly as they walked to Sverker and Filip's house. Andreas came out at the same time and joined them.

On the garden table were roses arranged in large vases, plump English teapots, baskets of scones, homemade marmalade, cream cheese, and pear brandy.

Inez handed over the book. Sverker's eyes opened wide. He flipped to the first page, read Inez's words, and blinked away the tears that appeared in the corners of his eyes.

"Thank you," he whispered.

They sat down and everyone helped themselves to scones, tea, and brandy. Meja snapped a few pictures. Filip complimented her dress.

"Is that also from the treasure trove?" said Andreas.

"Treasure trove?" said Filip curiously.

"Inez's closet," Meja explained.

Sverker grinned at Inez. "I bet it really is a treasure trove. You were a style icon." He turned to Meja and repeated emphatically, "An *icon*."

Meja nodded. "I can imagine."

Inez waved her hand dismissively.

Sverker flipped through the book again. "You dedicated all your books to M, didn't you?"

Inez reached for a scone. She had no desire to get into this.

"But nobody knows who M is, do they?" continued Sverker.

"Not even my publisher," replied Inez.

Inez caught Meja's eye and suddenly felt a fluttering panic in the pit of her stomach. Would Meja really be able to keep her new book secret, as requested? Words could slip out so easily. But she made up her mind to enjoy the afternoon and leave those thoughts for another day. Maybe she would ask Meja to sign a nondisclosure agreement.

"You're not dependent on your walking stick anymore, I've noticed," said Filip. "Almost good as new."

Inez nodded. "Yes. I barely think about it, actually. My hip doesn't hurt much anymore. I even went for a little walk without my stick."

"Well, that's worth a toast," said Filip, raising his teacup.

"Cheers to Inez's hip healing and to the best neighbors in the world," said Sverker.

Inez smiled and everyone raised their cups. As the rhubarb-and-vanilla tea trickled down her throat, it occurred to her that her new life was beginning.

Everything was going to be so much lighter from now on.

MEJA

After thanking Sverker and Filip several times for a fantastic afternoon, Meja, Inez, and Andreas went home as an odd trio, arm in arm.

They stopped at Inez's gate.

"I have something I'd like to show you," Andreas said to Meja.

Meja hesitated and looked at Inez awkwardly.

Inez rolled her eyes. "Go. I'm seventy years old. Fully capable of taking care of myself. In fact, I think I'd enjoy a couple of hours alone in the house."

"All right then," Meja said.

When they reached Andreas's porch door, he went in but made her wait outside a few minutes. When he let her in, she gasped. He had lit candles in a floor-standing candelabra, taken out two champagne glasses, and put a bottle of cava in an ice bucket. But that wasn't what made her gasp. It was the painting on the easel. The painting of her. She went to examine it.

"This isn't me. But it is who I would like to be," she said.

"This is exactly who you were the last time you were here."

"Really?" Meja looked closely at the painting.

"There was something different about you when you turned up in Inez's pantsuit smelling of cigar smoke before breakfast."

She laughed. "When you put it like that it sounds crazy."

"Maybe it's okay for life to be a little crazy sometimes," he said.

"Now *that* sounds like something Inez would say. Is she being a bad influence on you?"

Now it was Andreas's turn to laugh. He was just about to pop the cork when Meja stopped him.

"You know, I don't really like cava."

"Don't you?" He put the bottle down and brought out some sparkling water instead.

"Now those are bubbles I'll happily drink."

They sat on the couch and chatted about everything under the sun. She asked about his job as an art teacher, and he spoke about how creativity had the power to reach the challenging children, the boisterous and the withdrawn ones alike. His answer made her wonder who his ex-wife was. How could anyone let a man like Andreas go?

"Penny for your thoughts," he said.

Meja shrugged. "I was actually just wondering why you broke up. You and your wife. But you don't have to tell me."

Andreas looked up at the ceiling. "It's the classic story. We took each other for granted, grew apart, and, well, became superficial friends instead of lovers."

Meja's skin got goose bumps just hearing him say the word *lover*.

"What about you?" said Andreas. "Your relationship is struggling, isn't it?"

"It's over," said Meja. "We had also grown apart. Well, that's actually not entirely true. We never really grew together, but we both liked the idea of having someone. We liked each other, but I'm not sure we were ever really in love."

Andreas nodded thoughtfully. Then he looked up from behind his forelock of dark hair, made eye contact, and held it. She took a deep breath, wishing he had put some music on so he couldn't hear her breathing so clearly.

"You may not realize it, but you are special," he said.

Meja glanced at the painting of herself. Of a woman with sparkling eyes. Curious about the world. Then she did something she had wanted to do for a long time, though she'd never admitted it—even to herself. She moved closer to him and ran her hand through his dark, mid-length hair. She leaned in close, shut her eyes, and inhaled his scent of mild shampoo and masculine fragrance. He smiled, put his arms around her, and pulled her toward him.

The early morning was very quiet when Meja sneaked home. Every time the stairs creaked, she winced. When she entered her room, Ingrid started squeaking, and she fed her some pellets before collapsing on the bed and staring at the ceiling. She and Andreas. Something told her this hadn't been her smartest decision. He was bound to regret it, and then things would get awkward. But right now she didn't care. She had never experienced anything like that before. Curious, exploratory, reverent moments of intimacy. She smiled.

Her thoughts wandered back further, to yesterday at Sverker and Filip's. She heard Sverker's question in her head. *But nobody knows who M is?* She knew. Inez had dedicated every book she had ever written to her friend Mathilda. Once again, Meja had doubts about the book's ending. Was it really the truth?

Meja carefully took the key out of the jewelry box, opened the drawer, took out the black notebook, and crawled into bed. She ran her fingers over the leather cover before flicking through to the final pages:

Mathilda taught me to see signs. She didn't talk about fate or chance, just signs. These signs came and went. You could let them pass like woolly wisps of cloud in the sky, or catch them like snowflakes and shape them into something beautiful: a snowball lantern, a snow angel. There was always a choice. I had packed my bag that morning. I had decided to dive at the oyster bank near the seals, where we used to lie on the rocks and talk about life, where Mathilda left oyster shells with her engraved words—some I found, others her father probably found. Of course, that was where she had placed her most important message of all. The shell that would tell me where she had gone. Where Amelia and I would be going too.

But . . .

Meja turned the page with a trembling hand. But what?

. . . the news that my book would be published came just hours before I was about to dive for the shell. It was a sign. I didn't let it pass like a fleeting cloud. I caught it like a snowflake and shaped it into my dream.

I knew you would understand. What I didn't know is whether you would ever forgive me for not searching for the oyster shell.

Meja turned the page. Blank. What happened next? What happened to Mathilda?

She put the book back and went downstairs, making no effort to be quiet this time, and knocked on Inez's door. When no one answered, she knocked again.

Inez opened and looked at her with surprise and pillow lines on her cheeks.

"I want to know what happened," said Meja in a curt, clear tone.

Inez yawned. "I don't know what you're talking about. What time is it, anyway?"

"It's five o'clock, and I want to know what happened to Mathilda."

Inez rubbed her eyes and yawned again. "You know what happened. You read the last chapter. She moved to Palermo."

Meja crossed her arms over her chest and pursed her lips.

Inez sighed. "We need something warm and sweet."

She put on her dressing gown, ran a hand through her hair, and padded into the kitchen to make some hot chocolate with generous dollops of whipped cream. They settled into the living room armchairs, and Inez pulled a blanket over her legs.

"You wanted my opinions on your book," Meja said. "I think every chapter cuts straight to the heart. It all feels so real." She paused for emphasis. "Except the ending."

Inez put the mug down on the table and clasped her hands in her lap.

"And that's why I don't think it's true," continued Meja.

Inez sat quietly. Meja waited.

"The truth is," she said eventually, "I don't know what happened to Mathilda. Many people—who knew her or had only heard of her—concluded that she'd drowned herself. The daughter of the sea would never have survived behind bars if she was convicted."

"But what do *you* think happened?" Meja asked.

Inez shrugged. "I really don't know. I've looked for her at every single author signing in every country I've ever visited. Nothing. I went to her father to ask him if he knew anything, but he was confused, had difficulty answering questions, and seemed to think I was Mathilda. I went to Stockholm for my first meeting with Cristy instead of looking for the oyster shell with Mathilda's final message, and that's where I stayed. Nikolas and I had never married, and his sister inherited the house. I had no ties to Kobbholmen. So the bag I had packed for Mathilda's was unpacked in a small apartment in south Stockholm. I only went back once, and that was to testify in court."

"What did you say?"

"I told the truth: that I was in too bad a shape to know anything about what happened in that room."

"That was true?" Meja said.

Inez sighed. "Yes, but you know what? I could have said that I used my last ounce of strength to push him, that he hit his head and died, and that Mathilda showed up shortly after, called an ambulance, and took it upon herself to protect me."

"But you were under oath," Meja said.

Inez smiled tiredly. "If everyone was like you, Meja, the world would be a much better place."

Meja stirred her hot chocolate and took a sip. "A more boring place, you mean?"

Inez smiled. "A bit too straitlaced perhaps, but better all the same."

"Well, I certainly wasn't straitlaced at Andreas's house last night," said Meja, stretching her neck.

"Oh-ho!" Inez said and laughed. "So I have made a woman of you after all?"

Meja answered only in the form of a sly smile and drank the rest of her hot chocolate.

Inez grabbed the armrest of the chair and stood up. "I would like to get another hour's sleep, unless you have more burning questions that simply can't wait?"

Meja shook her head.

On her way back to her room, Inez turned to Meja. "So, what do you think I should do with the ending? Now that you know?"

"Keep it as it is. Let the world think she ended up in Palermo, but rewrite it as if that's what actually happened."

Inez nodded with a weak smile and disappeared into her bedroom.

As Meja crawled back into bed, she wondered if anyone had ever found that oyster shell. The one that told the truth about where Mathilda had gone.

INEZ

Inez had difficulty falling asleep after the early morning sugar high and conversation with Meja. She got out of bed and paced around downstairs. So many things had changed since Meja had come into her life. She snapped a few photos on her phone, of the tidy bookshelf, the uncluttered living room table, and the open blinds. She was about to send the pictures to Amelia but changed her mind and wrote instead: Are you busy? Wondering if I could visit for a couple of days?

Half an hour later the answer came: You'd be welcome. Inez wrote a note to tell Meja she could have the house to herself for a few days because she had gone to see Amelia. Then she packed a bag, booked a ticket, and ordered a cab to Central Station. Before she knew it, she was on the direct train to Copenhagen.

She got that flutter in the pit of her stomach, as she always did on trains. There was something special about watching the world pass by outside the window so quickly that you couldn't fix your eyes on anything. Meditative. Flying had never appealed. Being above the clouds gave her a feeling almost comparable to fear of death. She leaned her head back against the seat and let her thoughts fly by as fleetingly as the trees and houses outside.

They passed villages and fields, traveling through Malmö and over the bridge to Denmark. At Copenhagen Central Station, Inez stepped out into a teeming crowd. A man in a formal suit stood flipping through a business magazine next to a group of young backpackers sitting on the ground nibbling rice cakes. Out on the street, waves of children's screams came from the roller coasters in Tivoli Gardens. Copenhagen was a melting pot of people and life, and today Inez was in the perfect mood for it.

She walked down Strøget, the main shopping street, passing several street musicians and stopping to watch a group of acrobats form a human pyramid. A seat outside a café became available, and she sat down and ordered a coffee.

"Mange tak," she said to the waitress.

She thought about the last few times she had seen Amelia. She always looked forward to spending time with her daughter, but it tended to be a bit prickly. Like forcing the wrong puzzle pieces to fit together. The differences between them were at their most palpable at Amelia and Aksel's house, where all the unspoken conflicts that simmered below the surface seemed to seep out in little unnecessary comments and facial expressions. She was determined that today would be different. Because her life was different now. She had finished writing her story, the one that had been weighing on her more than she had known. She had cleared out all her books and papers and put flowers in the window. She had started socializing with people again!

In her head, she made a few rules for herself. Don't wear your sunglasses, despite the blinding whiteness. Change the subject when you notice Amelia getting stressed and maniacally cleaning. Answer when spoken to, even if you don't like what's being said. Speak softly. Ask questions. Most important: sound interested. Even better: *be* interested!

Inez arrived and buzzed Amelia's apartment. "It's me," Inez said in her most amicable voice.

Inez didn't like using the elevator with the grated door, but seeing as the apartment was on the top floor, she had no choice. She felt a rare flutter of nerves in her stomach as she ascended floor by floor.

Amelia greeted her with cool kisses on the cheek.

"You're looking fresh," she said.

Inez wished she could say the same about her daughter, who looked tired and weary.

"You should see my house," she said. "It's never been so fresh."

She took off her coat and Amelia hung it in the closet where all their coats were stored in a neat row, ordered by length.

"Have you finished your decluttering now?" Amelia asked, walking into the kitchen and pouring green tea into mugs so big you had to hold them with both hands. They sat down in the living room.

"Look," Inez said, showing Amelia the pictures she'd taken that morning.

"No way! It's like a brand-new house. Now, doesn't that feel better?"

It actually did feel a lot better, but Inez wasn't about to admit it. "So, how are you?"

"Good," said Amelia curtly. That meant she didn't want to talk about it. "Guess who's in town?"

Inez shrugged.

"Just you wait." Amelia started a FaceTime call and Cristy appeared on the screen.

"Inez! Are you at Amelia's? I'm coming over!" Cristy said in a shrill voice and hung up before either Inez or Amelia could respond.

Fifteen minutes later Cristy entered with outstretched arms.

"My star!" she exclaimed and gave Inez a hug. She was surprisingly strong, despite her slight frame. "What a wonderful surprise. Let me look at you." She looked her up and down. "What are these baggy clothes? And where's the rouge? You know my motto. A woman can get away with anything except not wearing rouge."

Inez just smiled in response. Cristy might be eighty years old, but she was guaranteed to be wearing colorful clothes and makeup.

"I remember the first time you came to me. I knew you were going to be big. That I would make you big." Cristy smiled at the memory. "What a life we lived."

Inez used to publish an average of one novel per year, writing for six months and promoting for six months. Always enthusiastically cheered on by Cristy, who soon became more than just her publisher. She was her friend, her savior. Cristy had bandaged Inez's wounds, topped up her champagne, and looked after Amelia when Inez needed to write or travel. Cristy never had a family of her own. She took care of Inez and Amelia.

"It was a wild life," said Inez. "Do you have any regrets about those years?"

Cristy shook her head, causing her large white curls—which Inez assumed was a wig—to bounce, then reconsidered.

"Actually, I do have one regret. That I didn't make you see a therapist back then, fifteen years ago. I should have helped you more. What the journalists wrote was nonsense, yet it resulted in your first ever case of writer's block, which meant you ended your career far too early and turned into a hermit."

"It wasn't all bad. I suddenly had a lot more free time," Inez said, looking at Amelia, who sat down on the couch on her other side. "Time for you."

Amelia sipped her tea and shrugged. "I was twenty-nine by then, Mom. It was kind of too late."

Inez frowned.

"Too late to start over, anyway," Amelia clarified.

This was no fun. Inez felt like she was on trial. But she was determined to prove that they could have a good time together.

"I wouldn't have agreed to see a therapist anyway, and I didn't have writer's block. It was a conscious decision I made. I was done with writing." She turned her gaze to Amelia. "And it's never too late."

Cristy snorted. "It didn't seem like you were done with writing, it seemed like you were hiding."

"I was. So that I could have some peace to decide what to do next. I took a break from writing to get away from all the chaos, but during that break I came to new ways of thinking."

She was lying. Giving up writing had been terrifying. It was the only thing she knew and loved. But she had been terrified of her past reappearing like a thistle in her beautiful flower bed. She was known as the author who celebrated friendship, but she had betrayed her own best friend in the worst way imaginable. The newspapers would have had a field day.

"Sure," said Cristy, who sounded like she didn't believe a word of what Inez was saying. "What did you decide to do with the rest of your life then? Or are you still thinking? I can't say I've seen many signs of life in you."

Inez smiled. "I spent a long time just thinking, but now I know. I just want to live. Spend time with my neighbors, enjoy the sea. Maybe pack a small bag, get on the train, and travel."

"Where?" Cristy said, rolling her eyes at Amelia to emphasize her dubiousness.

Inez thought. "I'd like to go back to Berlin."

"You've been to Berlin plenty of times," said Cristy. "I know—I booked the hotels every time."

"A hotel with a book signing in the lobby isn't the same as strolling around Unter den Linden, visiting galleries, and sitting outside at cafés."

Cristy took a sip of tea and bit into a sugar cookie that Amelia had set out. "True. Can I come with you?"

"You want to mooch around Berlin together?" Inez said with a laugh.

"Why not? Don't you think your mother and I should mooch around in Berlin?" Cristy said, looking at Amelia, who was smiling in amusement.

"Absolutely," she said.

"It could make a good book, about friendship in the golden years. Your readers would love it." Cristy nudged Inez in the side, spilling her tea. Inez reached for a napkin to save Amelia's presumably expensive couch.

Amelia had her head leaned back against the couch cushion, smiling, with her eyes closed.

Inez and Cristy drank and chatted about Cristy's recent travels. Soon they heard Amelia snoring gently.

"I think there's a bit of tug-of-war going on between her and Aksel," Cristy whispered.

"Yes, I suspected as much. She looks exhausted."

Inez looked at her daughter, then at Cristy. "Thank you," she whispered. "Thank you for everything you have done for her over the years. And still do."

"I love her like my own, you know that. Besides, there wouldn't have been any books otherwise."

Inez nodded. She was right about that.

Cristy yawned widely and rested her head back too. "I don't suppose you do feel like writing a book about friendship in Berlin, do you? I would very much like to work again."

Inez smiled, leaned her head back as well, and closed her eyes. A book about two friends having adventures in a big city in their golden years. It would make Sverker happy, at least. Then she remembered the oyster diver manuscript.

She looked at Cristy. She had done everything for Inez and never asked a single question. Never pried into who M was or what Inez raved about when she had her breakdowns. She was just there for her.

"Actually, I have written a book," she said.

Cristy sat up immediately. Inez put her finger over her lips and whispered so as not to wake Amelia.

"But I intend to have it published posthumously."

"Huh? Why?" Cristy whispered. "Are you sick?"

"No, I'm not sick. I'll probably live another twenty years, at least. But this is no ordinary book."

"It's no fun to publish a book without a launch party." Cristy sank back against the couch. "So you've written an out-of-the-ordinary book to be published after your death?"

Inez nodded.

"Well, that sounds ludicrous if you ask me, but I want to read it, of course. And maybe we could go to Berlin to celebrate when it's finished?"

Inez took a deep breath. She hoped telling Cristy had been the right decision. Her publisher's eye would undoubtedly make the manuscript better.

Cristy closed her eyes, and her breathing started to match Amelia's. Inez felt a rush of warmth at being in the presence of the two people she loved the most.

I hope it's not too late to show it, she thought, letting her heavy eyelids close too.

MEJA

The house felt very empty without Inez. Her note had said: *Make your-self at home.* But Meja certainly didn't feel at home. On the contrary. She was only here for Inez's sake. Without her, she had no job and nothing to do. Solitude brought Meja's lack of direction in life into clear focus. She had nothing.

Through the window she saw Andreas heading toward the sea carrying an easel and paints. She hid behind the curtain. The thought of their night together made her wince. It had been wonderful, but if she could go back in time and undo it, she would. They could have been great friends. Now everything was going to be more complicated.

Once he was out of sight, she pulled down the blinds.

"I'm turning into Inez," she said to herself. "I need to get a grip."

She sat down on the couch and thought about Inez's book. Was she really going to publish it posthumously? And use that phony ending? Even if she rewrote it more convincingly, it still wouldn't be the truth.

The oyster shell on the bookshelf caught her eye, and she went to inspect it. It made her wonder if anyone had ever found the shell with Mathilda's final message.

She peeked inside a small jewelry box on the bookshelf, then went over to the dresser by the window and opened one drawer after another. She didn't even know what she was looking for. After thoroughly searching downstairs, she went up to the walk-in closet and opened the shoeboxes containing memorabilia. Eventually she found a small yellowed newspaper clipping. An obituary and memorial text for someone called Mats Nilsson.

Apparently Mats had been Kobbholmen's first oyster diver and had put the village on the map as a prime spot for the delicacy. He lived alone with his daughter, also an oyster diver, who sadly went missing, but later remarried a woman named Louise Hedin. She and her two daughters, Anna and Ellen, were his principal mourners.

Meja put the clipping back and did her best to leave the room in the same state as she had found it. Then she went downstairs, heart racing, unsure what to do next.

After a while she picked up her phone and googled *Louise Hedin, Kobbholmen*. She had passed away ten years ago. She moved on and searched for Anna and Ellen. She found nothing on Anna, but Ellen had kept the last name, still lived in Kobbholmen, and even listed her cell number online. Meja typed out a message.

Hello! My name is Meja. Sorry to bother you. A friend of mine knew Mats and Mathilda and has a few questions she would like to ask someone who was close to them. About the oyster business. Looking forward to hearing from you.

Hours passed. Meja occupied herself with a crossword magazine. Eventually the reply came: How lovely. I don't know if I'll be able to answer many questions, but you are most welcome to call or visit.

Visit? She googled Kobbholmen again. About four hours by car. Through the gap in the blinds, she glimpsed Sverker outside with a rake, tidying a flower bed. She went outside.

"Thanks again for afternoon tea," she said.

"Oh no, thank *you*," Sverker replied. "It was our pleasure."

"I took some nice photos. I'll print them out to give to you later." She shifted her weight from one foot to the other. "There's something I wanted to ask you."

"Ask away. I have no secrets."

"It's about your car. I have an errand in Gothenburg today, out of the blue, and I get motion sickness from long train journeys."

"Of course you can borrow it. We rarely use it."

"Oh, thank you, that's so kind. It's just for one night," said Meja.

Sverker disappeared into the house, returned with the car keys, and gave her some instructions.

"Have a great time," he concluded.

Meja nodded in thanks. She felt like a scoundrel, first snooping through Inez's things and now lying to Sverker, which he seemed to suspect. But she was determined.

She went up to Inez's closet and tried on a wide denim skirt with a frill at the bottom and a yellow singlet top. She spun around in front of the mirror and took a photo that she sent to her mother with the caption: I may not have a great dream, but at least I've found my style.

It didn't take long for her to reply with two emojis, one with heart eyes and one with clapping hands. Had she ever gotten two happy emojis from Susanne before?

With a spring in her step, Meja quickly took care of Ingrid, packed a bag, and set off. Miles down the road, her heart was still pounding. She put the radio on to distract herself from the thought that she really ought to turn back and spend the day planting some nice things in Inez's garden.

But she didn't turn back.

Shortly after Gothenburg, she stopped for a hot dog, then continued. When she passed the sign for Smögen, she thought how lovely it would be to visit the charming seaside town on the way back and photograph the quay and its famous multicolored huts. Just under half an hour later, she arrived in Kobbholmen.

She checked in at a bed-and-breakfast fifty yards from the seafront, then drove straight down to Oyster Bay, where, according to Inez's manuscript, Mathilda's hut had once been. The construction was still there, with a sign that read TORSTEN'S OYSTERS. She stopped and took in the view.

Inez's book had painted such clear images in her mind that she could picture Mathilda right there in her boat, with a young Inez sitting on the high rocks, writing in her black notebook. Rocky little islands rose out of the sea, and Meja envisioned them lying on the rocks, talking about life and dreams. As Meja walked closer to the water, she could see white oyster shells glinting below the surface.

Air left her lungs with a sigh. Inez would be very unhappy about this. More than unhappy—she would consider it an invasion of her privacy and would regret ever having shared her book with Meja.

She was having second thoughts about talking to Ellen. Maybe just seeing the hut was enough. Why was she even here? She decided to go back to her bed-and-breakfast and think it all over carefully.

She was back in Kobbholmen in under ten minutes. She walked around the harbor and along the pier with its restaurants and shops, dodged tourists, and admired the rocky islets in the water, but she was finding it hard to focus. She returned to her room.

She collapsed on the bed with a big sigh of relief and stared up at the ceiling. She texted Ellen that she was nearby, and soon got a reply saying she was welcome. Meja's body felt heavy and reluctant. But she was here now. She may as well get on with it, even if she didn't know what she was really expecting.

Ten minutes later she rang the doorbell at the address Ellen had texted to her, and a dainty, well-dressed old lady with gray hair and a floral dress opened the door and welcomed her in.

"This is such a lovely village," said Meja.

"Yes, I can't imagine living anywhere else. It was too small for my sister; she went to Stockholm at a young age and stayed there."

Ellen served Meja some coffee and set out a plate of lemon muffins.

"Help yourself. Homemade."

Meja thanked her and took a muffin. It was fluffy and sweet and had that wonderful home-baked taste.

"Where are you from?" Ellen said.

"Helsingborg."

"Oh, that's a long way to travel."

"I had errands nearby," Meja said, wondering what had gotten into her. It was just one lie after another.

"So . . . ," said Ellen. "You wanted to know more about Mats's oyster business?"

Meja nodded and listened to Ellen's long story about changing ownership, the hard life of an oyster diver, the evolution of the profession and its importance to the village. In her head she tried to formulate a question that would lead the conversation to Mathilda, but Ellen just kept talking and didn't leave her time to think.

"My mother, sister, and I moved here from a small village in Småland. I remember my early childhood as idyllic, but that might just be nostalgia talking." She smiled. "My mother would always chide my father for crossing the train track on his way back from work. He claimed it was so he could get a few extra minutes with his girls." Ellen smiled and looked out the window. "Isn't it strange how life always rushes by, except when tragedies happen? Then each second is an eternity. Every millisecond becomes imprinted on the brain and heart."

Meja took a sip of coffee and let Ellen continue her story.

"I remember sitting in the kitchen doing my homework. I had asked my mother a math question. She was doing the dishes and drying a big glass bowl. We lived near the train station. The moment Mom heard the screech of the train's brakes on the rails, she knew. I saw her eyes open wide, she lost her grip on the bowl, and it smashed into a thousand pieces. She got several shards stuck in her legs, but didn't seem to feel them. She just turned and ran to the train tracks. Life was hard after he died."

Ellen fell silent and sipped her coffee before continuing.

"But my mother was strong and eventually she managed to pull herself together and get a job at a small manufacturing company. Then someone knew someone who needed an employee in Kobbholmen, and we moved here."

"That must have been an adjustment," said Meja.

"I had a strong sense of having come home. I think my mother always longed to return to the mossy woods, but I loved it here, and still do. I love the sea."

Ellen smiled at Meja. "Then she met Mats and they got married. She used to say that they were bound together by grief, that once you've experienced the worst loss imaginable, you could never live your life with someone who hadn't. He had lost his wife and daughter." Ellen tilted her head. "But I've been rambling on. Was there something in particular you wanted to ask about?"

Meja blushed. She felt bad for tricking Ellen into talking about Mats when she had an ulterior motive. But there was no backing out now.

She cleared her throat. "I'm actually rather interested in Mathilda."

"Aha," Ellen said, straightening the white tablecloth that was already perfectly neat. "A number of people have come asking about her over the years. Journalists—usually young, recently graduated—on the hunt for their first big story, or criminologists dreaming of cracking a real case."

"Do you know what happened to her?"

Ellen let out a chuckle. "No, I don't. I would say so if I did. I don't believe in keeping secrets."

"Do you think Mats knew?" Meja whispered almost inaudibly, well aware that she was poking her nose where it didn't belong.

Ellen pursed her lips slightly before saying, "I don't know. Perhaps. Or he decided on a likely outcome and stopped brooding. He was a smart man. He knew that brooding was like poison. Besides, we rarely talked about Mathilda. We rarely talked about my dad either. Mom used to say that life can only be enjoyed if you dedicate it to the living. I think she was right."

Ellen started clearing up. Meja understood that her time was running out.

"Did you save anything from Mats's time as an oyster diver?" she asked.

"Like tools and such?" Ellen asked.

"I guess . . ."

Ellen pondered. "No, I don't think so. Most of it passed to the people who took over from Mats."

"And there's nothing left of Mathilda's?"

Ellen beckoned Meja into the hall and held out her jacket. Meja understood that she was being too pushy, but she couldn't stop herself.

"There are a few photographs, but little else," said Ellen with some hesitation. "I understand that you haven't found what you're looking for, but I think it's best that Mathilda remains a mystery."

Ellen opened the door and let Meja out.

"But if you absolutely had to guess, what would you say happened?" Meja said in a last-ditch attempt to get something worthwhile from her visit.

Ellen shook her head with a smile. "You get to create your own ending. Isn't it better that way?"

Meja said thank you and goodbye, trying to contain her disappointment.

She walked up and down the winding alleyways and got takeout seafood pasta to eat in her room. Then she pulled down the blinds and collapsed into bed. She might not have learned anything about Mathilda that she didn't already know, but she was glad she had seen Kobbholmen. Inez had been very faithful to the location in her story. Her words were like a painting.

Tomorrow she would go back to Domsten. She found herself missing the place, and the people. Sverker, Filip, Inez . . . and Andreas. *I need to talk to Andreas,* she thought before closing her eyes and falling asleep.

MEJA

The next day, Meja woke full of energy. She got up, had a light breakfast in the dining room, and checked out. Then she drove the short distance back to Oyster Bay and the hut. This time she brought her camera and photographed the beach, which was covered in oyster shells. She walked along the path that wound through the forest and up the rocky mound. She thought of all the times Inez had walked here as a young woman, bearing bruises from Nikolas's fists, but still tending to her dream somewhere deep inside. The dream of writing a book. The dream that Mathilda encouraged her to realize.

She felt a rush in her stomach when she reached the top. It was a platform of softly rounded rocks undulating like solidified ocean waves as far as the eye could see. "Wow," she whispered. It was one of the most beautiful vistas she had ever seen.

She took a few pictures and sat on the edge gazing out to sea. Little islands poked out of the water here and there. *You get to create your own ending,* Ellen had said. That was exactly what Inez had done. And perhaps what Meja should do too.

It was time to go home. Time to close Inez's book and write her own story. Choose a direction. She felt a tingling in her stomach. Maybe her trip to Kobbholmen hadn't been in vain after all? Maybe it had nothing to do with Inez and Mathilda. It was about her.

Meja keyed Domsten into the GPS, turned on the car radio, and started humming along to pop music. When she came to the sign for Smögen, she turned off the main road. The small coastal town was one of Sweden's most popular tourist destinations and a lot of people had had the same idea today. She had to drive around for fifteen minutes before she found a parking space just a few minutes' walk from Smögenbryggan, the famous quay. She felt giddy with anticipation and proud of herself for coming on this little excursion all by herself. Instead of taking the straight, easy road back, she had chosen to experience something new along the way. It was very unlike her. It felt like a big step.

At first it felt like everyone was looking at her, but she soon realized that no one cared that she was walking along the quay alone. Everyone was minding their own business. She walked past restaurants, cafés, and small shops offering ceramics and clothes, continuing to the end of the quay where red, yellow, blue, and green huts stood all in a row. She snapped a few pictures.

She got a message: Hi, this is Ellen from yesterday. Are you still in Kobbholmen?

Meja typed back: I took a trip to Smögen.

If you come back, pop by. I have something I want to show you. Nothing too remarkable.

An hour later Meja knocked on Ellen's front door. Ellen let her in and served her coffee and muffins in the living room again.

"Your visit piqued my curiosity about what might be sitting up in the attic. My mother and Mats moved to this apartment in their later years, and I inherited it when Mom died. I replaced some furniture and put a few of my own boxes in the attic, but a lot of their things have been left untouched."

Ellen disappeared into another room and came back with a box. On the lid it said *M*. Could that stand for Mats or Mathilda? Meja nodded and tried to look nonchalant, when in reality her heart was pounding and making her feel very warm all of a sudden. She wanted to rip the lid off, but controlled herself and sipped her coffee instead.

"There is absolutely nothing of value, but since you were searching for Mathilda, I thought you might want to see it."

Ellen put the lid aside and carefully took out some children's drawings of boats, a seashell necklace, and some photographs of Mathilda from school graduations and around the islands. So that was what she looked like.

At the bottom of the box were lots of oyster shells.

Ellen smiled. "I remember when Mats decided to sell the business and retire. Mom and I helped him clean out the hut, and she was nagging him about these oyster shells that he had felt the need to bring home. She begged him to choose just one, but he insisted on keeping them all."

Ellen picked up one of the shells and turned it upside down. "Mathilda used to write a word on the shells and throw them back in the water. Mats found some, but I'm sure there are still others on the seabed. Mats said it was like finding treasure. After Mathilda disappeared, a whole box of shells appeared at the hut. Maybe it made him think she was alive after all. Who else would have put the box there? Old engraved shells were found long after she had disappeared."

Meja felt her cheeks flush hot and took a deep breath in an attempt to sound calmer than she was. "Can I have a peek?"

"Of course. I'm finding it hard to decipher them. They mainly just look like scribbles to me, but you have a look." She went to put on more coffee.

Meja inspected the shells: *Happiness, Friendship, Sea, Family, Intimacy, Love.* One of the shells stood out because it had several words carved into it. But it was too indistinct to be legible. She stuffed it into her purse and just had time to close the zipper before Ellen returned with the coffeepot.

"Refill?" she said.

Meja nodded. Her hand trembled slightly and she lifted up a shell.

"Sea," she read.

Ellen put on her reading glasses and held the shell some distance away. "Ah yes, you're right."

"You should put this on display," said Meja.

"Well, why not?" Ellen stood up and placed the shell on the dresser among lots of framed photographs. "Lovely."

"Thank you for showing these to me. And the photographs," Meja said. She finished her coffee and stood up. "I'd better get going. Thank you—you've been most kind and accommodating."

"It has been a pleasure," said Ellen.

Meja was about halfway home when she realized that she ought to bring back a thank-you gift for Sverker. She stopped to get an expensive bottle of champagne.

"You shouldn't have!" he said when he saw the bottle in her hand, but smiled gratefully.

When Meja came home she did what Inez always did: she took out a crystal glass and poured some port. She took a good sip before taking the shell out of her purse. Her palms were sweaty. She needed the flashlight on her cell phone to get a better look at the engraved words.

I'm waiting . . . Meja squinted but couldn't make out the rest of what was written. It started with a *B* or a *D*, with maybe an *I* in the middle and an *S* at the end. She got her camera and photographed the shell from different angles and with different lighting. Maybe she could enlarge the picture and decipher it on the computer.

Was this really *the* shell? The shell that Mathilda had thrown into the water for Inez to find? The shell that Inez had left at the bottom because she'd chosen a different path in life?

INEZ

It was nine o'clock at night when Inez got back. She breathed a sigh of relief. It was good to be home. Her visit with Amelia had gone unexpectedly well, as had seeing Cristy for the first time in four years.

Amelia had promised to visit in a couple of weeks, which had inspired Inez to start making plans already on the train. She would buy more plants and fill the fruit bowl on the table—Amelia would like that. She would have the blinds open and serve up a really good paella, which she loved but had never made herself. She would have plenty of time to practice.

She was excited and felt light on her feet as she stepped into the house. It was quiet and dark. She frowned in surprise at the closed blinds. Hadn't she left them up? She opened them. The evening sky was stunning.

Her old yellow purse was on the oak table. Inside was Meja's wallet. She smiled to herself. Then her eyes landed on an oyster shell she didn't recognize lying on the table. It was an incredibly beautiful shell with nine annual rings, like frills, in white, purple, and blue. Where had it come from? She only had one shell that Mathilda had given her a long time ago. The one she had shown Meja. But this one looked completely different, with a smooth, white surface.

She sat down with a thud on the nearest chair and turned the shell over. There was something carved into the underside. She squinted but couldn't quite make it out. *I'm waiting . . .* Inez's breathing became shallow. There was a rushing in her ears. She gasped for air.

There was a creak on the stairs, and Meja stopped abruptly when she saw Inez, then continued slowly and sat opposite her. The table formed a barrier between them.

Inez tossed the shell at Meja. "What is this?"

"It's . . ." Meja looked like she was trying to come up with a good explanation, but Inez knew she couldn't lie.

"It might be the ending of your book," whispered Meja.

"I don't understand," said Inez.

Meja sat quietly for a long time.

"I went to Kobbholmen. To see Ellen, Mats's stepdaughter." Meja's voice was as fragile as a whisper. "She's retired now."

Inez gasped for air again. Everything went dark. Meja went to Kobbholmen?

"She didn't know anything about Mathilda, but she found a box that Mats had saved. There were a lot of oyster shells with words engraved in them. And one of the shells stood out from the others because it consisted of several written words. This one."

The pieces of the puzzle slowly fell into place.

"*This* is the shell?" she whispered.

"I think so," said Meja. "I think this is the shell that Mathilda left for you to locate her. I think her father found it under the sea and put it in the box with the others. It starts with *I'm waiting . . .* and then . . ."

Inez's vision blurred. She reached for the shell, dropped it on the floor, and stamped on it with the shoes she hadn't taken off since returning home.

Meja put her hand over her mouth.

"You had no right!" Inez's voice broke. Her body was shaking and her fists were clenched so tightly they had turned white. "It's not your story. It's nobody else's story. Only ours!"

These last words came out as a scream.

Meja backed away and nodded.

"You have five minutes to get out of here. I never want to see you again. And if you say one word about my book to anyone, I will sue you."

Inez went into her bedroom, slammed the door, and collapsed on the floor, gasping for air. Half an hour later she heard the front door open and close a few times. When it remained closed, Inez came back out. Her legs refused to carry her so she had to crawl over to the broken oyster shell and lie down next to it. Hacking sobs rose within her.

She had told her daughter that it was never too late. But it wasn't true. It was too late for this. She didn't want to know now.

She sobbed until the morning sun shone through the window, but still didn't get up. For the first time in her life, she longed for her final breath. An eternal sleep with no decisions, choices, or regrets. No forgiveness or shame. Just floating slumber. She squeezed her eyes shut and wished for her time to come.

ONE MONTH LATER

INEZ

September swept into Domsten like a whirlwind. It howled around the roof ridges, and the waves thrashed wildly on the strait. Inez was still going for her walks. It was too windy for the pier today, so she sat on Viola's bench, where it was slightly calmer. It was only four in the morning. Since Meja had disappeared from her life, she only went for a walk very late in the evening or early in the morning. That way she didn't risk bumping into anyone and could sit in peace looking at the stars. And the sea.

She had forgotten her gloves and rubbed her cold hands together.

A lot had changed since Meja left. Or rather, everything had gone back to normal.

The blinds were closed again. She had thrown away all the plants that Meja had bought, except the old cactus, and returned to her old routine of eating the same dish for a week at a time. This week it was fish. Baked salmon.

She spent her days reading books. She ordered most of them from a secondhand store online. Every week new books arrived, and they were starting to form piles in her living room.

She had canceled Amelia's visit. She didn't want her daughter seeing her like this. She had apologized for the change of plans and said she was working on an exciting project and didn't wish to be disturbed. Maybe it would have been better to show her a dark, messy house and a mother who had lost all will to live, rather than blaming work. But it was done now. Inez had taken the easy, but painful, route. They hadn't spoken since.

She got up with a sigh and went home.

There were no lights on in the neighbors' houses. Sverker had knocked several times in the past month and resumed his habit of hanging flowers on the gate, but she didn't even bother to take them in and throw them away. They hung there until they withered and Sverker removed them himself.

Andreas had also knocked a few times. She hadn't opened the door for him, either, but had bumped into him early one morning when he was out to paint the dawn. He asked if she was okay. She replied that everything was fine. That Meja had stopped working for her and she was now busy with a writing project. He looked dubious but nodded. Then she had scurried home, grateful that he hadn't asked more questions.

She went back inside, hung her windbreaker up in the hall, and brewed some strong coffee. Then she sat down to continue reading *The Portrait of a Lady* by Henry James. Isabel Archer, one of the most notorious female characters in literature, made Inez forget herself for a while.

The rest of the day followed the same routine as any other. Toast for lunch, nap, coffee in the afternoon, port in the early evening, dinner. By the time the clock struck midnight, she had finished the book about Isabel and placed it on top of the newest pile of books growing on her floor.

She didn't know what day it was but had the feeling it was the weekend because she had spotted Sverker and Filip through the kitchen window getting into a cab wearing smart shirts and bow ties. They were good at enjoying life, those two.

She opened the front door just a crack to see if it was safe to go to the mailbox in peace. The street was quiet. She went out in her slippers and emptied the mailbox of several days' mail, then piled it on the oak table. Since it was probably the weekend, she decided to treat herself to a glass of wine or two. She opened a bottle of red and poured a glass. A fruity Portuguese. Then she put on her reading glasses and flipped through the mail hastily, leaving the bills in their own pile, unopened. One envelope stood out from the rest.

She inspected it. No return address. She pried it open with her letter opener, and out came another envelope and a small handwritten note.

Thanks for everything, and sorry about everything—again. The answer is in the envelope. I photographed the inside of the oyster shell and enlarged it on the computer. At first I considered throwing the picture away. But it didn't feel right. So now I am sending it to you. What you do with it is up to you. If you don't want to know, discard the envelope.

Warm wishes, Meja

Inez stared at the sealed white envelope. Her hands trembled as she took it in her hand. Impulsively, she reached for the lighter on the table and was about to set fire to one corner when she changed her mind and dropped both envelope and lighter. She leaned her forehead against the table and closed her eyes. She had no tears left to cry.

She remained there until her neck became stiff, then she took the envelope and hid it under the humidor in the closet upstairs and came back down. She wasn't going to look at it, but she had to keep it.

Maybe this was a sign that it was time to bring Mathilda back into her life. Edit that rough draft she had written. Go through the words again, sentence by sentence. Write a more convincing ending and send it to Cristy, as she had promised. She poured away the wine, turned on the computer, and wrapped herself in a writing bubble once again.

MEJA

Meja was standing on a stepladder and adjusting a spotlight to get the lighting perfect. She stepped down, stood a couple of yards back from the wall, looked around, and nodded contentedly to herself. Only two photographs to go and she will have filled the small gallery on Kullagatan with her pictures. Tomorrow night she would open the doors for the private viewing of her very first photography exhibition. She didn't really see the point. Who was going to come? But her mother and Bengt had insisted, saying a fancy opening night was obligatory for an exhibition of such fantastic pictures. So they had taken on the role of party planners and invited the entire theater ensemble. Meja's only request was that they serve oysters.

Susanne had cried tears of joy that her daughter finally understood the value of a colorful life. Meja didn't reveal that her choice of refreshment was actually connected to a tragic story. After all, that story was what had led, via some circuitous detours, to Meja standing where she was today.

She adjusted the photograph of Viola's bench—entitled *Take the Decision into Your Own Hands*—and stepped back to look at the result.

She had fallen hard that day when she was kicked out of Inez's house once again. But she had gotten back up, knowing that she had found something of value after all: a direction.

She was enjoying her new vintage style and continuing with her photography. She had swallowed her pride and moved into Susanne and Bengt's guest room, and she had started picking up shifts at the theater café. She smiled when she thought of her mother. They were and would remain very different people, but now at least there was a sort of understanding between them. They were still finding their way, but Meja felt that it was the beginning of something new. A relationship with bandaged wounds.

It had been an abrupt end with Inez, but she would be forever grateful for her time in Domsten. She had learned a lot about herself and about life.

She hadn't really intended to find out what the oyster shell said, but one night when she couldn't sleep and found herself staring at the ceiling for an hour, she got up and transferred the image to the computer. One printout clearly showed the words. She sent the picture to Inez, who would no doubt tear up the unopened envelope out of sheer stubbornness. So be it. It wasn't Meja's decision to make. As Inez had said, it wasn't her story.

She was folding the ladder when she suddenly caught sight of a familiar face outside the gallery window. Andreas? She felt her pulse start to race like a galloping horse. He stopped in his tracks, looked at Meja in surprise, and came in.

"Whoa," he said with wide eyes.

"Hello," she said.

"What are you . . . what is . . . ?" Andreas stuttered.

"Let me just put this away," said Meja, pointing at the ladder.

She disappeared into the back room and took a few deep breaths before returning.

Andreas was moving slowly from photograph to photograph. He didn't say a word until he had done a full circuit. "Did you take all these pictures?"

"Yes, I did." She hoped he couldn't hear her pounding heart. "There's going to be a private exhibit tomorrow, so all feedback is welcome. If there's a picture hanging askew, say so."

"They're hung perfectly," he said.

Meja swallowed hard and wiped the corners of her eyes.

When it came down to it, they were still strangers to each other, yet somehow she felt like he knew her better than anyone. He actually understood her. She could tell from the way he had painted her.

"Sorry," she said. "Opening night jitters, as my mother would say."

He smiled and stroked her arm gently. "It's really nice to see you again."

"How are you?" she said, making a concerted effort to stay composed.

"Good," said Andreas. "Except . . ." He trailed off.

"Except what?"

"I miss you. You disappeared so suddenly."

"I was going to get in touch, but it all got so messy. Long story," said Meja. She looked away. "Are you driving, or shall we dip into the bubbles for the opening?"

He laughed. "I thought you didn't drink bubbles?"

"My mother has taught me to like it. It was her number one priority when I moved in with her and her partner."

"Well, then," he said. "Let's sneak a bottle."

Meja got one of the bottles from the fridge and two glasses. They sat down in the armchairs by the window and clinked glasses.

"So what happened?" he said.

"I can't really explain. My life hit a standstill, and I dragged Inez down with me. Or was it the other way around? It's complicated, but either way I couldn't stay there anymore. Two drowning people cannot save each other."

Andreas frowned. "That sounds dramatic."

"More than you know," she said.

"So you didn't leave because of me?"

Meja shook her head insistently. "No, not at all. Is that what you thought?"

He shrugged. "That night we spent together was wonderful, but we don't know each other very well. I thought maybe things had moved too fast, that you regretted it."

"I didn't," she said, sipping her drink and glancing at him with hot cheeks. "How is she?" she asked cautiously.

"You want an honest answer or a reassuring one?"

Meja bit her lower lip. "Honest."

"I don't think she's doing well. I never see her during the day, and the house is all shut up. But I see her from my bedroom window at night sometimes. She goes to sit on the bench or walks to the pier."

Meja looked down at the floor.

Andreas fiddled with his glass. "We all really want to support her, but she doesn't open the door when we knock. Do you think there's anything we can do as her neighbors? You know her better than we do."

Meja shrugged. "No, probably not. She is the most stubborn person I have ever met."

Andreas nodded slowly. "I understand. Well, I'm glad I finally got a chance to talk to you anyway. I was worried."

"Sorry, I should have reached out. I was just so busy picking up the pieces of myself."

He glanced at the photograph that Meja had taken of him and Kattis.

"Am I invited tomorrow, seeing as I contributed to the artwork? I can drink water since I've already had my ration of booze."

"Of course you can come to the opening," said Meja, smiling. "And Kattis too, of course, if she's in town."

"She's in Gothenburg. Thank you for sending her those pictures, like you promised. She's delighted with them."

Meja nodded, wrote his name on a printed invitation, and gave it to him. "There, now you're officially invited."

She paused for a moment and then wrote one for Sverker and Filip as well.

"Could you give this to them?"

"Absolutely. And what about . . . ?"

Meja shook her head. "Don't think so."

"Okay." Andreas drank up and got ready to leave, but lingered.

Meja took a step forward, wrapped her arms around him, and leaned her head against his chest. He hugged her back gently.

"See you tomorrow," he said. "I'm not supposed to say good luck, am I?"

"I think it's only actors that are superstitious like that. You can wish me luck."

"Good luck," he whispered. He kissed her lightly on the cheek, and left.

Meja leaned against the wall to catch her breath. Suddenly she didn't care if no one else came tomorrow. Andreas was coming. Nothing else mattered.

It was time for the opening. Meja couldn't remember having ever been so nervous before. Susanne, on the other hand, was in her element, setting out canapés, oysters with lemon and pepper, chilled bottles, and champagne flutes. Perhaps the dress that her daughter was wearing also contributed to her radiant mood. Meja had found an Audrey Hepburn–inspired dark-green dress with a flared skirt and bare shoulders at a vintage store. It fit her perfectly.

Bengt handed Meja a glass. "You look like you need a stiff drink. You're not going to faint, are you?"

Meja shook her head and accepted the glass. "But I'm not made for this sort of thing. I'm not a dazzling socialite like my mother."

"Sure you are. You're just not used to it. Can't blame you for being nervous."

"Thank you, Bengt. For everything. For the guest room, for inviting half the theater, for making my mother's dream come true."

He patted her lightly on the arm. "There's no need to talk as if you're on your deathbed. Everything is going to be great. This is the beginning of your new life!"

Meja laughed nervously. That morning, she had found out that she had been accepted into a one-year photography course in London. She hadn't told anyone yet. She was waiting until after the opening.

The bell on the door rang, and Andreas came in. Her pulse quickened.

"Welcome," said Susanne, reaching forward to take his jacket. Bengt handed him a glass and Meja went over to say hello. He was holding a gift. It must be a painting—the painting of her.

"You can open it later," he said, smiling. She nodded and leaned it against the gift table that Susanne had set out, despite Meja's protests.

"And you are?" Susanne said, clinking her glass against his.

"I'm a . . . friend . . . of Meja's."

His short pause before and after the word "friend" made Susanne raise her eyebrows at Meja. Just then, the bell rang again, and in came a few members of the theater crowd. They covered the gift table with bottles, chocolates, and flowers, and kissed Meja on the cheek before walking around the venue to admire the pictures. More theater folk trickled in, and then came Johan, accompanied by a short, dark-haired young woman.

Meja raised her hand in a wave and couldn't help but enjoy his puzzled expression for a brief second when he saw her new look. "Wow," he mouthed, looking at her wide-eyed.

She smiled and walked over to greet them.

She had invited Johan because she'd worried that no one would come. He replied that he would love to come and asked if he could bring a friend. When Meja asked if he meant a girlfriend, he said that it was very new. It felt good to say yes. Like drawing a big line under the past. They had both moved on.

She politely greeted the girl, who looked a little shy, holding tightly onto Johan's hand.

"Grab a drink and see if you can find yourself somewhere on the walls."

Before he could respond, they were interrupted by a shrill howl. Sverker and Filip arrived, dressed in fancy dark-blue suits and holding the biggest bouquet of flowers she had ever seen.

"You have no idea how happy we were when Andreas gave us the invitation! We were so worried about you," Sverker said, giving her a long hug. Filip followed with a more modest embrace.

Meja's eyes moistened. It was so wonderful to see them again.

"Oh no, oh dear," said Sverker. "Don't cry and ruin your mascara now. We'll talk later. But, Meja? That dress. You are pretty as a picture—and a thousand words."

"Pretty as a whole picture book," added Filip.

"Pretty as a whole art gallery of pictures, and the postcards in the gift shop."

Meja laughed and took a napkin to wipe the corners of her eyes without smearing her mascara.

"Thank you so much for coming. Have a look—see if you can find yourselves."

Sverker and Filip hugged her once more and started browsing the photographs. They chatted to several members of the theater company, showering the pictures with compliments all the while. Meja sipped her champagne and watched them. By the time they had done half a lap around the venue, they had already mingled enough to receive free tickets to tomorrow's performance from one of their new acquaintances. When Sverker passed Meja, he slapped her lightly on the arm.

"You never said your mother was an actress."

"I only just recently found out myself," said Meja.

"And you couldn't have passed on the information straightaway?" he said, tilting his head.

Meja laughed. "You're right, how silly of me. I promise not to keep such important information to myself in the future."

"Good. So that means we're going to stay in touch from now on?"

Meja didn't dare say anything for fear of crying. This exhibition wasn't just the celebration of a fresh start, it might also be a sad farewell.

But no one knew about her potential London plans, so she forced a smile and played along as Sverker spoke about autumnal dinner parties at his and Filip's house.

Bengt tapped his glass to get everyone's attention and then gestured to Meja.

She took a deep breath.

"Thank you, everyone, for coming. Recently I have been on a transformative journey, based on decisions made in fleeting moments. The kind of moments that you might let pass by like tufts of clouds in the sky, or catch like snowflakes and shape into something beautiful, as I once read."

Everyone looked around the room at the photographs with new eyes now that they knew the theme was seized, or unseized, moments. Meja raised her glass, expressed her appreciation for Susanne and Bengt's help in making this event possible, and thanked everyone for coming.

The gallery filled with conversation and laughter again. Meja saw Susanne talking to Johan for a long time. Then she strode across the room, picking up another glass of champagne on the way, and stood next to Meja.

"You probably did the right thing," she said, sipping her drink.

Meja looked at her questioningly, though she knew she was talking about Johan.

"He's nice enough, but he's not for you. *He*, on the other hand . . ." She nodded at Andreas, who was helping Bengt write notes with the word **SOLD**, which went up on picture after picture.

"He's a good friend," said Meja, with concerted effort to sound believable.

Susanne snorted. "Why can't you just seize an opportunity when it—" She stopped, forced a smile, patted Meja lightly on the arm, and continued. "Of course you know best. But he is lovely, your *friend*."

Meja gave her mother a gentle hug and turned to Filip, who was standing on her other side.

"I can't tell you how happy I am to be here and see this. Sverker has been so worried," he said. "You should have seen him when he received the invitation from Andreas. Not even a spring-blooming magnolia could make him so happy."

Meja laughed.

Sverker, who was standing on the other side of the room, waved at Filip. Catching his attention, he pointed to the painting of the two of them in their pergola, each with a glass in hand. It was by far the happiest picture in the exhibition. Which was why it had been important to Meja to include it. Among all the wisps of passing clouds, there were some that turned into something truly beautiful. Sverker and Filip were Meja's best example. Filip gave a thumbs-up and mouthed, "Buy it." Sverker went over to talk to Bengt, and a **SOLD** note was soon stuck on that picture as well.

Johan left his girlfriend by one of the pictures and came over to Meja. He looked a little embarrassed.

"I can hardly believe this is you." He cleared his throat. "Look, I'm really sorry—"

Meja interrupted him. "You have nothing to be sorry for. This was the best thing for both of us. We just needed a push to see it. I'm happy for you. Because you have moved on."

"It's very new. I don't know if it's right yet."

"No, but you'll never know if you don't try. It's good that you're giving it a shot."

She cast a quick glance at Andreas, who was looking at her and Johan.

"Good luck," she said, clinking her glass against Johan's and walking over to Andreas.

"What an evening," he said, shoving his hands deep into his pockets.

Meja wanted to brush away that lock of hair that had slipped into his eyes, wanted to warm her cold, nervous hands on his warm, rosy cheeks and slip her arm around his waist.

She thought back to that day in Fahlman's café when she had been forced to leave Johan's apartment. How she had looked at him when he was ordering their coffee and thought that he looked perfectly average, and that was no bad thing.

He didn't look average anymore. His dark curls had grown a bit too long and become unruly, his hazel eyes had splashes of amber that made them sparkle, and he had a way of smiling that crooked little smirk that always made him look so enchanted by life. An enchanted person couldn't be average. An enchanted person was special.

She peered into her glass and nodded. "Yes, it's been better than perfect."

Two hours passed quickly. After the party finished, only Andreas, Susanne, and Bengt remained.

Bengt washed up the glasses while Susanne loaded up the car with Meja's gifts. Then she put her arm around Bengt's waist as he rolled down his shirtsleeves.

"Shall we leave the young ones to it?" she said.

Meja could tell from her tone of voice that she had already interpreted Andreas as a potential boyfriend, no matter what Meja said.

"Thanks for everything. See you at home soon," said Meja.

Susanne waved her hand. "You come and go as you please, day or night."

Meja avoided looking at Andreas. Susanne was hardly being subtle.

When Susanne and Bengt had left, Meja sank into an armchair and kicked off her high-heeled shoes. Her stomach rumbled. She laughed.

"Sorry, food hasn't really been a priority of late."

"Understandable. Hey, why not come to my house for some mushroom risotto?"

There was uncertainty in his voice. It made her want to scream *Yes!* but she took a calm breath instead and said, "I need to decompress a bit first. What if I took a cab to your place in an hour?"

He smiled, relieved. "Perfect."

After a quick hug, he left her alone in the gallery. Meja walked around the room, looking at each photograph in turn. All but five were sold.

She was fixated on the photograph of Sverker and Filip in the pergola when the bell on the door rang. Meja turned around to say that the gallery was closed but stopped in her tracks. It was Inez with a gift in her hand.

"You missed the party," she said in a faltering voice.

"Was I even invited?" Inez said sulkily before handing Meja the package and walking around the gallery.

"This looks suspiciously like a book," said Meja, trying, but failing, to smile. She unwrapped it. *The Portrait of a Lady*. She didn't recognize it as one of the books in the save pile. "Thank you."

"I think it's appropriate for your new life," Inez answered with her back to her.

Meja put the book down and watched Inez walk around the gallery. She had stopped at the picture of herself standing on the porch with her face to the sky and her eyes closed. When she turned to Meja, her expression was softer.

"That was the very moment I decided to write the truth. To lighten my own yoke, and to honor my friendship with Mathilda. But it didn't turn out that way. I took the cowardly path."

"It's a difficult story to tell," Meja said, almost too quietly to hear.

"That's why it's so important to get it right," Inez said.

They both sat down.

"The ending isn't right," said Inez.

Meja didn't dare say anything. They sat in silence for a long time.

"Will you come with me?" Inez said finally.

Meja looked up. "Back to your house?"

Inez smiled sadly. "No, to Bouzigues."

Meja put her hand over her mouth. *I'm waiting in Bouzigues.* That was what it said on the oyster.

"Are you serious?"

"I've never been so serious about anything in all my life," said Inez. "I don't expect to run into her there. Frankly, who knows if she's still alive. I'm sure we would have met again at some point if she were. But I need to go there and see the place anyway. It will make a good ending. Don't you think?"

"Yes, it really will," said Meja, wiping the corners of her eyes. "Sorry. It's been a long and emotional day. I'm going over to Andreas's for risotto, by the way. Shall we share a cab?"

"Aha," said Inez, smiling widely. "I knew it."

Meja smiled. "You sound like my mother."

They got up to leave, and Meja locked up behind them.

"Meja. I'm the one who should be saying thank you and sorry. Not you," said Inez as they stood arm in arm waiting for the cab.

Meja blinked the tears away, thinking of the note she had written to Inez along with the answer to the riddle of the oyster shell. "You're welcome, and I forgive you," she said with a smile.

MEJA

Andreas drove Meja and Inez to Copenhagen Airport. Inez grew quieter and quieter over the course of the journey. When Andreas hugged them both goodbye, she didn't respond. Meja glanced at her. She had pallid cheeks and a vacant stare. Meja gestured for her to sit on a bench while she checked their luggage, and Inez didn't protest, which was telling. Normally, she would have announced that she was perfectly capable of checking her own luggage like everyone else.

Meja followed the slowly winding line. She knew that Inez didn't like to think *what if*. But right now, Meja couldn't help it. What if she had known everything that last week's exhibition was going to set into motion? She had never wanted to do it in the first place; it was all Susanne and Bengt's idea. What if Andreas hadn't been in town on an errand that day and had never passed the gallery? She might never have seen him again. And he wouldn't have given the invitation to Sverker and Filip, who had in turn invited Inez. And they wouldn't be sitting here now. On their way to France.

She checked their luggage and they went through security. Meja had only flown on holiday once before, when she and Johan went to Crete. They had ended up in an all-inclusive hotel in the middle of nowhere, where most of the guests were families with children. She hadn't been able to eat at a buffet restaurant since. It had not been a trip to remember. But what she did remember enjoying was the airport.

She glanced at all the duty-free stores, cafés, and restaurants as they moved at a slow pace. She could spend all day here just taking pictures. People's facial expressions were so particular when they were in transit. So easy to read. So filled with anticipation, worry, stress, excitement.

Inez scrolled through her text messages and looked up.

"They're at Le Sommelier Bar & Bistro."

Meja nodded. "Let's carry on walking; I'm sure we'll see it."

Inez had invited Amelia on the trip too. If Meja understood correctly, her daughter had refused at first but was persuaded by Inez's publisher and friend, Cristy. Amelia had finally agreed, on the condition that Cristy come too. So now they were sitting at a bar somewhere, waiting for Inez and Meja.

"There," said Inez, pointing at a bar with a bistro feel.

A glamorous older woman in a purple hat and matching jacket waved at them. Meja assumed she must be Cristy. She came and kissed both Inez and Meja on the cheek.

"Wonderful to see you. This is going to be so much fun! Can't you just feel the atmosphere in this *French* bistro?" Cristy gestured around the bar.

Inez tried to smile, but it came out as more of a grimace.

Amelia also greeted them, in a more restrained way, and they sat down.

"A group vacation. Almost too good to be true. This calls for a celebration," Cristy said, ordering a bottle of wine.

Meja leaned closer to Inez. "Do they know why we're going?" she whispered.

Inez shook her head.

Oh dear, Meja thought and smiled at Cristy as she poured them all drinks.

"I read a bit about the place. Bouzigues is known for its vast salt-water lagoon and is the oyster and mussel capital of the Mediterranean. Not exactly Berlin," she said, winking at Inez. "But it takes about three and a half hours to drive to Cannes, so if the town is too sleepy we can just hire a car and drive around. With all those oysters in our belly, we could have the time of our lives." She chuckled, giving Inez a nudge. Then she turned to Meja. "And am I right in saying you're Inez's cleaner?"

"I was," said Meja.

"Now she's a friend," Inez said, in such a clipped tone that Cristy dropped the subject.

She continued talking about their destination instead. Inez sat in composed silence, and Amelia scrolled and typed on her cell phone. Meja tried to nod and look interested for the sake of politeness but felt nerves creeping under her skin. What was this trip really going to achieve? Inez was going in search of a past that neither Amelia nor Cristy knew about. Wouldn't it be better just to tell them?

They finished the wine and went to their gate. Meja shuddered at the sight of the plane outside the large panoramic windows.

"I know," Inez whispered. "I hate flying too. The things a person will do to write the ending of their final book."

They boarded and found their seats. Inez had the window seat with Cristy next to her, then Meja and Amelia were on the other side of the aisle. Cristy placed an eye mask, hand cream, a water bottle, and a fashion magazine in the pocket of the seat in front of her.

"There we go," she said, pulling a miniature spray bottle in a sealed bag from her purse. "This is just as important for us ladies as a Bible is to a devout Christian," she said and took off the lid. She pointed it at Meja and spritzed some mist right in her face.

Meja flinched and was about to wipe it off with her hand when Cristy stopped her and demonstrated on herself. She closed her eyes, sprayed, and slowly opened her eyes.

"Ahhh, lovely." She rolled her eyes at Meja's uncomprehending expression. "You have a lot to learn, my girl. The face needs moisture, and the air indoors is dry—especially on airplanes—so you need a face mist. You can even use it over makeup." She leaned forward to inspect Meja's face, even though they were already close to each other. "Not that

I see a trace of makeup on you." She put the spray bottle in the seat pocket along with her other things and buckled her belt. "Rouge," she said, nodding convincingly. "It's the only makeup you need."

The plane's engines rumbled. Meja glanced at Inez, who was sitting with her eyes closed and head tilted back.

Once they were in the air, Cristy ordered wine and chatted animatedly with her neighbors in front and behind. Amelia, Inez, and Meja slept or pretended to sleep—Meja wasn't sure—until the plane landed in Paris, where they transferred to a plane to Montpellier.

When they landed at their final destination, Cristy sprayed herself and Meja in the face again, and off they went. Meja and Amelia hurried off to baggage claim while Cristy and Inez went out to find them a cab.

"Mom and her whims," said Amelia, more to herself than to Meja. "We'd decided that I would come and visit her to see what a good job you'd done of sorting out the house. Then suddenly I wasn't welcome because she had an important project to work on. I didn't think she even worked anymore. I don't hear a peep from her for several weeks and then she expects me to drop everything and just go on vacation." The luggage belt began moving. She shook her head. "This is exactly how she was when I was growing up. Colleagues, parties, meetings, interviews, writing, research, planning, editing, book launches, photo shoots . . . all of it, and more besides, came before me. I just had to tag along. Or stay in a hotel room with Cristy."

"I'm glad Cristy is joining us. She seems like a breath of fresh air," Meja chirped, for lack of anything else to say. She really didn't like the fact that Amelia and Cristy were unaware of the true purpose of the trip. It meant she would constantly have to watch herself and not say the wrong thing. But this was Inez's trip, and it was her decision.

Amelia looked at Meja with weary eyes. "I wouldn't have come without Cristy. She has always been like a second mother to me. All the times Mom has been elsewhere—physically or mentally."

Meja nodded, relieved to see Inez's leather suitcase roll toward her on the conveyor belt. Once they all had their luggage, they walked toward the cabstand, where Cristy was waving at them.

They all squeezed into the cab, with Cristy in front. Meja assumed Cristy's French was a little off, judging by the driver's amused smile. In what was probably equally broken English, he replied, "Oyster very good there. Eat many."

Cristy clapped her hands together in delight and turned to the party in the back seat, then frowned. "You ladies look like you're going to a funeral. If you don't lighten up, I'll run away with this handsome cabdriver instead. You can keep your oysters."

Meja couldn't help but smile. Cristy was the saving grace of the trip. She continued to chatter away to the driver about similarities and differences between Sweden and France. Amelia was scrolling through her phone again. It looked like she was working. Inez sat quietly looking out the window.

After about half an hour they turned off at the sign pointing to Bouzigues and followed small streets through a residential area. Just the sight of house numbers in beautiful ceramic tiles made Meja want to jump out of the car and take pictures. They passed a vineyard and some houses mid-construction before arriving at the village itself, where the driver wound his way through narrow alleys.

Soon they could see snatches of water between buildings. They came to a small port, but instead of stopping there, the driver continued along the coast past restaurants and cafés. He pointed at the sea and at tall wooden structures of some kind. "Oyster," he said.

Meja and Inez craned to see. They continued past stately residential buildings in white or light terra-cotta plaster with palms and pines in the gardens, past a sandy beach, and then a short distance to a sort of industrial area right by the sea. There were docks lined with boats, ready to sail out to the large, wooden, scaffolding-like structures. Each jetty had its own building that Meja assumed housed oyster vendors. Business was bustling behind the wide-open doors with shutters on either side. There were nets, plastic baskets, and utensils everywhere, and people sitting on plastic chairs scraping oysters.

Meja and Inez exchanged a glance.

The driver went slowly through the area before turning back to the harbor, where their pink hotel was situated right on the waterfront.

Cristy paid—Meja assumed she tipped generously—then flashed a beaming smile at the women as they all got out of the cab.

"There, you see what happens when you make an effort to be *friendly*? We got a free sightseeing tour too."

She craned her neck as they passed the outdoor dining area of the hotel restaurant, where staff cruised between the tables holding platters overflowing with seafood delicacies, and entered the lobby.

Meja took a brochure and flipped through it while the others handled the check-in. The lagoon outside was enormous, and a close-up of the wooden scaffolding showed that it resembled large tables where clams, oysters, and shells were farmed on ropes. She was about to show Inez but noticed how tired she looked and decided to put the brochure in her pocket instead.

Once everyone had their keys, they took the elevator up and parted ways. In her room, Meja dumped her bag, pulled open the heavy drapes, and breathed deeply. They had arrived.

She could hardly believe she had tracked down Ellen in Kobbholmen, found the oyster shell, and deciphered the place name. And now they were all here.

She freshened up and went to check on Inez.

"Wow," said Meja when Inez let her in. She had the tower room with a balcony facing the harbor. Meja went out and admired the view of the lagoon. Thoughts of Andreas fluttered through her mind. He would love to paint this view. She was just about to say so to Inez, who was standing next to her, when the older woman suddenly took her hand.

"Do you think she's still here?" Meja whispered.

Inez slowly shook her head. "No, I don't. I would feel it in my heart if she were."

She went back inside and took a small box out of her luggage. Inside were the remains of the smashed oyster shell with Mathilda's final message.

"Tonight I will scatter the shards in the water. And that will be the ending." She smiled weakly at Meja. "Then we will have oysters and champagne in one of the restaurants here and then go to Cannes tomorrow so Cristy can have her party. When I get home, I'll rewrite the ending more honestly. The way I hope and believe it was for Mathilda in this place."

"That sounds good," said Meja. "Authentic."

There was a knock on the door, and Inez opened it to reveal Cristy wearing a wide-brimmed sun hat and sunglasses. Behind her stood Amelia.

"Time to cause some trouble in the village," said Cristy.

They left the room, and Cristy paused in the hallway to dab a little rouge on Inez's and Meja's cheeks. "There. Now you look a little more alive." Then she tottered off in her high-heeled sandals.

"Are you really going to wear those?" Inez said.

"What if I run into the love of my life and miss my chance because I'm going around like *that*?" she said, pointing at Inez's orthopedic sneakers.

"If he was really the love of your life, wouldn't he be able to see past your shoes?" Inez said.

"Hello!? He would be French. Of course he would care about the shoes." Cristy rolled her eyes.

Amelia smirked at Meja, who smiled back. Maybe this trip was going to be fun after all.

They walked around the village. Meja took out her camera and immortalized the coiling green wrought iron balconies, house facades with flaking plaster, and laundry hung out to dry on lines.

A visit to the small oyster museum right by the sea was vehemently vetoed by Cristy, whose feet had started to swell up so much that her sandal straps were chafing, and they started walking back to the hotel. Cristy suggested they take a siesta and meet at the restaurant downstairs at seven o'clock. No one objected.

Back in the hotel room, Meja lay on the bed and googled Cannes. She fell asleep with the image of a palm-lined beach and turquoise water on the back of her eyelids.

INEZ

The view from the balcony was beautiful, but the location didn't suit Mathilda. It was too manicured. Inez had done some research before the trip and learned that small oyster larvae were attached to ropes with cement, three by three. These cords were hung down into the water from the wooden structures in the lagoon and removed after three years. It was completely different from Mathilda's method of wild picking. And yet, there was something beautiful about this dedication to the sea's delicacies. There was a certain reverence in this village, a pride in growing, harvesting, cooking, and serving "the best oysters in France."

Inez fingered the box in her pocket and went for a solo walk while the others were taking their siesta. Whenever she passed a restaurant, she showed the staff the note she had written in English: *Excuse me, do you know a Swedish oyster diver who lives here? Her name is Mathilda.*

They all shook their heads. An hour and a half later, she returned to the hotel and the one restaurant she had yet to ask, the one where they would be eating that evening. She held out the note in a slightly tremulous hand. The man thought for a moment and then said in stilted English, "I get grandmother. She knows everyone, remembers everything."

Fatigue suddenly caught up with Inez after the long walk, the flight, and all the excitement. The man pulled out a chair for her.

"Please, sit and enjoy the view," he said.

A few minutes later he came back with a short woman with long gray hair tied up in a loose bun. He served Inez a glass of white wine, which he told her was made from local grapes, and asked his grandmother the question in French.

The woman mumbled to herself. Inez felt her heart fluttering. Then the woman shook her head and said something to her grandson. The man splayed his hands in an apologetic gesture.

"No Swedish oyster diver."

"Thank you, anyway. Let me pay for the wine; it was delicious."

He shook his head. "On the house."

Inez didn't have the energy to protest. She raised her glass to them and stayed where she was, sipping the cool drink. When she had finished, she went back to her room for a nap and a shower. Then she went down to the restaurant again in a fresh linen shirt and pants.

She heard her group in the distance. Cristy was speaking animatedly in French to the waiter, who laughed and spoke just as enthusiastically back. Amelia and Meja were reading from the same menu. Inez felt warmth ripple through her, similar to what she had felt sitting on Amelia's couch with her daughter and Cristy sleeping next to her. A sense of harmony. She had people in her life that she cared about. So why spend her time chasing ghosts?

"Inez!" Cristy exclaimed, motioning for her to sit down.

Just then the waiter came out with a large platter of fresh oysters and champagne.

"Cheers to Inez for taking us on this unexpected but wonderful adventure."

Everyone raised their glasses.

As Amelia and Cristy entered into a lively conversation about Copenhagen's art scene, Meja leaned closer to Inez.

"You look . . . rested."

Inez smiled and patted her hand. "You know what? A nap did the trick. I'm happy to be here. Happy about getting an ending." She adjusted the napkin in her lap. "I'm almost looking forward to leaving this behind and going to Cannes for a couple of days of extravagance."

Meja smiled. "That makes me really happy. So this trip was worth-while after all."

Cristy turned to them. "Cannes? Did I hear Cannes?"

Inez smiled. "I think we've seen all there is to see here, especially after the driver took us sightseeing, so if you want to go to Cannes tomorrow, I think we should."

Cristy clapped her hands in delight. "Yes, yes, yes!"

"I'll book a rental car for us," said Amelia.

Cristy turned to Amelia and told her that she had been to Cannes several times. "I'll show you all the sights."

Inez smiled. In Cristy's world that meant places where you might catch sight of celebrities. She doubted Amelia would find this as fasci-nating as Cristy did.

Bowls of mussels and sliced baguettes were placed on the table.

"Wonderful," Inez said, smiling at the three women around her.

The warm evening settled like a soft velvet blanket around Inez's shoulders. She was enjoying the present moment in a way she rarely ever had. It was a feeling she wanted to capture, like a clam in its shell, to revisit on the dark autumn days soon to come.

Evening faded into night, and Cristy let out a big yawn.

"Right, lovely ladies. This girl needs her beauty sleep if she's going to cause trouble in Cannes tomorrow."

They agreed to leave straight after breakfast. Back in the hotel, Amelia, Meja, and Cristy said good night and went to their rooms. Inez pretended to do the same but turned back and went down to the harbor pier instead.

She had spent so much time standing on the pier at Domsten, feeling Mathilda's presence. Here she felt nothing. But it was very likely that Mathilda had once come to this precise spot, and this was where her oyster shell would rest at the bottom of the sea forevermore.

It was a dark night, and the stars shone with a rare clarity. Inez took the box out of her pocket.

"Thank you for everything," she whispered. "My heart tells me that you did find happiness at last." She scattered the crushed shell into the water. Then she put the empty box in her pocket, raised her hand in a brief farewell, and turned back to the hotel.

MEJA

When Meja came downstairs, Inez was sitting alone at the breakfast table. She had coffee, juice, and a plate piled high with eggs, bread, cheese, croissants, and oysters. She brightened when she caught sight of Meja, who sat down across from her.

"Do you realize that you can have oysters for breakfast here?"

Meja smiled and ordered coffee and a croissant.

Inez tilted her head. "You look a little pale."

"Too much wine and champagne for me," she said, looking out over the lagoon. "But it was worth it. What an evening!"

"Yes, we won't forget it in a hurry. Even Amelia was laughing out loud. It's been a long time since I've heard that."

"I saw you from my window last night. On the pier."

Inez ate an oyster and nodded. "I scattered the crushed oyster shell in the water, in the place where Mathilda might once have been, or where she had planned to go, at least."

"I wonder what happened to her," said Meja.

"You know what?" said Inez, wiping her mouth with the cloth napkin. "I don't, not anymore. I'm satisfied with the way it's turned out. Returning the shell to the sea, being here with you, having written my story and knowing it will make a fascinating book one day. Because Mathilda was a fascinating person. I have borne this cross for long enough, and I feel I have been forgiven now." She shrugged. "Maybe it's the atmosphere here, all the wine and good food playing tricks on me, but that's how it feels right now."

"Well, I think that sounds pretty great. So, are you ready for a celebration?"

Inez nodded. Just then, Cristy and Amelia emerged with their luggage.

"I thought you were still sleeping," Inez said.

Cristy scoffed. "Sleep? I'll sleep when I'm ninety. Come on, chop-chop. We've got things to do."

Amelia was already sitting in the driver's seat of a rented white Audi when Meja and Inez came out. They got in the back seat, and Cristy sat up front.

"To Cannes!" Cristy said, letting out a small squeal of joy.

They followed the coast to avoid the crowded village streets, but the road came to a dead end at the oyster museum, with nothing but beach beyond.

"Hmm. I guess we're going to have to turn back and take another route," said Amelia.

Just then, Inez grabbed the seat in front of her with both hands and craned her neck. "Wait!" she cried. "Stop the car!"

Amelia pulled to the side.

"What now?" said Cristy. "Did you forget something?"

Inez got out and slowly started walking along the beach, her eyes fixed on the jetty in front of the museum. Meja moved over to Inez's side of the car to see. A wooden boat with a small cabin in the stern was puttering toward the jetty.

A woman was standing at the wheel. Meja couldn't see much from this distance, except that the woman was slim and straight-backed and had long, dark-gray hair that fluttered in the breeze.

"What is Mom doing now?" Amelia said with a sigh.

She got out of the car, followed by Meja and Cristy. But when Amelia started to head toward Inez, Meja held her back. Amelia looked at her in surprise but stopped.

The woman in the boat docked at the jetty and unloaded a plastic basket of oysters.

Inez covered her mouth with both hands, as if to stifle the sounds that wanted to come out. But instead of approaching the woman, she walked away from her, away from the museum and the rental car. She just walked and walked with quick steps farther down the wide sandy beach.

"What is she doing?" Amelia said, starting to walk after her.

Cristy and Meja followed.

The woman on the jetty had caught sight of Inez from behind and shielded her eyes with her hand to see. When Inez turned around again, she raised her hand in the air, questioningly. Inez raised hers back, and the woman started walking in Inez's direction.

Meja, Amelia, and Cristy slowed their steps, keeping their eyes fixed on this woman. She reached Inez. They stared at each other. The woman placed a hand on Inez's cheek, then Inez placed a hand on hers, and they just stood like that, completely still.

"I don't think we're going to Cannes today," said Meja.

"Huh? Why not?" said Cristy.

"Because Inez has found what she came here for."

"I have no idea what's going on," said Amelia, raising her eyebrows in surprise as Meja wiped a tear from the corner of her eye. "Can you explain?"

"It's Inez's story. She'll have to tell you herself."

INEZ

All was calm. Inez heard no sounds, saw no people. She didn't know if her heart was still beating. She couldn't feel it. Everything was a blur. Except Mathilda. Her contours were as sharp as ever. She was standing right in front of her. Alive and well.

"I knew you would come," said Mathilda.

Inez swallowed hard. "It took a lifetime, and a cleaner, for me to get here," she whispered.

She gathered the strength to utter the words she had come here to say. It was painful, but nowhere near as painful as all the guilt she had endured over the years.

"I'm sorry," she said.

Mathilda tilted her head. "There's no need to be sorry, Inez."

"Yes, there is." Tears clouded her vision. "You sacrificed your whole life for me. I was supposed to come and find you . . ."

Mathilda put her finger on her lips. "Shhhh."

Inez wiped the corners of her eyes and saw Amelia, Meja, and Cristy coming toward them.

Amelia looked worried. "Are you okay, Mom?"

Inez nodded. "Yes, I'm good."

"What's going on?" said Cristy. "Meja says that this wasn't just a tourist trip at all, that you came here for . . ." She made a gesture of uncertainty.

Inez smiled weakly. "She's right. This is what I came here for." She looked at Mathilda. "To find the oyster diver."

Cristy and Amelia exchanged confused glances. Mathilda held out her hand and introduced herself. She held Amelia's hand for an extra-long time.

"You're Swedish?" Amelia said in surprise.

Mathilda nodded and smiled. "I moved here half a lifetime ago and married into an oyster-loving family. We founded this museum in the early 1990s. My son and his family run it now, but I help."

"But how do you know—?" Amelia began, but Mathilda interrupted her.

"Are you in a hurry, or would you like to give me a hand? In truth I'm far too old for this sort of thing, but I love being able to offer the museum's visitors handpicked oysters."

Amelia and Cristy looked at Inez for answers to their many questions, but Inez only answered Mathilda's.

"We're not in a hurry, and we're happy to help. Right?"

Cristy and Amelia nodded uncomprehendingly and followed Mathilda along the beach.

Inez and Meja followed behind. Inez was having to concentrate on her breathing so as not to pass out, and her body was trembling as though from fever.

"Is this really happening?" she whispered.

Meja squeezed her hand. "Seems so."

The jetty boasted a colorful line of blue and red boats, and Mathilda's was docked beside a blue-painted wooden hut. They all helped her unload the oysters. When Mathilda opened the door to the hut, Inez gasped. The tools, the shells, the smell of the sea. It was like traveling back in time, to Kobbholmen, to her youth.

Mathilda gave Amelia an oyster knife and showed her how to open the shell. Just as she had when Inez first met her in the café on the pier in Kobbholmen.

"A natural," she said when Amelia succeeded on the first try.

Amelia smiled in surprise. "And you can eat them right away?"

"That's when they're most flavorful," said Mathilda, giving Meja and Cristy a knife each. Meja got her shell open on the second try and then helped Cristy.

Mathilda gazed at Inez with moist eyes. Clearly, she too was over-whelmed by this turn of events. It was slowly sinking in for both of them. Inez nodded almost imperceptibly. Here they were. Standing over a basket of oysters. Not even in her wildest dreams could she have hoped for such an ending to her book.

Mathilda picked up her cell phone and made a short call in fluent French.

"My good friend Javier will be here soon. He's a chef at a bistro a few minutes' walk from the museum. Let me treat you to a meal there. I have to work a little longer, but he'll take care of you. When you've finished eating, I'd like to take Inez out on a short boat ride before you carry on to wherever you're going. Is that okay?"

Everyone exchanged glances and nodded.

"Oh, and by the way," said Mathilda. "No one here knows that I'm Swedish. They think my name is Monique and I'm from Denmark, just so you know." She winked.

Amelia glanced curiously at Inez, who avoided eye contact. Soon a man appeared from the other side of the museum.

"Be back here in an hour," Mathilda whispered to Inez.

Inez nodded and followed the others, but paused to watch Mathilda step into the boat and steer away from the shore. It was a sight she thought she'd never see again.

Meja took her by the arm, and they followed the others to the restaurant in silence.

The man spoke to them in French and served the most amazing concoctions to accompany the oysters, but Cristy didn't even let out her usual squeals of joy. Everyone was engrossed in their own thoughts as they ate.

"What did that woman say her name was?" Cristy said to Inez.

"Mathilda."

Cristy thought, then narrowed her eyes. "Your dedications . . . M for Mathilda?"

Inez nodded slowly and looked back in the direction they had just come from. If the others hadn't still been talking about Mathilda, she might have thought she had imagined it. Mathilda hadn't changed. The same curious, alert eyes, straight posture, long hair. Tears began to flow.

"Mom," Amelia said, concerned, reaching her hand across the table. Inez took it and held it tightly. "Who is she? You have to tell us."

"A friend," said Inez, picking up a napkin to wipe her wet cheeks.

"A friend?" Cristy repeated. "Why have I never heard of her?"

"Because she's a friend from my past. We lost touch, in quite a dramatic fashion. I promise I'll tell you everything. Later."

"So what now?" Amelia said.

Cristy took a deep, pensive breath. "I think we should enjoy this feast, stay in the village one more night, and take it from there."

Inez looked at her gratefully.

Meja poured them all wine from the carafe. "Cheers," she said.

"Cheers to what?" said Amelia, who still sounded a bit shocked by all this.

"To life's crossroads," said Inez.

Amelia turned to her. "Have you taken us to one of life's crossroads?"

"It would seem so," said Inez.

Cristy tilted her head. "So this was never a spontaneous holiday? You came here to find a friend?"

"Why didn't you just say so?" Amelia said.

"Because I really didn't think she would still be here. I just wanted to see the place. It felt too complicated to explain."

"But *you* knew?" Amelia said, looking reproachfully at Meja.

Meja squirmed.

"Yes, she knows because she has read my manuscript about the oyster diver," Inez said.

Cristy narrowed her eyes. "Manuscript? The one I'm going to get to read?"

Inez nodded.

"Are you writing again, for real?" Amelia's voice was getting continuously shriller.

Inez raised her glass in a trembling hand.

"All will be revealed. In time. For now I only ask one thing of you. Eat, enjoy, and wait for me." She checked the time, clinked glasses with the others, took one last sip, and stood up. Amelia got up as well.

"Stay with the others. I have to do this alone," she said, patting Amelia lightly on the arm.

"But what if . . . ?" Amelia said, with a worried tremor in her voice.

"I never think *what if.*" Inez smiled and turned away.

Out of the corner of her eye, she saw Amelia sit back down and Cristy put an arm around her shoulders.

Inez followed the same route back and turned onto the jetty. Mathilda was already waiting by her boat. She held out a hand and helped Inez get in. They said nothing. Didn't even look at each other. There was no need.

Their proximity alone was enough to make the air tremble.

Mathilda steered the boat along the rocky shore. A shiver ran through Inez. Everything was as before, yet completely different. Her boat was almost the same as the one in Kobbholmen, the water just as still, though it was more turquoise here. And dolphins were more likely to follow in the boat's wake than seals.

They docked at a rickety jetty and disembarked. Mathilda took off her shoes, rolled up her pant legs, and waded out with the aquascope and net. Then she nodded for Inez to do the same.

"Are we going to look for oysters here?" Inez asked in a voice so thin it sounded like a whisper.

Mathilda nodded.

Inez followed, lowered the aquascope, and began searching the bottom. After a while she raised her head. "This doesn't look like an oyster bed."

Mathilda gestured for her to keep searching, and after a while Inez saw something white glimmer on the bottom some distance away. She walked over carefully so as not to slip on the stones. It was an oyster. She bent down and picked it up.

"I found one!" she shouted, but fell silent when she saw Mathilda. She looked pale despite her tanned skin.

Inez looked at the oyster in her hand. It wasn't a whole oyster, just a shell. She swallowed hard. She knew what that meant. Mathilda must have left this while Inez was at the restaurant. For her to find.

"I told you I would do anything for you, and this is why," Mathilda whispered.

Inez slowly turned the shell over and saw letters carved into it. She read them slowly, one by one.

My sister.

INEZ

The air was harsh, forlorn. As if she had been gone for six months, not five days. They hadn't gone to Cannes in the end, staying in Bouzigues instead.

Inez dropped her bags on the hall floor and looked around the living room. It was just as she had left it: stacks of books, blinds down, dry cactus on the windowsill. Papers piled on the oak table. Mathilda's story. At the top of the pile was Meja's photograph of the words in the oyster shell. *I'm waiting in Bouzigues.*

After redrafting the manuscript, opening Meja's envelope had felt like the natural thing to do.

At first she didn't even google the place. She just let it rest in her mind. It wasn't until Sverker knocked on her door—so persistently that she had no choice but to open—and told her about Meja's exhibition in town that the idea took root. She had grown tired of solitude. Tired of hiding. And she had missed Meja. Missed the cups of coffee left outside her door, their walks to the pier, casual chats in the armchairs, sharing a port. The time had come to look the truth in the eye. The truth was Bouzigues. And the truth was she wanted Meja to go with her. It was all thanks to her.

Inez opened the blinds. Never in her wildest dreams had she expected that Mathilda would still be there. She swallowed hard. The thought of Mathilda gave rise to so many emotions: amazement, joy, and something else as well. She had let Mathilda down, but Mathilda had let her down too. Why, for all these years, despite all their intimacy, had she chosen to keep it a secret that they were sisters? What had given her that right? What if Inez had known then that Mats was her father too? And why didn't Mathilda try to contact her in their later years? It wasn't like she'd been difficult to find.

Inez stepped onto the porch and gave herself a little shake. She didn't want to get stuck in negative thought spirals. Didn't want to think *what if*. There was no point.

A bunch of flowers hung on the gate. A bouquet of delicate, white, fall-blooming anemones. She displayed it in a vase on the window for Sverker to see. Then she took a picture and sent it to Amelia with the words A new era.

Amelia had broken down when they landed at Copenhagen Airport. She felt cheated by Inez's lie about the purpose of the trip, and years of repressed emotions had manifested in tears, disappointment, sadness, and a heartbreaking smallness. Meja had returned to Helsingborg alone while both Cristy and Inez accompanied Amelia home.

As soon as they arrived, Amelia told them that she and Aksel had separated. Then they spent the rest of the day talking about everything they should have hashed out long ago, starting with the most painful: Amelia's sense that she had always come second in Inez's life, and her feeling lost behind the perfect facade of her life with Aksel.

When all the words had been said, Amelia looked at Inez, then at Cristy, who had both been listening in silence, and burst into a peal of exhausted laughter. This elicited even more tears, and they all hugged each other, laughing and crying in turn.

Cristy poured them a brandy each and they entered round two of the conversation. Something else they should have spent more time talking about over the years: all the good times. Of which there were plenty. Certainly more than sad times.

They talked about all the trips they had taken. Cristy would tutor Amelia but always end up doing the teachers' worksheets herself because she considered the topics entirely irrelevant to children—who cared about chemical formulas and how many politicians there were in parliament? She taught Amelia about what she considered important: art, music, literature, food, and drink.

Amelia wiped away tears of laughter when Cristy told her how proud she'd been of Amelia when she, age nine, walked up to a man at a publishers' party and told him about the grape in the wine he was drinking. Inez told Amelia about how she had dressed up in her mother's clothes and waved from the balcony to devoted fans below their hotel in Madrid. And Amelia added that some of her fondest childhood memories were of curling up with a pillow and blanket to sleep under Inez's desk. Nothing made her feel safer than the clatter of her mother's fingers on the keyboard.

"Sorry for being so grumpy and only focusing on the negatives," Amelia said finally. "You always included me; you treated me as an equal. You didn't indulge me, and deep down I'm grateful for that. Grateful for everything I got to be a part of."

"And I'm sorry for all the times I shut you out and didn't realize that I *should* have indulged you a little, because you were only a child," Inez replied.

And they had embraced, with a strong sense of having embarked on a new chapter.

Inez's cell phone beeped. It was a picture of Amelia's bedroom floor, where a few items of clothing lay on the floor by an unmade bed. New era here too, she wrote with a laughing emoji.

Inez smiled. After all that had happened, the most important thing now was for Amelia to find herself. Inez had found herself. Meja had found herself. Now it was her daughter's turn, and Inez would do everything in her power to help her along the way.

She put on her sheepskin slippers and was about to pour a glass of port when she saw a familiar figure approaching the house. Meja opened the gate, in a well-practiced movement, and waved when she caught sight of Inez through the window. Inez opened the door with a smile.

"I was coming to see Andreas but saw that the blinds were open and realized you must be home."

"Oh, I thought you could smell the port," said Inez and went to pour a glass for Meja as well.

"That too," she said with a chuckle.

They sat down and clinked glasses.

"How's Amelia?" Meja asked.

Inez smiled. "She's well. The trip brought up a lot of emotions that pushed her over the edge, but that's exactly what one needs sometimes. We spent a full twenty-four hours talking and drinking brandy, punctuated by naps. It was cleansing. I could see it in Amelia's eyes when I left. There was a determination there that I have never seen before." Inez patted Meja on the hand. "Just think what your curiosity has set in motion."

Meja sipped her port with a smile.

Inez had so many questions, starting with How had Meja ended up with Ellen in Kobbholmen? But she thought it might be better not to know. It was what it was, and it had all turned out to be for the best.

"What about you?" she asked instead. "What are you going to do with your life?"

On the flight home, Meja had told her about the course in London and how it had coincided with her and Andreas falling in love. She said she didn't know what to do, but Inez assumed she would choose love. That was the most important thing, after all.

"You've taught me the importance of following your dream, your calling," said Meja. "And the importance of choosing carefully at those crucial crossroads. Catching the passing clouds. So I'm going to London."

"Oh," said Inez with a frown. "Perhaps you should take my advice with a pinch of salt."

Meja smiled. "We'll try a long-distance relationship for one year. If our love can't survive that, it probably won't survive all the other challenges that will no doubt await us in the future."

Inez smiled, feeling tears well up. She was so proud of Meja's journey.

"There's just one problem," said Meja.

"What's that?"

"Ingrid. She has nowhere to stay when I go to London. My mother doesn't like having her around. I thought . . . she's a good companion, and she likes it here."

Inez raised her eyebrows and scoffed. Then again, she needed someone to talk to about her day. Who better than Ingrid Bergman? She nodded briefly to hide her enthusiasm.

Meja gave her a big hug. "Thank you."

"One year," said Inez. "Not a day longer."

"One year," Meja said and stood up, straight-backed. "Wish me luck. I'm going to talk to Andreas."

"Good luck," said Inez. "You'll be all right. I don't think I've ever come across a better-suited couple. Well, maybe Sverker and Filip."

Meja left, waving heartily. Inez waved in return and choked back tears.

Who would have thought it? She remembered that first day when Meja had arrived and fumbled with the gate latch. Inez looked around the living room. Time for another clear-out. She needed to make the place fit for guests, even guests with standards as high as Sverker and Filip's.

ONE YEAR LATER

INEZ

The string lights hanging in the trees shone in yellow, blue, green, and red. The table was laden with seafood canapés, oysters, clams, lobster au gratin, and shrimp, along with several bottles of champagne. It was the fifteenth of August, and the weather gods were smiling on Inez, offering a warm, windless evening. Sverker received guests in his garden with lavish gestures and tight hugs, and Filip made sure that everyone partook in the treats on offer. Meja was standing with her arms around Andreas. It was impossible to tear them apart.

Inez smiled. There was something cinematic about the scene. She stood in her guest room and looked down on the spectacle. She was wearing an elegant green silk dress and had found some gold trinkets with matching emeralds in the jewelry box in the guest room. On opening the lid, she had noticed that the key to the desk drawer was in the wrong compartment. Which could only mean that Meja had used it.

Inez had taken the little black book out of its drawer. Now she stood with it pressed to her chest as she gazed down at the people anticipating her long-awaited entrance.

So that's how Meja had known the ending wasn't true when she confronted her early that morning. She had read it in the black notebook.

Inez clenched her jaw as she flipped through the pages. She could feel the hands of time caress her cheek. She paused on the last page: *I knew you would understand. What I didn't know is whether you would ever forgive me . . .*

She craned her neck to see further into Sverker and Filip's garden. There she was. Mathilda. Tall, slim, and straight-backed. She was standing next to Amelia. They were so similar that it made Inez's stomach flutter.

Amelia had blossomed into a completely different person over the past year. She had gained peace of mind. They had gotten to know each other again, as mother and daughter, and there was a new gentleness to their relationship.

Amelia had realized that she finally had what she'd so desperately wanted all along: a family. She had found an aunt in Mathilda and a whole new French family. To Inez's surprise, Amelia had gone back to Bouzigues, studied the language, and worked at the museum, which had really benefited from her help. Inez watched in amazement as her daughter, who had always been a rose with thorns to protect herself from life, bloomed into a strong and independent lily.

Inez found a pen to add one final sentence to her black book.

She forgave, as sisters do.

Then she put the book back but left the drawer unlocked.

"So, what do you think?" she asked Ingrid, who squeaked contentedly.

Inez chuckled and left. Carefully, so as not to tread on her dress, she walked through her yard, which Sverker had decorated with a Mediterranean theme. Silver willow, lemon tree, marjoram, and thyme. He had offered to build her an oasis, and this time she had accepted.

There was a murmur of voices in Sverker and Filip's yard. She greeted everyone—neighbors, publishers, old writer friends she had gotten back in touch with—and went to stand on the porch. Filip handed her a glass. Everyone fell silent and all eyes turned to her.

"This story began with death—that of my neighbor Viola—and was originally intended to end with death. My own." She saw Amelia frown. "But it didn't turn out that way. The vital, vivacious people in my life saw to it that this book got published now, while I am very much still alive. In the words of my dear publisher, Cristy, a launch party is much more fun than a wake."

There was a ripple of scattered laughter. Amelia shook her head with a wry smile. Inez raised her glass in a toast.

"Thank you all for coming; thank you, Meja, for forcing me to open my blinds; thank you, Sverker, for turning my weedy yard into an oasis; thank you, Cristy, for casting your keen eye over another of my manuscripts; thank you, Amelia, for taking my hand, despite everything. Thank you, Mathilda, for . . . well, you know. Now if I may ask Filip to do the honors and remove the veil, I present my new book, *The Oyster Diver's Secret*. I was about to say 'my final book,' but I might have promised my publisher that I would write another book about female friendship in the twilight years. I think it's going to be about two mature ladies causing trouble in Berlin. Cheers!"

Cristy let out a squeal of joy, and everyone shouted "Cheers!"

Filip removed the veil, and the guests came forward to take a copy of the book. Inez signed them all and exchanged a few words with everyone.

As the evening grew dark, the music was turned up, and the wine bottles came out. Spontaneous dancing erupted on the porch, and lively discussions were going on in every corner.

Meja came over to give Inez a hug. "I almost want to pinch myself."

Inez patted her lightly on the cheek and smiled. "I have you to thank for much more than the blinds."

"I understood what you meant," said Meja.

"To think that you, the lost cleaner, have turned out to be something of a wild child."

"I learned from the best."

"Maybe so," said Inez. "But the courage was all yours. The courage to make difficult decisions, walk the line, uncover the truth. You didn't get that from me."

"But it was your story that brought it all out."

Inez clinked her glass and looked around. "By the way, have you seen Mathilda?"

Meja also looked around. "Not for a little while."

Inez left Sverker's house and walked toward the sea. On Viola's bench, she saw a figure with long gray hair fluttering gently in the late evening breeze. Inez took off her shoes and walked barefoot in the sand. She sat down next to her sister and took her hand. Together they gazed at the dark sea.

"The truth is out now. The oyster diver's secret," said Inez, glancing at Mathilda.

Her sister stared longingly at the sea, as usual. Then she turned to her and gave her a subtle, silent nod. Inez's pulse quickened. Something about that tiny movement sent a surge of unease through her whole body. There was something she wasn't saying.

Her eyes were fixed on Mathilda.

The truth was out now . . . wasn't it?

Inez wiped her sweaty palms on her silk dress, her eyes still staring into Mathilda's.

Memories swept past like hazy specters. She blinked. That fateful night with Nikolas standing above her, rubbing his hand, sore from all the punching. Opening her swollen eyes just enough to see him walk toward the bedroom where Amelia lay screaming. The surreal feeling of her whole body being broken and crushed, yet numb, and still managing to get up and grab the kitchen knife.

Inez gasped and slowly brought her hand to her mouth. She heard herself screaming at him, saw him turn around, and . . . the final look of shock on his face.

There was a metallic taste in her mouth. She had bitten her lip.

Mathilda took a handkerchief out of her purse and dabbed it. Inez stared at her. Her whole body trembled. Had *she* done it? It hadn't been Mathilda after all?

Mathilda returned her gaze to the sea. Her breathing was as calm as the waves. Inez, on the other hand, gasped as if she were drowning.

"I think my calling in life was to help you, so that you, through your books, could help others," Mathilda said softly.

"I write trash, according to the critics." Inez's voice faltered.

Mathilda turned to her and smiled. "Your writing goes straight to the heart, and it's with the heart that we make the most important decisions."

Tears flowed down Inez's face.

Mathilda brushed them away. "You always say that you never think *what if*. Don't start now. I did what was right then, in the moment. And I have a wonderful life, a happy home, and family. What more could I ask for?"

Inez thought of Mats. Had he known? Or had Mathilda sacrificed her father for Inez's sake? But before she could ask, Mathilda got up and tugged on Inez's arm. "We've been given the rarest gift of all. Time together. Let's *live*."

Inez swallowed and nodded weakly.

"Come now," said Mathilda. "There's a party in your honor, and I'm dying to dance."

"But what are we going to do? About the ending, the truth?"

Mathilda smiled again. "Officially, the book is fiction, isn't it?"

Inez quickly blinked away the tears and nodded.

"So let's keep the truth between us." She linked arms with Inez. "Now I think we should have a dance and a proper drink. I noticed Cristy had a hip flask in her purse. She said that wine and champagne were mealtime drinks—parties need hard liquor."

"That sounds like Cristy," Inez said, squeezing Mathilda's hand.

"Love you, sis," said Mathilda.

"Love you more," said Inez.

THE OYSTER DIVER

Mathilda was fourteen years old when she and her father, Mats, had gone fishing, despite the storm warnings. When they were far out to sea, the sky turned black as night. They worked quickly to turn around and return to land. But the sea had other plans. The waves became furious jaws snapping at their little fishing boat again and again. Mathilda attached herself to the boat with a rope and clung to the railing to keep from falling overboard. Thunder rumbled angrily overhead, and rain hammered down so hard she could barely see.

"Keep talking to me!" she shouted to her father. "So I know you're still there!"

Mats kept talking to keep Mathilda calm. It was the worst storm they had ever experienced, and Mathilda heard fear creep into his voice. Would they survive? Or sink below tempestuous waters?

When Mathilda sobbed from exhaustion and said she couldn't hold on anymore, her father shouted, "You can't let go. I have something important to tell you!"

When the waves were at their highest, he revealed to Mathilda that she had a sister, who had only been a week old when their mother had passed away. He had known he wasn't capable of bringing up both girls on his own and decided to keep Mathilda.

Mathilda listened to the incredible story. About the couple in Kobbholmen who couldn't have children and so adopted the girl with the heart-shaped birthmark on her temple.

They made it out of the storm, but Mats refused to elaborate. "She doesn't belong to us anymore," he said. The only thing Mathilda managed to press out of him was that the family had moved away when the girl was four years old.

But Mathilda never stopped thinking about her sister, and when she saw that young woman on the pier gently raise her hand to taste an oyster for the first time, Mathilda knew it was her. She felt it in every cell of her body. The next time they met, she saw the heart-shaped birthmark on her temple, which confirmed it. She made up her mind that she would do anything for her little sister. Anything. No love could be stronger. No decision more important.

ACKNOWLEDGMENTS

Thank you to everyone who has helped bring Inez and Meja's story to life in this book, which is very close to my heart.

Thanks to Bokförlaget Forum and my dream team: publisher Ebba Östberg, who knows where I want my stories to go; Marie Jungsand and Josefina Karlström, who pull the strings and think outside the box when it comes to marketing; editor Kerstin Ödeen, who has a keen eye for the things I miss; and everyone else who works on my books.

Thanks to Emma Graves, who created the Swedish cover, and to everyone at Enberg Agency, who have taken the oyster diver into their hearts and out beyond Sweden.

Thanks to friends, book bloggers, and all my amazing, committed readers and listeners. You are the best!

Many thanks also to Lotta Klemming, who answered all my questions about oysters and the oyster-diving profession. Your passion is my inspiration.

And the biggest hugs to my everything: Peter, Kelvin, and Elliot. If the world is an oyster, you are my pearls.

P.S. The book takes place in real locations, but I allow myself to be a little inventive sometimes. Kobbholmen doesn't really exist, but almost . . .

ABOUT THE AUTHOR

Photo © Lisa Wikstrand

Caroline Säfstrand is a writer from Helsingborg in the south of Sweden. She is the author of ten novels. Her books are published in several countries and have been nominated for various book awards. *The Oyster Diver's Secret* won the Feel-Good Book of the Year Award in Sweden in 2023, and it's her first novel to be translated into English. Caroline loves to write about the secrets and people at life's crossroads, and she imbues her stories with warmth and depth. She lives with her husband, two sons, and two dogs. Learn more at www.carolinesafstrand.se.

ABOUT THE TRANSLATOR

A. A. Prime (Annie Prime) is an award-winning translator of Swedish literature. Her works include the Red Abbey Chronicles trilogy by Maria Turtschaninoff, which won the GLLI Translated Young Adult Book Prize and nominations for the Marsh Award for Children's Literature in Translation, the Carnegie Medal, and the International Dublin Literary Award; *Slugger* by Martin Holmén, which was shortlisted for the Dagger Award for crime fiction; and *The Night Raven* by Johan Rundberg, a Kirkus Best Book of the Year. She holds an MA in translation from University College London.